ICE MAIDEN

A Psychic Visions Novel
Book #18

Dale Mayer

ICE MAIDEN
Dale Mayer
Valley Publishing

ISBN-13: 978-1-773363-97-4
Print Edition

Books in This Series:

About This Book

Gabby Mulder was loving her winter in Aspen, Colorado, until a dangerous event with a ghost nearly killed her. Not that she was a believer but, given the circumstances, she had to be open to such a possibility. When one of her roommates is brutally murdered in their shared apartment, rumors circulate of a serial killer returning, which just adds to Gabby's pain. Confused and grieving, Gabby is forced to move to a new residence, while the police investigate the death, the crime scene at the apartment, and her.

Detective Damon Fletcher considered Gabby a flighty troublemaker after an incident at the bookstore where she worked and then later on the slopes. But when one of her roommates is murdered, his interest in her grows to a whole new level.

When another of Gabby's roommates is killed, Gabby is caught in the middle, as suspicious gazes turn her way. What had she gotten mixed up in? Even worse how are these deaths connected to several cold cases? The danger escalates as events, ghostly and otherwise, strike closer to both Gabby and all those who she holds dear.

Your Free Book Awaits!

KILL OR BE KILLED

Part of an elite SEAL team, Mason takes on the dangerous jobs no one else wants to do – or can do. When he's on a mission, he's focused and dedicated. When he's not, he plays as hard as he fights.

Until he meets a woman he can't have but can't forget. Software developer, Tesla lost her brother in combat and has no intention of getting close to someone else in the military. Determined to save other US soldiers from a similar fate, she's created a program that could save lives. But other countries know about the program, and they won't stop until they get it – and get her.

Time is running out ... For her ... For him ... For them ...

DOWNLOAD *free military romance*? Just tell me where to send it!

http://dalemayer.com/sealsmason/

PROLOGUE

THIRTY-YEAR-OLD GABBY MULDER called out to her friends and roommates, "Go!"

They all dove down the ski slope, racing to the bottom of the hill, on the last run of the day. The sun was high; the snow shone brightly on a wonderful Aspen day. Gabby was tired after a long but eventful day of snowboarding, looking forward to hitting the hot tub. The others had wanted to do one more run, and she'd been willing to go along, knowing she could take it easy afterward. Snowboarding was such a great way to combat stress.

Something she had in spades.

Especially after yesterday.

She worked as a clerk at a local Aspen bookstore—a job she'd quickly fallen in love with, even though she'd been in the resort town only for the winter and planned to leave when ski season was over. She and her best friend, Wendy, had been planning a winter here since forever. Now the end of March was near, and she couldn't bear to think about leaving. She loved it here, … the town, the atmosphere, her job. Even her boss, although sometimes morose and cranky, most of the time was great.

He had been looking for a gimmick to bring in more customers. As a lark she had picked up a pack of tarot cards she'd found on the counter and offered free readings. It was all fun and games, until several people confirmed that her readings had been right on. Then somebody else had returned, upset at the horrible message she'd been given because it all happened, just as described. The woman was now a widow and felt Gabby could have done something to save her husband's life.

That was followed by a visit from one of Aspen's finest, and Detective Damon Fletcher had definitely not understood nor had he been impressed. In fact, it's almost as if he thought Gabby had something to do with the man's death, to somehow make her prophecy come true. She wasn't sure if the detective thought she was a scam artist or a murderer. Neither helped her sleep last night.

His parting words, "Don't leave town," had been a sobering reality check. It wasn't like she could anyway, as she had no car.

Her boss had been furious with her, saying, "Gabby, these readings are supposed to be fun and positive. Nothing else. You don't believe that stuff, do you?"

She just looked at him mutely.

"Stop them now," he ordered. "Our business depends on the goodwill of the community. A bad reputation and ugly rumors will finish us. No more. I mean it. Your job is on the line over this."

She immediately nodded because she needed the job. The cost of living in Aspen was brutal. Gabby shared an apartment with four other women, none of whom could afford to move. Only about seven thousand people lived here year-round, but the influx of tourists during ski season brought in tons more people, both to sightsee and to serve the rich.

Her roommates knew about the tarot readings. Gabby

had done several for them in the last few weeks. She had even done readings for them during breakfast this morning and hadn't thought anything of it. When they'd asked her to pull a card for herself, that had been fine too. Until she pulled the one card that made them all gasp.

The Death card.

She laughed and said, "Whatever," then tucked it back in the box, as they'd all looked on with worried expressions. She smiled and said, "Come on. The Death card doesn't mean literal death, as in I die. It could just mean the death of a relationship or a job even." Although she hoped it wasn't the latter.

Unconvinced, they all headed to the slopes. And now, here Gabby was at the end of the day, happy that the dire card hadn't proven to be a bad omen.

With a pleased smile at the beautiful sunny view of white-capped mountains around her, Gabby rode the mountain, leaned into the next corner, loving the power and the sense of control she had, as her board bit into the icy surface.

Just then a hard push sent her careening diagonally across the mountain. She cried out as her body instinctively bent and twisted to stay upright, her arms flaring, even as she tried to see who'd pushed her. She struggled to brake. She was a good snowboarder, not racer material, but she'd have said better than average at least. Until now. Nothing she did brought her board back under her control. Or her speed. She dug in the edge of her board, her body almost scraping along the snow, but it wasn't working. An out-of-bounds marker flashed in warning up ahead.

Panic hit her, as the wind slashed her cheeks, and icy-cold tears stung her eyes. Still, her out-of-control board propelled her forward, as if guided by unseen hands.

She hurtled toward the cliff's edge, screaming at the top of her lungs in terror. Her friends hollered and waved at her, telling her to get back.

In desperation, she threw herself to the ground to try to stop. Her displaced goggles allowed snow and ice to burn her exposed skin and eyes, as she hurtled downward into a snowball of board and limbs that never seemed to stop spinning.

Splat.

She slammed into a small upward jut of the cliff, sending a cloud of snow falling on top of her. Gasping for air and terrified to move, she couldn't even see for the instant whiteout. When her world finally stopped moving, she peeked through her lashes. The snow no longer fell, and she could see the ski hill stretch high above her to the right, as she laid on her back. That emboldened her to test out her limbs. She moved her fingers and toes, and no pain ripped through her. She sighed softly in relief, rolling her head slowly to the left to test her neck as well as to see how close to the edge she was.

It. Was. Right. There.

The cliff dropped away at her cheek. Her bent left knee was suspended over the edge into nothingness.

Oh, hell, no. Too terrified to move—in case her small perch gave way—her heart slamming against her ribs, she froze in place. Not much more than a tiny jut of rock kept her from falling to her death below. Her mind couldn't wrap around it. What the hell just happened?

Then she remembered the tarot card. *Death.*

No way was this about the Death card. Couldn't be.

A voice whispered in her head, *Death comes to us all.*

Sometimes earlier than we want. Sometimes by another hand. You live this time.

Shocked, she cried out, "Who are you? What do you want?"

The same voice chuckled, a sound of triumph and joy. *You can call me Death. And what do I want? That's easy. I want you.*

And, with that, the voice disappeared.

Terrified, and still in shock at how close she came to flying off a cliff, she lay pinned against the mountainside, afraid to move.

Calls behind her had her raising her hand to let those racing toward her know she was okay. But was she really? She didn't dare check further, too paralyzed with cold and fear.

Minutes later, Wendy, her face red and puffy from exertion, finally neared Gabby. Wendy stood a safe distance back and above her best friend, calling out, "Oh, my God. Are you okay? What happened to you? Ski patrol is on their way. Don't move."

Gabby had no plans to move ... ever. In fact, the longer she lay here, the more rigid and panicked she became at the thought.

"What happened? Did I hear you yelling at someone earlier?" Wendy asked hesitantly.

Gabby rolled her head to look at her best friend in confusion. "I don't know," she said. "I thought somebody just spoke to me." She couldn't very well tell Wendy about the message. She wouldn't believe her. No one would.

"It's all right," Wendy said. "Take it easy. You probably just hit your head."

In truth, Gabby felt fine, which she shouldn't have because that was a hell of a tumble. She could have—should have, in fact—broken several bones. Even her board was still attached to her bindings, her feet locked into place.

Just then the ski patrol arrived. Thank God. The first man unclipped his skis and carefully made his way down to her. At her side, he stopped and stared. "You."

She bolstered her courage to smile at the detective—also ski patrol, it seemed—who only yesterday had told her not to leave town, while they investigated her and the tarot card mess. "Uh, hi. Sorry about all this."

He snorted. "What the hell was that all about? I saw you start down the mountain. Then you went nuts. That was incredibly irresponsible. You're lucky to be alive."

She shuddered, shrank as small as she could, and said, "I don't know what happened." She could almost see a sneer forming on his face. "It wasn't me," she rushed to add. "I was pushed."

His gaze sharpened. He studied her, as she lay here, not daring to even breathe deeply, in case that shifted her balance somehow. "Who pushed you?"

"You won't believe me."

"Try me."

She looked up at him and whispered, "A ghost."

"A GHOST?" DAMON muttered for the umpteenth time, as he paced outside the curtained-off room in the ER area, where everybody, including him, insisted that Gabby be checked over. Although it was just good common sense, it was taking way too long. Finally he cleared his throat and said, "So?"

Just then the white curtain was thrust back in front of

him. Gabby sat on the side of the bed, fully dressed and looking completely fine. The doctor, however, stared at her, clearly puzzled. Damon looked from the doctor to the patient and back again, then said, "Well?"

"She's fine," he said, shaking his head. "Not only is she fine but she's better than fine."

"How can she be better than fine?" Damon asked in confusion.

"For somebody who took a great tumble, like you all say she did," the doctor said, "it's amazing that no damage was done."

"So you're just saying that she's lucky?"

"Maybe lucky," the doc said slowly.

Damon gritted his teeth, as he waited for the aged doctor to finally cough up whatever bothered him. Dr. Mitchie McGonigi had been in practice for what must be at least fifty years, it seemed—making him, counting all the years in training, close to eighty years old—and the man didn't seem to be slowing down or inclined to retire. But he had a wealth of experience he wasn't reticent about putting to use, and today was no different.

Apparently something nagged him about this case, as he continued to study Gabby, and the doc would tell Damon what that was whenever he was good and ready, not a moment before.

Finally the old man released a heavy sigh and said, "She should be bruised. She should be in shock. She should have signs, physical signs, that she went through what she went through."

"And she doesn't," Damon said. "So what does that mean?"

"I don't know what it means," he said in frustration.

"My brain isn't quite the same as it used to be, but I think I've seen this before."

"Seen what?" Damon asked in frustration. "So she got lucky and walked away unscathed. We've seen that time and time again with many people—from car accidents to any other kind of an injury. This is no different. She's just lucky."

What else could it be? He glared at Gabby, who still sat here. As soon as she saw him, she immediately wiped the smile off her face. He upped the wattage of his glare. He wanted her to know that she wouldn't get away from here without talking to him.

"Well, she's certainly fine to go home," the doctor said. He turned back to Gabby and said, "Now, if you get any delayed symptoms, please let me know."

"Thank you," she said with a bright smile. "I'll be sure to call if anything changes." She hopped off the bed and tried to brush past the detective.

He shook his head and said, "Oh no, you don't."

"I have nothing more to say. I told you that I don't know what happened."

"No, I disagree," he said. "So instead of taking responsibility for going out-of-bounds and almost killing yourself," he said, "you immediately tried to mock the rest of us by saying a ghost made you do it."

She appeared slightly tongue-tied, as if not knowing what to say, and he liked that. He hated to think that she was getting off being smug and difficult, when she should be thanking everybody around her for saving her. They all were put into dangerous positions themselves, trying to get her off the mountain.

But the doctor turned to her and said, "Did you say, *ghost*?"

She flashed a grim smile. "Well, maybe," she said, but, even to her, her tone sounded lame.

The doc nodded thoughtfully. "Yes, that's what I remember."

"*That's* what you remember?" Damon asked. "What are you talking about, Doc?"

"It was the other case."

"What other case?" he snapped, striving for patience but wanting to pull out his hair.

"The one I thought of earlier," he said in a pensive tone. "It was fifty-plus years ago. ... No, maybe even longer. It's hard to remember the exact dates. I'll look up the details. But a series of odd murders remind me of something similar, but, like I said, I can't remember all the details."

"You do that," Damon said. He watched as the doctor moved toward his office. Then he returned his attention to Gabby. "Again? Really? A ghost?"

"Look. I wasn't trying to be irresponsible. It was the last run of the day," she said in an earnest tone. "I don't know what happened, but I was pushed."

"Nobody was behind you," he said.

"It *felt* like I was being pushed," she corrected. "I didn't see anybody either."

"And, if you didn't see anybody," he said, "how do you explain what happened?"

"I don't know how to explain it," she said, her jaw shoving forward and her gaze snapping at him. "I don't have an explanation. I told you that."

"Well, at least that's honest," he muttered. "Something really weird is going on with you right now," he said. "I haven't decided if you're just a charlatan or a busybody or one of those no-good crystal readers who's looking to cause chaos wherever you go."

She stared at him, her eyes dark and deep. "I'm none of those," she said. "I'm just somebody spending a winter here in Colorado. I told you before that my boss asked me to do something to bring more business into the store. So, on impulse, I picked up that pack of tarot cards. That's it."

"Then you go snowboarding today," he said, "and, on the very last run of the day, you headed straight across the mountain, even the uphill part, so that you could end up hanging on that peak."

"Well, … wait." She stopped, looked at him, and said, "What do you mean, *across the mountain?*"

"Did you not see the direction you were going?"

She shook her head. "No, I don't understand. Why would I go there?" She frowned.

"I don't know," he said, his own voice going quiet. "But if ever a hill to catch everybody's attention on, it's that one."

"I don't understand," she said.

"How long have you been in town?"

"Since the first of October," she said.

"Oh, so then you haven't heard the rumors?"

"No," she said, raising her hands in frustration. "Rumors about what? I don't know what you're talking about."

He was tempted to believe her, but he'd been gullible before, and his years on the force had made him anything but stupid at this point in his life. "Look," he said. "That particular peak? One of the reasons it is considered so dangerous is because we've already had a suspicious death there."

"When?" she asked. "Who?"

"It was a long time ago," he said evasively, not wanting to give her anything more salacious to help her work her con or whatever it was she was pulling.

"Okay," she said, "so, if I keep digging, I'll find it?"

"Probably," he said, "I don't know." And, with that, he added, "I don't want you going back up the mountain and pulling another stunt like that."

"As I said, I didn't pull this stunt," she shot back, and he could see the anger building in her eyes. "I have no problem with not repeating it."

He frowned. "Look. We have a lot of good people working ski patrol up there," he said. "It's very traumatizing when somebody ends up dead."

"Yeah. Same could also be said about the person who ended up dead," she said, her gaze wide, yet holding a hint of sarcasm.

"I don't think that's as much of an issue as it is for the people who are left behind," he said. "But these ski patrol people spend a lot of time and energy trying to keep idiots safe, and, when the idiots won't comply and end up dying, despite the best efforts of the rescuers, well, it's hard on them."

"You know something? I can actually see that," she said in a quiet voice. "However, I wasn't planning on being stupid or difficult or dying."

"No," he said. "I'm half inclined to believe you on that. The trouble is, I can't decide if you're just a fool or somebody who just likes trouble, or if you're just a silly schoolgirl."

At that, his barb hit home, and, with a visible wince, she clammed up.

He nodded. "Stay away from the mountain for a while, would you? And, if you do ever go back up there," he said, "be smart about it." And, with that, he turned and walked out.

CHAPTER ONE

G ABBY WALKED THROUGH the hospital out the front door. She didn't know where Wendy was, she'd expected her best friend to be waiting here at the hospital. She pulled out her phone, surprised that it had survived, feeling way better than she apparently had any right to. When she called Wendy, her girlfriend answered right away, asking about her mountain tumble.

"Oh, my God. Oh, my God. Are you okay?"

"Sure. Then I was okay up on the mountain," she said, "so this doesn't exactly change anything."

"Maybe not," her girlfriend said, "but I was really worried about you."

Yet you weren't here. Why is that? "Well, I came to the hospital to placate you guys," she said, "and the detective is still pissed off at me."

"Yeah, he sounded like it when he was here," she said. "As cranky as your boss is, will he think this is another publicity stunt of yours, which just makes his bookstore look bad again? Do you think you'll lose your job over it?"

She winced at that. "I hope not," she said. "I came here to snowboard for the winter. Arriving a couple of months before the season, I really got going to find work so I could pay my way. The last thing I want to do is end up in so much trouble that I don't even have a way to support myself here. Aspen is not exactly a place for the faint of heart."

"No, it certainly isn't," Wendy said. "Are you coming home?"

"Well, I'd like to," she said. "Would you mind coming to pick me up?"

"I'll be there in ten minutes," she said.

"Fine. I'll be sitting outside."

"It's cold out," she said. "You should wait inside."

"I'm good. I'm fine," she said.

"Good for you," Wendy retorted. "I can't get warm since we got home."

"Yeah, well, I probably should be freezing or in shock or something. Even the doctor seems to think I'm in better shape than I should be."

"Well, after that fall, you must admit that you are pretty lucky to have walked away from it."

"I know," she said quietly. "But I can't really do anything to change things, now can I?"

"No, of course not," she said. "It's just really lucky that you have the opportunity to rethink your life now." At that, her friend hung up.

Gabby was left staring at her phone. "What are you talking about? Rethinking my life?" she said. "I just wanted a winter to snowboard. Is that really so much to ask for?"

Apparently it was because, ever since Gabby had started work at the bookstore, it seemed like everything had gone off-kilter somehow. She didn't understand why nothing ever seemed to work out. It was frustrating as heck. As she stood here in the front entrance, leaning against the hospital's brick wall, she took several long slow deep breaths, not sure if it was just her weird clarity at the moment or if everybody else was in a fog.

She didn't understand this clarity, but she did feel different somehow. She rotated her neck slowly and stretched her arms high above her head. As she brought her arms back down again, the detective drove by, staring at her. She flushed and gave him a quick little wave of friendship, hoping that he wouldn't see her as any more of an oddball than she already was in his eyes.

She figured from the glare he sent her way that she'd failed.

She wasn't exactly sure what was going on, but something had set him off too. Then some people thought her odd here in Aspen. She didn't know why. What was wrong with being a happy-go-lucky person? Despite her circumstances, she had always been like this.

However, something about this place deemed her a little weird to everybody. It wasn't Aspen itself. It wasn't the bookstore. Not really. Just sometimes. And now the fact that she had survived that tremendous fall without so much as a scratch would just add fuel to the fire. She didn't know how to combat that, except to do what she'd always done, which was ignore them.

She really wasn't insensitive to other people; it's just that either people really got her or they didn't. Finding her tribe was something she had hoped to do a long time ago, but instead here it seemed like she'd ended up with a whole group of female misfits, who Gabby felt a lot older than, only to find out they all thought she was younger. She shook her head at that.

"Now I'll just be even more of an oddity," she said. "Pretty soon they'll come into the bookstore just so they can see me. That would be a heck of a deal." And not something she even wanted to think about. If her boss ever thought that would work, he'd be all over it.

By the time Wendy arrived to pick her up, Gabby was bored and tired of waiting. She jumped into the front seat and let her girlfriend drive her back home again. Once there, the other women, her roommates, were exclaiming, and some were even crying over her.

She just gave them all a smile and said, "I'm fine. Really. I'll go have a bath and get to bed."

Immediately they shared commiserating looks, and one of them spoke up. "Yes. Yes, that's a good idea. You need that."

Gabby went in to have her bath, but, instead of soaking and relaxing, she found herself full of energy and all keyed up. Instead of that fall wiping her out and shaking her up, it seemed like it had energized her. That worried her more than anything. Once in her small bedroom, the only space that was hers alone, she closed the door, pretending to need to sleep, when really she just wanted to be alone to think things through.

She hadn't told anybody about the crazy message she'd received while she was on the mountain, and now she wasn't even sure if she had actually heard it. It was just too far-fetched to believe. At the same time, if she had heard correctly, then somebody had whispered in her ear, in her head, and she needed to figure out how that worked, what that meant.

He'd said that he was Death. But since when did Death speak? So that part made no sense. She frowned, as she lay here in bed, looking on her phone, surfing for anything about the person that Damon had said died up on the mountain. It took a good hour, trying to stay quiet, hoping that her friends would all leave her alone.

Finally she found it. Or at least she had found out about one death on an Aspen mountain. Just a small article about this woman who had been hiding out in Aspen just seven years ago. After her death, the authorities found out she had been accused of murder in another state, although nothing could ever be pinned on her. The article didn't explain how she died, just that it happened on the local mountain. The gossip about her took the forefront of that piece.

Immediately chills went up and down Gabby's back. *Murder?* Since when did somebody come to Aspen to get away from murder charges?

She always thought of this as a resort town, a place where everybody came for fun and a holiday. Maybe that's what a murderer had done? Maybe that's how she enjoyed life and was coming here to get away? Gabby couldn't find any of the details on who this woman supposedly murdered, only that she had died in a bad fall up on the mountain. And with one puzzle solved in her world—yet more murders happening here than she liked to know about—Gabby closed her eyes and somehow fell asleep.

DAMON WALKED INTO the office several hours later, after checking out a stuck vehicle and some party revelers who were a little too drunk to make their way home safely. Damon was tired and fed up. He didn't even know why he was here. He should have gone straight home. But something about that Gabby woman had him keyed up.

"What are you doing here?" asked his partner, Jake Perkins.

"I don't know," he said. "I should be home, sleeping."

"Especially after boarding all day on ski patrol duty. And

I hear you had quite an incident on your watch."

"Bad news always travels fast, doesn't it?" he muttered, shaking his head. "If you can believe it, she was that same idiot passing off the tarot card readings as being real."

"Oh, her," Jake said, then laughed hysterically. "That's funny."

"I don't think it's very funny," he said. "Matter of fact, it feels very unfunny."

"I don't know about that," Jake said. "For the rest of us, that whole tarot deal is bad news. But it's not ugly news."

"I get it," he said. "She's probably just fleecing a few bucks off some people. But more than that, she's setting off a raging panic with those readings."

"Sure, I suppose," he said. "But it sounds like the mountain tried to teach her a lesson today. And you and I both know how ugly that mountain can get when she's in a pissy mood," he said. "The last thing we need is any more deaths."

"I know. We were all hoping to get through a winter without any for once. Hasn't happened yet."

"Nope, it sure hasn't. But we keep trying."

"True enough," he said. "It's hard though. Out of nowhere, she just went flying, so badly I thought for sure she was a goner. When she took that last drop down, I couldn't believe it when I came up over the rise to see her, sitting up, tucked against the mountain, petrified at where she landed. Any other person would have gone over the cliff."

"True enough," his partner said. "Obviously it was one hell of a lucky fall."

"I know, and then she had the nerve to blame it on a ghost."

Jake looked at him and sniggered again.

"It's not funny," Damon snapped. "When I asked her

what the hell happened, she said she was pushed."

"Pushed?" Jake stared at his partner in surprise.

"I know," he said. "And I did see her out snowboarding, not that I knew who it was immediately, but I didn't see anybody around her at the time, when suddenly she was careening off the mountain."

"No, you're right," he said quietly. "That's really strange."

"It is, and I just don't know what the hell is going on."

"Well, you already thought she was two bricks short of a load after the tarot card stunt, right?"

At that, Damon rolled his eyes. "Can you believe it?" he said. "Like we haven't got real crimes here to worry about."

"Well, apparently not," Jake said with another snigger.

Damon glared at his friend and said, "What? Am I supposed to put that ghost remark in the report?"

"Why not?" he replied. "It's what she said."

"True." He thought about it, then shrugged. "Well, I can put it in italics at least. They can laugh all they want, but it's the truth."

"Exactly. Besides, we must be truthful. And, hey, maybe she's setting up an insanity defense."

"It's not like she's ripping people off though by almost falling to her death from the mountain," Damon said, suddenly feeling the need to defend her. "And we only had the one anonymous complaint on her readings."

"But what were they complaining about then?"

"Well, the woman lost her husband," he said. "So she's obviously acting out of grief. But she feels like Gabby should have known that what she said in the reading was the truth and should have done something to protect the woman's husband."

"Really?" Jake stared at him. "How does somebody protect somebody else from death? If she could bottle some of that, she'll be a trillionaire in a heartbeat, right?"

"It just didn't bear thinking about. And that's assuming Gabby's even correct in any of these premonitions, which, so far, we haven't seen any actual proof of."

"So what do tarot card readings have to do with her flying down the mountain? Or being pushed?"

"Well, that's the part that doesn't make much sense," Damon said. "Because, if she was pushed, you would think that somebody would have seen something."

"Did you get a chance to interview anybody at the scene?" Jake asked.

"No, I was bringing her down off the precipice, then to the ER. I do know a few people who were out there, but I'm not sure I know anybody there at that time."

"We still have to follow up, work our due diligence," Jake said.

"You mean, head off any complaints about us not doing a thorough job, even though it's all for the loony bin?" A note of humor was in Damon's voice because even he could see just how ludicrous it was. But the fact of the matter was that Gabby remained convinced that somebody had pushed her. Damon frowned and then nodded. "Even if she hadn't said that and even if I didn't know she was part of that tarot card mess," he said, "you know we would have done everything we could to reassure her that she hadn't been pushed."

"And, if she were," he said, "you know it's a crime, so we need to follow it up anyway."

"Right," Damon said. "So I'll have a talk with the mountain safety officers and see if they have any idea of who all were around there at the time of her fall."

"You said her friends were there too, right?"

"Yes, one for sure was at her side when I arrived. I can question her and ask what she saw," Damon said.

"I'd question everybody, just to make sure our backs are covered," he said.

With that, Damon nodded. "You know what? For now, I think I'll head home."

"I think you should. I doubt you got any sleep, did you?"

"What's sleep?" he said, "Especially these days."

"Grief won't last forever," Jake said.

"I'm not sure about that," Damon replied. "It feels like a life sentence."

"Man, it's been two years. It's time to cut loose."

"Yeah, but I'm not ready," he said instantly.

"You only keep saying that because it's a reflex," he said.

At that, Damon stopped, thought about it, and then shrugged. "You know what? That may be true," he said. "Or maybe it's still the way I feel."

With that, he walked out and headed home. Two years and four days. Couldn't forget the four days. Everybody thought he was overcome with grief. Nobody knew the hell he'd endured for the four years of his marriage and how relieved he was that she was gone. Not relieved enough to have had a hand in her accident because that just wasn't his way. But every time he brought up divorce or any attempt to get out of the situation that was choking him, she'd tried to commit suicide.

Damon knew that the psychologist had said it was an attention-grabbing action, but Damon couldn't just sit there and let her go down the tubes because of his need to be free. He'd been caught in a nightmare that he'd found no way out of. And the two years since had been even worse. Survivor's guilt? Or PTSD? Or just plain not letting go of the trauma of those years? It took time to get back to normal. And he felt he would get there. Eventually.

Damon knew Jake was probably right in the sense that Damon should get back into the dating game and have some sort of normal life, but he just didn't want to. Not yet. Absolutely nothing inside him said he should either. Maybe the truth was that he was too damn scared.

After all, he'd hooked up with somebody he thought was the most brilliant person in the world, and she ended up being so emotionally unstable that he'd been living a nightmare the entire time with her. He just didn't want to repeat something like that. And every time he met somebody like Gabby, it reminded him of how many people in the world were just a little off, and he didn't even know Gabby well. It wasn't that he was trying to judge her, but dealing with her so far made it easy to do so.

CHAPTER TWO

G ABBY WOKE THE next morning, feeling rested and well. She bounced out of bed, got dressed, then raced out and put on the coffeepot. After her day off—she rolled her eyes—she was supposed to go to work today. Her roommates, minus Tessa, looked up at her in surprise. Gabby turned and said, "Oh, I didn't realize you guys were up already."

"Yeah, we didn't get any sleep," Wendy groused. "I had nightmares all night."

"Nightmares about what?" Gabby asked in commiseration, as she sat down beside her friend.

"You," Wendy said, "going over that cliff. I may never snowboard or ski again."

"I'm sorry," Gabby said with remorse. "That must have been terrifying to watch."

Liz and Betty nodded.

"You don't even know the half of it," Wendy replied. "I think all I did was scream because my throat is so raw today."

And, in truth, her friend's voice did sound gravelly. "Hey," Gabby said, "I'm really sorry. I don't even know what happened, but I feel really good today."

"How can you possibly feel good?" she said. "I don't know how you could have slept either."

"Stress, exhaustion, I don't know," she said, showing her palms, "but I feel good, and, for that, I'm grateful. I do have to go to work today."

"You're going to work?" Liz asked in horror. "You need to stay home and recuperate."

"Yeah, not happening. I have expenses to pay. Remember? So I have a job. And I need to keep it."

They watched mutely as she poured coffee into a thermos, checked her watch, and said, "Of course I overslept."

"How about food?" Wendy asked.

"I'm okay," she said. "I'll grab something at work."

"Remember the money thing?" Wendy asked. "You weren't going to buy lunch out anymore."

"I know," she said, "but I'm late."

"We have some muffins here that Tessa made. Grab a couple," Wendy urged. "At least take that much."

Gabby looked around and saw them, then snagged two without even wrapping them. "Thanks," she said, as she headed out the door and walked down the street to work.

When she got around the corner, she raced toward the bookstore, reveling in the crisp cold air. There was something to be said about living in a place like this. She thoroughly enjoyed every minute of it. The five of them together had done decently as roommates, and it was nice that Wendy had shared some of Tessa's muffins.

They often did that. Somebody would cook a batch of something, and everybody would share it together. But other times it didn't work out quite that way. But none of them liked wasting food, so, when someone had too much to eat themselves, they usually passed it around to the others. It worked out well.

And it saved all of them a few dollars along the way,

which was good because Gabby made what seemed like pennies off her job. As she walked into the bookstore, her boss looked at her and then pointed at his watch. She checked, smiled, and said, "Look at that? I'm right on time."

He checked his watch, frowned, and said, "Oh, I thought it was a few minutes later than this."

"Nope, I'm on time," she said, giving him a bright, cheerful smile. "How was it yesterday?"

"It was fine," he said. "I did ask if you could work yesterday too."

"And I probably should have," she said, "since my trip up the mountain yesterday turned out quite differently than what I had intended."

"*Huh.* I heard somebody had a near miss," he said.

She glanced at him, but he wasn't looking at her. "There are always a lot of near misses," she said and got right to work. A couple hours later, when she grabbed yet another cup of coffee, her boss looked at her and cleared his throat before speaking.

"Did you come up with anything else to bring in some business?"

She looked around and saw four or five people already in the store. "Today seems pretty good, business-wise."

"Sure, but tomorrow won't be," he said, in that perpetually glum tone of his.

"Maybe it will be," she said. She was the eternal optimist, and he was the eternal pessimist. But somehow, most of the time, they got along very well. She had to admit she had messed up a time or two, and he hadn't really appreciated that, but what could he do when it was all a learning experience for her? She'd thought about other marketing ideas to bring in more customers but wasn't sure that he'd be up for any of her ideas after the last one.

He had a tendency to claw onto the negative and to hang onto it way too long. She was the opposite. She liked to keep trying new things, until she found something that worked. While she sat here at the front counter, she polished off the first muffin and then ate the second.

He looked at her and asked, "Did you not eat this morning?"

"No," she said. "I brought these two muffins, but I'm still hungry. I'll get lunch from across the street, maybe grab a sandwich."

"I brought a bunch of sandwiches," he said. "You can have one of those."

She looked at him in surprise. He wasn't well-known for his generosity. She beamed and said, "Thank you. I could really use it."

He motioned toward the small fridge he kept in the office. "Go ahead and grab one. I think I brought like four today. I don't know what I was thinking."

"Hey, it's perfect for me," she said with a bright smile. She raced into the office, as no customers were at the cash register, then snagged the top sandwich, and came back out. Even before she got back to the cash register, she'd taken several bites.

"You must be really hungry."

"I am," she said. "Must have been the day on the mountain."

"Maybe," he said. "It's been a long time since I skied."

"Go back to it," she said, in that encouraging voice.

He shook his head. "No, people die on the mountain."

At that, she stopped, froze for a long moment, and then nodded slowly. "That's very true," she said. "They do." She frowned because it seemed like her voice suddenly got thick, almost tense, and she didn't know why. She turned and looked at him and asked, "Did anybody you know die on the mountain?"

"Why would you think that?"

"I just thought it would be a horribly personal thing to have happened."

"Well, it would be," he said. "It's bad enough to lose anybody you care about, but, on a mountain like this, even worse."

"Why a mountain *like this?*"

"It's very unforgiving," he said, staring at her in surprise.

"I just never looked at it that way," she said.

"That's because you don't live here," he said with a nod.

She found that almost insulting. "Well, I do live here," she said. "I just haven't been here for very long."

"I meant, you're a newcomer," he said, by way of explanation.

"Well, everybody is a newcomer," she said, in that matter-of-fact tone of voice, "until they've been here long enough."

He rolled his eyes at her. "Meaning, you aren't an old-timer because you don't know all the old stories or some of the old happenings."

"Like what?"

"Well, we had a serial killer at one point in time," he said, "and he murdered young women on the mountain."

"Really?"

"He was a ski instructor at the time, and he'd pick his victims from his students."

"Wasn't that like setting himself up to get caught? It seems a little too obvious."

"Well, it still took a long time for him to get caught, if that's the case," he said with a shrug. "I don't know much about it, but it took them over a decade to actually find him. I think it was because he was poisoning his victims. Once the cops figured that out, then further autopsies and drug panels helped solve those cases. They did get him in the end though. He died in jail a few years back."

"Wow," she said. "That's terrible."

"Yes, it was," he said. "I lived here during that decade, and it was a terrible time."

"Is that why you don't go skiing now?"

"That's one of the reasons. But it really doesn't matter. It's not like I'll be taking any ski lessons, and it's not like some serial killer will target me," he said with a shrug.

She wasn't so sure about that. A lot of women—young women—went after old men, if they had assets. And Aspen was full of very wealthy people. On second thought, her boss, Jerry, wasn't exactly a wealthy old man. "I don't think you have enough money for somebody to murder you," she said cheerfully.

He snorted. "If that is one of the prerequisites, then, no, I definitely don't."

She grinned at him. "Besides, isn't it time you got a girl-friend?"

"What is the correlation between our last conversation and this one?" he asked in exasperation.

Blithely she shook her head and said, "No clue. But, hey, it's what came to mind."

"And it seems like whatever comes to your mind," he snapped, "comes flying out of your mouth, without any regard for the conversation at hand."

"I've always been this way," she said, trying not to dim

her enthusiasm.

"Well, you're even worse today," he said, groaning. "I'll head back to my office and get some work done."

"Okay," she said, "I'll be right here."

As a customer came toward her to check-out, Gabby turned with a smile. "Hi," she said. "Let me help you with those." As she reached for the items to ring them up, she started in on a conversation, asking if the woman had found what she was looking for, if she needed anything else, and was she looking for any other books. By the time the woman had left, her boss was back out again, a glare on his face.

"Now what?" she said, raising her hands.

"Don't be so chatty," the boss growled. "That poor woman was trying to get away from you, and you were talking so much."

She looked at him, feeling hurt. "That's not true," she said. "It's not even fair to say something like that."

He groaned. "Not everybody is a social butterfly," he snapped. "So just keep it under control."

After that, she tried hard to keep her natural enthusiasm down, but it seemed even harder today. Instead of being shell-shocked and lifeless from her nearly catastrophic event up on the mountain, it seemed like she'd been energized by it instead. She frowned at the thought. Just then, one of the customers came up and said, "Hi, I was looking for a book on the history of Aspen."

"Sure," she said with a bright smile. "Let me show you where those are." She walked her around to the section where the local books were and pointed out two that discussed local history. The woman picked up one and bought it. Later in the day Gabby remembered she'd wanted to look at the same thing herself. When a lull in the bookstore's traffic came, she headed back to the two books she had pointed out to the woman. Gabby wanted one for herself but winced when she saw the price of them.

Of course, as was so very typical of the bookstore, these were thirty dollar books. She needed to find something less expensive to match her measly income. She flipped through the first book and didn't find anything too interesting, and then, as she picked up the second one, her boss came by and said, "If you're looking for a good book on the history of Aspen, there's another one, only it's about the dark history."

"Oh," she said, "where do you keep that one? I don't remember seeing it."

"That's because I don't sell it," he said.

"Why not?"

"Because things like that shouldn't be perpetuated. It's gruesome."

"And yet," she said, with a slight smile, "you're telling me about it, so I can go look it up."

"Yes, but then that's you."

Frowning, she didn't know what to say to that but made a note of the book he was talking about. "Is it something we can order in?"

"Probably," he said. "Anything like that has a great sell-through rate."

This just made her itching to again ask why he didn't carry it here, but she held her tongue because either he was in a weird mood or she was. It didn't matter. She thought she'd go by the secondhand bookstore when she got off work. Seemed like the wrong thing to do, but she couldn't afford to pay for brand-new books. By the time the end of the day rolled around, she still wasn't the least bit tired. She had enough energy to spare that she could easily walk the few blocks over to the other bookstore.

Saying goodbye and leaving Jerry to lock up, Gabby headed out the door and down the street and turned at the corner. She'd been into the secondhand bookstore a couple times, and the woman there knew where she worked. As she walked in, Emily looked up, smiled, and said, "You've only got a few minutes. I need to close up on time tonight."

"Yeah, you usually open and close a half hour later than we do," she said. "I was looking for a book on the local history," she said and gave her the title that her boss had mentioned to her.

"Ah, you're talking about *The Dark Past*. That's its actual title." She walked over to one wall, quickly thumbed through several books that she had there, then nodded and said, "Here we go, one copy."

"Oh, perfect," she said. "How much is it?"

"Well, it's in nearly perfect condition," she said, "so it should be fifteen dollars."

At that, Gabby winced.

"But, for you," she said, "how about ten?"

"That would be great," she replied, smiling with relief. "I can just about manage that."

"I'd suggest you get another job, but I know jobs in town are hard to come by."

"They are if you can't do restaurant duty," Gabby said. "I'm just way too klutzy for waitress work."

At that, Emily laughed and said, "Here you go. Enjoy the book." She handed it over, after ringing up the sale.

With the purchase tucked inside her oversize purse, Gabby headed home. The snow had picked up, and it was blustery out. But still it was a beautiful day. She just loved Aspen, almost dancing along on her way home.

As she neared her apartment, she thought she heard her name called.

You're mine, Gabby.

But she didn't understand what that meant.

Oh, you understood, the voice in her head said. *You just don't want to listen.*

Then it disappeared.

DAMON DROVE THROUGH town, heading toward the apartment that Gabby had listed as her address. He had stopped in at the bookstore at the end of the day but had just missed her. As the owner of the bookstore had said, she'd left already. He took a few minutes to walk the area and then hopped into his vehicle to give her enough time to get home. But, once he arrived at her place, nobody answered.

He waited in his car until she showed up, and, when she did, she looked quite pleased with herself. She ran through the snow, bouncy and fresh looking. He wondered at that. He hopped out and called to her. "Gabby?"

She immediately froze, a frown taking over her features, but she didn't acknowledge Damon.

"Gabby?" he called out again.

She stopped, turned, and looked at him. He could see that she recognized him, and then she bolstered up a smile for him.

He sighed. "Hey, I'm just checking in to make sure you're okay from yesterday."

Immediately the fake smile disappeared, and she beamed at him. "I'm doing great," she said. "Thank you very much."

"No aftereffects?" he probed gently.

"No, I feel really great," she said.

"I figured you'd be home, spending the day recuperating in bed."

"No, not at all," she said. "And you're not the first one to point that out to me. But I feel fine, honest."

"Well, that's good," he said, frowning. "I really expected you to have some residual effects today. You know? Bruises, abrasions, sore muscles, something. That was a hell of a fall."

"Hey, I got a second opportunity at life. I'm determined to live it."

"But do you really realize how lucky you were?"

"Yes. I'm trying not to dwell on the accident part," she said, on a more serious note.

He nodded to himself. At least she understood how close she'd come to losing that life she found so precious. "So," he said, crossing his arms, hating that he did it defensively, but finding it hard not to. "Yesterday you said that you were pushed."

"Yes," she said immediately. "I was. I know it."

"Did you see who did it?"

"I already told you that I didn't," she said. "You just don't like the other answer I gave you."

"Not when it doesn't make sense," he said.

"Well, I can't make it make sense for you, can I?" she said. "You'll have to investigate and make it make sense for me."

He stared at her in confusion.

"It's what you do, right?" she said helpfully.

"And how do you figure that?"

"You're a detective," she said. "You solve puzzles." And, with that, she gave him a beaming smile and added, "If that's all, I'll go inside and make some dinner."

"I do have a few questions for some of your roommates.

Who was out on the mountain with you when I arrived?"

"That's Wendy," Gabby said. She unlocked the main entrance door, pushed it open, and asked, "Do you want to come up and see if she's there?"

"Well, I knocked a while ago, and nobody answered."

"Nobody likes to answer anyway," she said candidly. "Nobody here likes to come down three flights of stairs just to open the door either. Essentially we're all a lazy lot."

"So, if somebody is coming over, you don't open the main entrance door for them?"

"Well, of course, if we know they're coming," she said. "But nobody was expecting you, were they?"

A little lost in the conversation, he nodded slowly.

"See? So it's not like anybody was planning on you coming, so why would they let you in? You could have been anybody, like a serial killer or something."

"Ah," he said, "you mean, you don't open the door to strangers?"

"Isn't that what I said?"

He looked at her, frowned, and said, "Uh, no. You gave some convoluted explanation that made absolutely no sense whatsoever."

At that, another voice joined them. "Well, that's our Gabby," Wendy said.

He looked over and recognized her friend, who had been on the mountain. "And she's like this all the time?" he asked humorously.

"Yes," she said. "I've known her a long time. We came to Aspen together."

The threesome headed up three flights of stairs in silence. Wendy watched as Gabby walked into their apartment and headed to the living room, then flopped on the couch.

"You could at least invite him in," Wendy said.

"Come on in," Gabby said, with a wave of her hand.

He stepped inside, wondering at the odd turn of affairs. He looked at Wendy and said, "I wanted to speak to you. To ask if you saw who pushed her on the mountain yesterday."

"I didn't," she said immediately. "It was the darnedest thing. We were all just about to head down the mountain, and she was right there beside me. The next thing I know, she's careening off at breakneck speeds, heading off the mountain," she said, shuddering. "I didn't sleep a wink last night."

"And yet she slept fine apparently," he said, nodding at Gabby.

Gabby just lay there, watching the two of them. "I don't know why," she said. "It's only you guys who seem to think it's weird."

"Yeah, you'd think it's weird too if you were me. You're the one feeling good and energetic," Wendy said. "Me, on the other hand, the one who's feeling like death warmed over, does find it weird. Very weird."

At that, Gabby grinned. "You know I'm always a little bit on the high-energy side."

"More than a little bit, I would say," she said, "and that's okay too. We love you anyway."

Immediately Gabby hopped up, and the two women exchanged a quick hug. She sat back down on the couch, now beside the detective. "I really don't know what to tell you. I didn't see who pushed me. Wendy didn't see who pushed me. I was hoping somebody might have seen something."

"Well, we were hoping for that too," he said, "but we haven't found anybody else who was up there at the same time who might have seen the incident."

"That's too bad," she said. "They would help me feel like I wasn't making it up."

"Are you making it up?"

"I said, I wasn't making it up," she snapped.

He grinned. "Okay," he said, "I'll take that at face value."

"Good," she said. "It would be nice if somebody did."

"How was your boss today?" Wendy asked, changing the subject.

"Oh, the usual. Glum, depressing, dour. You know, all the downer words."

"Old man Jerry?" Damon asked. "He's always been like that."

"Always? Something must have happened to make him that way."

"Well, he's old and alone," he said. "That might do it. His world is probably pretty dark sometimes."

"No wonder he doesn't carry the book with Aspen's dark history in the store," she said with a chuckle.

"Dark history?" Damon asked.

Gabby hopped up, as he watched, and walked to her purse that she'd set on the counter and took out the book. "He told me this was the book with the dark history of the area, but he refused to carry it in the store."

"Well, it's a tourist town. He probably thinks it's best for Aspen to put its best foot forward."

"I feel so sorry for him," Gabby whispered. "It never occurred to me how lonely he probably is. Yet he doesn't welcome any extra conversation or anything. I guess that's why I know so little about him. Who knows what his life may have been like?"

"Everybody's got a story," Damon said. "People just generally don't like to share."

"True enough," she said. "Anyway, I need to get cooking. Is there anything else you wanted to ask me?"

He shook his head. "No, but please keep an eye on your injuries," he said.

"Well, I would," she said, in exasperation, "but, as I keep telling you, there aren't any."

"And that's just the damnedest thing too," Wendy said, staring at Gabby.

"I'm doing well, and I won't feel guilty about it. I'm blessed that a scary tumble was all there was to it. For once, something went right in my life."

On that note, Damon looked at Wendy to see her studying her friend Gabby with an odd speculative glance. "Is there something you want to tell me?"

Wendy looked at him in surprise, shook her head, and said, "No. It's just Gabby. She's a very unique person."

"I can see that," he said. "I just don't know if I should hear anything else about this."

"I don't know," Wendy said in surprise. "I'm not sure what to tell you."

"But you've known her for a long time."

From the kitchen, Gabby called back, "I can hear you two."

"Good," Wendy said, "because we're talking about you."

Gabby poked her head around the corner, then grinned and asked, "Nachos for dinner?"

"Perfect," Wendy said. "I might get a few of those down."

"Not a problem. If you don't want them, I do. I've been starving all day."

At that, Damon looked at her. "How hungry?"

"*Starving*," she said, her tone exaggerated. She flashed that bright grin that he started to find a little too attractive for his peace of mind. "I mean, I ate sandwich upon sandwich today. I just couldn't get full. Jerry even gave me one of his. But I was still hungry and had to buy more."

Damon frowned.

She looked at him in surprise. "Detective, do you ever do anything but frown?"

He glared at her.

"Okay, okay. I shouldn't tease you. I'm sorry," she said. "But really, I'm fine. I keep telling you that."

"And then you tell me things like you've been superhungry all day, and you can't get full," he said.

"What difference does that make?" Both Wendy and Gabby turned to look at him.

"Nothing, I guess. It's just, maybe it's an odd thing."

"Maybe," she said. "But hopefully it's not a bad thing."

He shook his head. "Just an odd something I heard once."

"Well, don't keep us in suspense," Gabby said lightly. "What did you hear?"

But he didn't dare tell her. "Oh, nothing," he said, as he stood. "I've disturbed you ladies enough. Please have a good evening." And, with that, he turned and walked out. He hoped he was wrong, but he remembered hearing something at a psychologists' forum on some of the more oddball cases that they had seen. One of them, a Dr. Maddy something, had mentioned that detail about, in the presence of psychic ghosts, people have experienced an incredible insatiable hunger. He couldn't remember exactly what else she had said, but he would find out.

When he returned to his office, he immediately searched for Dr. Maddy. Found the right one obviously, with all the psychic-related mentions about her, including confirmation of the connection between insatiable hunger and ghosts. Damon checked her website for her contact info, but she was booked a year out for consultations. However, she recommended Stefan Kronos, if anybody needed urgent help sooner.

Damon shook his head. *Stefan Kronos?* His captain would hate this angle.

CHAPTER THREE

"WHAT WAS THAT all about?" Wendy asked Gabby, who was busy stuffing raw carrots in her mouth, to which Wendy just shook her head.

When Gabby had finally swallowed, she said, "I have no idea. Something about my appetite bothered him but then, whatever."

"Are you sure you're feeling okay?" Wendy asked slowly.

She looked at her friend and frowned. "Don't you start," she said. "I'm fine."

"But you're even more high energy than usual," she said.

"Yeah, but I feel like my old self."

At that, Wendy went silent, lowered her head.

Gabby looked at her friend, worried. "What about that bothers you?" she asked, placing her hands on the counter and glaring at her friend.

"I don't know," she said. "You just haven't been like this in quite a while."

"In how long?"

"At least since your adoptive father died."

"Ah," she said. "Well, maybe I'm finally coming to terms with the fact that I have no father, birth or adoptive or foster or whatever."

"Maybe," Wendy said, but her tone was doubtful.

At that, Gabby raised both hands. "If I'm down and depressed, you worry about me," she said. "Then, if I'm up and happy, you worry about me. Where's the happy medium here?"

"I know it sounds funny," Wendy said, "but it's just ... you're not acting like yourself."

At that, Gabby stopped and fully faced her. "What does that mean?"

"I don't know," Wendy said, frowning. "It's just that you're different."

"Is different bad?"

At that, Wendy didn't appear to have any answers either. "I wish we hadn't gone up that stupid mountain," Wendy said.

"Hey, I'm starting to feel the same way," Gabby snapped back.

"I don't know what happened up there, but something did."

"Well, whatever it was," she said, "it's over with. And I'm fine. I don't know why I'm fine, but I am, and I'm grateful."

"Me too," Wendy said with a rush. She got up, hugged her friend again, and said, "Come on. Let me get the cheese out and help you make the nachos." Together, the atmosphere was restored once again, the two of them laughing and joking, as they made nachos and sat down to eat.

"Where are the others?"

"Well, Liz is working," Wendy said, "and I have no idea about the other three."

As it was, nobody else showed up. Not even before they went to bed, which was unusual but not that unusual. Liz had a boyfriend, and she was working late shifts, so she might not even come back tonight. Besides, her boyfriend had a room to himself. There wasn't much in it, but he had his own bathroom and a hot pot. More important, it was private, so she often stayed over there.

"I'm beginning to wonder if Liz will move out," Wendy said, as she got ready for bed.

"Maybe, and, if she does, we'll have to find somebody else in a hurry," Gabby said. "You know the rent here is outrageous."

"I know. I can't imagine trying to pay her share as well. Have you thought about what you want to do after this?"

"No, because this has been our dream since forever. Remember?"

"Oh, I remember," Wendy said, "and I was willing to go the distance, but I don't know for how much longer."

"*Ugh*," Gabby said, turning to look at her. "You want to leave?"

"I just feel like we could do so much more with our lives if we weren't here."

"I know, and that's why we said one winter. Remember?"

"I remember," she said. "It's almost April. Remember that?"

Gabby frowned. "Meaning?"

"Meaning, when is winter over here? It's not like we set any guidelines for that."

"I know," Gabby whispered. "Let's not talk about it tonight though, okay?"

"Okay," she said, "but it's not something we can keep pushing off."

"Maybe we can, though."

"And maybe we can't."

With that in mind, the two friends split to their separate

bedrooms. As she curled up in bed, Gabby realized that Wendy was right, of course. They had made the decision to come for a winter but had never discussed at what point winter was to be considered over. She hated to think that her best friend would move away because this wasn't where Wendy wanted to be. But, at the same time, it was exactly where Gabby wanted to be, so she had some decisions to make herself. One of the realities of living here was that it was very expensive, particularly when they had low-end paying jobs.

She groaned on that note, determined to get through the night with some rest and to wake up nice and happy again tomorrow. Soon she drifted off to sleep. The next thing she knew, she heard all kinds of odd sounds in the apartment. She sat up in bed, wondering if one of the windows had been left open. She walked over and opened her door just a hair, only to hear an odd wail coming from the living room. Wendy's door beside Gabby's door opened up, and the two of them stared at each other, terrified.

"What the hell is that?" Gabby whispered.

Wendy immediately shook her head. "I have no idea," she said, "but I don't like the sound of it."

Both of them were too terrified to go into the living room.

"You should call somebody," Wendy said.

Gabby grabbed her phone and called the police. And, for whatever reason, her fingers ended up connecting her to the same detective. When his sleep-clogged voice answered, she said, "I don't know if you can hear this going on in the background," she said, "but that's happening in my living room."

He came awake almost instantly. "What the hell is that?"

"I don't know," she wailed, as softly as she could. "I don't know. It's coming from the living room."

"Stay in your room," he said, "and lock your door, if you can. I'm on my way."

As she turned, Wendy was here in the room with her, shutting the door quietly, and the two of them sat and waited on the floor, their backs against the door. Then, all of a sudden, the noises stopped.

They looked at each other, and Gabby jumped up. "I don't know, but maybe it's safe to look now."

"Hell no, it's not safe," Wendy said, in an adamant voice, rising to her feet. "We'll wait for the detective to come through."

"But what if he doesn't come?" Gabby said.

"I'm not going anywhere until the detective gets here! Did he say he was coming?"

"Yes. He said he's on his way," she replied. She turned to the door, put her ear against it, and looked at her friend. "It's quiet out there."

"I know," Wendy said, "and somehow, *somehow* that seems even worse."

Gabby hated to agree with her, but, when she opened the door a bit, she heard just this weird deathly silence. She immediately slammed the door shut again, then turned to look at her friend.

When a loud *bang* came from the living room, the two women jumped together, arms around each other, as they clung tightly. Then they heard footsteps coming toward the bedroom door.

"Oh, my God. Oh, my God. Oh, my God," Wendy whispered, and they backed up toward the window, where they could look out of their third-floor apartment. "We're never getting a third-floor apartment again," Wendy whispered. "If we were on the first floor, we could be out and gone by now."

The two women trembled as the footsteps stopped just outside the bedroom door. Gabby's phone rang. With their arms clenched around each other, Gabby was too scared to even look at her cell. "Shit, shit, shit, shit," she said, quickly trying to turn off the noise. If the intruder didn't know someone was here, he did now. But her cell rang on, and, as her fingers fumbled, she answered it.

"It's me. I'm outside your building now."

"Oh, my God," she said. "Come in. Come in. Come in. He's right at our bedroom door."

"I'm here," he said. "Just stay on the phone with me. I'm on my way in. Did you see him?"

"I can't see anything," she said. "Whoever it was stopped just outside my bedroom door. Some horrible noises were out there."

"Okay. I'm at the front door. I'm putting the phone in my pocket, just stay on the line."

And, with that, the two women grabbed hold and waited. They heard something more in their apartment, but Gabby didn't know what it was. Then more footsteps. Finally the bedroom door opened, and it was Damon. She looked at him in shock; then she raced toward him. "Oh, my God," she said. "What happened?" And then, as he reached out to her, she didn't give a damn. She threw herself into his arms, and he wrapped them around her.

Damon said, "I'm here. Easy now. Take it easy."

Now Wendy clutched him, right beside Gabby. With his arms around both women, they burrowed close, looking for that reassurance that whatever hell had gone on was okay now. Finally they calmed down enough to look up at him, questions written all over their expressions.

"Give me a moment. Just step back in your room and stay here."

"No problem," Gabby said. The women both stepped back, but, with the door open, they could watch as he headed back out to the living room. Then she heard him on the phone but couldn't understand what he said. Gabby looked at Wendy, the two of them standing there, close to each other.

When he finally came back, his face was grim.

"What did you find?" Gabby asked.

"I think it's one of your roommates," he said hesitantly.

"Oh, my God, who?" Gabby asked.

"Who's here right now?"

"We don't know," Gabby said. "When we went to bed last night, it was just the two of us."

"And would you have expected your roommates to be home by then?"

"Sure," she said. "We all live here. Well, except Liz. She stays with her boyfriend sometimes."

He pulled out his notepad. "Liz who?"

They immediately shared the names of their three other roommates.

"Okay, I want descriptions," he said.

"Can we leave here?" Gabby asked.

Wendy said suddenly, "I want to go out in the living room."

He looked at each of them, shook his head, and said, "No, you can't."

And then Gabby realized. "Oh, my God," she said, "something really bad happened to somebody out there, didn't it?"

He looked at her slowly, then nodded and said, "Yes."

Gabby took a deep breath and then another deep breath, but she felt herself starting to hyperventilate.

Wendy grabbed her friend's arm and said, "Come sit down. Come on. Come sit down. It'll be okay."

"It doesn't feel like it'll be okay," Gabby said. "Don't you realize somebody died in our living room?" she cried out. "Somebody we know?"

"I know. I know. Let's sit down." Wendy pulled Gabby over until the two women sat on the bed. Then Wendy described her other three roommates to Damon. "Liz is tall, like five-eight or maybe five-ten," she said, correcting herself quickly with a shake of her head. "Long dark hair, almost black. Tessa is smaller, brown hair, a little bit more mousy, scrawny. And Betty is shorter, a little stockier build. Auburn hair."

He wrote everything down, then nodded and said, "You both stay in here. Do you hear me? Don't move."

Gabby stared up at him, her eyes huge. "Who is it?" she asked in a voice barely over a whisper.

"I don't know yet," he said. "Promise me that you'll stay here?"

She looked at the door and wished she didn't want to see beyond, then nodded. "Yes," she said, "we'll stay."

He nodded, then closed the door and left them alone.

DAMON WALKED OUT from the last bedroom down the hallway, checking on the other two bedrooms, but nobody was in them. For five women, only three bedrooms were in this apartment. At this point he wasn't even sure who the body belonged to or whether it was male or female. Of course it didn't help that the head was missing. As he walked back, carefully retracing his steps, he waited for his partner and the forensics team to show up. When he heard noises outside the apartment complex, he pulled out his phone and checked with his partner.

Jake answered, "Yeah, we're coming up. What have you got?"

"You won't believe what I've got," he said, "so come in carefully." As soon as a knock came on the door, Damon opened it and let everybody in.

They all stood at the front door in shock. "Oh, my God," Jake said. "Where's the head?"

"I don't know," Damon said. "And I also don't know what sex the body is. Because the whole front of the body had been flayed. The bottom half was wearing jeans, but it was impossible to tell if it was a male or a female from that quick glance."

One of the guys behind him started to gag.

Damon turned, glared at him, and said, "You will not add to the mess in here, or I'll have your badge."

The kid was green, literally, and had only been on the job for a few months. He quickly raced outside.

"Remember," Jake said. "Not everybody has seen the action you have." Even Jake's voice cracked, and his face was a tinge green.

"I know," Damon said. "I still can't have him messing this up."

"Where are the two women who called this in? Are they in their rooms? Are you thinking they have nothing to do with this?"

"I know, at first thought, it seems impossible they

couldn't have been involved because they're here," he said. "But they're not covered in blood, and their rooms are spotless. They also called me, apparently with all this going on in the background. I did hear screaming, but it wasn't normal screaming, neither male nor female. More like animal screams."

"Yeah, that fits," Jake said, staring in horrified fascination at the mess in front of them. "Where's the coroner anyway?"

"He's coming," Damon said. "He's not too thrilled about being called either."

"Doesn't matter if he is or not," Jake said. "This one is big."

"The biggest. And that's not cool."

"Nope, it isn't. It won't change anything though," he said. "This one will bring the media from all over the world."

"Shit," Damon said, "that's not what we want." He looked at Jake, who stared at the corpse in fascination. "Jake, smarten up."

"Oh, I'm here," he said. "But you know something? This is triggering all kinds of things."

"What things?"

"Remember when we were talking about serial killers in the past?"

"Yeah. What about it?"

"This," he said, pointing at the scene before them, "*this* was the MO of one of them."

Damon turned to look at what was left of the body. "What are you talking about? Mutilation was the MO?"

"This and, I mean, this right here is the MO. They completely defaced the chest and removed the head."

Damon stared at his partner, his stomach sinking.

"You're telling me that you had a serial killer here in town with this same MO?"

"Oh, yeah, I'm not kidding."

"Well, where's the killer now?"

"He's dead."

Damon looked at him shock. "Dead?"

"Dead." Jake held up his hands. "And heads-up. No one is supposed to talk about that case. Ever."

CHAPTER FOUR

B Y THE TIME the authorities had spent another three hours in the living room, both women were fed up and frustrated. Nobody would tell them anything, including Damon. When Gabby finally got him back in her bedroom to talk to them, Damon looked at the two women and asked, "Do you have another place where you can sleep tonight?"

Gabby's jaw dropped. "Are you serious?"

"I'm very serious," he said. "After all, somebody has been murdered here."

The women sagged onto Gabby's bed, burying their faces in their hands. "We barely got into this place," Gabby said. "You know what housing is like here."

"Do you have friends? Somebody with a couch you could sleep on?"

"No," Gabby said.

"Well, I do," Wendy said, a little awkwardly.

Gabby looked at her in surprise. "You do?"

She shrugged in an *I was going to tell you* motion, then said, "Yeah, I've been seeing someone."

"You didn't tell me," Gabby said in surprise.

"I haven't had a chance, and you've been kind of depressed lately, so I didn't want to add to it."

"Of course I'd have been happy for you," she said. "That's crazy. Who is it?"

"Well, that's the other reason I didn't want to tell you."

"Why? I don't understand."

And, from what Damon could see, Gabby really didn't understand. He looked at Wendy and asked, "Who's the boyfriend?"

She took a deep breath and said, "It's not a boyfriend." She winced as she looked at Gabby and said, "I got back together with Meghan."

Damon caught the startled and then angry look on Gabby's face, and he realized what Wendy had said. "So is this an ex-girlfriend?"

"Yes," Gabby bit off, "a woman who was terrible to her."

"But she has changed," Wendy said.

"In what way? And why was she bad?" Damon asked. "And please keep to the facts. I don't want all the drama."

"She beat up Wendy," Gabby said. "Is that factual enough?"

He turned and looked at Wendy. "Is that true?"

"She got drunk and hit me a couple times. She was really frustrated because she doesn't want to be lesbian." She shrugged. "But we're good together."

"Oh, my God," Gabby said, then lifted a hand to her chest, shaking her head. "Go to her place," she said. "You might as well get out of this nightmare. If Meghan has a place for you, take it."

"I could probably get her to let you stay there too."

"Hell no. Meghan and I had quite the words after what she did to you," she said. "I wouldn't want to sleep anywhere close to that viper."

"You know she's not that bad."

"I know she's not that good," she said quietly.

Wendy stood and a little helplessly said, "I would have

told you."

"I know you would have," she said, "at least when you were ready." She watched sadly as her friend walked out of the room.

Damon wasn't exactly sure what to say, but he turned to Gabby and asked, "What about you?"

"I don't have anywhere to go," she said. "Can't I stay here, in my bedroom?" Her voice was ever-so-soft and quiet, but he heard grief inside. He motioned at the doorway, where Wendy had just gone. "Is this likely to be a long-term problem?"

"I don't know," she said, "but you can only lead a horse to water."

He thought he understood what she said but held back from making any comment. This was the last place he wanted to be—in a domestic mess like this, on top of a brutal murder.

"Can you at least tell me who died out there?" she said. "I don't know which of our friends it is, but we should contact the others."

"We're looking for them," he said. "We've already located Liz. She is with her boyfriend."

"Good, she better stay there," she said softly.

"That was our recommendation to her."

Gabby nodded slowly. "Yeah," she said, "everybody has somebody."

"What about Betty, does she?"

"Yes, she did. She had a boyfriend. They were kind of off and on. But I think they were more on again lately."

"Well, hopefully we'll find her with him," he said, "and hopefully she can stay there."

"And Tessa?"

"We'll find her too."

"Right, and what do I do?"

"You need to find a place to go," he said firmly.

"So, by law, I have to leave?" she asked.

He stared at her. "Surely you don't want to stay."

"I have no place to go," she said.

And, for the first time, he saw her for what she really was—a young woman completely alone and caught up in a tragedy. "I'm sure you've got a friend you could call," he said, his voice turning gruff.

"Well, all my friends lived here," she said, "and yet somehow I stand alone. So maybe they're not friends so much as roommates." She walked over to the bed, sat down, and leaned against the headboard.

"GABBY, ARE YOU sure you don't have anywhere to go?" Damon's mind spun, thinking about options.

"No," she said quietly. "I don't. How many times do I have to tell you?"

"Pack up something," he said, "because you can't stay here. Do you need a garbage bag, or do you have an overnight bag?"

She got up and walked to the closet. She pulled out two suitcases, one carry bag, and opened them up.

In a furious set of motions she quickly emptied the dresser and the closet. She really didn't have much. In the one suitcase, she put in her boots, along with her ski pants and jacket, all her snowboard gear, minus her board. Damaged in the accident. The other suitcase was for everyday clothing. With that done, she looked at her bedding and said, "The only other thing in the entire apartment that's mine is the bedding and my toiletries in the bathroom."

So whatever she had was literally right here.

"Let me go get something for the linens," he said.

"Garbage bags are under the sink," she said, as she gathered her bathroom stuff into her carry bag.

He nodded, walked out to the kitchen, and came right back with a garbage bag. She quickly packed up her little bit of bedding and then said, "I don't even know where to go, and I can't afford a hotel overnight."

He looked at her in surprise.

"I've spent all winter working, and all it does is give me a roof over my head and food on the table, sometimes," she said quietly. "I came here to work for the winter, so I could enjoy the boarding. And somehow everything went absolutely wrong."

"Come on," he said. "I'm sure I can find you a place for the night."

"I could stay here," she said again hopefully.

He shook his head. "No way. That can't happen."

"Damn." Finally she nodded.

"Don't move. I'll pick up the bags and take them outside." He grabbed both suitcases and looped the trash bag through his fingers, leaving the carry bag with her. "I'll be right back." He walked out with them, stopped in the hallway when he saw Jake walking toward him, and said, "Don't let her leave."

"What are you doing with those things?"

"Taking her out of here for the night. Everybody else has gone."

"Good," he said, "this is ugly."

"Yeah, and she's got no place to go."

"What will you do with her?"

"I was thinking about my aunt's house. There's the room over the garage."

"I thought you were renting that out."

"Yeah, but I haven't yet," he said. "So it's empty at the moment."

"Slippery slope, you know? She's now somebody in need."

"She is," Damon said. "So what else am I supposed to do? Turn her out on the street?"

"No room in the shelters either," he said. "I just checked."

"I know. I double-checked too. Every one of her friends has a friend to stay with, except for her."

"Fine," Jake said. "I won't let her out but hurry up."

Damon walked down the steps, loaded up her gear into the back of his car, and raced back up. By the time he got there, she stood outside her apartment door, now shut to her.

She wrapped her arms around her chest and stared at him in horror. "They held up a blanket as I went past. Is it that bad?"

"Yes," he said, "it's that bad."

She didn't say another word and followed him downstairs. He noticed that she at least had her winter coat and winter boots on. "Did you have anything else in there?"

"No. Not even food," she said. "I usually buy enough just for a day or two. I grabbed the last of the muffins that Tessa made this morning for breakfast."

"Are you that broke?"

"The rents are really high here," she said. "If I want to keep a cell phone, then, yeah, it's that bad."

"You need another job then," he said.

"Wouldn't that be easy?" she said. "Except I'm really clumsy and don't do well in a restaurant environment. The bookstore is perfect, but Jerry doesn't have enough hours for me." Damon helped her into the front seat of his car. She asked, "How come it's not a cop car?"

"It is, but, because I'm a detective," he said, "it's unmarked. I've got all the lights and sirens, if I need them, just not out on display all the time."

"Oh," she said, settling beside him.

"You ready to go?"

"Sure," she said, "but where to?"

"I've got a place for you," he said, "at least for tonight." And he started up the engine and drove off.

"Where?" she asked suddenly.

"My aunt's house," he said. "There's a studio above the garage."

"In this town you could rent that for like five grand a month," she said almost bitterly.

"And I've thought about it," he said, "but it needs some work done, and I haven't got that far yet."

"Well, at least now you know you could," she said. "And thank you. I really appreciate it."

"It's fine," he said. He pulled up to his aunt's place, and she looked at it in shock. "Wow, this is gorgeous."

"It is. I haven't decided if I'll sell it yet."

"Is it yours then?"

"Yeah, it is," he said. "My aunt died a couple years back, and the estate was tied up for a long time. But it's mine, free and clear now."

"Lucky you," she said.

He looked at her, gave her half a smile, and said, "I'd do

anything to have my aunt back. Including giving this all back. She was everything to me."

"I'm sorry," she said. "I don't know what that feels like."

"No? Too bad. Everybody needs the security and love of family," he said. "Come on. Let's get you inside."

CHAPTER FIVE

G ABBY WALKED INTO the open side door and up the inside stairwell. She was grateful for indoor steps, given the wintery conditions here. At the top, she opened the suite door and stopped in amazement because, when she thought about a room over a garage, she certainly wasn't thinking about the quality high-end furnishings that this complete suite appeared to have. Granite countertops were in a tiny-ass kitchen; what looked like leather furniture was in a small living room with a big TV and a small gas fireplace. The bed in the corner was partially surrounded by tapestries, giving privacy, but, at the same time, making the one room seem divided, so somehow bigger. She shook her head, looked at him, and asked, "Are you sure you want me to stay here?"

He raised an eyebrow. "Why not?"

She frowned. "Because you could get a lot of money for this."

"It's been sitting idle so far," he said. "And, yes, I could rent the place, but again we're back to not having made those decisions yet."

"Wow," she said, "lucky you."

He snorted. "Well, let's make that *lucky you* right now."

"Thank you," she said sincerely. "I really do appreciate it."

"You okay here for the night?"

"I'm fine," she said quietly. "Not a whole lot left of the night anyway."

He nodded. "Stay inside, please. I'll check in with you in the morning."

"Fine," she said, watching as he left. She dropped her large carry-on bag beside the suitcases he'd brought up for her. Absolutely everything she owned sat at her feet. Except for her board, which was getting repaired, but she wasn't even sure how she was supposed to get the money for that. If it was even worth fixing. She didn't work tomorrow morning—this morning actually—and that was a good thing.

On the other hand, it wasn't good because she really needed the money. She reached up and scrubbed her face, wandering toward the bed and stopping in amazement at the room she found herself in. The cost for a room like this at one of the local hotels would be hundreds and hundreds of dollars, something she surely couldn't afford.

Aspen was well-known as an expensive tourist destination, and she had never expected to spend a night in a fancy place like this. The trouble was, she couldn't enjoy this fully. In light of the murder, none of it mattered. And, even more distressing, she didn't know which of her roommates was dead, only that one of them was. She used the bathroom and found her nightie in among all the rest of the clothing she'd piled into the one suitcase, changed into it, and curled up in bed.

Staring at the window with its curtains wide open and the snow falling outside, she wondered how her life had ended up here, with her in this corner. And how utterly alone she suddenly felt. She used to be incredibly good friends with Wendy, but somehow Wendy had been keeping a secret from Gabby and a major one at that. It was distressing in a completely different way. She had no clue what she was supposed to do with that.

Obviously Wendy could do whatever she wanted to do, but, at the same time, it was tough to wonder how long the relationship with Meghan had been back up and running.

Gabby hated to say it, but it was almost a betrayal because she and Wendy used to tell each other everything, and yet this had obviously been hidden from Gabby. And the fact that Wendy was afraid of Gabby's response meant that Gabby had also failed their friendship. She shook her head as she burrowed deeper into the blankets.

She loved Aspen—like, seriously loved being here—and it would break her heart to leave. Even with the murder, Gabby felt at home here, more so than at any other place she'd ever lived.

However, apparently Wendy was ready to leave. So how did that work out with her partner, Meghan?

With so many unknowns rolling around in Gabby's mind, it seemed her life was so confusing, and she didn't know what to think. But true sleep was further off. She lay here, dozing in and out, yet never getting into a deep fulfilling sleep for the bulk of the night.

When she finally woke up, her eyes were gritty with tears—tears stuck in the back of her head. She groaned and rolled over.

"Imagine if I'd paid for this," she wondered aloud. "It would be worse to think that a wonderful night in this beautiful place was unappreciated because of a bad night's sleep." She sighed heavily. "But now, since I'm off today, what will I do?" she whispered to herself, as she propped up against the headboard.

She didn't bring any foodstuffs with her because she had

none, but could something be here? Even if old and stale, she'd really appreciate some food and coffee. Heck, a hot cup of tea sitting in bed would be lovely too. She crept out of bed, surprised that it was still fairly warm in here. At her apartment they used to turn the heat down to save those pennies. It was so cold, but they could pile on the blankets, and the first person up would turn the heat back up again.

She reached the little kitchenette, found a coffeepot, one of those individual-serving things, where you stuck in a pod. But were pods even here too? After a little digging in the kitchen, when she opened a drawer, she crowed in delight to find several of them inside. She wondered if it would be overextending the hospitality that had been given her if she made use of the coffee.

Then she decided she could simply offer to pay for it, if nothing else. She made herself a single cup and found an unopened package of shortbread cookies. At first she hesitated, then figured she was in for a penny, why not a pound, and grabbed the package and took it to the bed.

There she crawled under the covers and pushed the pillows up behind her and sat back, looking at the view from her window of the snow swirling outside. It was morning, and the sky was light, but she still felt sad. It was a new day and a new dawn, and, although she was normally an optimist, it was hard to find something really positive to think about today.

When her phone rang, she knew it would be Wendy.

"Where are you?" Wendy asked, her voice raised.

"Why do you care?" she muttered. And then groaned. "I'm sorry. That wasn't fair. I'm at a small studio apartment for the night. Where are you?"

"I'm at Meghan's," she said.

"Good."

"Look. I feel like I deserted you last night, and I'm sorry."

"Yeah, it felt a little like that too," she said, "but at least you had a place to go. I'm fine though, so don't worry about me." It was hard to have this conversation because everything felt odd and unusual between them right now.

"And, Gabby, I'm really sorry I didn't tell you about starting the relationship again."

"You have your reasons," she said quietly.

"I do," she said. "And I know that you don't agree with it, and I knew you would be upset with me, so I didn't tell you."

"Uh-huh," she said.

"She has promised not to hit me anymore," Wendy said.

Gabby pinched the bridge of her nose, wondering how many women had said the same thing about their partners over the years. She didn't say anything.

Wendy added, "Anyway, I just wanted to make sure you were okay."

"I've removed everything of mine from the apartment. I wasn't allowed to stay there last night," she said, "and that's when I realized how little I actually had."

"We came with nothing," she said, "so it's not like it's a hardship to move out."

"No, but we're still on the hook for the rent next month, and we still have to hand in our notice."

"Do you think everybody is moving out?" Wendy's voice rose.

"Well, I never did get any details last night, but I understand the victim was one of the five of us," she said. "Only I don't know who. It breaks my heart to think about it."

"In which case we'll find another roommate."

"Yeah, and, once the news gets out, do you think we'll get one? Besides, I don't know if we can go back. Ever."

Wendy gasped. "No," she said, "I guess not."

"Right, so we'll all be in a similar circumstance right now. Unless you're moving in with your girlfriend."

Wendy hesitated and said, "I don't know that we're ready for that."

"No, I don't know that you are either," she said, "but I'm where I am just for today, and I don't have any place after this."

"So what will you do?"

"I don't know," she said, feeling a crushing fatigue, the complete opposite to the high energy she'd had yesterday. What she wouldn't give for a dose of that right now. "That's a problem I'll face somewhere along the line."

"Okay, well, I guess I need to talk to Meghan and just see about our situation," she said hesitantly.

"Yep, and, if you find out anything about the murder, let me know. We'll contact the others as well."

"Don't you think the police did?" Wendy asked.

"Yes, but we still have the logistics of a month's rent to pay."

"I don't think anybody'll want to pay April's rent."

"We still owe it though," she said quietly. "It doesn't matter if you want to or not."

"Do you think the police will come after us if we don't?"

Gabby stared at the phone in her hand. "That doesn't sound like you," Gabby said.

"I don't have any money," Wendy said. "I was struggling to figure out how to pay my share of April's rent as it is."

She frowned at that. "Haven't you been working?"

"Just a little bit," she said.

At that, Gabby stared at the phone in shock. "Why didn't you tell me?" she asked.

"I didn't know what to tell you," she burst out. "It's just been really rough. I lost so many hours at my job, and then it was just basically a case of 'Don't bother coming in anymore,' so I didn't know what to do."

"When did you last work?" Gabby cried out.

"Last week," she said. "Not since last week."

That was a death knoll in Aspen because a week of lost wages when they were living so tight was unworkable. "Wow," Gabby said, stumped. "And you didn't think you could tell me that either?"

"Well, I did say I wanted to leave."

"Were you planning on leaving, like in the middle of the night, before the rent was due, leaving the other women on the hook for our rent too?"

"Well, I was hoping we could pay the rent, stay until the end of April, and then let them know we were leaving, so they could get somebody else to move in. You know it was around that time frame that we would leave anyway."

"Sure," she said, "but what about Meghan?"

"Well, that's another one of those conversations that I need to have," she said. "I don't know. I just ... I don't know," and she started to cry.

All Gabby could do was sit back and try to sort out all this. She'd never ever heard of Wendy proposing anything like this. She was always a very honest, upright, and fair person. "Wendy, are you in some kind of trouble?" she asked cautiously because it just brought back echoes of the abusive history with her and that same partner.

"No, no, no," she said, "well, outside of the fact that I

have no money."

"Well, that's a big one. You at least have some family you might call on," she suggested.

"My mother told me not to call and ask for help anymore," she confessed, "and I just didn't tell you that."

"Sounds like you haven't told me a whole lot of what's been going on in your life," she said, hurt beyond belief. "I'm sorry. I didn't know things were so rough with your family."

"I think they blame you," she said.

"Me?" Gabby cried out in surprise. "Why? What did I do?"

"You convinced me to come here for the winter."

"But we've been planning this since we were kids."

"Right," she said, "and my mother didn't really understand it, and I walked away from a good job there and didn't have any money problems at all, and now, of course, I've nothing but."

"But you also had a savings account that you could rely on, unlike me," she said. "I mean, I had a little bit of savings, but nothing like you did."

"Yes, I know, but I've been out of work so much that I've had to tap into it."

"Well, you've been living happily enough," she said, surprised. "Buying lots of takeout, going out for meals."

"Yes, but all those days and months that you thought I was working, I wasn't," she confessed. "I was with Meghan."

"Oh, my God," Gabby said, sagging back against the headboard. "So you haven't hardly worked since we moved here, and you've been living off your savings this whole winter?"

"Yes."

Gabby didn't even know what to say to that. "You know we made plans for this," she said, "and I thought we understood what we would be doing, moneywise."

"Sure, and then I couldn't get more hours. I couldn't get more work."

"But I don't understand," she said. "You were working in the restaurant industry. Aspen always needs people, even if only washing dishes."

"Right, but remember I had a problem with the one manager."

"Sure, but what's that got to do with it?"

"Well, he'd spread some nasty rumors about me, about me stealing money."

"And you didn't tell me that either?"

"No, because, once again, it sounded like I was a failure and having to confess something I didn't want to confess."

"I'm never ashamed of you," she said. "But we set it all up with fairly strict rules so that something like this wouldn't happen. What really distresses me is that you didn't tell me. Not when you ran into financial difficulties, when I probably could have got you a job somewhere or at least helped you look," she said quietly. "But then, when you went back with Meghan, you didn't tell me either."

"One lie led to another," Wendy said sadly.

"And now?"

"I don't know what *now* is. Everything has shifted."

"Well, I guess, in the worst case, you can go home. You can blame me, and your mother will welcome you back with open arms and help you get back on your feet again."

"Yes," Wendy said. "She probably would. But that's not what I want to do."

"Maybe not, but maybe, at this point, it's what you

should do," she said, wondering if that would separate Wendy from her girlfriend, Meghan. Gabby hated to even try to be an architect of that kind of change, but Wendy had been the one who had wound up in the hospital when they first arrived. "It's been a very tumultuous trip here," Gabby said. "I mean, right from the beginning, when you hooked up with Meghan."

"Please don't bring that up," Wendy said. "I know you'll never let go of that, but I'm trying to forget it."

It was on the tip of Gabby's tongue to suggest that Wendy walk away, but Gabby knew Wendy wouldn't, couldn't do it. "All I can say is that I hope you'll be happy together," Gabby said. "But, if you're planning on staying with her, how is it that you're looking at going home then?"

"I don't know. That's one of the conversations we must have. She's been talking about leaving for a long time."

"Is that smart?"

"Again, I don't know, but she can get a job anywhere. She's a physical trainer."

"That's true, but I'm sure this is a good place for her too."

"I'm not staying," Wendy said mutely. "At least not under these circumstances."

"No, but what if you moved in with her and found yourself in a much better situation, would that help?"

"It would, but I don't know that I want to push the relationship to that point."

"What did you tell her about last night?"

"I basically told her that one of the women was dead in the apartment, and the cops made us clear out."

"Well, that's true as far as it went," she said.

"I know," Wendy said, her voice sad. "Oh, she's up now.

I've got to go." And, just like that, Wendy hung up.

Gabby stared down at the phone, her lips twisting, because that was exactly what Wendy used to do. She always used to run and hide, so that her partner wouldn't know who Wendy was talking to. Just like Wendy's mother didn't like Gabby and blamed her for them moving to Aspen for the winter, Wendy's girlfriend, Meghan, also didn't appreciate Gabby's *interference* either.

And that was just too damn bad because anybody who put her friend in the hospital needed to be interfered with. Gabby was just sorry she wasn't a six-foot-tall three-hundred-pound male who could have pounded Meghan in the ground. Meghan was one of those women who used her physical strength to overpower others. She was a physical trainer, but she was also a bully. And when it came to Wendy—who was obviously somebody who had trouble standing up for herself and standing confidently in her own decisions—that had been a match that Meghan would have thought was made in heaven.

But, for Gabby, it had been a nightmare. She got up, made herself a second cup of coffee, and polished off another four cookies. By the time those cookies were gone, she felt a little bit better. The snow had picked up outside, and it looked to be a raw blustery day. She knew Damon had said she could stay last night, but could she stay longer? She was even now wondering what she was supposed to do for tonight.

She knew, besides Jerry's apartment upstairs, a little guest room was above the bookstore, but she didn't think her boss would let her stay there. She might be wrong, and being in a position of having no choice but to ask him wouldn't be fun. Since Jerry had lived upstairs forever, a bathroom must be upstairs as well, but the whole apartment and that one guest room all connected to the bookstore below. She didn't know just how far his trust would extend.

As she sat here, contemplating what she was supposed to do now, her phone rang again. She looked down and didn't recognize the number. "Hello?"

"Did you get any sleep?"

She smiled at the detective's voice. "No, not really," she confessed. "I kind of drifted in and out. Can I return to the apartment now, live there?" she asked hopefully.

"No," he said. "We've contacted the landlord too. He's coming to look at the damage."

"What damage?" she asked, her voice rising.

He hesitated and said, "Just some damage."

"And can you now tell us who it is?"

"It's Tessa," he said, as she gasped in shock. "Yes," he said, "she's been identified."

"By whom?" she asked.

"Her boyfriend." Then he mentioned the name, but she didn't know it.

"I didn't know her all that well," she confessed. "So I'm not terribly surprised she had a boyfriend too. Everybody seems to have partners here."

"How about you? Do you have one?"

"No," she said, "I don't."

"And you just have Wendy as your alibi for last night, right?"

"Alibi?" she asked, her voice rising into a squeak.

"Yes," he said, "alibi."

"You heard it going on over the phone," she said.

"I know," he said, in that soothing voice that she was coming to crave. "But I'll check everybody's whereabouts."

She quickly explained about her and Wendy being home for the whole evening and going to bed early.

"That's fine," he said. "We'll get a statement from you anyway."

"Are you telling me that I can't move back there?"

"At the moment you certainly can't, no."

"And it might not be something I can move back into anytime soon?"

"Quite possibly not."

"Wow," she said, sagging back onto the bed. "So I don't even know where to go now," she whispered to herself.

"Well, at the moment you have a place," he said, "so let's deal with this one step at a time."

"Well, I can hardly sit here on your goodwill," she said, "and no way I could possibly afford to rent this."

He asked, "How much were you paying for your apartment?" She mentioned her part, and that had him laughing. "Seriously?"

"Yes," she said, "we were splitting the full amount, and that was my share of it."

"Wow," he said. "I've owned my own place, so I've forgotten what rents are like here."

"Especially being a tourist town," she said quietly.

"Well, let me think about it," he said. "I'll see what I can come up with."

"But I need to find a place for today," she said, fretting.

"You can stay there today and tonight," he said shortly.

She stopped and said, "Are you sure?"

"Well, I won't kick you out into the snow," he said. "Obviously, as a long-term plan, that's not a great solution, but it will get us through this immediate problem."

"That's great," she said, "and thank you. To know that

I'm even okay for today is huge right now."

"Right," he said, and she wondered if he was already wishing he hadn't made the offer.

"Can you tell me anything about what happened in our apartment?"

"Not yet," he said. "I'll pop over in a little bit."

"Oh, okay," she said. "And I didn't mean to impose," she said, "but I found some coffee in the drawer, and I had some."

With a note of surprise, he said, "Coffee and stuff are still there?"

"Cookies and some coffee," she said, "so that was my breakfast."

"Good," he said. "If you find any food that you can use, go ahead. I don't know how old or stale it might be though."

"That's fine," she said. "It's amazing what you'll eat when you're hungry."

"I guess you haven't eaten either, have you?"

"Just the cookies," she said, "but that was fine."

"Okay, I'll take a look when I get there and see what else might be around." And, with that, he hung up.

She wasn't sure what he meant by that, but she wouldn't argue, since he said she could have the coffee, and now she was tempted to get another cup.

She got up and checked if there was more than one cup. If so, then she would indulge, but otherwise she would hold off for later today or even tomorrow. As it was, she opened the cupboard below and found an entire case. She stared at the gold mine with joy. She pulled it out to find more cookies, saltines, some rye crackers, and several cans of tuna. She stared at the tuna. "What an odd thing to find."

But not. Of course it could be kept for a long time without perishing, so it made sense, depending on who'd been here last. And she didn't mind because this helped her out tremendously. After finding that, she made a thorough search of every cupboard to see if any other gems could be put to use.

As it was, she found a little tiny fridge, hidden behind those fancy doors to hide the ugly appliances. Only these appliances were pretty on their own. Nothing perishable was in it, but she found mustard, ketchup, and mayonnaise. She was good with that. She checked the dates on them, and they were all still fine, so she pulled out some crackers and the mayo, opened up one of the cans of tuna, and had it on crackers. It was a cold meal to go along with the cookies she'd had earlier, but it was something.

She didn't even think about what food they all had back at the apartment. Probably a little bit remained but not a whole lot. They'd been pretty skimpy on the food lately, and now she knew why; everybody seemed to have partners that they were eating with, while Gabby had been sticking to her little budget and trying to stay alive on it. She shook her head at that—again feeling abandoned by her roommates, her supposed friends—and, by the time she'd finished eating, she remained seated at the small table, watching the snowfall from the windows.

She watched as a vehicle pulled up and parked outside the garage. As she watched, the detective got out, and she checked her phone to see it was already ten o'clock. She hurriedly rose to clean up whatever mess she'd made, to make sure he understood how much she appreciated being here and that she would make sure it would be well taken care of.

When he knocked at the door, she opened it with a

smile and said, "Hi."

"Hi," he said. As he looked around the small apartment, he said, "It's actually a nice little space, isn't it?"

"It is," she said, "and it's lovely to see the snow falling and not being in it." She rolled her eyes at his glance. "I know. I know. It's part of being in Aspen, but there's also something nice about enjoying it from inside and not having to go out in it."

He walked in and had a large bag with him. He placed it on the counter and said, "I didn't even think to ask if you could use any of this stuff," he said, "but I brought over a few things."

She looked at the bag in surprise. "Where did you get this stuff from?"

"My place," he said in a short voice. He unloaded a dozen eggs, half a block of cheese, what looked like some sliced ham, a loaf of bread, some peanut butter, jam, and honey. It was basically a care package.

She stared at the food and then at him, her heart swelling at his generosity. "Thank you."

He looked at her, shrugged, and said, "It's the least I can do."

"Maybe so, but it's also way more than most people would do," she said. "You know that, right?"

"I'm not most people," he said briskly. He proceeded to put away the food and said, "Help yourself to anything here you want and can use. I didn't know exactly all that you needed."

"Well, the bread and peanut butter is a staple," she said humorously.

He chuckled. "For almost everybody, yes." He looked around at the apartment and said, "You should be safe enough here."

At his wording, she stopped, stared at him, and said, *"Safe enough?"*

He just gave her a shuttered look.

"Is there any reason to think that what happened to Tessa will happen to anybody else?" she asked, as she held her breath, waiting for his answer.

"Until we've done our investigation," he said, "we have no way to know anything yet."

She stopped and took a long slow deep breath. "I'm really confused."

"So are we," he said bluntly. "Your friend was butchered."

She stared, her hand at her throat, as she took several steps back to come up against the kitchen chair and slowly sat down. "Butchered?"

"Decapitated, and her chest was completely flayed apart."

Her stomach rose, and her throat closed. Suddenly she was bent over, her head between her knees.

"Take it easy."

She nodded, took a deep breath, and slowly straightened. "So how did anybody identify her?"

"Well, that's the trick. The boyfriend identified several tattoos on her hip and lower spine, and she was wearing a ring that he'd given her. But, without the head, we can't really be sure until the coroner confirms ID."

She shuddered at the thought. "My God. Why would anybody do that to her?" she asked, her voice trembling, as she wrapped her arms around her chest.

"That's what we're still trying to find out," he said.

"And how fast it all happened." She stared at him in

shock. "We heard these horrible noises," she whispered. "But we had no idea what was going on. Then we called you."

"And that call was recorded," he said, "which is a good thing because we heard the noises in the distance, but it did sound more like an animal."

"I know," she said. "That's all we could think of too. But definitely no animal was involved in this." She stared at him. "She was really butchered?"

He held back from telling her that basically the butchering happened as part of the murder. The killer wasn't kind enough to wait until Tessa was dead before he flayed her.

Gabby just continued to stare at him.

He worried about the paleness of her skin. Jake had warned him about not giving her too many of the details, but it was hard not to give her some answers, when she'd been there in the apartment at the time.

"Oh, my God," she said, reaching up with trembling hands to cup her face. "I just don't understand what's going on anymore."

"Has something else happened?" he asked in a sharp tone.

"No, not really," she said.

"*Not really* isn't good enough," he said.

She looked at him in surprise, then waved her hand, as if to push it off to the side, and said, "I just didn't realize that Wendy had been lying about her situation and basically hadn't been telling me anything about what had gone on for the last few months. We're best friends. We came here together, and I only found out through this nightmare that she'd been keeping all this stuff from me."

"You mean, the girlfriend?"

"Yes, that's part of it," she said, "but also the fact that

Wendy had no income and that she's been living off her savings, while pretending to work."

"Lots of jobs are in town," he said, frowning.

"There are, but she had a confrontation with one of the managers in the kitchen where she worked. According to her, he spread some rumors that made her hard to hire again."

"What kind of rumors?"

"He said she was stealing," she said quietly.

"Would she have stolen from him? Because that'll definitely get you kicked out of any kitchen," he said curiously, "which is almost like a self-sabotaging kind of thing, unless she was hungry and stole food."

She stared at him, surprised. "I'm not even sure," she said. "I only found out about it this morning. Wendy had a decent amount of money set aside, and we were all supposed to head back to our normal world when this winter was over. But apparently, while she's been here, she has gone through the bulk of her money, and her parents blame me for this entire fiasco."

"WOW," DAMON SAID, leaning against the counter as he studied her for a long moment. "Sounds like it's been an interesting winter so far."

"Is that the word for it?" she asked. She shook her head, staring back out the window. "Everything has just been so bizarre."

"Sometimes life is like that," he said.

"Maybe," she said. "I don't appreciate it."

He snorted. "Welcome to life." She gave him a lopsided grin that he found endearing. She looked pretty cute in that moment. Even as he warned himself not to go down that pathway, his heart tugged him there nonetheless. "I'm sorry," he said, looking at his watch. "I have to go."

"Fine," she said. "If there's anything I can do to help, let me know."

"Stay out of trouble. How's that?" he said. "It's hard enough for me to get through all this as it is without you bringing up tarot cards and ghosts."

She winced. "Yeah, I'd like to never bring it up myself again," she said, "but, after what he said, it's hard for me to think of anything else."

"What who said?"

She turned to him. "The guy who pushed me."

He stared. "You never said anything about him speaking to you."

"Well, that's probably because I knew you didn't believe me in the first place," she said, frowning.

"I can't believe anything you say," he said, "if you don't tell me the truth."

"It's the truth as I remember it," she said. "I was in a panic, trying to save myself. Remember?"

Everything she said sounded right. Everything had the right tone, the right tenor, to make him believe she was telling the truth. "So what exactly was it that he said to you?"

She walked him through the little bit that she remembered.

"And he said, he was *Death*?"

"Yes," she said.

"So somebody is just messing with you?"

"Well, in theory, yes," she said. But then she stopped and said, "The problem is, I didn't see anybody."

"No, of course not," he said. "But then, you were also pretty busy, weren't you?"

"Yeah, that's one way to look at it," she said. "It was just insane while I was hurled down the mountain. I did hear his voice while I was resting on the bottom, but that's all."

"I think that's probably quite enough," he said.

"It just makes no sense," she whispered.

"Well, it *will* make sense," he said. "You just aren't necessarily aware of it yet."

She looked at him and said, "Have you ever had any psychic experiences?"

He shook his head immediately, even as a voice inside called him a liar. "No," he said, "none." She looked at him for a long moment and just something in that gaze of hers had him shifting uneasily on his feet.

"Interesting," she murmured. "You don't like telling the truth about that either."

He glared at her. "I haven't had anything like that."

She nodded slowly. "I don't know," she said. "Nowadays everything is different. It's like I can see things more clearly. I can hear things a little bit better, or maybe it's my intuition. I don't know. Yesterday I had superhigh energy and was happy, but today it's like a completely different world."

"Well, yesterday you were thankful you were still alive after a terribly traumatic accident," he said, "and today a friend has been murdered."

Her shoulders sagged at the reminder. "Great," she said, reaching up to cover her eyes for a moment, her shoulders shaking. "She didn't deserve that," she cried out, and the tears dripped down her cheeks. "She was a lovely girl."

"Well, hold on to that thought," he said. "Also I need a list of anybody you ever saw around the apartment or who knew where you lived and who knew her."

She stared at him in shock. "You're thinking it's somebody I know?"

"What I'm thinking is that somebody saw her and went after her. But I don't have a motivation, and I don't know how he knew she was there. I'm sure you have all the information as far as where she was working and the people she worked with," he said.

She replied, "Kinda. I know the restaurant name, and you can check out the rest there. That's one official line of inquiry, but that's not the same as checking in with her friends. I don't think I ever met anybody," she said, frowning, trying to remember.

"Well, while you're here, relaxing and trying to recuperate," he said, "I want as much information as you can think to give me. I've got to go back to the office now."

"Fine," she said. "I'll text you if I come up with anything."

"I'll stop by later this afternoon," he said, and, with that, he turned and headed out the door.

CHAPTER SIX

"**W**ELL, THAT WAS fast," Gabby said. "I wonder if he's coming back to check up on me, or if there's some other reason." She sighed to herself.

A voice in the back of her head said, *He's checking up on you.*

She snorted at that. "You don't know that."

Yes, I do.

"No, you don't."

Yes, I do!

"No, you don't."

Yes, I do.

She stopped, took a long slow deep breath. "That's it. I'm officially going nuts."

You are nuts.

"I am not," she said, then stopped. "Am I arguing with myself?"

No, you're arguing with me, said the voice in her head. Then it started to laugh like a crazy man and said, *You didn't even recognize me. How simple are you?* And, with that, he disappeared.

She *had* lost her mind.

Then she realized that the other voice in her head may have actually happened. She wrapped her arms around her chest and rocked herself back and forth, whispering, "Oh, my God. Oh, my God. Oh, my God." When her phone rang, she dashed to pick it up. "Hello?"

"What's the matter?" Damon asked in a sharp voice.

"What?" she asked, confusion in her voice, trying to figure out what he was talking about.

"You called out to me," he said. "What the hell is going on?"

"I called out to you?" She stared around the apartment, certain now that she was going completely mad. "What do you mean, I called out?"

He hesitated, then asked, "Are you okay?"

"No," she said, "I'm not okay. The damn ghost is talking to me again." And, with that, she burst into tears. He kept trying to talk to her on the phone, and she ended up just putting the phone down as her hands were trembling and couldn't hold it any longer. She didn't know how many minutes she sat here, but, when she heard footsteps on the stairs, she wasn't surprised to see Damon burst through the door. He dropped down in front of her, and she just threw her arms around his neck and started to cry. "Am I going crazy?" she murmured against his chest.

He held her close and let her bawl.

When she finally regained some semblance of control, she pulled back and wiped her eyes on her sleeve, like a child. She sniffled several times and took several big deep gulps of air and said, "I swear to God, that ghost who pushed me talked to me again." She stared up at his gaze that was deep and dark and gave nothing away. She sat back and said, "You don't believe me."

"I don't know what to believe," he said. "In theory, no. I mean, I can't believe because it doesn't make any sense."

She nodded. "I know. I know that. I mean, in theory, I

really do understand that," she whispered. "I just don't know what to say because it's what happened."

"And what did he say?"

"It's like I was having an argument with myself," she said. "And it just made no sense. Then he said I was actually arguing with him, not me, and he laughed at me, like I was some kind of an idiot for not having figured that out."

"And how would you possibly figure it out?" he said. "When you, in theory, don't really have any exposure to this kind of stuff." He looked at her closely. "Or do you?"

"*This kind of stuff?*" she repeated with a slight sarcastic overtone. "I don't even know what *this* is."

"You're the one who keeps calling it a ghost."

"As far as I know," she said, "it is. Yet I've never spoken to a ghost in my life before."

"I want you to talk to somebody," he said abruptly.

She looked at him and asked, "A shrink?"

"A specialist," he temporized.

"A shrink," she said, her shoulders sagging.

"Don't you want to figure out if there are voices in your head or if something else is going on?"

"They won't be open to the idea of ghosts. They'll start talking multiple personalities and all kinds of crap like that."

"I don't know," he said. "We have a very interesting psychologist on staff."

"I'll do it," she said, sighing loudly. "If for nothing else than to see if I'm going crazy. I don't want to be on any medication though," she fretted.

"Medication isn't always bad," he said.

"It always makes me feel funny."

"But you don't know what this medication is," he said with a wry twist.

She groaned. "No. I know that." She shrugged. "But I'll try to listen to anything he says."

"That's fine." Then he straightened up and said, "Let me make a call and see what we can set up."

She nodded, as he walked a few feet away. She walked over to the small kitchen and made herself a cup of coffee. Thank heavens for the big case of coffee under the counter that would keep her supplied for a long time. At the same time, she wasn't sure that she should even be drinking this much, as if she were running purely on nerves.

She stared around the living room, now very dry-eyed, as she huddled into the single oversize recliner. Gazing out the window, she hugged her coffee cup to her. This was such a uniquely comfortable spot, full of luxury, and made her feel like she was in a surreal environment, but it just went along with everything else.

She thought briefly about the other women she shared the apartment with, wondering why nobody had contacted her, but, then again, she hadn't reached out to them either. It said a lot about who they were really. More roommates, not so much friends.

Gabby was still hurting from Wendy's lack of sharing and her inability to tell Gabby about Meghan again. Friends were for telling things like that. Had Gabby really been so hard on Meghan? Maybe Gabby had; maybe that had been her fault entirely. That just sent her down another ugly path.

When Damon stepped in front of her, she looked up at him and said, "And?"

"We can get you in this afternoon."

She winced. "Meaning that I'm really a head case, and they want to know if I had anything to do with my friend's death?"

He stared at her in surprise. "How did you segue to all that from one appointment being scheduled?"

"It's the only reason you could get me in so fast," she said. "You have a murder to solve, and I'm a likely suspect."

"I don't know about a likely suspect," he said, "but I will concede that, because you are a part of the case, the appointment is a little bit faster than normal."

She nodded. "How long do I have?"

"About an hour," he said, "and I'll drive you myself."

"Wow," she said, "they must have really made an opening then."

"Yep, they did," he said cheerfully.

She nodded glumly. "I guess thanks are in order then."

"Don't sound so unimpressed about it," he said.

"Hard to be impressed," she replied. "When you think about it, it's just all bad news."

"Well, it would be easy to say that except, in theory, you don't understand how this works."

"I understand a lot," she said, "but I don't understand what's going on in my head at all."

"Which is why we'll let you talk to somebody."

She nodded slowly. "If you say so."

He stayed with her, and they had half an hour of basic general conversations about the town, the people, and snowboarding, until he looked at his watch and said, "Finish up the last of your coffee and let's go."

She winced, and, tossing back the last of the caffeine, she got up, grabbed her jacket, put on her boots, and stood here, waiting for him to tell her what was next. He led her down to his vehicle, and the snow bit at her skin, as she stepped outside. She looked up at the dark stormy clouds and said, "This is about how I feel right now."

"Yeah," he said, "let's not forget that you are at least feeling something and that your girlfriend no longer has that opportunity."

With that bitter reminder, she hopped into his vehicle and didn't say another word.

DAMON PROBABLY SHOULDN'T have said that to Gabby, but it was something that most people needed to be reminded of. They were lucky that they were even alive. Lucky they were here and doing what they were doing, versus all the people who could no longer do that. He was pretty damn sure that Tessa wanted to have a life as she chose to lead it, not ending up in the morgue as she was now.

It was all just a little too weird. Her death has caused quite a stir among Damon's team too. He, for one, was still trying to figure out what could possibly have done that kind of damage to the body, and the other guys were muttering about the dark side of the history of Aspen. Damon hadn't had a chance to read up on that, but apparently a somewhat similar death had happened. He hoped that it wasn't truly similar, but that, over time, general gossip had expanded it.

He pulled up in front of Dr. Mica's office and parked. He looked at Gabby to see her fingers intertwined in a white-knuckle grip. "It'll be okay, you know?"

She nodded mutely and didn't say anything.

He'd been aware of a rising tension, the closer and closer they got to their destination, but he hadn't realized how unnerved she was. "Are you worried about meeting her," he said, "or about what's happening to you?"

"Both, and the explosive combination of when they come together," she said starkly.

That made him pause, and he realized just how important the outcome of this visit was. He nodded slowly. "I hadn't considered that." He hesitated and said, "Do you want me to come in with you?"

She looked at him in surprise, yet he could see the relief in her eyes, but almost immediately she masked it and then shook her head.

"No, that probably wouldn't be right. But thank you for offering." And, as if she had a gust of courage, she quickly opened the car door, hopped out, and slammed the door shut, racing up to the front steps, where she stood under the eaves, out from under the weather. He got out slower, locked the vehicle, and joined her.

As he opened the front door and headed toward the office, she asked, "How do you know this doctor?"

"She's a consultant for the police force," he said. "I've had a few times where I've needed to see her myself." He caught her staring at him in surprise, then gave her a smile. "Think about it. Think about the work I do and how hard it is sometimes. When you save some abused woman from violence, only to turn around and save her again a week later because she went back? How do you think that makes me feel?"

She winced at that. "Thanks. That just brought it a little bit too close to home. I don't think Wendy sees herself as an abused woman."

"Honestly, they never do," he said sadly. "Until it's too late."

"And is it often too late?" she asked, worry in her voice.

"Unfortunately, yes," he said. "A lot of times it's too late. And I'm not saying that's what'll happen to your friend, but it is a problem," he said. She nodded, and slowly he reached out a hand, grabbed hers, and said, "Hey, it'll be okay."

She snorted. "No," she said, "I'm not sure anything will be okay anymore."

"Well, that is something you'll have to decide for yourself. Because life happens, and you can just react, or you can choose to take your reaction and make something out of that." He said, "It doesn't all have to be negative."

She took a deep breath, nodded slowly. "I know that," she said. "I guess I'm just not to the point of feeling like I'm in control of anything right now."

"Well, let's go talk to Dr. Mica and see." He pushed open the door to the office to find Dr. Mica standing in the reception area with a stack of papers in her hands.

She looked up, smiled, and said, "There you are."

"Thank you for seeing us so quickly," he said. With that, he introduced them and said, "Some interesting things have been happening."

Dr. Mica looked at him and then looked at Gabby. "Come on into my office," she said. "We can talk there."

As they walked into the office, Damon didn't know what he should do.

When Gabby got to the doorway of Dr. Mica's office, she turned to look at him, frowned, and said, "You might as well come in."

"If you want me there," he said.

"Well, if I don't, I guess I'll ask you to step out," she said in a tight voice.

He nodded, giving her emotional support, as he walked in. Dr. Mica's eyebrows were raised, but, as she looked at him, he gave an almost imperceptible shrug, as if to say it was all good. Then he sat down in one of the chairs.

"So tell me what's going on," Dr. Mica said.

"It started with me being pushed down the mountain and almost dying the day before yesterday," she said, "and it ended, so far, with my roommate being murdered last night, and me being hounded by a ghost."

It all came out in such a fast rush that Damon could see Dr. Mica trying to blink and process at the same time.

"Okay," she said slowly. "That's a lot of information, so let's unpack that a bit. Who pushed you down the mountain?"

"I don't know," Gabby said. "I was standing there on my board, completely in control, and, the next thing I know, I was going at a speed that was way more than anything I could have produced on my own, taking me out of bounds over a hump, where I landed on this tiny outreach of rock. The detective here, on his side job with ski patrol, came and helped rescue me."

"Well, good job there, Damon," she said with a bright smile. Damon tilted his head, acknowledging but not entering the conversation. She turned back to Gabby. "Then what happened?"

"I was pretty traumatized. He insisted I go to the hospital, but I was completely fine, and I felt good, which made no sense, considering the terrible fall I took, but I was fine," she said with a shake of her head. "The next morning, I woke up superenergized, superhungry, having a wonderful day. Everything was great. I woke up today feeling off, and it was just—I don't know—it was the antithesis of what should have been."

"That's not necessarily true," Dr. Mica said. "You came close to death, and, instead of dying, you had a realization that life was something very special and worth living."

"Potentially," she said. "In the meantime, last night I

was home with one of my roommates. Five of us share a place, due to the high rents here," she said. "We woke up to a strange sound, and my girlfriend came into my room. We were too scared to go out to the living room, and then we heard these absolutely horrible noises, terrifying noises," she said, stopping, taking several deep breaths.

"And that's when we called the detective here, who came running, and told us to stay locked up in my room, which we did. We thought we heard somebody coming down the hallway toward us, but then the sirens started," she said, starting to shake, caught up in the memory. Damon reached out a hand and grabbed her fingers, and she clutched his fingers supertight. "And then all of a sudden Damon showed up."

"You didn't tell me that the killer walked down the hallway toward you," he said.

"Didn't we?" She looked at him in surprise and then shook her head. "I'm surprised I was even coherent enough to talk."

"Okay, so that was a horribly traumatic session last night," the doctor said. "Now what else has happened?"

"I ended up leaving the apartment because, well, it was a horrible murder scene, and I'm all alone because my best friend apparently had another relationship to go to that she hadn't told me about."

"And was that some sort of a betrayal for you?"

"Yes," she said. "I know it sounds foolish, but, yes. We came here together for the winter to enjoy snowboarding, and I thought she was part of it all and onboard. We had all these plans on how we would make it work financially, but the other thing I didn't know was that she had lost her job early on and didn't tell me. So she has been spending her savings this whole time and now has no money left. Her parents blame me for the loss of all her savings, and I didn't even know that was going on," she said in bewilderment, as the words spilled out of her.

"Anyway, Damon found me a place to spend the night," she said. "Then this morning, I started to rehash everything that was going on, after Damon told me which of my roommates was murdered, and it seemed like I was having this ongoing argument in my head. And of course—" She stopped.

"*Of course*, what?"

"Well, in some ways, it makes sense that you argue in your head. I mean, lots of people do it." She looked from Damon to the doc. "Right?"

"Yes, of course," the doctor said. "We argue with ourselves at times. It's completely normal."

Gabby took a deep breath of relief. "Right, so that's what I thought, but then he said that I wasn't arguing with myself. That I was arguing with him and that, if I thought I could hide, I was wrong," she whispered.

"And who do you mean by *he*?"

"When I first got pushed off the mountain," she said, "it felt like an unseen force pushed me between my shoulder blades."

Damon looked at her in surprise because that was also a detail she hadn't mentioned.

"And when I finally came to rest, and I was still alive, he said something to me." She went on to explain how he'd said it and what he had said, then continued, "And so it was that same voice that I heard again."

"And that was earlier today?"

"Yes," she said, and she held out her hands, which were

trembling. "I get that I've been through a couple really horrible experiences, and I'm sure that shock is playing into all this to some degree. I just don't know what else it is."

"It's all very interesting," Dr. Mica said. She studied Gabby, but in an odd way, like Dr. Mica was focused on something almost slightly to the side of Gabby.

Damon looked at the doc. "What is it you're thinking?"

She looked at him and smiled. "Well, it's hard to say," she said. "An awful lot of trauma is happening here, like she just said, and that can mess with our minds. The thing is, she believes that this is what's going on and that another entity is involved, yet is determined that she shouldn't be believing it."

"Well, of course I shouldn't be," Gabby said. "There's no such thing as ghosts."

"Isn't there?" Dr. Mica said with a smile. They both stared at her.

"Are you saying you believe there are?" Gabby asked.

"I come from a different vantage point than you guys do," she said, "and we do believe that there is life after death and that our ancestors have a life once they have passed from this realm. So I won't tell you right now that you're being possessed or that there's a ghost or anything else like that. But I won't knock it either."

"Wow," Gabby said, staring in shock. "I thought for sure you would tell me that I was crazy and would want to give me some pills to make life come back to something resembling normality."

"If I thought life was that easily handled," she said, "I would. But I don't know that that's the answer right now."

"I don't think it is," Gabby said quietly.

"Why is that?"

"Because this entity, this person that I keep fussing about," she said, "I think he's here right now."

Damon leaned forward and looked at her. "What are you talking about?"

She started to shake. "I feel like he's right here," she said, and she put her hand out to the space on the right side of where she sat. "It's cold right here. Like really cold."

He immediately ran his hand through the space too, and, indeed, it was cold. He reared back slightly, then looked at Dr. Mica to see an odd look on her face. He stopped and stared at her. "What is it you're not telling us, Doc?"

She looked at him with a frown. "I'm not exactly sure," she said. She looked at Gabby. "Can you talk to him?"

"I don't want to," Gabby whispered.

"Well, maybe you should try, if you believe he's here," she said gently. "Maybe he'll tell you what he wants."

"He told me that he wants me to die," she said in a rush. "He told me that before."

"And why should you die?"

"I don't know," she cried out.

"Easy, *shh*. Take it easy," Dr. Mica said. "Let's see what we can figure out here."

"There's nothing to figure out," she said, bolting to her feet. She looked at Damon. "I told you this wouldn't work."

"Don't panic," he said, standing and reaching for her, but he had to step through the space that had been cold before. Instantly a chill wafted through him. He was struck by almost a darkness inside it, and, for the first time, he wondered if maybe she was telling the truth, if something completely abnormal was going on here, something super-natural? He turned to look at Dr. Mica to find her still staring at the same spot, and he knew that something was going on in her world that she didn't want to share.

She looked up at him and said, "Maybe you should take her home and look after her tonight."

He said, "If you know anybody who can help her—" He left it wide open for interpretation because, if Dr. Mica wasn't prepared to say anything to him, she might not be prepared to get anybody in to help. Yet obviously they needed help of some kind.

"Let me think about it," she said quietly.

He took a deep breath. "Okay." Then he said, "Come on, Gabby. Let's get you back to the apartment."

She nodded and stepped closer to him. He found he could do nothing else but wrap his arms around her and hold her close. Even as he walked her out of the doctor's office, Damon turned to look at the strange cold spot in the office. And the doctor was staring at it in the same way that Damon was. He still couldn't see a thing, but he was pretty damn sure she did.

CHAPTER SEVEN

BACK IN THE vehicle Gabby sat here, shaking almost uncontrollably. She whispered, her teeth chattering, "Can we turn up the heat?" Damon did so immediately, until she was blasted by hot air, as he slowly drove through town and the snow back to the garage apartment. When she got out, she asked, "Are you okay if I stay here for the rest of the day?"

"I told you that you're fine here," he said, bristling.

She looked at him gratefully. "Thanks," she said, and she raced up the stairs. She didn't know if he would follow or not, but she needed to be alone. She needed time to think, time to sort through just what was going on in her world, and yet she knew that the more time she had, the fewer answers there would really be.

When she entered the small studio suite, Damon came up the stairs behind her. She was torn between relief and the need to be alone. "I'm not good company," she said, when he walked in.

"Not expecting you to be," he said, "but you need real food."

"I ate some tuna on crackers and those cookies that were here."

"They were probably ancient," he said in disgust.

"It was food," she said, with a shrug. "I haven't really

bothered too much about quality lately."

"That may be, but I brought some fresh stuff." He opened the fridge and started pulling out food.

She noted how dark it was getting outside. "I've totally lost track of time," she murmured.

"It's okay," he said. "You don't need to be keeping track."

"Well, you can't just babysit me all the time," she said.

"Wasn't planning on it," he replied.

She immediately headed for the chair by the corner window and pulled out a blanket and wrapped herself up in it. "What are you making?" she asked.

"I figured an omelet," he said, as he chopped onions and bacon, which he quickly popped into a frying pan and sautéed while she watched.

"I don't know if I can eat anything," she confessed.

"I know that," he said, "but you'll need to."

"What was Dr. Mica looking at?"

He looked up at her and said, "You saw that too, huh?"

"Oh, yeah," she said. "I did, and it kind of freaked me out."

"Yeah, me too, but I'm not sure it was for the same reason."

"What was your reason?" she asked.

"I've been to her and spoken with her many times," he said. "So I already know who she is as a person, but her reaction today to some of what you had to say was a little different than I expected."

"Is that what you call it?" she said, turning to stare out the window.

"But she's not responsible for any of this," he said, "so we track down the methodology for you to deal with the trauma that you're dealing with. That'll require a medical professional, while we're still tracking down the killer."

"And yet," she said, turning to look at him, "you're right here, babysitting me."

"I am," but he didn't elaborate.

"You think I'm a suspect, don't you?" Her heart sank. "Oh, my God. Do you actually think I could do something like that to Tessa? To even think that you might have considered that for a single moment," she said, "that's just so incredibly wrong."

"You're not a suspect, and I'm not sure that you're in any danger," he said.

"*Not sure?*" she said, pouncing on the phrase.

"No," he said. "We're not sure of anything at this moment. I'm trying to keep an eye on you to ensure that you get through this."

"Oh," she said, as she sank back into her chair, uncertain what to say to that. "Have we found any evidence or anything to point to who it was?"

"It's an ongoing case," he said. "I can't talk about it."

"Maybe not," she said, "but obviously something is going on, and you have some evidence."

"Is there?" he asked. "Because seriously, when you think about it, not a whole lot is out there."

"Forensics?"

"It's too early for anything to come back," he said.

She sagged in place. "Of course," she said, "that would make life way too easy, wouldn't it?"

"We need to look at everybody. You want us to find the killer, don't you?"

"Of course," she said, curling up tighter into a ball. "It's just so hard to believe that anybody would have killed

Tessa."

"I'm still looking at Tessa's background, and I'm still trying to find a motive in my head that makes any sense. You must know more than I do about her life. So what did you do when you spent time with her?"

"I'm not sure I ever really did," she said, shaking her head. "It was more a case of spending time with Wendy, and Liz to a certain extent, but Tessa? No. It was more like she was here, and then she was gone more than she was here, the same as Betty. Because they must have been with their boyfriends all the time. I guess they were just not quite ready to move in and make that kind of commitment to each other."

"And that's understandable."

"Sure, but it's pretty hard to pay the rent in town here, but Tessa managed to get away from the tight living quarters because she had the boyfriend."

"Exactly," he said, "whereas you and Wendy were here with a plan and a date and thought everything was moving in the direction you expected it to."

"And, boy, was I wrong," she said. "I'm still not sure. She was talking to me about leaving and leaving soon, and then she pulls that about Meghan, so I don't know if she's thinking Meghan will leave with her or if she's using that as an excuse to get away from Meghan. I really don't understand," she said. "I need to talk to her, and we did briefly on the phone earlier, but I haven't heard from anybody else so far."

"Did you try to contact them?"

"No," she said quietly, "I haven't."

"And they haven't contacted you for probably the same reason."

"And what reason is that?"

"You tell me," he said, looking at her with that considering glance of his.

She shrugged. "I didn't reach out to Wendy because I don't really know what to say."

"I get it," he said. "What about the others?"

"I'm not even sure I have their contact information," she said. "I'm wasn't kidding when I told you that we didn't have much of anything to do with them."

"So, just five strangers rooming together for a winter?"

"Pretty much, though I probably would have said that we were friends before all this, until you asked all these questions, and suddenly I wasn't sure I knew anything about anybody."

"I think that's fairly standard actually. Often you can get away with a certain level of social niceties that make you think that you actually know somebody, but you really don't."

"So, did you check to see if anybody had a criminal record?" she asked. "Did you check where Tessa worked? Did you check, you know, I don't know. Her friend group?" she said. "She was really active and busy, so I imagine she had a wide social group."

"She did," he said. "We're still checking."

"Right, and of course the murder you described is just a little to the left of normal," she said, "if any murder is normal."

"It's very far to the left, if that's what you want to call it," he said. "And that's another reason why we're not necessarily looking at a woman."

"Why is that?"

"Because a tremendous amount of strength was required," he said.

"Oh," she said, in a small voice, hating to even imagine what he said.

"It is what it is," he said, "but don't worry, we're on it."

"Yes, as long as there isn't another one."

"Let's hope not," he said.

She shivered.

He called her over and said, "Come on. You have an omelet here to eat."

She got up slowly, walked over, and said, "I'm really not sure I can eat it."

"Remember that part about you needing to eat?"

She sat down at the counter, and he placed a plate in front of her. "It looks really good," she said in surprise.

"I do like to cook," he said, with a note of humor.

"Maybe, but," she started, "I'm really—"

"Stop," he cut in. "You need to eat. You need it for your strength, just in case more emotional shocks are coming your way. You need reserves in order to recover somehow."

Slowly she picked up her fork and cut a small bite and put it in her mouth. She gave a happy sigh. "It is really good."

"Exactly," he said, "and that makes it easier to get a lot more food down. So eat, please."

She nodded, and, while she ate, his phone rang. He stepped away and answered it. She only heard part of the conversation, but it sounded like he was talking to another team member or somebody in forensics. When he finally hung up, she sat here, determined not to quiz him about the call. "Do you get to share that information?" she blurted out, despite her best intentions.

"The only information so far is that there is nothing and

nothing and more nothing. Forensics didn't come up with anything meaningful. All the friends say they had no idea where Tessa was. Her boyfriend says that she was home that night and that he had just talked to her on the phone around dinnertime, when she was at work. They confirmed that she was only missing or not accounted for in those hours after work."

"And she could have been there," she said, "but I didn't wake up and hear her come home."

"And that's where the problem is," he said. "No cameras are in that building."

She looked at him in surprise. "I thought there was. That's one of the reasons why we were supposed to pay so much money," she said indignantly. "We were told the cost was higher because it was so well secured."

"The cameras were down," he said.

She stared at him in horror. "On purpose?"

"I don't know," he said. "We're not there yet."

"*Not there yet.*" She shook her head and took another bite of the omelet. She swallowed and continued to shake her head.

"When do you go back to work?" he asked.

"Tomorrow," she said, her voice shaky. "If I still have a job."

"Why wouldn't you?"

"My boss is superstitious. He brought me on because he thought I would bring in business. Then he told me to try anything that would bring in more business because the store was suffering. So I started the tarot stuff, and, as you know, that blew up in my face too."

He snorted. "You think? Whatever made you think of it in the first place?"

"A pack of cards was just sitting there on the counter," she said. "It had been something he had for sale, and the packaging was damaged. So I asked what he wanted to do with it, since it's hard to sell stuff with damaged packaging. He just blew me off and walked away, muttering to himself. So I picked them up and decided I might as well put them to good use."

"So you had no ulterior motive or anything beyond that?"

"No, not at all," she said. "I had no clue that would start any of this."

"And yet when you gave these messages in the readings, they were just in jest?"

"Well, what else would they be?" she asked, staring at him. "I get the idea that you think there could be something to all this stuff, but you don't want to actually say so."

"I don't know what *there* is," he said, in a strange tone. "But several people followed your lead in the readings, and apparently you said certain events would happen, and they did."

"Sure, but I was just reading the cards," she said. "And, besides, I pulled the Death card before I went snowboarding that day, and I didn't die."

"But you almost did," he said. "Surely that counts for something." He grabbed his coat and said, "I've got to take off now."

"Okay," she said, "I'll be right here."

He gave her a hint of a smile. "Do that and stay safe."

Something about his tone when he said that though had her bolting to her feet. "So you do think I'm in danger?"

He looked at her in surprise and said, "No, I don't have any reason to believe that."

She frowned, then watched as he turned and left. Just what had that phone call been all about? Though he'd tried to cover it with a bit of conversation, he'd left pretty abruptly after the call. Too abruptly. With that, she realized that either he got a break in the case or something else happened that was connected to the case. She quickly snatched up her phone and then texted him. **Has there been another victim?**

He texted back **Yes.**

"Oh, my God," she said, texting him again. **Please tell me that it's not one of my friends.**

I don't know who it is, he typed, **at least not yet.**

Please let me know, she wrote.

But he didn't answer.

THE CONVERSATION HADN'T been an easy one, and Damon had hoped he would get out of there without Gabby realizing that they potentially had a break in the case. But not the one that they wanted. It was another victim, and, as he drove to the location, he wished the snow would let up, at least a little bit. He loved winter and all that it entailed, so living in Aspen meant they got more than their fair share than a lot of the country. Here lately, they were in an ugly lull of just plain old dark and stormy weather.

As he arrived at the crime scene, his phone rang. It was Dr. Mica. "Dr. Mica, what, uh, what can I do for you?"

"Are you distracted? Did I call at a bad time?"

"I'm at a new case," he said, "so potentially, yes. But if it's quick—"

"I'd like her to meet somebody," she said abruptly.

There was silence while he thought about that. "Who?"

"Stefan Kronos," she said.

At that, he stilled. "The psychic?"

She took a deep breath. "Yes. I know it's very unorthodox, and it doesn't fit with anything else but ..."

"I think it's a good idea," he said after a moment. "If he's in town."

"He's not, but that's no problem. He'll contact you." Dr. Mica chuckled.

"If he's willing, then that would be great. But I don't think Gabby should be alone during that."

"You're very protective of her," the doctor said quietly.

"Yes," he said. "Is that a problem?"

"Not for me. I just don't know if it is for you." With that, she said, "I'll call you back as soon as I have something arranged."

"Okay. I'm not certain when I can be available," he said. "Like I said, I've just arrived at a new scene here."

"Fine, I'll be in touch," she said and hung up on him.

He had no idea yet what he would face at this new crime scene. As he got out of the vehicle, he pocketed his phone and walked up to Jake, who had a grim look on his face. "What's up?"

"Another one," he said.

"Another one what?"

"Just like Tessa," he said.

Damon stopped and stared. "Are you serious?"

"Very."

"The same methodology?"

"Very same. She's been butchered."

"Jesus." The forensics team was in high gear, documenting all they could find. Damon moved carefully amid the scene and stopped where the sheet-covered body was. The coroner lifted the sheet for him to see underneath, and he stared in shock. "This one is even more violent," he said in surprise.

"I wondered that myself," Jake said. "It's kind of hard to separate where the violence starts and stops."

"It's unbelievable," he said. "There's no rhyme or reason to it."

"I know, but, Jesus, we must stop this guy."

The coroner straightened to stand with Damon.

Damon nodded his head in recognition. "Dr. Keto, how are you?"

"I'd be a hell of a lot better if you'd stop bringing me these bodies," he said. "You need to find this guy and find him fast."

"Yes, sir," he nodded. "Believe me. I don't want to see any more like this either."

"It's pretty bad," he said. "She suffered. It was over fast, but she still suffered."

"That's motivation, if I didn't have enough proof of that one already. I'm trying to envision who could even possibly do this," he said. "Do you have any idea what was used to flay the chest open?"

"At this point, I'll say some kind of a sword," he said. "I know that sounds strange, but it's the only thing I can really think of. When I get back to the lab, we'll compare the two victims. But it doesn't make a whole lot of sense otherwise."

"Otherwise," he said, "it doesn't make *any* sense."

"The heads are decapitated and removed from the scene, and that same tool makes a single cut down the breast bone, then shears off the skin from the ribs, pulling the torso back and off."

"Opening them up? Exposing them for something?"

Damon said, tossing out ideas.

"It could be either or could be anything," the coroner said. "When you think about it, that's your department. Mine is just trying to figure out what happened."

"Was she alive when they did this to her?" Jake asked.

The doctor looked up at him and nodded. "I'd say that the chest was done first and then the head."

Jake added, "We can't confirm ID yet, but I think this is another one of the roommates."

Damon stopped and stared. "Are you serious?"

"Yes. It looks to be Liz. Her boyfriend just called her phone, which rang here, looking for her. When we asked when he'd seen her last, he said he had dropped her off here for a couple hours, while he went to the pub with his friends. I could hear pub sounds in the background. He was calling to see if she was feeling better and wanting to come join him."

"So this is his place?"

"It is. They've been back and forth for a few months trying to decide if this is the direction they want to go, but she was still living with the women, figuring it out. They had just decided that it was a go for them, and she knew it would be a problem because it was hard to get roommates, and the women were all needed to pay the rent."

"Ah," he said, "that's fascinating and bizarre at the same time." He stopped, looked around, and said, "So two of the same original five."

"Yeah. So what shape is that girlfriend of yours in?"

"Hardly a girlfriend," he said, "and she's pretty un-nerved. I took her to Dr. Mica today."

"Good. If anybody can sort that out, she can."

"Maybe. She wants Gabby to see a specialist."

"Oh, good. Who is that?"

He knew this would cause quite the reaction, so he gave a half smile and said, "Stefan Kronos."

Jake stopped and said, "Wait? As in the psychic, the guy who helps solve all those police cases?"

"Yeah."

"Shit. Maybe we should use him."

"It's not a bad idea, but I doubt the captain would okay it," he said, "and you know how he feels about ugly publicity."

"Well, he'll get a shit ton of ugly publicity when the media gets a hold of the fact that now two dead women have been brutalized like this," he said, with a hand motioning at the body in the room.

"And, of course, nobody was here at the time. The boyfriend knows nothing, and nobody heard anything, correct?"

"Well, I'm not sure about the *never heard anything* part. I haven't had a chance to canvass the other apartment dwellers here," Jake said. "So why don't we do that now?"

Damon nodded, and they went apartment by apartment, knocking on doors to see if anybody had heard or seen anything. Without giving too many details, the same answers kept coming back. No, no, and finally, no.

When they got to the very last apartment, not expecting anything different, the door opened to an older man with a cane. When Damon asked him the same questions, he nodded and said, "A horrible ruckus came from that corner of the apartment," he said. "It butts up against mine."

"What do you mean, it butts up against yours?" As he walked in through the apartment, he saw it was L-shaped, and the tenant was correct that part of it would have been close to the apartment in question. "What did you hear?"

"Well, I didn't have my hearing aid in, but I still heard that," he said. "Like some screaming or roaring. Very animalistic."

"Ah, and how long did it last?" he asked.

"Not very long, maybe a couple minutes, and then it stopped. I wondered if it was some of that newfangled music all these young people are putting on. Aspen used to be a nice little town. Then it got rich and popular, and now it's just this drug-infested mess."

"Have you lived here long?"

"All my life," he said. "But *all my life* means a different thing when you're my age. Never heard anything like that before though."

"Any idea what it could have been?"

"Young man, if I didn't know better, I'd have said it was some supernatural being torturing the poor girl. You better find out who it was, so it doesn't happen again. I'll cheerfully go to my grave never hearing that sound again."

"And you didn't see anybody?"

"No. I opened the door and looked out," he said, "but I didn't see anyone."

"Are security cameras here?"

"Sure," he said, "you better check them too. Because, if he got in, he had to get out."

"True enough," he said. He thanked the man, took his name and number so he could add it to the file, and said, "If we have any more questions, we'll come back."

"Well, if you expect me to remember anything, don't take too long," he said with a cackle. "My memory is not exactly what it used to be."

"Got it," he said with half a smile. He stepped back and looked at his partner. "That was interesting. Same MO, same creepy sounds."

"Yeah, and no luck with the security cams. Nobody caught on tape. Our team will go over them again, just to be sure."

"So what do you know about this Stefan Kronos guy? It would be nice to know more. I've never met the man."

"Neither have I," Jake said. "I always wanted to though. He's legendary."

"That's because you're from what, Oregon? Is that where he's from?"

"That area anyway, but he has started to really branch out and help more PDs. Usually long-term serial killers are who he's focusing his time on these days."

"Sounds lovely," Damon said, and he meant it. Because any help they could get, as long as it was legit, was worthwhile. He didn't know about using psychics though, and that just brought back thoughts of Gabby and her tarot card sessions. "Hell, if he's willing to take a look at Gabby, I mean, do you think it would help?"

"I don't know," Jake said, "but it's more a case of whether the doc thinks so."

"Funny thing to suggest though."

Jake stopped and looked at him and said, "Does Dr. Mica think there's anything about the ghost stuff Gabby's talking about?" he asked Damon directly, as if the light had suddenly come on.

"I have no idea," Damon said. "It didn't make any sense to me either."

"Interesting," he said.

When they were done here, Damon turned and headed back to his vehicle. He wasn't even sure where to go with this now.

Dr. Keto called him over and said, "I'm hearing rumors about other cases with similarities."

"I've heard of some but haven't checked into them yet. Surely it's just town gossip, right?"

He said, "I went to some of our records, wondering the same thing. I had to go back many years, but I did find some similar cases. You have to pick through all the murders to find those like this."

"And that means what?"

He snorted. "I have no clue. That's for you to figure out."

At that, Damon rolled his eyes and said, "Thanks, and if you want to forward me the case numbers, I'd appreciate it."

The doctor nodded and said, "I can do that."

"Great, thanks." With that, he walked back to his car to find Jake standing there.

"Plan of attack?" Jake asked.

"Well, for one thing, the other three women are in danger," Damon said succinctly.

"Yeah, that was my take on it too. This is personal."

"Not only personal but it's also vicious," Damon said. "I don't understand the chest being flayed like that."

"Neither do I," he said. "If the victims are all females, it makes you wonder if it is sexually motivated or whether it's jealousy or something along that line."

"More questions for Dr. Mica, and I haven't even brought her in on this death yet."

"Well, you did bring her in, just not about the perp," he said. "You're too busy taking care of the victim." And he waggled his eyebrows.

"There is something about her," Damon admitted. "I don't understand the attraction, but it's there."

"That's dangerous talk," Jake said, yet he was smiling at his buddy.

"The coroner will send me some case file numbers he was looking into. He said he has a couple that have similarities in a few of these aspects but not to all of it."

"Good. That at least will give us something to go on. Notification of next of kin?"

Damon winced at that. "You want to?"

"Hell no, I don't want to, but I will," he said. "But, if I do that, you take notification of the roommates."

He sighed. "I can do that. Besides, we have a hell of a lot more questions we need to ask them."

"That's the truth," Jake said. "And not only do we need to start with what the hell is going on but who do they know who is even capable of doing something like this."

"You know that they'll all say they don't know anybody capable of this, right?" he said. "We'll also take into account that these women worked in multiple service industries in town. So they knew hundreds of people between them. And, even if they knew just one, or if somebody was friends with just one, that didn't mean they weren't watching them all."

"Why these two victims?" Jake asked, leaning against the car's rooftop with Jake. "Why these two? Why not the other three?"

"Opportunity perhaps," Damon said. "When you think about it, did the killer even know that the other two women were in the apartment that night? Not only that, I think he was on his way to check them out," he said and told Jake what Gabby had said about the footsteps coming down the bedroom hallway.

"But that would imply that the guy was there, even as you arrived."

"I know," Damon admitted. "I've been trying to wrap my mind around that. Did I see anybody? No. But that doesn't mean somebody wasn't just ahead of me. Somebody who went out the window or went down the hallway and darted into another apartment," he said. "For all I know, he was still hiding in the apartment, and I might have missed him. That'll eat away at me, while I think about it, because that would mean this death was on me."

"Don't even go there," Jake said. "Do not. We can't start taking on that kind of guilt. We can only do the best we can do for the victims and try to keep as many alive as we can."

"I know. I know," he said. "But, Jesus, did you see what they did to her?" He stared at his partner.

"And I'm thinking from that alone we're probably talking male, huh?"

"The trouble is," he said, "I was reminded of Wendy's girlfriend, who has a history of violence and is a fitness trainer. It's possible that she could be quite capable of doing something like this."

"And the dead women are not her girlfriend, so maybe she's attacking those who opposed their relationship?"

"In which case," he said, "that would put Gabby at the top of the list."

"And why is that?"

"Apparently she helped rescue Wendy from that relationship once. She was very unhappy to hear that Wendy had gone back. So much so that Wendy had kept it a secret from Gabby until now."

"Until before this?"

"No," he said, thinking back onto the conversation. "Gabby just found out because of the first murder, when we were looking at places for the women to go for the night, to get them out of the crime scene. Wendy admitted then that she was back with Meghan again."

"Interesting," he said. "I wonder if the other victim already knew about Wendy and Meghan and had expressed some kind of negativity over the relationship."

"I suggest we go talk to Wendy first."

"I agree," he said. "Are you okay to leave Gabby alone for the moment?"

"I have to," he said. "We don't necessarily have the manpower to put a guard on her."

"We could always call the captain and suggest it anyway," he said. "You never know."

"Good idea."

Jake offered to drive them in his car, while Damon contacted the captain. Captain Meyer hemmed and hawed and said, "Talk to the other roommates and see what we have for motivation that led this murderer to go for those two women. I get that we have two victims, and there's a group of five potentially, and, if we only appoint one guard, then that's possible too," he said, "but you know what our budget is like."

"Sure, but we've never hesitated whether to spend money versus to save a life before," Damon argued.

"Talk to me after you interview this third roommate." And, with that, he hung up.

"Same old, same old," Damon said, shaking his head.

"But you know he doesn't have a whole lot of choice," Jake replied. "He's got his hands tied too."

"I know. It still just pisses me off," Damon said. "We shouldn't be arguing over saving a life."

"Nope, we shouldn't," Jake said, as he pulled up to the apartment. It was one of the chic new contemporary-looking places, two blocks from where Meghan worked.

"This is a pretty decent place," Damon said. "Much more high-level than the place the women were sharing."

"Maybe that's part of the problem," he said. "When you think about it, one has money, and the other has none."

"Right, so it easily became an abusive situation, a controlling environment."

"Well, it can be. It can also easily be viewed as simply a step up in her living space."

"Right."

They knocked on the door, and Damon checked the time. "It's already nine o'clock."

"I know. It's been a very long day."

When Meghan opened the door, Damon studied her face, seeing a strong jaw, high-bridged nose, and high cheekbones. This was a woman who knew what she wanted and went after it. Damon introduced himself and his partner.

She raised an eyebrow and asked, "Is this to do with Tessa?"

"Well, we certainly need to talk to you and to Wendy. Is she in?"

Meghan hesitated, then nodded. "Yes." She backed away and said, "Come on in."

She led them to a small living room with a gas fireplace, where Wendy was curled up under a blanket. She looked up at the police, and immediately her skin blanched. "Do you have any news?"

"We have some, but more than that we have more questions," Damon said instantly.

Her shoulders sagged. "Of course. What do you need to know?"

Damon started in, asking about Tessa's family, friends, relatives, or anybody who knew where the five women had lived. Had they had any male friends over? Had they had anybody over? And then he started in on the latest victim's family and relationships.

Wendy answered those questions about Liz almost blindly.

But finally Meghan stepped in and asked, "Why are you asking about her?"

Damon looked at Meghan, then at Wendy, and said, "Liz was found dead tonight."

Immediately Wendy cried out and bolted to her feet. "What?"

"Yes, she was murdered," he said.

She stood there, almost hyperventilating. Meghan walked over and wrapped her arms around Wendy in a big strong hug and said, "It's okay, sweetie. It's okay."

"It can't be okay," she said, crying. "How can this ever be okay?" She stared at the cops. "Please tell me it's not the same man."

The two detectives shared a look and hesitated. Then Damon nodded. "It looks to be the same killer. Yes."

"Oh, my God," Wendy said, and, with that, her knees buckled.

Meghan helped Wendy sit back down on the couch, while Meghan glared at the cops. "Wasn't there an easier way to tell her?"

"No," he said succinctly. "Not really." There was never an easy way to share this kind of information.

"Jesus," she said, rocking Wendy, who sobbed uncontrollably in her arms.

"How long have you been here tonight?"

Meghan said, "All evening. We brought in Chinese food. We were just sitting here and enjoying the fire. We were talking about the future and where we wanted it to go," she admitted.

"That sounds like a deep talk. What was the decision?"

"No decision," Meghan said. "We don't really have answers at the moment. And now that Wendy's dealing with so much trauma, I'm not sure she's capable of making the decisions that need to be made."

"Right," he said. "So, Meghan, what is your relationship with the other women in the group, the other roommates at Wendy's apartment?"

"Rough," she said. "I made some mistakes early on, and they haven't forgiven me for that. But then they're Wendy's friends, and so they're very protective of her. I wasn't a good influence at the time."

"What happened?" he asked.

She gave him a lopsided smile. "I drank too much, got angry and frustrated, and took it out on her. I'm bigger, fitter, and stronger, so it became a difficult scenario. Wendy ended up telling the others about it, and I think she actually called Gabby for help, so Gabby came and 'rescued' her," she said, with a mocking eye roll. "Gabby took Wendy to the hospital, and there was a big stink about it all. Wendy here didn't want to press charges, and we've been slowly making back up again, as I try to find a way to have her forgive me."

"It seems like she has forgiven you, if she's here now."

"I'd like to think so," she said. "I certainly haven't crossed that line again, and I don't want to."

"Is anger a big problem for you?"

"I didn't think so, but I don't know. I'd never really been in that position," she said. "I just saw red."

"Do you know what caused it?"

"Wendy was talking about leaving," she admitted. "Saying that she and Gabby were only here for the winter, and I just got really mad about it. I'd finally found somebody I really cared about, and she wouldn't even give me a chance. She would just up and leave, like it was no big deal."

"And I believe that conversation happened yesterday as well," he said, looking directly at Wendy. "Isn't that correct?"

Wendy looked at him, her eyes widening; then she looked hesitantly at Meghan. "Well, somewhat," Wendy said, "I was talking to Gabby about what we were supposed to do when she was ready to leave."

"So you're still looking at leaving?" Meghan said in a hard voice.

"We don't have anything settled between us," Wendy said, "so, of course, I have to look at leaving. It's not definite though."

"Right," she said with half a smile. "If we stay together, you'll stay, but, if we aren't, you're leaving. Is that it?"

"Pretty much," Wendy admitted. "Pretty much."

"Do you really think your friend will let you stay here with me? After all, I'm such a danger to you."

Damon again heard that same mocking tone and still didn't like it. He was looking for signs of an abusive relationship, and he saw bits of controlling behavior. It was enough to make him concerned too. From experience, he had learned that he could only get somebody to change so much or to even see the truth in another person. None of this would change until Wendy herself put a stop to it. And he waited for anything to explode the tenuous relationship between Meghan and Wendy.

Wendy's shoulders sagged, and she said, "You know perfectly well I can't afford to stay in Aspen," she said. "I have almost wiped out the financial nest egg I had before I arrived, and it hasn't been easy."

"That's not my fault," Meghan said. "I have a good job here. I've always pulled my own weight."

"Meaning, I haven't?" Wendy's smile slipped. "And you're right. I haven't," she said. "I'm not sure what the problem is in this town, but I've been blacklisted."

"You got on the wrong side of somebody," Meghan said, "but I'm sure you could find other jobs."

"And you're right, but I guess my self-confidence took a big hit, and I just never really pulled myself back up again," she said.

"So you have to make a decision about what you want to do," Meghan said quietly. "And I would prefer it if you would make that decision sooner rather than later. It's a little hard on me to sit around and to wait, while you decide whether you're leaving with your *friend*," she said, "or staying here with me."

"You haven't even asked me to stay," Wendy said.

"Nor have you said you wanted to," Meghan replied.

At that, Damon realized he'd had enough. He stood and said, "You two work out your relationship on your own time, please," he said. "What I really need is a list of anybody who would know where you lived and would possibly have anything against the two women who were killed."

"I have no clue," Wendy said. "Honestly I spent most of my time with Meghan, and I just didn't tell Gabby."

"Is that why you have no money?"

"She can't blame me for that," Meghan said.

"And yet I should," Wendy said, "at least for some of it.

How many times did you tell me not to go to work so I could stay here with you because it was your day off?"

Meghan had the grace to flush at least. "Well, I didn't know you were that bad off," she said.

"I lost my job because of it," Wendy replied.

"Well, not really," she said. "You lost your job for a lot of other reasons too."

"Maybe, but it's been a struggle to find something else."

"And like you said," Meghan reminded her, "your self-confidence took a hit, so I don't know how much you've even been trying."

At that, Damon held up his hand. "And again, stop, please. You can have that conversation on your own time."

Meghan rounded on him. "This *is* our time," she said. "We have no answers for you. Go do your job, and find your killer. You'll have to get your clues somewhere else."

And, with that, Damon was dismissed. He stopped and glared at her for a long moment and said, "Interesting that you want to obstruct justice."

"I'm obstructing nothing," she said with a snort. "But I do know my rights. You've asked questions, and we gave you answers. Now be gone with you. Otherwise I'll call my lawyer about police harassment."

Rather than sit here and argue with her, he nodded and said, "Have it your way." And as he walked out, he sent one final shot. "While you're patting yourself on the back for throwing us out, you might remember that two of Wendy's friends are dead now. She could be next." And he closed the door hard behind him.

It was a low blow, but, at this point in time, he really didn't care. Meghan's attitude was beyond grating and irritating as hell. If Wendy wanted that for her life, then she was already nicely settled in for it. But it wasn't his idea of a good relationship at all. And he could see how Gabby would have chewed away at the restraints holding her back from saying anything. But it also wasn't his job to help Wendy get out of a situation she obviously didn't want out of.

If she'd asked for help, for an escort or even a ride to get away, that was a different story, but she hadn't. She remained there with Meghan 100 percent, and that then meant it was Wendy's own problem. He just hoped that it didn't become a police case and end up being his problem.

As for Meghan being the guilty party, he wasn't about to write her off the list. She was aggressive, bitter, and strong enough to have done the job. She also had the motivation and the opportunity.

As far as he was concerned, she topped the damn list.

CHAPTER EIGHT

W HEN SHE WOKE the next morning, Gabby was turned
inside out. She'd slept somehow, but it seemed
impossible to sleep when her friends were being killed. Yet
she couldn't do anything to stop the murders either. She
dragged herself out of bed, had a hot shower, and got
dressed. She didn't have the healthy bank account that
Wendy had had when first coming to Aspen, but Gabby had
always worked to earn her own way. But she was still
bemused that Wendy could have gone through all that
money so fast. She'd easily had a year's worth of living
expenses saved. At least Gabby thought so. But now she
wondered if she really knew anything about her best friend.

Still thinking on this, Gabby walked to the kitchen and
scrounged through the food Damon had left behind. She put
on toast and a couple fried eggs. As soon as she'd finished
eating, she bundled herself up and stepped outside and
prepared to go to work. She didn't have a vehicle and had
walked or taken public transit everywhere since she'd come
Aspen. She was a little farther away from the bookstore this
time.

Actually she was quite a bit farther away, and that was
poor planning on her part. She hadn't taken that into
account when deciding her departure time for work today.
Setting out at a brisk walk, she quickly texted her boss and

said that she might be a bit late, but she was on her way. He would get mad when she was late, but, if she showed up, he would be happy to see her, though he'd never show it.

A text came back almost immediately, saying, **Don't bother coming in.**

Instead of texting him, she dialed his number. "What do you mean, don't come in?" she said. "I'm over halfway there. What are you talking about?"

He stopped and said, "People are talking."

"Talking about what?"

"Your dead friends."

She groaned. "And that's my fault?"

"No." He paused a moment, then added, "The detective stopped by at closing two nights ago, looking for you."

"He found me at my apartment."

Jerry appeared to be thinking about it and said, "Fine, but, if the customers don't like it, I'll have to lay you off."

She felt a darkness inside her at that thought, knowing that then she would really be screwed. "Please don't do that," she said desperately. "You know I need this job."

"And I need business at the bookstore too," he said, "and I can't have somebody working here who's suspected of murder."

"Oh, Jesus," she said. "I'm not on the suspect list. You can talk to the detective and confirm that."

He hesitated. "Are you sure?"

"Of course I'm sure," she said. "It's not me. These were my friends. I wouldn't do that!"

"Well, somebody is doing that," he said. "How can anybody be sure who is guilty and who isn't?"

She took a long slow breath. "Please don't fire me or lay me off," she said. "I need this job, and I can only tell you—

in as sincere a way as possible—that I had nothing to do with it. They were my friends. I can only hope that the police will get a break in the case and will find out who did this."

She continued talking to him as she walked, keeping him on the phone until she could see him in person. Or at least tried to. He hung up on her before she made the final block to the bookstore. He generally was easy to talk to and had been more than fair in his dealings with her. But she also knew that the bookstore was his lifeblood, and it must be hard enough to make a living with what she feared was the cost of the lease on the place. She wasn't sure if owning the place was any better cost-wise in Aspen.

She'd often suggested that he move to a new location, but it would be a lot of work, and he didn't sound like he was up for it. She could hardly blame him, as it would be a ton of work. She loved the bookstore, and something like that would be exactly what she'd like to have for herself someday.

Her adoptive parents had had no plan to send Gabby to college, so she had worked for years, saved up her money, then still attended college during the day while working nights and weekends to support herself. She was older than most college kids, but she got some small business training, just hadn't had a chance to really apply it. She'd stuck with the same call center job she'd had all through college and had taken this Aspen trip as her celebratory break after finishing up her program, before starting a full-time job.

Working at the bookstore had been a perfect opportunity because it had allowed her to see firsthand just what her training could do with something like this. But unfortunately Jerry wasn't interested in applying anything that she'd learned. She could hardly blame him, when it seemed like everything she'd done had gone sideways instead of upward. But to blame her for the murders was not fair at all.

The bookstore loomed up ahead. The weather was decent, and a few people were out on the streets, but it was still early, and anybody who was anybody living in Aspen would be up on the mountain today. Fresh powder was everywhere.

She stared wistfully up at the white-capped mountains around her, wishing she could go, but her board had been damaged, and she still didn't know if it would be possible to salvage it. She might not even get any more snowboarding in this season. She wondered if Wendy was using her board and how she'd feel about letting Gabby use it, since Wendy had only been skiing so far this year. But that didn't mean she'd want Gabby to have her board. It would make life a whole lot easier for Gabby, as Wendy well knew, but their relationship was a whole different story right now with Meghan in the mix.

Gabby rushed toward the bookstore, and, when she threw open the door and stepped inside, several customers were here, and they all looked up at her. She recognized one and waved a hand. "Hi, Reggie. How are you doing?"

"There you are," he said. "I came in early to see if you could help me find a couple books."

"Absolutely," she said, in a bright, cheerful voice and stepped forward to help him. If nothing else, she would make herself useful enough, and maybe she could keep this job after all. A few hours later she had a chance to lift her head from the steady stream of work she'd been at the whole time, finding her boss standing there, staring at her.

"So, what's the verdict?" she asked with a fatalistic attitude.

He shrugged. "Nobody seemed to care today."

"Why would they?" she asked gently. "I'm not strong enough to do what they did to the victims. I'm not on the suspect list. If anything, people should probably sympathize that I have been through a horrible ordeal."

"The trouble with any crime like this is," he said, "that we're up against people who don't always think logically," he said. "And I can't have any added stigma over my store."

She took a slow deep breath. "So why don't we take it day by day?" she asked.

He thought about it and then nodded. "We can do that," he said. "I really need somebody here. I just wish you didn't come with all this baggage."

"It's not baggage that I would have wanted," she said, "and I'm sorry. But I'm sorrier for my friends who are no longer here."

He nodded at that. "Good point. You want to start unpacking those boxes?" he asked. "We had a big freight order come in this morning, and I know some of them are special orders."

"I got it," she said and immediately set to work. Around lunchtime she heard the doorbell ring. She turned with a bright smile, determined to make the most of every opportunity on the job while she had it. The detective walked toward her. She immediately frowned and joined him. "Please stop coming here. I almost lost my job this morning."

He looked at her in surprise, then looked around at the place and said, "I'm the only customer at the moment."

"I know, but that's got nothing to do with it. Jerry seems to think I'm bringing in bad energy or the bookstore will get a bad reputation for having hired somebody on the suspect list."

"Which you are not," he said.

"And I told him that, but then he said it didn't really matter and that people would interpret my presence here in a lot of different ways, but none of them would be positive."

"And that might be quite correct," he said thoughtfully. "Anyway I came for a book."

She stared at him in surprise.

"Seriously," he said with a nod. "I do read, you know?"

"Sorry." She flushed at the thought. "That was very rude of me. What book are you looking for?" she asked, returning to business mode.

"The book you mentioned on the dark history of Aspen."

"Ah," she said, "we've actually had a run on that. Jerry didn't want to but brought in a few copies." She headed to the other side of the bookstore. "Okay," she said. "This is them." And she pointed to the last two copies.

He shook his head. "I can talk to him, if you want," he said quietly.

She looked at him gratefully. "I hate to even ask, but, yes, if you could at least reassure him a little bit. I really need this job."

She felt his gaze as he studied her for a long moment; then he nodded slowly. "Where is he?"

"He's in the back," she said.

Damon snagged one of the books and said, "You want to ring this up for me? Meanwhile, I'll go talk to him."

"He's likely to have a heart attack when he sees you as it is," she said.

"Is he that worried?"

"His health is not good," she said quietly, "and this is his main source of income."

"And yet, depending on what his rent is here, he could do much better at a different location."

"I've mentioned that," she said, "and gotten mixed messages. I'm not sure about this, but I'm beginning to wonder if he owns the land or something."

"If that's the case, if he owns the property, he should have more control over expenses and can always sell to get a cheaper place elsewhere."

"Well, we don't have a whole lot of business," she said quietly. She rang up the purchase for him, and, as he looked at the thirty-two dollar total, he nodded. "That could be one of the reasons."

"It's the book publisher's pricing," she said. "It's not our pricing." And she pointed to the back cover, where the barcode was.

He shook his head. "I don't have time to read much for fun, but, when I do, it's more the epic fantasy type stories," he said, "and they're generally half this price."

"True," she said. "And we have a bunch of those here too, if you're interested," she said with a bright clerk-ish smile.

He rolled his eyes at her. "I get you're trying to work the system to keep your job," he said, "but I came in for something, and I got it, so thanks."

Her smile fell away, and she nodded. He looked up to see something behind her shoulder. She turned and gave her boss a bright smile. "Hey," she said, "he came in to pick up one of those books on the dark history."

Her boss looked at the book and shuddered. "Why is everybody so obsessed with all that stuff?" he asked.

"I don't know," Damon said, "but I appreciate Gabby

here giving me the heads-up on it."

"She should be trying to sell other books," he said fretfully, "not advertising the kind of stuff that brings the wrong kind of clients in."

"I'm not the wrong kind of client," Damon said quietly. "And she's doing a good job here."

"But for how long? I really can't afford any negative publicity."

"I get that, and I don't know if it'll reassure you or not, but Gabby is not a suspect."

Jerry looked at him seriously. "Do you mean that?"

"Yes, of course I mean that," he said, sounding surprised.

Her boss took a long moment. "I see," he said. "Well, the sooner you solve it, the better."

"Oh, absolutely," he said. "I'm all for solving it fast. We just need to have a better rundown on possible suspects."

At that, her boss looked at Gabby. "Surely you can help with that, can't you?"

"I've helped all I can," she admitted. "If I could do something else, I would."

Jerry snorted. "Pull a bloody tarot card and see what you get," he said. "It seems like you've been stupidly accurate with them so far." And, with that, he turned to the back of the store, walking unevenly.

She frowned as she watched his progress.

"You're right," Damon said. "He doesn't look that healthy. Anything specific you know of?"

"I don't know," she said. "Of course he's old. When I first hired on, I was afraid he wouldn't make it through the winter."

"Well, I'm not sure I would argue with that," he said. "He's an interesting character though."

"He is, but he's basically good-hearted, and he gave me this job, so I am grateful for that," she said.

"Maybe if you're lucky, you'll get to keep it too," he said.

She smiled, feeling a little bit of relief. "I hope so," she said. "As we head into summer, we have lots of tourists. I really think we should be getting more tourist-type books in."

"Maybe you could suggest that," he said.

"He doesn't like my suggestions too much. I'm the one who suggested the tarot cards, and look at what happened from that."

"And you had no clue where that information came from, for those readings? You just made it up?"

"The information came to me when I was staring at the cards," she said. "I didn't expect that one lady's husband to die."

"And did you say anything about methodology or give any details?"

She shook her head again. "No, I didn't have too many details. I just said that somebody close to her would die soon and that she needed to remember that every day was a gift and that she should make the most of it."

"Which is fairly inane," he said, "and anybody could have made a comment like that."

"Exactly," she said. "I wasn't trying to cause trouble. I was trying to give a reading based on the cards."

"So, you really were attempting to read the tarot cards?"

"Sure, but I didn't have any training. It's not like I know what I'm doing or anything."

"Some people do believe in them," he said, studying the unopened packs around her. "You do sell them."

"Again," she said, "they're a tourist thing. And it's hard not to sell them if it'll bring in some money."

"Kind of like these books," he said, as he held it up in his hand.

"Exactly like that," she said.

"Well," he said, "let me take my book away and see what I can find out for information."

"I hope you enjoy it," she said with a bright smile.

He nodded. "What time do you get off?" he asked.

"Five o'clock," she said, "so I'll be closing the store."

He nodded. "I'll come by then." With that, he left.

She didn't know why he would come back by, whether to check up on her or not, but it was nice. She didn't know the last time anybody had come to check up on her in person. It seemed like she spent her life checking up on others. And, with that thought, her mind immediately went to Wendy, and Gabby winced. She sent a text to her friend.

How are you doing?

When Gabby got no answer, she shrugged, because, of course, Wendy was still mad at her. And that was too bad. She was the only friend she'd had. Gabby had felt like a redheaded stepchild all her life, even though Bernadette and her husband had taken Gabby in permanently, or at least until she was eighteen. That relationship hadn't been easy, and Gabby had felt like a second thought in the background of her adoptive parents' lives, which made Gabby's life a little bit more difficult.

Gabby had grown up knowing that Bernadette and her husband had taken Gabby in, keeping her out of the foster system, and Gabby was grateful. But she didn't feel like she could stay past her public-school years, like her adoptive parents had done their duty, and now was time for Gabby to move on. Actually Bernadette had made that pretty clear. So, when Gabby had any kind of trouble, whether a child or an adult, she didn't feel like she could call and ask for help either.

Whereas Wendy had a loving, supporting family, full of siblings, aunts, uncles, and cousins. Wendy leaned on others a little more, and Gabby knew she couldn't lean on others because she had no other family. She was desperate for this job. She really needed it, and she'd do a whole lot to keep it. But, at the same time, she already knew that she should probably be looking around to see if something else was out there that she should be doing instead—something that she could get a little further with. But to even think about leaving the bookstore sent a dagger through her heart. She looked around at the old building and sighed. "I really love this place," she said.

Her boss commented from behind her, "Well, you're probably the only person in town who does."

She smiled up at him. "I really do. I love the atmosphere. I love the history behind it. Just so much of it seeps into your soul here."

He chuckled. "I forgot what a romantic you are," he said.

She looked at him in surprise.

"That's how romantics talk all about the good things. They forget about the broken plumbing and the electrical that needs to be updated and the heater that doesn't work. Romantics never see those kinds of things."

"I admit I hadn't considered them," she said cheerfully.

He smiled and nodded.

She asked, "You've been here in this bookstore for a long time, haven't you?"

"Over thirty years by now," he said, quietly staring at the window to the snowy street outside. "Lived in the apartment above for almost as long."

"When I had to move out of my apartment," she said, "I wondered for a fraction of a second if that room up at the top of the stairs was even available."

"I'd forgotten you had to get out," he said. "What did you end up with?"

"I found an apartment over a garage, just a little studio, where I could stay temporarily," she said. "But I'll need to find new housing anyway."

"Can't you get back into your apartment?"

"I'm not sure that'll work," she said. "Five of us were paying the rent before, and now we'll be short two. Regardless I can only imagine how hard it would be to get anybody else to join us to live at a murder site."

"Sure," he said, "they could worry they would be next on the murder list."

She winced at that. "God, I hope not," she said, "but, either way, I can't pay that kind of rent on my own."

"Can you stay where you are?"

"No," she said. "It's only out of the generosity of the owner that I get to stay for now."

"Huh," he said, muttering to himself. "I don't know about the spare room." He looked up in that direction. "The room above the stairs has a bathroom right there, but it's hardly safe and secure. And it's all attached to the bookstore."

"Which is why I thought you wouldn't go for it," she said.

"I'm not sure I would go for it," he said. "Let me think about it."

Brightened by that idea, she smiled up at him. "Thank you," she said. "Even that is more than I had hoped for."

"Not everybody is after the bottom dollar," he said.

She replied, "Maybe not, but we also know that the bookstore doesn't make a lot of money and that you need to bring in more business."

"And that works both ways," he said, "because new business also means bringing in more money. And, if you'll pay money for rent, then ..."

"Right," she said with a smile. "Anyway, think about it." She gave a one-arm shrug. "I'd love to stay here."

And she would. She honestly would. Noting what time it was, she quickly went through the lock-up process with Jerry and then headed outside. As she stepped out, she heard someone calling her. She turned, and there Damon was.

She smiled up at him. "So, what's this?" she asked. "Are you afraid I won't make it back to your place and might freeze on the road? Or are you afraid somebody's coming after me?"

"Well, not the first one," he said, "because that doesn't make any sense. But the second one? ... Maybe."

Her smile fell away. "Do you really?"

"I'm not sure you are a target, but we have had two deaths, both roommates of yours. We can't ignore that pattern," he said. "I don't want to err on the wrong side and have a third person of a group of five dead in the morgue."

She took a long slow deep breath and said, "Reality sucks."

"Sometimes," he said, "sometimes it sure does."

DAMON HELPED GABBY into his car and then drove her

back to his aunt's house. He still thought of it as his aunt's house, even though it was now officially his. He couldn't really wrap his mind around the idea of owning it because it was a big beautiful fancy house—not exactly his style, he thought. He hadn't moved in fully because he was contemplating selling it. An awful lot of money was tied up in it that he could convert to cash if he sold it. Compared to just sitting here tied up in his aunt's place, the ready cash seemed better.

Yet something was so cozy and homey about his aunt's home, and Damon had so many good memories from here that he wasn't sure he wanted to get rid of it. And he'd also had a long hard fight with family members and had bought out several of them to make this his. So why did he go through all that agony and expense and then not plan to keep it, to enjoy it? But the mind was a wondrous thing, and he seemed to do things for different reasons that a lot of people didn't understand, including himself sometimes.

As they walked up to the garage apartment, Gabby noted a bag in his arm. "What's that?"

"More groceries."

She stared at him in surprise. "You don't have to feed me and give me a room too. I should at least buy my own food."

"So, if I didn't bring food tonight," he said, "what would you eat for dinner?"

She stopped, stared, and said, "You know what? I didn't even think about it. I was so on edge—after Jerry telling me not to go in this morning and that he would lay me off—that I did everything I could to be perfect and to make sure he didn't follow through."

"Did he say anything after I left?"

She shook her head. "No, not about that, but I did mention the room above the store at the top of the stairs. It's got a lock, but it's connected to the store, so I'm not sure he would be comfortable with me staying there."

"Is it just a room?"

"A bathroom's next door," she said, "but, yes, it's just the room."

"I'm not sure I'm comfortable with you staying there," he said.

"Well, it's not like I have a whole lot of choices," she said. "The price of rent here in Aspen means multiple people need to stay together to make anything affordable."

"And you don't have another group of friends to live with?"

"Not only do I not have another group of friends but I highly doubt that I'd find anybody wanting to share an apartment with me after what happened."

"Do you have to tell them?"

"No," she said slowly, "but won't they already know with the news? Even if they don't, if they ask, what am I supposed to say?"

"I'm not sure," he said. "It's definitely something I can see as a problem."

"Well, if you found one person who was now looking for new roommates after two had already been murdered, what would you think?"

"Nothing good," he said cheerfully.

"Exactly," she said. "So, what am I supposed to do?"

"Tread carefully," he said, "because you also don't know if the murderer is somebody looking to rent an apartment either and might know you have a need for a roommate."

With that thought, she grimaced, while Damon opened up the garage apartment and let her inside.

"It's so beautiful here," she said quietly. "Thank you so much for being generous enough to let me stay here."

"Well, it surprised me too," he said, "but seriously, it's empty, so why wouldn't I? Almost any human being would."

She gave him a sideways glance and shook her head. "That's not my experience," she admitted. "They might let me have it but at an outrageous rate I couldn't afford."

"Well, that's one of the reasons why I wondered if you had friends who you could rent it with."

"Only if I have Wendy plus a couple more," she said, "and Wendy is not answering my calls."

"Wendy is dealing with her own losses and her relationship with Meghan," he said.

She looked at him hopefully. "Did you talk to her?"

"I saw her earlier," he said.

"Is she okay?"

Gabby asked in such a hopeful voice that he looked at her and shrugged. "She is, at the moment, yes. Obviously she and Meghan are working on their issues, and that has some pluses and minuses as well. On top of those domestic issues, lack of money is one of Wendy's problems, plus her lack of plans and her lack of a job."

"I do worry about her," she said.

"I know that," he said. "I saw it today. But you can't help her if she doesn't want to help herself. And yet she's still talking about leaving Aspen, and I got the impression that she felt she had to leave. Otherwise I don't know."

"What *otherwise*?" she asked helplessly.

"She's not in any danger. At least she didn't look to be," he said. "Do you understand the history of what happened?"

She looked at him and nodded. "It was pretty ugly," she said. "Wendy was absolutely devastated, but somehow she went back. And I didn't understand that, and I probably wasn't the nicest about it."

"It's easy to judge," he said, "and much harder to understand the pattern that happens when people get into these abusive relationships," he said.

"Well, it was definitely that kind of a relationship."

"But the fact is, Wendy went back, and she also hid the fact from you that she was seeing Meghan again."

CHAPTER NINE

"T HAT'S NOT SOMETHING I want to really look at," Gabby said softly. "Maybe I'm better off leaving now too." She looked around the studio and shook her head. "Nothing to stop me. Jerry doesn't really want me to work at the bookstore. I don't have a permanent place to live, so why am I fighting it?" she said, in a sudden awakening to her plight. "I can't even snowboard, now that mine is wrecked."

"I'm sure you could get another board, if you wanted to," he said gently. "Don't make too many decisions right now, when dealing with this fresh trauma. Besides, we have an ongoing investigation, and I need you to stay in town."

She raised her gaze and stared at him in shock. "Seriously? So I can't leave, even if I chose to?"

"No," he said, "you can't. Neither can Wendy."

Gabby sagged into the chair and stared out the window. "I don't know what to do," she said softly. "To think that two of my friends are dead is just beyond belief."

"And that's why we must get to the bottom of what happened," he said.

"That's your job," she said. "I don't know how to solve this."

"Did you give us that list?"

"You mean, people who know us?" She shrugged. "Half the damn town," she said. "There's five of us, and two of the women worked at bars part-time, and four were always in bars. I have no idea who could possibly know or not know anything about us. How am I to know about other people who may know me but who I have no knowledge of knowing them?"

"That's the problem," he said, actually following along this time with the Gabby logic. "Why don't you borrow a board and go up the mountain?" he said.

"You mean when I have a day off? Or when my boss decides to fire me?" Frustrated and upset, she scrubbed her face. "It's just such an odd state of life."

"Do you have anybody to call? Any support system?"

She looked up at him, frowned, and said, "No, I do not."

He nodded. "Okay, any idea why something like this would be happening in your life?"

She stared at him in shock and started to laugh, an almost hysterical edge to it. "What do you mean when you say something like that? Are you talking about a ghostly thing or about somebody trying to murder my friends?"

He looked at her, his head tilted. "So do you think somebody is after your friends?"

She blinked. "Is that what you're saying? Do you want to go for a walk?" she asked suddenly.

He turned to look at her. "Are you trying to change the conversation?"

"No," she said. "I'm frustrated, angry, and upset. Even the thought that somebody is killing my friends puts all the guilt back on my shoulders."

"The guilt is not on your shoulders," he said quietly. "You can't take that on."

"How can I not, if they died because they know me?

How is that anything other than making me feel guilty?"

"If you didn't do anything," he said, "then that makes no sense."

She wouldn't argue with him. "Is that a yes or no on the walk?"

"I have to get back to work," he admitted.

"Good," she said. "I'll go for a walk then." He hesitated, so she looked at him and asked, "Is there any reason I can't walk outside alone?"

"Not that I know of," he said.

"Good," she snapped. "In that case, I need to get out for a bit."

"You just came home from work."

"Sure, *work*, where he's considering taking away my job almost every moment of the day," she said. "So there I was, on absolutely perfect behavior all day, to make sure I had a job to go to tomorrow. Today will be over soon enough, and then I'll be back in the same stressful environment tomorrow."

"Keep remembering," he said, "you do have today. And a tomorrow to wake up to."

She winced. "Right, but that's not exactly helping me right at the moment."

"I know," he said, standing. "Come on. Let's go for a short walk."

"I thought you had to go to work."

"I do," he said, "but I can afford to take a short walk."

She frowned and then shrugged. She got up, put on her boots, grabbed her winter coat and her vest, and said, "Let's go." They made their way down to the garage and stepped outside. The snow was coming down heavily. "I don't know why," she said, "but I really like the snow."

"Well, that means you're in the right place," he said. "Lots of people like to come for a visit and then go home, where they can leave it all behind."

"Not me," she said. "I should have been born and raised here. I'm definitely a winter bunny."

"At least you know it," he said.

"Sure, but I can't afford to stay here, and everything that's happened since I got here is telling me to go home, to run, and to get far away from this nightmare."

"Maybe," he said quietly. "But, at the same time, maybe it's not that bad."

"Oh, it's that bad," she said sadly. "I just don't know what I'm supposed to do about it." She shoved her fists into her coat pockets and tilted her head up, smiling as the snowflakes fell in her hair.

"You'll need a hot bath when you go back inside," he said.

"Maybe," she said. Outside, the cold air was brushing through her. It was hard to even feel the cold; she felt such a sense of welcoming here.

"Are you okay?"

She looked at him in surprise. "Of course."

"You're not cold?"

"No." She looked at him and frowned. "Are you?"

"A little on the chilly side," he admitted, "but it's not bad."

"We can go back if you want," she said, hoping that he didn't want to.

"No, it's fine," he said. "I'm just surprised you're not cold."

"Why?"

"Well, your jacket is wide open, and you have no hat or

144

gloves on," he said, "and it's a bitterly cold night."

She looked at him in surprise, down at her hands, frowned, and said, "You're right. And normally I feel the cold. But I'm not today."

"Too much going on inside?"

"Too much going on in my head, yes," she said with a shrug. "But I'm not sure what I'm supposed to do with any of it."

"Maybe there's nothing you can do," he said. "When you think about it, if that's just what it is, then that's just what it is."

"I guess I'm waiting for you to solve this thing."

"Believe me. We would like to."

"And yet you're escorting me around on a walk."

"I do need some time off from work too, you know?" he reminded her gently.

She flushed. "I'm sorry. That was rude of me."

"We often don't get any time off in between cases like this," he said, "and particularly right now. But everybody else is working hard, and I haven't had a whole lot of sleep."

She realized that he'd taken her criticism a little harder than she'd intended. "I said I'm sorry," she said. "Look. Why don't you go back to work? I just want to be outside in the cold for a bit."

He looked at her curiously, frowned, and said, "No, that's okay."

"No, I insist," she said. "I just want to be alone. I'm really crappy company."

"I'm not here for the company."

"No, I know you're trying to keep an eye on me, but I'm fine," she insisted. And he hesitated still, but she said, "Go. I promise I won't be very long. I just wanted to cool down a little bit."

He frowned and nodded and said, "Well, I'll go pick up a few things at the office."

"Go," she said.

"Fine." He turned and walked back toward the main house. She was just at the property line at the street, and, as she watched, he went into his aunt's house. She frowned at that. Maybe he was living there? But he told her that he was thinking about selling it but hadn't quite figured out what to do. And, for the first time, she realized he *was* living here himself. Somehow that made her feel even better.

She wasn't alone in this world, and he was nothing but a call away.

Gabby walked down the block a little bit, where a river was more or less frozen over the top. Some really unique ice formations had been created here from the last time it was running. As she stood here, she heard his vehicle come out of the driveway. She turned to look, lifted a hand in greeting, and he drove away. She smiled at that, and, staring down at the water again, she realized that she really wasn't cold at all. She was like warm, as in, seriously warm.

She tilted her head back, loving the feel of the snow coming down and landing on her face. She wondered if it was safe to take off her jacket because she was very warm. So she pulled it off and laid it over the railing of the bridge and wanted to just dance with the freedom of being outside in the fresh air. Away from all that horror and nightmare going on. She didn't know if she was going crazy or not, and, after the talk that she'd had with the shrink, she figured that she may definitely come out on the crazy side. Maybe.

She started to laugh and dance a little more and then a little more. Finally she just sat down on the railing and stared out at the world. It was gorgeous out here. Why was every-body locked up inside? She didn't know how long she stayed here, but eventually she heard her name. She looked over to see Damon, standing there, a frown on his face.

"What are you doing?" he asked.

She looked at him in surprise. "What do you mean, what am I doing? I'm out here in the snow, enjoying it."

"You have no coat on," he said, in a sharp tone, his gaze searching. "You're completely covered in snow."

She looked up and down and then gave her shoulders and head a shrug, and, sure enough, snow went spraying everywhere. She laughed. "I didn't realize."

"How can you not realize that you're covered in snow?" he asked, walking toward her. "Hold out your hands."

She did as he asked, and, taking hold of one, he bit off an oath, exclaiming, "Gabby, your hands are like ice!"

"Sure," she said, "I've been outside."

"No, they're getting seriously frostbit," he said. "What is going on?" He grabbed her other hand now.

"Nothing," she said, staring at him in shock. She tried to pull her hands back, but he wouldn't let her.

"No," he said, "let's get you inside."

"I don't want to go," she said stubbornly.

He stopped, stared at her, and asked, "And why is that?"

"I told you," she said. "I like it out here. It's so beauti-ful."

"It's too cold. You need to come in. It's not safe any-more."

She stared at him. "Why on earth would you say that?"

He took a long slow deep breath. "And now you're being argumentative, something I haven't seen from you before."

"But you don't know me that well, do you?" she said,

tilting her head back up to the snow and spreading her arms wide. "It's beautiful out here."

"You're not equipped for it. You have no jacket on, and your body temperature is dropping."

She opened her eyes wide, turned to look at him slowly. She felt something odd inside, almost a rumbling. "I'm not sure what that means," she said. "But, if you think I'm suicidal, you're wrong."

"Good," he said shortly, "because I'm not seeing responsible behavior out of you right now."

She frowned. "Wanting to be outside makes me suicidal?"

"You're past being outside," he said. "Your fingers are blue. Your face is completely covered in snow, your head is wearing a big snowcap," he said. "I doubt any of your friends would consider this normal behavior."

She stopped, looked at him, and felt a tinge of fear inside. "If I'm not being normal," she asked slowly, "what am I being?"

He didn't say anything and just stared at her.

"You'd call me crazy?"

"I didn't say that," he said.

"No, but you're thinking it."

"I didn't say that either," he said. "Don't put words in my mouth."

"No," she said, as she looked down, hesitating. "Is something wrong with me?"

"I don't know," he said, "but you're really worrying me."

"I wonder why," she said, sending him an odd look, catching a really curious look on his face. "What do you see?" At that moment he studied her, not with horror but with something odd in his gaze. "Damon, talk to me."

"I want you to step away from the river for a moment."

She looked at the river, shrugged, and took several steps away from the railing. "What?"

He let out a long exhale. "I just thought I saw something there beside you."

"Like what?"

"I don't know," he bit off. "Now can we go inside, please?"

She wanted to push it and still stay outside, but something else was warring inside her, telling her not to do it. Slowly she nodded. "I guess, if I have to."

"Thank you," he said, but he stood there waiting for her, watching to see if she would actually follow through.

She felt the resistance inside her, wanting to stay here. Yet at the same time something else was going on inside. "I feel really strange," she said. "Like, *really* strange."

"I wonder why," he muttered.

She glared at him and took two steps, before letting out a weird sound, just before the ground rushed up to meet her face.

Damon dropped beside her, still figuring out what had just gone on and why she'd acted so oddly. He swore to God that he saw this weird shadow behind her. And it kind of freaked him out, but he wasn't sure if it was the light playing with his vision or something else. That's why he had asked Gabby to move away from the river. Yet it hadn't helped clarify anything.

Gabby had been off since he got here. Hell, she might have been off for a long time. For the first time he wondered if maybe she could be guilty of these crimes somehow. Yet she'd been home with him at the time of the second murder, so that made no sense.

But something was wrong, something was going on here that he needed to check out. He ran his hands over her after her collapse and couldn't find evidence of anything being broken, but she was cold, so very cold. He hesitated, wondering if he should call for an ambulance, but decided that he'd get her into the garage apartment first.

He picked her up, wondering how she could be so light. He raced her back to the garage as fast as he could, then made his way up to her suite, where he put her on the couch. Throwing some blankets on top of her, he then rubbed her hands, her face, and her feet, just to get some circulation going. When she finally moaned, he kept it up.

"Stop," she whispered, "it hurts."

"Maybe it hurts," he said, "but at least you're alive."

"So cold," she said, her teeth chattering.

"I know," he said, "and I need you to work hard to get warmed back up again."

"I don't know what happened," she said. "How did I get so cold?"

"Well, you were standing outside without a coat on for at least an hour," he said. "That'll do it."

"Why? That makes no sense," she whispered. "I always wear my jacket. I know how cold it can get out there."

"Yeah, I hear you," he said. "But that's what you were doing. Since I left apparently, which means I shouldn't have left you in the first place."

She opened her eyes, gave him a lopsided grin, and said, "Well, I'm still alive."

"Sure, but at what cost?" he said, shaking his head. "I want you to get up and move around. Get the blood circulating through your system. Then I'll put on the teakettle."

He helped her to her feet and assisted her so she could move initially. "Come on. Come on. Keep walking," he said. "Let's push that frostbite away."

"Doesn't help that I'm so c-c-cold."

"Once I know that you can walk by yourself," he said, "I'll run you a hot bath."

"Now that," she said, "sounds about perfect."

"I don't know about perfect," he said, "but it's something."

"And helpful," she said.

As soon as she could stand on her own, he got the teakettle on. Then he checked to see if she was still on her feet. She was, so he raced to the bathroom and ran the hot water in the bathtub. "Do you want some bubble bath in it?"

"If you have some here," she said, "then, yes. That would be great."

He nodded and headed back into the bathroom again, finding some stuff in the back corner that smelled like lavender. As soon as he poured in a big dollop, bubbles rose up. In a flash he stepped from the bathroom to see her huddled in a chair. He shook his head. "Move it. Come on. You've got to keep moving."

She glared at him, but, with his assistance, she stood and walked about a bit again. "Why was I out there for so long?" she muttered. "I don't even think it's possible that an hour went by."

"I was gone for an hour," he said. "Maybe even an hour and a half."

She shook her head. "Not possible," she announced.

"Well, keep arguing with me," he said. "It will keep your blood pressure moving."

"You're making it up," she muttered.

"Yeah, like I've got time for that crap," he snapped.

"Maybe you do. I don't know. Maybe you're just making it all up."

"You're the one who's freezing, not me. Why the hell wasn't your coat on?"

She looked at him, surprised, and he motioned to her coat off to the side. "Feel your hair."

"I often go out without a hat on," she admitted.

"I get that," he said. "I really do, but why on earth would you have taken off your coat?"

"I didn't," she said.

He stopped, looked at her, and said, "If you didn't, then who did?"

She stared at him in shock. "I didn't have a coat on?" she asked hesitantly.

"No. You didn't. Check your shoulders," he said. "You're still in a wet sweater. I should have taken it off you as soon as I got you home."

She reached over and patted her shoulders. "Who took off my coat?" she asked. "I thought you took it off when you brought me inside."

"No," he said, "it was off when I found you. And you were doing some weird dance movement on the bridge."

"Oh, hell, no," she said. "I was doing no such thing."

He groaned. "I don't have time to argue with you, Gabby," he said. "Let's get you stripped down and into the bath."

"I can do it myself," she snapped, and she took three hesitant steps toward the bath and fell.

Swearing, he picked her up, carried her into the bathroom, and said, "This is not the time."

"For what?"

"For sensibilities and modesty," he said. "We need to get you in that hot water. Otherwise I'm calling an ambulance, and you're going with them."

"No, no, no," she said, "I can't afford that."

"I hear you," he said, "but I don't really care right now. You get yourself warm, and, if you can't do it yourself, I'll help you."

CHAPTER TEN

GABBY DIDN'T KNOW what to think. It didn't make any sense to her. As she tried to grab her sweater with her fingers, it kept slipping from her hands. She stared up at him. "I don't think I can do this," she whispered.

Immediately he had her sweater up over her head and tossed to the floor, her bra unclipped, and her pants down to her ankles. He held her, while she stepped out of them, and he took off her socks as well. Her panties hit the floor seconds later, and she was picked up and lowered slowly into the warm water. She cried out in relief as the warm water encased her body, and her teeth started to chatter.

"Good," he said, "let your teeth chatter. It's a sign that your body is trying to warm itself up."

"If y-you s-s-say so," she whispered. She sank under the water to her chin and tried to get out something about a hot tub.

He shook his head. "Nope, I don't have one."

She nodded, closed her eyes, and pulled herself right under, allowing the heat to soak into her scalp. When she needed air, she came up to find him staring at her, looking worried.

"I'm good. I'm okay," she said. "I don't know what that was all about, but I'm okay now."

"Well, when you're feeling a little bit better," he said,

"you'll explain to me why you were out there without your coat. Your coat was right there on the ground beside you, but why would you take it off?"

She felt the waves of anger coming off him. But, at this point, she figured it was more worry about her than anything. "I don't know," she whispered. "I don't remember taking it off." She looked up to see that he didn't believe her. "Honest."

He shook his head and disappeared.

She figured to see to the tea. She sank back under the water, feeling the bathtub fill more and more. Some of it going into the overflow as she went under, but she didn't care. As long as it didn't overflow the actual bathtub, she wasn't moving.

When he returned, he had a hot cup of something and a shot glass. She looked at both. He bent down, turned off the water, and said, "The bathtub is full. I want you to drink this shot of whiskey, and this is hot tea for afterward."

She looked at the whiskey, then looked at him and said, "I really don't like whiskey."

"I *really* don't care," he said. "It'll light a fire inside."

She snorted.

"Come on. Just do it already. Please?"

She groaned, sat up slightly, took the whiskey, and threw it back, then immediately started coughing.

He grinned. "At least you're not used to it."

"What do you mean by *at least?* Why on earth would anybody want to drink this?"

He laughed at that. "Now," he said, "get back under the water."

"I would if I could breathe," she said, still coughing a little bit. She sank back under the water, feeling her body shaking and quivering some more.

"The shivers are good," he said. "It means your body is trying to raise its temperature back to normal."

"Sure, but that doesn't tell me why I was out there without a coat on though," she muttered.

"No, it doesn't," he said. "We must find out, and we must find out fast."

She nodded. "Well, I don't know who you're supposed to interview to find out," she said, "because I can't tell you jack shit."

"Yeah, you just stay in here and warm up. I'll go make some calls."

She nodded and didn't know what to say. What could he do? When he came back twenty minutes later, he had an odd look on his face.

"Are you still okay in here?" He bent down, tested the water temperature with his hand, and nodded.

"I'm fine," she whispered. "I don't want to get out yet, if that's what you're asking."

"No, you need to stay in there for a while," he said. "When it cools down, we'll drain some and put more hot water in."

"And since I can talk now, can I ask why the hell you don't have a hot tub?" she said with half a smile.

"Well, I hadn't planned on rescuing an ice maiden. If I'd known ahead of time," he said casually, "I might have been more prepared."

"That would make sense," she said, and then she yawned unexpectedly.

"I don't want you falling asleep yet," he said. "You're not out of danger."

She sighed and said, "Did you find out anything?"

"I did," he said. "I want to show you something on my laptop." He disappeared to grab his laptop and returned quickly. "Can you tell me what I'm looking at?"

She watched as a street camera zoomed in on the bridge, and there she was, standing on the bridge with no sign of him. She noted that date and time stamp. So it was definitely after he had left, and there she stood, twirling around, her face to the sky. Then she took off her coat, threw it to the side, and just stood there for the next twenty minutes. He had it on Fast Forward, so that they could confirm that nobody else was with her.

"I don't remember that," she said softly. "Like, as in, I *seriously* don't remember it."

"And that's what worries me," he said. "If I hadn't come when I did, what do you think the chances of you surviving this night are?"

She shook her head. "But I don't remember taking off my coat," she said. "I wouldn't normally do that. I'm not suicidal at all."

He just nodded, but his gaze was searching.

She knew with a sinking heart that he didn't believe her, but then why would he? She stared at the video herself and didn't believe it. "I don't know what's going on," she whispered. "Everything has not been okay since that snowboard accident."

At that, he frowned, settled back, and studied her for a long moment.

"Now what?" she asked in exasperation.

"Nothing," he said. "Drink your tea."

"It's empty."

"Good," he said. "I'll go get you more."

He disappeared again, and she heard him on the phone,

talking to somebody a few minutes later, but had no clue who it was. As long as it wasn't the paramedics. Things like that were expensive, and she was out of money in a big way. And, although she kept hoping she'd retain her job, she had no guarantee that would happen. As more strange things happened, and things got weirder, chances were good her job would be gone without any warning. It's not like she could blame her boss either. If she were a detriment to his business, he had to deal with it. He needed to survive too.

But still, she needed more than that to live on anyway, and, once again, she was brought back to what had brought her here in the first place. She'd always thought about coming to Aspen ever since she learned to snowboard in school. And, of course, it didn't hurt that her adoptive parents had told her that they had picked her up here, and sometimes she wanted to come back to wherever that was.

They didn't tell her that she'd been born here; they just said that they had taken possession of her here. Like picking up a puppy. Something for her to contemplate. She hadn't thought anything was weird about it until now, and all she could think about was what if she were driven to come here for some other godforsaken reason? That didn't bear thinking about because the what-ifs would drive her crazy. And there are no what-if answers. Just something in her world had gone seriously wrong, but what was she to do about it?

"I KNOW, DR. Mica. All I can tell you is that the video shows her all alone. Yet I saw something bizarre that isn't showing up on the video, and that concerns me even more."

The doctor continued, "I've made a couple calls," she

said, "but I haven't made any connection yet. Stefan is crazy busy."

"I don't even know who to take her to," he said. "I don't know who can even help her."

"But you don't think she's suicidal?"

"I don't think so," he said. "I'm not exactly sure what's going on, but I need to get back to her."

"Will she be okay, or do you want me to call an ambulance?"

"Well, she's against the ambulance idea because of the expense, and she is warming up in the bath, but I really don't feel comfortable leaving her alone right now."

"Do you think she'll do something else that's—Let me try Stefan again," she said. "It's out of the ordinary, I know. But I don't want to say anything until I've confirmed with him."

"Fine," he said. "I guess it's her mental state I'm worried about."

"Keep an eye on her," she said. "If you need me to, I can come talk to her."

"I could bring her to the office tomorrow maybe," he said. "She's quite worried about losing her job, and, considering all that's been going on, that is a possibility."

"No, I could come to her," Dr. Mica said. "I don't know what hours she works, but I could always make a house call after she's home. If you think she'll be well enough to go to work?"

"I'm not sure," he said. "That's just part of the unknowns right now."

"Right. Well, let's take a look and see what's going on. I'll call you back as soon as I can." And, with that, Dr. Mica hung up.

Damon walked back into the bathroom to check on her and found her dozing lightly. "Make sure you don't fall asleep," he warned.

"I'm not," she said. "I'm just relaxing. My teeth have stopped chattering, so don't worry about taking me to the hospital."

"Well, I'll keep worrying," he said, "because, whatever you were doing out there, you can't explain. But it's right there on the video."

"Thanks," she said, "I was trying to forget that."

"I don't think we can," he said. "I don't think we should."

She opened her eyes and stared at him. "What do you think it is?"

"I don't know," he said, and, with that, he went back to the living room. He returned to check up on her a few minutes later, and she was fine, eyes closed, dozing calmly. He tested the water and turned on the faucet to add some hot water, forcing her to open her eyes and to look at him. "I'm just making sure it's still warm."

"The shivers have stopped," she said, with half a smile.

"Good, now let's get some more heat in the tub, and I'll go make some more tea."

"I'm starting to feel waterlogged inside now," she announced.

He chuckled. "It doesn't matter if you are or if you're not." When his phone rang, he looked down at it in surprise and said, "I'll be right back." He walked into the living room to answer it. "Hello?"

"Right," said the man on the other end. "My name is Stefan Kronos, and Dr. Mica asked me to contact you."

Damon didn't know what to say, other than, "Oh."

"Yes," he said, "I get that response a lot."

"You're *the* Stefan Kronos?"

"I'm not exactly sure who *the* would be," he said, "but I am a psychic, an artist, and a consultant for the police."

"Okay," Damon said with a nod, his mind filling in all the details of what he'd heard and read since. "Thank you for contacting us. I'm not sure you can do anything to help though."

"What did the shadow around her look like?"

"Honestly it looked like a normal person, only higher and off to the right."

"Depends what normal is. Could you see any facial features?"

"No, it looked like she was wearing a hood."

"She?" he asked immediately, as if pouncing on a clue.

By then, Damon had relaxed a bit. "I'm not sure, but, yes, I feel like it was a she."

"Interesting," he said. "Could you tell anything else?"

"No, but it was almost like it was smiling."

"And did your friend appear to recognize that this thing was there?"

"No, I don't think she did, but she was out there for an hour without a coat in freezing temperatures. When we first went outside for a walk, she said she was hot, that she was really warm. I didn't want to leave her, but I had to go to the office and get some stuff. By the time I came back, she'd been out there without a coat on, according to the video footage, basically since the time I left."

"And she was fine?"

"She was fine, until somehow she wasn't, and she collapsed and pitched forward into the snow. Then she almost seemed to come back to herself."

"Can you explain what happened just before that?"

He did the best he could. "I didn't know what I should be looking for," he said. "She just acted so bizarrely, not like herself at all."

"Okay, so what kind of run-up was there to this event?"

"Run-up?"

"What other strange incidences?"

"Well, there's been a few," and Damon quickly filled in Stefan on what he knew.

"Plus these recent murders?"

"Yes," he said, staring at the phone. "But I wasn't thinking they were connected."

"Interesting," Stefan said.

"You're not really thinking they can be connected, are you?"

"Haven't had much experience in this line, have you?"

"Depends on what you mean by *this line*," he said. "I've never worked with a psychic before, if that's what you mean."

"When did she open the tarot cards?"

"As I understand, the package was already torn," he said for clarity, "and it was a few days before her snowboarding accident. Some people report that Gabby had apparently come in with readings that were way too accurate, and not all of them were terribly proper or nice. She hadn't really worried about it because she'd been having fun, making it up. But then one of the customers came back and raised a stink because her husband had died in an accident. She made an accusation of negligence, saying Gabby should have told her exactly what would happen, so the wife could have done something to save her husband."

"Well, Gabby couldn't have done anything to save him,

if that was the way his life was to go," Mr. Kronos said, in an almost absentminded way.

"Maybe," Damon said, "but there's no talking to the grieving widow."

"Of course not," he said. "Then Gabby went snow-boarding that day?"

"Well, it was a few days later, yes, and had this terrible accident. She said somebody spoke to her, but she couldn't see anybody, and she felt like she'd been pushed off the course down the mountain."

"What did they say?"

Damon answered and, as far as he could tell, gave an accurate rendition of everything. "I have it all written down in the statement, if you want to see it."

"Yes," he said, "I do."

"I'll send it. So, I don't really know what you expect all this to mean," Damon said.

"I don't know that I'm *expecting* it to mean anything," he said. "No matter what, for you, it'll seem like a far-off theory anyway."

"Why is that?"

"Well, because, at the moment, I'm thinking posses-sion."

Damon closed his eyes, took a long slow deep breath, and swallowed hard. "As in a spirit possessing her?"

"Well, at least you're not accusing me of being a charla-tan and a fraud," he said, with some humor in his tone.

"No, but it's on the tip of my tongue," Damon replied.

"Of course it is," he said, "but, until you actually know what's going on, keep an open mind."

"Well, I would have kept an open mind, except these things have been so bizarre that I can't actually explain them away in any normal manner. And, when all else fails," he said, "we must look at the abnormal answers. But possession is way out there."

"It is," Stefan said quietly. "Particularly if this is new to you."

"Isn't it new to everyone?"

"For 99.9 percent of the world, absolutely," he said, "but that doesn't mean that it's not out there for all of us."

"Okay, this is just too awful to even contemplate. But, if it is a case of possession, where and what would she be possessed by?"

"Well, that is the question, isn't it? We'll figure that out because then we'll determine why this spirit is still around and what it is doing with her."

"Do you think it's actually affecting her? Like affecting how she acts and reacts?"

"Let me ask you this question," he said. "Would you have expected her to go out in the snow, take off her heavy winter coat, and dance around like that?"

"No, but remember. I don't know her all that well. Although I'm not sure what bothered me more. The dancing or the standing still, just letting the falling snow stack up on her head and shoulders."

"Then something suddenly changes, and she pitches forward into the snow like that and goes from being really hot to freezing. That was weird," Stefan said.

"That was definitely weird."

"Good," Stefan said, "at least you can latch on to that bit. That's common."

"But then what? How did the possession start? How does the spirit just decide all of a sudden that she's *it*?"

"I suspect it'll have something to do with the tarot

cards," he said. "Maybe you can find out what happened and how they got torn open."

He stared at the phone. "Seriously?"

"Absolutely," he said with a hard voice. "I get that this is all new to you, but don't mock it or knock it, for that matter. It's about the only line we have to go on right now."

"How do we tell for sure?"

"I have the means, and I'll get back to you in a few minutes," he said, and then the line went silent.

Damon stared down at his phone. "Okay, now I'm wondering if I've lost it," he muttered, as he stared around the room. "If any of the guys had heard that, I'd be the one getting fired."

He wondered what he had just done to his career. His mind struggled to grab some sanity in all this, but it just wasn't coming. What the hell had happened, and why? He just didn't know what to do. He made another cup of tea and took it back into the bathroom. He checked on her, and she was lying there, resting peacefully. Her skin was still too waxy for his comfort, but at least she looked to be recovering.

"I'm fine," she said. "And any more looks would be of the Peeping Tom variety, so go away."

He snorted at that. "Hey, I like a warm body in my bed," he said, "not an ice maiden."

"Don't say that," she whispered. "That's just not nice."

"I'm sorry," he said and quickly disappeared. He wasn't sure what about the phrase had triggered such a reaction, but he immediately felt like he'd pulled the wings off a butterfly. He shook his head, wondering what the hell had happened to him. When the phone rang again, he figured it was Stefan, even though the number came up as Unknown Caller.

"Hello?"

"At least you recognized it was me this time."

"Why is that?" he said. "Your number came up as an Unknown Caller, but the first time it came up with something weird."

"It tends to change, depending on what time of day I'm calling."

"Why?"

"I don't know," he said. "Technology doesn't always like me."

"Just technology?" Damon said with a note of humor.

"Glad you've got a sense of humor," he said, "because we have a problem."

"What kind of problem?"

"She's definitely got a possession situation going on," he said, "and, more than that, I think it's a murderous one."

CHAPTER ELEVEN

G ABBY HUDDLED DOWN in the warm water but kept her ears up and heard some discussion going on from the latest phone calls Damon had been getting. She didn't know what he heard on those calls, but she felt a chill deep inside that had nothing to do with her body temperature. Upon seeing that video, she tried hard to hide her reaction, but damn, it was scary to see herself doing something so ridiculous out there. Something she would never have done, and yet there she was, being a fool, and it didn't even look like it was her. Maybe that was the part that really got to her. It just didn't seem like it was really her; it seemed like it was somebody else being completely stupid out there. And it scared her. ... It all scared her.

When Damon came in the next time, he looked at her, and his expression said that something was wrong.

"Who was that on the phone?" she asked.

"Stefan Kronos," he said.

She stared up at him. "And who's that?" she asked. "That name means nothing to me."

"Maybe that's a good thing," he said. "It means nothing to me either, or at least it didn't, but apparently he's a consultant for the police."

"Ah," she said, "so is that a good thing then, because honestly you sound quite disturbed by it all."

"Yeah," he said, "*disturbed* is a good way to look at it."

"Now you're talking in circles, and you're scaring me again."

"Actually I'm a little scared myself."

She waited for him to explain, but he remained silent, and then she said, "Okay, Detective, enough with the puzzles. What's going on?"

"He thinks you're being possessed by a ghost."

She stopped and stared; then she started to giggle and then giggled and giggled some more. "Oh my, so you get some crazy person phoning you, and now you believe him?"

He grinned. "You know what? That was my initial reaction too, but this guy is pretty legit. He does all kinds of work for the police all over the world."

"All kinds of people do all kinds of work for the police," she said blissfully. "That does not make somebody legit."

He nodded slowly. "And I must admit, I don't really know what to think."

"Well, I'm not being possessed. How is that even possible?"

"So how do you explain your behavior earlier? You just closed down with a hard snap." And she stared at him wordlessly. He nodded. "That's the thing. If you're not possessed, what is the explanation for that behavior?"

"I don't know," she whispered. "I was really hoping we could just ignore that footage."

"Or the fact that you're in a hot bath because you've got hypothermia."

She winced. "You didn't have to tell anybody."

"Maybe," he said, "but I did have to tell some people because we must get to the bottom of this."

"Doesn't sound like there's much of a bottom," she said.

"Maybe not, but, at the same time, we need answers because, the next time you do it, I might not be around to rescue you."

"Oh," she said and stared off in the distance. "I don't know what to say."

"Neither do I," he said shortly. "So talking to Stefan wasn't exactly something that I thought to do. Dr. Mica contacted him."

She stared at him in shock. "The psychiatrist?"

He nodded slowly.

"She thought something serious enough was going on that I needed to talk to somebody else about this? Not just any somebody ... but a psychic?"

"I think she is just as disturbed as I was," he said, "and I must admit that I'm still pretty disturbed."

"*Duh*," she said, "I am too. Just think. Now we have somebody else, a completely different element to consider. And what would have caused this ...?" she said, waving her hand in the air, sending bathwater everywhere. "What if I was possessed by a spirit?" she said. "Why would this spirit want me to go dancing outside in the middle of a bridge in the midst of a winter snowstorm?"

"I don't know," he said. "I was hoping that maybe you would know."

She stared at him, seeing the quirk of his lips at his attempt at humor.

"I haven't a clue," she said. "That makes absolutely no sense to me."

"No?" he said. "Me neither."

"Honestly it's all just so bizarre," she said.

"It is, but we also have to consider the murders."

"Oh, my God," she said, staring at him in horror.

"Please tell me that they're not related."

"I don't know. I have no idea," he said, holding out his hands, hoping to calm her down.

"What do you know?"

"I know that I talked to Stefan on the phone. I asked him how we could tell if you were actually possessed, and he said he had a way of finding out. He got off the phone to do his check or whatever. Then he called me back and said it was official."

She snorted. "And you believe it because he said so over a phone call?"

"Maybe," he said. "I don't know what to say. I'm still kind of in shock myself."

"Well, it's not exactly your normal diagnosis, is it? I was thinking you would contact somebody to get me mentally examined to see if I were sane or not."

"It crossed my mind," he said, "and honestly it would be preferable to what we're talking about here."

She thought about it and nodded slowly. "I hear you," she said. "That actually sounds like it would be a better deal right now." She sat up, reached for the towel he had dropped beside her, and said, "I guess I want to get out now."

"All right," he said. "Are you okay to stand up on your own?"

She pulled the towel up to cover herself. "I think so."

"Take it slow," he said.

She nodded, and he closed the door behind him for the first time. She sat there at the edge of the bathtub, totally shaken. Possession? What the hell? Was that even possible? And how would it have happened? What did it even mean? And who was this person driving her world crazy, and why? What could she do about it? Then she heard another voice in her head.

I can help, he said, *but I'm not sure how easy it will be.*

"You're the one who got me into this," she said in a snarky tone.

First came a moment of surprise, and then the voice said, *No, I'm not.*

"What do you mean?"

I've never spoken to you this way before.

"Who are you?"

My name is Stefan. I just spoke to Damon on the phone.

She took a long slow breath, looking around the bathroom. "Are you in my head?" she asked furiously. "How did you get in my head?" she asked. "You realize you're making me crazy?"

Well, I'm not making you crazy, he said in a humorous tone. *But who else is talking to you in your head?*

"I don't know," she whispered, "but I thought I heard someone in there."

You thought you heard someone?

"Meaning," she said, "somebody has been talking to me, laughing at me, and, at first, I assumed it was my imagination, but then I heard it a couple more times."

Explain. Details, please.

She told him the little bit that she could remember and then said, "I just figured I was going crazy."

Interesting.

"What? That I'm going crazy?"

No, not necessarily, he said, *just that you're hearing these voices.*

"No, not voices," she said. "One voice. Well, *voices* I guess, counting you. But, if I'm hearing you, maybe you're making me crazy," she cried out. At that, a knock came at the door.

"Are you okay?" Damon asked. "What's taking you so long?"

"I'm okay," she said. "Sorry."

"Just get dressed and get out here, will you?"

As soon as Damon backed away, she whispered out loud, "See? This is what happens when people talk to me in my head. People look at me like I'm nuts."

So, don't talk out loud, he said. *Talk to me the way I'm talking to you.*

She blanked out at that and then closed her eyes for some reason, finding that way easier, and said, *Like this?*

Exactly like that, he said with a note of surprise. *You're doing this very easily.*

No, she said, *I don't think so.*

Oh, I do, he said. *Why are you in this area, at this location? I'm trying to figure out why this spirit is after you.*

I have no clue why I'm being possessed, she said. *I came here for the winter, for the snowboarding, just for fun. It was supposed to be like our one season before we settled down to full-time jobs, and my best friend was here with me.*

Was? Is that one of the dead women? he asked.

She winced. *No, Wendy and I came here for the winter to spend it together,* she said. *We've been best friends for years. She always knew that I wanted to come, and she also said she wanted to come, so we had this planned out for a couple years. We finally made the trip, and, since we got here, it's been just nothing but a nightmare.*

I'm sorry, he said. *Plans like that are supposed to be relaxing, not end up in some traumatic murders.*

Well, the nightmare part is happening, she said, *and I have no idea what I'm supposed to do about it.*

First, let's see if we can figure out the how and the why.

I'm getting a hell of a headache.

Okay, he said, *let's take a break. Get dressed, go out and visit with Damon. Then we'll switch and talk on the phone.*

And, just like that, he disappeared from her mind. Thinking for sure she was going crazy, she got dressed. She opened the door and stepped out and walked over to the gas fireplace, where she sagged onto the floor.

"Are you okay?"

"I'm not sure I'll ever be okay again," she said. "I just had the most bizarre reaction ever."

"In what way?"

"I think Stefan was just talking to me in my head." At that, she felt Damon immediately withdrawing. She held up her hands. "I know. I know. You'll think I'm crazy. But he did."

"You also said this other person spoke to you in your head."

She winced. "Right, so that's just more confirmation that I'm losing it. Great."

Just then his phone rang. He pulled it out, shook his head, and said, "Wow." He held it up, so she could read the Caller ID. *Psychic.*

She frowned. "Well, I gather that's Stefan?"

"Maybe, but the last time said Private Call or Unknown Caller or whatever, and the time before that showed something completely different." He shook his head. "Bizarre. Yes, Stefan. I'm here," he said. He put it on Speakerphone and set it beside her.

"I told him that you were talking to me in my head," she said. "Damon thinks I'm crazy now."

Stefan sighed. "It's never this easy," he said, "but, yes, I was using telecommunication."

"Seriously?" Damon asked, clearly not convinced.

"Yes."

"Well, that's just a little hard to believe," he said. "I'm a detective, and this sort of thing is not normal for me."

"Nothing is normal about this," he said, "but just because it's not normal doesn't make it wrong. And, of course, I'll prove it to you, which is not what I wanted to do."

"In what way can you prove it?"

WITH THAT, STEFAN jumped into Damon's mind. *Now I'm inside your head. Are you crazy too?*

Damon bolted to his feet, then looked around to see his phone still on the floor. "You're not on the phone call anymore."

She looked up at him, puzzled, then held up his phone, but the call had ended. "He's gone."

No, Stefan said. *I'm in your head. So, just like she got to experience it, now you've gotten to experience it.*

But I didn't want you in my head.

Neither did she, Stefan said cheerfully. *But it's not all that hard to do.*

Oh, my God, he said. *Seriously? You're really there, aren't you?*

My voice is there, he said, *that doesn't mean I'm physically in your head.*

Damon sat down into the big recliner, staring at Gabby. *That's what you did to her?*

Yes. Now I'll jump out, he said, *and you'll see a golden orb.* And, with that, Stefan jumped out of Damon's head.

Damon slowly sagged down beside her, snatched up his

phone, and said, "I can't believe he just did that."

"Was he talking in your head too?" she asked, her eyes huge.

"Yes," he said.

"Oh, my gosh, that's so good," she said.

"What the hell is good about it?" he asked, staring at her.

"It means I'm not crazy," she said.

"Maybe, but does it mean that I am?"

She stared at him in shock, shook her head, and said, "No, surely not."

And just then came a weird buzz. She moved closer to Damon, until they sat beside each other on the hearth. And right in front of them formed this great big golden orb.

"He said that he would get out of my mind, and next I'd see a golden ball."

"And that's me," Stefan said out loud, and the ball vibrated with the slightest of shimmers. They stared slack-jawed at the vision. "Now, could you guys just close your jaws, accept that life is different than what you always thought it was, so we can move on?"

"I'm all for moving on," she said, "and you can bet I'll never tell anybody about this, since nobody would believe me."

"Nope, they sure wouldn't," he said. "Now back to you. I want to run some scans, and I want you to share the history on those tarot cards."

She stopped and stared. "What do you mean by a history on the tarot cards?"

"I mean, I want you to find out why the package was open and who might have touched it before you did."

"Okay," she said, puzzled. "I can ask my boss, Jerry, but I don't think anyone knows the answers to those questions.

And what good will that do?"

"I'm not sure," he said. "Then I want a list of all the people you talked to and gave a reading for."

"I'm not sure I know exactly who they were," she admitted, "but I can try. I'm new to the area, and, if they were a tourist or a resident, I wouldn't necessarily know them. And if they paid cash …"

"Well, do your best," he said. "We need it. Listen. I can't keep this form for long. California is a hell of a long way from Aspen," he said, with half a laugh. "But I wanted to make sure that you were on the same page and that both of you believe in each other because that's really important."

"Why is that?" Damon asked.

"Because, whatever the spirit is doing, they're not done."

"But what do you mean?" she said. "What is the spirit doing? I mean, if it's just a case of me out in the snow without a coat, dancing like a fool, that's not so bad."

"I'm pretty sure the spirit is doing a whole lot more than that," he said. "Remember the Death card? Remember the message you got from him?"

"Yes," she said. "What's that got to do with it?"

"I suspect—and I mean I highly suspect—that this person is capable of moving from one person to another."

"What?" She stared at Damon. Damon stared at her. "I don't get it."

"I'm sure you don't," he said. "But the fact of the matter is, you don't understand an awful lot here. We are dealing with something that is much more sophisticated than I would have expected, but that's what we always end up finding in these cases."

"Okay, you're losing me here," she said, staring at Damon.

Damon stared back, then asked Stefan, "What do you think this person is doing?"

"I thought it was obvious," he said. "This person is using Gabby to further their own ends."

"What ends are those?" she asked.

Damon interrupted, "Are you saying the murders are involved?"

"I can't say for sure yet," Stefan said, "but I can tell you for sure that this person has a purpose, a reason why they've come back. Now I don't know what or why or how long they've been trying to make this happen, but, Gabby, you're now the weak link, via touching those tarot cards, I presume, allowing the ghost back into existence."

She swallowed hard. "I don't like the sound of that," she whispered.

"I will stay in touch," he said. "I don't want you two to separate."

"We have to," she said. "We both have jobs, different jobs in different places."

There was silence for a moment. "Then I don't want Gabby to ever be alone, let's put it that way."

"I don't know that I have that choice," she said.

"We'll work it out," Damon said in a harsh voice.

"Good," Stefan said. "I'll get back as soon as I can."

"But how—" Only it was too late. The golden orb disappeared right in front of them.

She bolted to her feet and walked over to where it had been, using her hand to waft through the area. "Dear God," she said, "what did we just see?"

"I'm not sure," said Damon, "but that was pretty incredible."

"No, it's incredibly scary," she snapped. "*Incredible*

doesn't even begin to describe it."

"Whatever it is," he said, "we must deal with it."

"But what is going on here?"

"From what Stefan said, he thinks somebody is here on a revenge mission, and they found a weakness when you opened those tarot cards. Now they are using you to get back at whomever."

"But how are we supposed to know what that is?" she asked.

"I'm pretty damn sure we won't like the answer, but I'll pop it out there anyway."

"What are you talking about?"

"I think what we must do is follow the bodies."

She stared at him in shock and horror and slowly fell silent.

CHAPTER TWELVE

W HAT DID DAMON mean by, *follow the bodies?* There had been two so far. Two of her friends. Were there more? Had Gabby missed something? Had he known something as a detective on the case that he wasn't willing to share? Did he think she knew more than she had told him? She didn't know what to even say, but she stared at Damon, struggling with whatever nightmare this was, trying to figure out how to get to the bottom of it.

She was also struck by Stefan's comment about using the tarot cards as an opening. She reverted back to that because it was a whole lot easier than the other discussion. "What did Stefan and you mean by the tarot cards being an opening to my system?"

"That's one of those questions I don't know the answer to," he said. "And I don't understand much about using tarot cards. We always hear rumors about Ouija boards being nothing that you should play with because of that, you know, open-door type of thought process."

She looked at him. "Tarot cards are nothing like Ouija boards."

"How do you figure?" he asked curiously.

"Well, they're just not," she said lamely. "I don't know. They're … they're just a way to talk to … A Ouija board's a way to talk to dead people supposedly, and tarot cards are like reading … getting a reading about your future."

"Well, that's interesting," he said. "I don't know then. I really don't know. Maybe, … maybe this ghost has some connection to you that we can't see."

"Well, that's even scarier," she muttered. "Who wants a ghost to have any kind of connection to them?"

He smiled. "The good news is," he said, "apparently this ghost has some connection, and, if he does, then surely we can find it."

"That's not very reassuring," she snapped. She glared at him, as she tried to think her way through this. But then she couldn't. It just didn't make any sense. "Can Stefan do anything to follow or track this person?"

"Follow or track?" he asked curiously. "Like, in what way?"

"I don't know. All that comes to mind is the damn Ghostbuster movie," she said, and then she started to laugh. "And I don't think he'd take kindly to that."

"I'm sure the joke's been made many times," he said. "Stefan didn't strike me as somebody who would get offended by a joke like that."

"Maybe not," she said, "but we don't … We seem to be completely in the dark here."

"So how do we learn more?" he asked.

"The internet," she said instantly. "That's where everybody learns everything."

He nodded slowly. "Is that something you want to take on?"

"Hell no," she said, "but I'm not sure we have a choice, do we?"

"I'm not sure either," he said, "but we can do some digging."

"We really need to talk to Stefan again."

"Not until we know more," he muttered. "We really need to do our homework before we get there."

"Maybe," she said, "and I guess you're right. I don't know. It just … It all feels wrong."

"Well, it might feel wrong," he said, "but, if we can get any answers for Stefan, you know that will help us."

She nodded, picked up her phone, and started researching tarot cards and possession. "Not even the internet has anything to say about it," she said.

"You were supposed to check on how they got ripped. Remember?"

"Right," she groaned. "I can ask Jerry, but I don't even know if I'll work tomorrow."

"Well, you're going," he said, "because you need the job."

"Right. Well, in that case," she said, "I'm off to bed. I'll say good night, and we'll see what tomorrow brings." He got up and left her soon afterward.

With her head still spinning, and confusion reigning as the utmost thought process, she headed to bed. But when she woke the next morning, she had not a single ounce of more clarity. Neither were there any strange or ghostly visits, so she was happy with that. She got up and looked around a little uneasily to see if she'd been dancing in the nude or something, but everything in the apartment looked and appeared normal.

She wished that, prior to that dancing-on-the-bridge event happening, she'd had some kind of warning. That was the troubling thing, the fact that it had happened without any warning. That really disturbed her because she felt like it could happen again without any warning. She wasn't comfortable with that. As she got dressed and raced to work, she thought about how she felt just before the event.

It was the heat. It had been the heat that sent her out of the house because she was looking for the cold. So was this spirit bound in ice or something? Why would the heat bother it? And, if she stayed in the heat and resisted, would that do the job? She frowned as she walked into the store.

Her boss looked quizzically at her. "Another bad night?"

She looked up, shrugged, and said, "It was okay."

He nodded. "Time to get to work then."

She started immediately unpacking the parcels that had just come in. When she got a chance, she asked him about the cards. "Remember that tarot deck I used originally? You said the package was ripped, and so you couldn't sell it. Do you know how it got ripped?"

"No clue," he said, "it was an old set in the back, down on the bottom shelf underneath the cash register there." And he pointed down behind the counter.

She squatted down and took a look. "*Hmm*, I wonder what it was even doing back here."

"No idea," he said, and he carried on.

She didn't know if she believed him or not because something odd had been in his voice. But then lately all she could see was odd everywhere. At lunchtime she asked him again.

He looked at her and said, "What difference does it make?"

"I don't know," she said. "I just ... I just wondered because I kind of felt a connection to whoever it was who had the deck." He snorted at that and didn't say anything. She wondered about bringing it up again, when he got an odd look on his face and walked over, bent down, and started digging into the crap stored in the back underneath the front counter.

Then he pulled out a small notebook and tossed it on the counter. "This notebook was with the cards, but I don't know where either of them came from," he said, "but they were both together in there. I looked at the notebook briefly and realized I couldn't sell it. I got the cards out and got mad because I couldn't sell them either, damaged like that. But they also shouldn't have been in there in the first place."

She picked up the little notebook and said, "Do you think it was a special order, set aside for somebody?"

"Well, if it was, who opened each one? Nobody came and picked them up, though I certainly don't remember taking a special order for any of this stuff," he said. "But who knows?"

"No, that's ... that's quite true," she said, trying to ease back some of his tension. "Have you had a lot of people work here?"

"For a long time, I had a lot of different people," he said. "And then, well, I stopped it."

She knew a story was behind this and desperately wanted to ask him because somehow it had to be connected. "Stopped hiring staff? But, Jerry, you'd be overwhelmed here, trying to do it all by yourself."

"But the business isn't overwhelming," he said.

"So how do you pay for—"

"For staff? I wouldn't have you here either if I thought I could get by without you."

She felt the hurt, striking hard and swift. But she understood. "I get it," she said carefully. "And you're used to being alone."

He shook his head. "That's got nothing to do with it. I

think you're in danger, but I don't know what from."

She stopped, slowly turned to look at him, and then said, "Pardon?"

He just glared at her, instead of answering.

She could see that whatever was bothering him had put him in a hell of a temper.

"I don't get what's going on," he said, "but it's something weird."

"In what way?"

"These books were out of place when I got in," he said, "but all the doors were locked."

She stared at him. "Which books?"

He just stared at her mutely and shook his head.

"Which books?" she said, her tone harder. "Come on, Jerry. You know this is important."

"Very difficult, yes. It's not important. It's all BS," he snapped. "I shouldn't even have mentioned it."

"But now that you did," she said, striving for calm and control, "which books?"

He walked over to the front counter and picked up two books sitting just off to the side and brought them over, slamming them down on the reception counter. "These two."

"And where were they when you found them?" she asked, reaching for them.

"They were on the floor over there."

"As if somebody slammed them against the wall?"

He gave her a look as to say, Are you stupid? "They fell obviously."

As she looked at the wall he was pointing at, literally hundreds of books were on the shelves there.

"But then why these ones, right?" she said with a shrug.

"It doesn't make any sense." She looked down at the titles and froze. "Possession and the occult. Well, maybe it does make sense," she said.

"You're back to that woo-woo stuff again, aren't you?"

"Well, when you tell me that something is going on and that … I'm in danger," she said, "I don't know what else to think. There's been plenty of woo-woo stuff going on around this place, and I have no idea what or why."

"I don't know either," he said. "All of it's a stretch."

She then asked, "But, when you've tried to explain everything away, and none of it's explainable, what's left?"

"I don't know," he said, with a tired sigh, "but you're not the first one to go down this pathway."

"What? Who else did?"

"Jenny. She used to work for me," he said. "She used to be in all that stuff too."

"What happened to her?"

"She left," he said in a dismissive tone.

"Did you fire her, or did she quit?"

"She quit," he snapped. "I only fire people who steal or do me wrong in some way. Otherwise the only reason I hire people is that I need help. What's the point of hiring the help and then firing the help? That defeats the purpose."

She blinked at the rambled explanation but slowly nodded. "Well, it's good to know you still need help," she said cheerfully, "because I still need a job."

"Maybe," he said, "or you'd be just like her and up and walk out one day."

"Did you have a fight or something?"

"I don't fight," he said. "I'm far too old for that. I come into work because that's what old-timers do." He continued, "We know the value of a full day, and we put it in and don't expect to get freebies out of it."

She wasn't exactly sure if that was a dig at her, but she decided to keep her mouth shut on that topic. "I'm sorry that she upset you in some way."

"She was one of those people who always dug into mysteries," he said, "and dug into private lives. She had no boundaries."

"Ah. Well, you have plenty. Lots of walls and lots of boundaries."

"Nothing wrong with that." He glared at her.

"Not at all," she said ever-so-quietly. "Everybody's entitled to have a few secrets of their own." He sniffed at that, and she nodded slowly. "And that's what she was trying to do, wasn't it? Digging into your history and your family?"

"None of your business," he snapped, glaring at her.

She smiled gently. "I'm not a threat to you."

"Anything that brings all that shit back up is a threat to me," he said. "I am not interested in going over old ground at any point in time." And, with that, he turned, and he stormed off. She sat here at the front counter, watching her view of his back as he walked right outside. For him to leave the building was huge. His apartment was upstairs, and he almost never left, preferring to order in his groceries and most of the extras in life. He always got a lot of personal parcels.

She had no idea what he did up there, all on his own, but the store was his life. She knew that and knew he would do nothing to hurt it. Not only did he need the measly income that came from it, but it was his only focus. But now, for the first time, she had to wonder just what else had been going on in his life that he was so desperately eager to keep quiet about.

IT WAS ALMOST lunchtime when Damon's phone rang. He looked down to see Gabby's number. Smiling, he answered. "Hey, how's your morning been?"

"It's been pretty good," she said, her voice low.

"Why the low voice?" he asked.

"I don't want my boss to hear me. He just came back, and he's gone into the office. I meant to call while he was out, but I didn't get a chance. It got busy here."

"So what did you find out?"

"The tarot cards were under the front desk with another little notebook," she said. "And he's had lots of people work for him, but he has some drama in his past that he doesn't want talked about. That he doesn't want anybody to poke around in. Somebody did quit once after having a confab with him and asking a lot of personal questions."

"But was it related to the tarot cards?"

"I don't know," she said. "He's not speaking about them, though he did say this former employee was into all that woo woo stuff too, as he put it."

"What kind of notebook was it? Was it one somebody was buying?"

"That's what I thought originally," she said, "but, on the very last page, a name is scrawled. *Andrea.*"

"How big is this notebook?"

"About three by four," she said, "so purse size. Not the most common size for something like this. But I don't know ... It ... I don't know," she said. "It's just this little brown leather thing. It's a little crumpled, as if it's been sitting here for a while, maybe jammed into the back of the shelf by something else."

"Do you think it was something the store sold? Like

maybe it was set off to the side for a customer to come back and pick up later?"

"I don't know," she said. "I asked if the tarot cards and the notebook could have been things someone special ordered but never picked up, but Jerry had no memory of that."

"What are you thinking?"

"Honestly I just thought that maybe it was something he found on the shelves damaged, like maybe a kid had written their name in the back, or somebody accidentally thought it was their notebook and realized what they'd done and didn't want to pay for it. It's a fifteen dollar notebook."

"A three-by-four-inch notebook is fifteen bucks?" he asked, his voice rising ever-so-slightly.

"When brand new from a bookstore, yeah," she said. "And the cover is leather. Remember?"

"Is it in the inventory?"

"I'm not sure what you're asking."

"If you ring it up, does it come up as being something you still sell?"

She said, "Oh, hang on a minute." And he heard the clicking of keys and a series of beeps go off. "No, the computer can't find it."

"Right. So do you have access to older records? I'm just wondering how long ago you actually carried a notebook like that."

"If we ever did," she reminded him. "It could also have been personal property lost by somebody."

"That's true too," he said, "so I'm not sure what to say then."

"I'm taking a picture of both the notebook and the tarot cards and where they were found, just for posterity," she said, "and I'll text them to you. But I wonder if you could look into Jerry's background and see if you find anything there."

"Your boss?"

"Yes," she said, "I just ... He gets so obviously upset every time I bring it up that I don't want to bring it up again. But, at the same time, you know? His past is a mystery to me. And not all mysteries are murderous ones," she said, "but the tarot cards came from here, and, of course, Jerry's a permanent resident above the bookstore."

"I'll take a look," he said. "I'll just add it to my list of other things to take a look into."

"Do you have any update on my friends?"

"No. Wendy is still with Meghan, and I spoke to Betty this morning, and she's still staying with her boyfriend too."

"Right. So it's up to me to find a new place. I haven't mentioned the room above the stairs to Jerry again."

"If you think he has anything odd or weird in his history," he said, "you're better off not to go there."

"Sure, but the streets are looking mighty cold," she said, her voice rising. "And I can't stay at your place and pay you the kind of rent you need for that."

"Need? It's been sitting empty. Remember?"

"Yeah, I'm still struggling with that," she said. "You could be making thousands of dollars a week on it."

"Maybe," he said in a mild tone. "I also hadn't decided what I would do with it either. Remember?"

"Nor have you said I can stay there," she said. "So it's a day-to-day arrangement for me as to whether I go to a homeless shelter."

"Okay, you can stay there for the rest of the week. How's that?"

"Well, that's a start," she said in a humorous voice. "Thank you. That gives me a few more days to find a place."

"Are you finding anything?"

She sighed. "Well, I've tried when I have a minute here," she said. "I'm trying to be discreet, since I'm supposed to be working, but, so far, looking in the papers and online, I haven't seen anything even remotely affordable yet. Listen to me whining. I'm sorry. I'm not trying to bother you at work with this."

"It's not an issue. Besides, Stefan needed more details, and I asked you to find out more about the tarot cards. Remember? Anyway, you've got this next week to keep looking for a place to live, and we'll see what you come up with then." At that, he watched Captain Meyer walk across the floor toward him. "I gotta go," he said and quickly hung up.

THE CAPTAIN LOOKED down at Damon. "Who was that?"

"The friend who's still alive after the murders."

"Getting anywhere with her?"

"A little," he said, "but not too far."

"She's a weird one, from what I hear."

"Hey, Captain, you've been here a long time," he said. "Do you know anything about the bookstore owner?"

"Jerry?"

Damon nodded. "Yeah, him."

"Odd duck. Even odder after his wife died."

"What happened to her again?"

"She was murdered," he said briefly, "a long time ago."

"How?"

"She was thrown off a cliff," he said. "We actually

looked at him at the time, wondering if he had been the one who had done it, but we couldn't find anything to prove it."

"She was thrown off a cliff?"

He nodded. "A whole group of them were up on a mountain, doing a big helicopter ski trip," he said, "and somehow, according to reports from the scene, they said she was basically thrown off."

"So it wasn't an accident?"

"Well, according to everybody who was there, she was thrown. But nobody saw anything or did anything about it, so it became this big mess. The coroner said that she died from blunt force trauma as she landed. And a lot of possible witnesses were around, like fifty or sixty of them, and yet nobody saw anything."

Damon stopped and stared. "Seriously?"

"Yeah, seriously."

"Wow. Surely somebody saw something."

"Well, it was before cell phones took over the world," he said. "A few people were taking pictures with the cameras of that day, but they were all around the mountain. Nobody was keeping track of Jerry's wife. She was a little bit off to the side, and another major group was there around her, but still nobody saw anything."

"Where was the husband?"

"Jerry was getting coffee," he said, "so he was definitely cleared. When he came back out, she was gone. She was found at the bottom of the cliff."

"But how do we know she was thrown?"

"Because she screamed all the way down," he said.

"And again, how do we know that she was thrown and that it wasn't just an accident."

"Nobody else was close to her," he said, "at least as far as we could tell. We had all kinds of suspects to look at, but we couldn't put anything together."

Damon stopped and stared. "Hang on. Let me just get this clear. A woman dies after falling from a height, lots of people around, nobody saw anything, and yet you guys determined that she was pushed?"

"Well, somebody else was at the top of the mountain that day, who said that she had been pushed too, but her husband managed to grab on and save her. She was pretty hung up about it, when she saw this other woman go over the edge. She said it looked like she was pushed."

"So, you had one witness who was already traumatized because of what she went through, and she said this other woman was pushed."

"As I said," he said, "the whole thing was crazy. Everybody says it was murder. Officially it was left as 'unknown cause of death,' which was pretty unsatisfying for all concerned."

"Wow. How often does something like that happen around here?"

"Not often at all, believe me. It was a mess, and people were pretty damn upset about it."

"Well, I can see why," he said, "but that's pretty bizarre."

"What can I say? It was like thirty years ago or something."

"Were you one of the ones who looked into the potential of Jerry being a part of it?"

"Well, we all had to look at him, but everybody said that he was in the restaurant at the time, so he was cleared."

"Unless he had somebody else push her."

"And we looked at that," he said. "Believe me. We did

know how to do our jobs, even back then. But, in the end, we had nothing to move forward with. No proof of anything."

"Was she suicidal at all?"

"Not as far as any of us could tell. According to everything that we found, her marriage was happy, and her husband was good to her."

The captain gave him a one-arm shrug. "It's been decades. Not sure even Jerry remembers accurately."

Damon frowned. "Did his wife work?"

"Yes. She worked in the bookstore, and she was into occult studies or some weird thing."

At that, Damon felt ripples going up and down his back. "Occult studies?"

"Yeah, and that didn't help at all. Everybody was bringing up all kinds of woo-woo stuff. Believe me," he said. "It's all garbage."

"Have you ever met Stefan Kronos?"

He snorted. "Do you know how many cops have asked me about that guy? I've never met him, never worked with him, don't want to," he said. "The world is black-and-white. There isn't room for all that weird stuff he keeps bringing up."

"You don't think he's ever helped any cops?"

"I think they would have gotten to the same point on their own in time."

"Interesting. I know a lot of cops believe in him," Damon said.

"I didn't think you believed in any of this stuff."

"I'm not sure I do," he said, "but that doesn't mean I'll dismiss it out of hand."

"Well, you better, if you work for me," he said.

"Were you up on the mountain that day Jerry's wife went over?"

"I was. I was on ski patrol. A lot of us did ski patrol back then," he said, with a shake of his head. "A whole pile of us was around at the time."

"And you didn't see what happened?"

"I saw her go ass over teakettle over the edge. But I saw no sign that she had done anything but literally get picked up and chucked off the mountain. Her footsteps were back about four feet from the edge. No snow crumbled over the edge with her. It was just really weird."

Weird didn't even begin to fit what Damon was starting to think. "Interesting," he muttered. He wasn't sure what to say or how to get more information from his captain.

"Nothing interesting about it."

"Sounds like maybe she took a run and a jump."

"That was definitely a theory at the time too," he said, "but the evidence on the ground didn't support it." Again he shrugged. "So, in the end, it's one of those things that you just walk away from."

"Those kinds of cases drive me batty," Damon said with feeling.

Captain Meyer laughed. "Yep. But, after the amount of time we've had to deal with it," he said, "there's really nothing more you can do but let it go."

"Has it ever happened again? Anything else weird like that around here?"

"Well, we had another husband who supposedly knocked his wife off the mountain. He protested and said he never did it, but we've got others who said he did. So, we went with the eyewitnesses, and he was charged with manslaughter."

"Wow," Damon said. "When was this? What's his status now?"

"He was supposedly writing a book about the case at one point," he said thoughtfully, "but I never did figure out what happened to him."

"What do you mean?"

"Well, I heard the rumors about him writing this book, but then I never heard any more about it."

"Is he even alive?"

"Why wouldn't he be?" his captain asked, looking at him.

He realized just how clueless Captain Meyer was when it came to this kind of stuff or just how closed-minded he was about these stranger cases. "Just a bad joke," Damon said. "Seems like a lot of people are dying around here."

"Our death rate's actually fairly low," he said breezily. "And we want to keep it that way. I don't like unsolved cases."

"How many do you have?"

"None," he said, which stopped Damon in his tracks.

He looked up at him and said, "How is that possible? You just said that Jerry's wife was murdered, but it wasn't solved."

"Sure, but we put down *Indeterminate* on the books because there was no way to solve it."

"Couldn't you have just said it was *accidental?*"

"Maybe, but it didn't feel right. I felt like somebody was behind it."

"So it's an unsolved case then."

"Nope, we changed the paperwork to *Indeterminate*. Case closed." And, with that, he turned and walked out.

Damon looked around at the other detectives nearby.

One, another young guy, looked at him and shrugged. "Did he just say that?" Damon asked with a frown.

"Yeah, I think he did."

"I remember the case he's talking about," Dave said from farther back in a room. He was another grizzled old-timer. "It wasn't so much that it was a murder but just that nobody understood what happened. Some people thought she took a running jump and went over the edge, but the marks on the ground definitely looked like she'd been picked up and chucked over the edge."

"Interesting," Damon muttered once more.

"Not very," he said. "We didn't have any explanation and weren't about to ruin the guy's life over it. It was obvious that Jerry wasn't at fault, so what are you gonna do?"

"I don't know," Damon said, "but you'd think there would be something."

"Maybe, maybe not."

He shook his head at that. "I guess, but it doesn't make any sense. Are there any other 'unsolved' murders that are now solved because of a change in paperwork designation?"

Dave gave him a hard look. "Don't make it sound like we doctored the books to give us a good rep," he said, "but, if there's any doubt in our investigative findings, you know we can't press any charges."

"Why wouldn't we keep them marked open, in case any new evidence came in?"

"What's the point of that?" he asked. "These are all old, old cases."

"So wouldn't it be nice to solve some of these old, old cases?" Damon asked.

"You find a way to solve them, good for you," he said, "but we've got current cases to deal with, in case you've forgotten."

"I get that," he said quietly. "But it doesn't sit well to just change the paperwork."

"It's not that we just changed the paperwork to suit what we wanted it to say," Dave said, losing patience. "But we had the coroner relook at the files to see what was going on, and, if he couldn't tell us anything new, then it was put down as unknown causes."

"But then it's not a murder."

"Exactly. The captain shouldn't have said it that way, but he's always felt in the back of his mind that foul play was involved, and it's always bugged him that nothing could be done about it."

"Well, we all get cases like that," Damon said.

"Exactly, so don't get hung up on terminology."

He watched as Dave got up and walked out of the room. Damon understood, but, at the same time, he didn't know what Captain Meyer's problem was. As Damon got up to refill his coffee cup, he heard his captain and Dave talking.

"Why the hell did you go stirring that shit up for?" Dave asked.

"Because it's a little too close to the kind of shit that's happening right now, and you damn well know it."

"Well, it wasn't a murder back then, and it isn't a murder now," Dave said.

"Back then we didn't know what the hell we heard or saw," he said. "But just trying to ignore it all doesn't fit either."

"Why not? Ignoring it worked well for the last thirty years. Why the hell do you want to stir that up now?" he repeated.

"Because something's wrong out there, Dave. Has been

for years."

"Maybe, but we can't fix it now if we didn't do it back then."

"Dammit, I don't know. Just something about this case's bugging me."

"Well, we got two murdered young women. Why don't we focus on that?" Dave snapped.

"We are," his captain said. "We are."

"We don't need to bring Damon in on all those old cases. No good can come from it. Hell, your own nephew got all spun up, digging into that mess, and drove himself into a solid rock wall over it. Your brother near drank himself to death after that."

At that, Damon stopped. *All those old cases.* How many were they talking about? And what was the deal with the captain's nephew? Damon slowly walked back so he wasn't seen by the two still conversing in the captain's office and looked at Jake. "*All those old cases?*"

Jake shrugged. "I ain't been here that long. Got no clue what he's talking about, but I did get the word to not talk about certain cases. These seem to be the ones to avoid," he said. "And, if you don't wanna rock the boat, you probably should forget you heard anything."

"Maybe. Not sure that's gonna sit very well either."

"If it doesn't pertain to these two young women …"

CHAPTER THIRTEEN

LATER THAT AFTERNOON, Gabby pulled out the notebook once again and took a picture of the name in the back. As she put it away, her boss stepped up and asked, "What is that?"

"It's that little notebook you brought out this morning," she said. "A name's written in the back."

He looked at her in surprise and said, "I didn't see that."

"It's just on the one page and not the last one either," she said. "Still, it's obviously not something that we could sell."

"I must have figured it belonged to somebody and was left in the store," he said, "but I don't know."

"Maybe," she said cheerfully.

"What's the name?"

"Andrea," she said, looking up at him. When his face turned completely white, she raced toward him. "Jerry, are you okay?"

While he stared at her, his breathing became heavy and labored.

"Jeez, sit down," she pleaded. "Please, take it easy."

He slowly sagged into the chair that she pushed up behind him. She had him bend over, so his head was down, and had him focus on his breathing.

"I don't know what just happened," she said, "but you

are terrifying me."

He took another long deep breath and then another. Finally his color returned, and he looked like he would make it.

"Do you need to go to the hospital?"

He slowly shook his head, but he looked old, as if the last few minutes had aged him terribly. He stared at the notebook, like it was a viper about to strike him.

"What's wrong?" she asked, crouching in front of him.

He looked at her, terrified. He shook his head. "There's no way else to explain it."

"Well, it would help if you would at least try," she said. "You're scaring me."

He gave a broken laugh. "You need to be scared," he said, "because it's happening all over again."

"What is? What's happening?" she asked.

"The deaths," he whispered. "The deaths are happening all over again."

She took a long breath and searched his eyes. His cheeks were pink, but he still looked shaken, as if something major had rocked his world. "Which deaths?" she asked quietly.

He continued to stare at her wordlessly.

"Come on, Jerry. You need to tell me," she said quietly.

"No. It could put you in danger," he said.

"It can't be any more danger than I'm already in now."

He shook his head and reached out to grip her hand. "Promise me that you'll have nothing more to do with those things," he said, his hand motioning to the tarot cards and the notebook.

"I wasn't planning on it," she said. "Do you know who they belong to?"

"If it says Andrea," he said, "that was my wife."

She stared up at him. "Your wife? What happened to her?"

He stared at her, his gaze haunted. "She died," he said quietly, "on the mountain."

"How?" she asked.

He raised his shoulders in a shrug. "She went over the edge. The speculation at the time was that I might have pushed her or that somebody else might have thrown her off. Even worse was the suspicion that she took a running leap and went off on her own," he said.

"Oh, gosh, she was suicidal?"

Tears filled his eyes. "I didn't think so," he murmured. "I'd have given anything for a chance to have found out what was so wrong that she would do something like that," he said, "because I loved her to death." And then he winced at the phrase.

"Maybe somebody else pushed her?" she asked quietly.

"The police looked into it for months, but nobody saw anything. So many people were out there with cameras, taking pictures, yet nobody *saw* anything," he said in a teary voice.

"How long ago was this?"

"Thirty years," he said in a broken whisper.

She turned to look back at the notebook. "And do you think that notebook was hers?"

"I don't know," he said. "She often had little notebooks like that."

"How long has it been since you cleaned out underneath that counter?"

He stared at the shelf in question and then said, "I have no idea. But surely not thirty years."

"Maybe you missed these. They were in the back," she

said. "I'm not sure how you found the tarot cards."

He looked at her and said, "You found them."

"No, you gave them to me," she said. "At least I thought that's why you put them on the counter and told me to try them."

"No, they were already on the counter," he said. "I figured you found them somewhere."

"Well, they were underneath, you said."

He stopped, pondered, and then shrugged. "I don't remember," he said. "I don't remember anything about them."

"Okay," she said, hating how similar what he just said was to her dancing around in the cold yesterday and not remembering anything about it afterward. "Did you recover your wife's body?"

He nodded. "A friend of mine with a helicopter took on the extremely dangerous task of going down after her," he said. "He and a team from the local search and rescue group."

"I'm sorry. It must have been a very difficult time for you."

"It was awful," he said. "She's the only woman I've ever loved. I just went in to get coffee for the two of us," he said, "and, when I came back out, she was already gone."

Such a lost and faraway look was on his face that she realized, in many ways, Jerry hadn't moved on from Andrea's death. "That must have been incredibly hard," she said. "I'm so sorry for your loss."

He nodded slowly. "It was just such a sudden shock."

"And you've been staying here ever since?"

He stared up and out the front windows at the mountain. "In some ways I feel like I'm waiting for her to come home," he whispered. "We never had a chance to say goodbye."

"Is there any chance, do you think that she jumped?"

He turned that gaze to her. "I hope not," he said. "I know it sounds terrible, but it's easier to ... to think that she was murdered than that she chose to do this," he said. "How do you reconcile yourself to the fact that your beloved wife chose death over life with you? She could have gotten a divorce, if she were so unhappy. I mean, I would have fought her all the way because I loved her so much, but to think that this is what she saw as her only option is just horrific."

"But then again, maybe somebody did throw her over the edge," she said quietly.

"A good thirty or more people were up there at the time. The cops kept asking me who was up there, who had opportunity, who had motive, but I didn't have any answers. I didn't know who could have done this because, to me, nobody could have done it. Why would they? She was beautiful inside and out," he said in a broken voice.

"I'm sorry," she whispered. "That's so terribly hard."

"You have no idea," he said in little more than a whisper. "She was everything to me. Absolutely everything."

"I can see that," she said. "And maybe what you're really waiting for is your time to die, so you can join her."

He looked at Gabby slowly. "I'm in my mid-seventies, and I'm not very healthy," he said. "That day can't come soon enough for me."

She slowly straightened, feeling her heart tug at the thought of a man who'd rather die early than recover from the death of his wife. "What are you gonna do with all this?" she said, looking around.

"The bookstore was hers," he said. "It was her dream, not mine."

She said, "Ah, that explains some things."

"You mean, the fact that some of it I don't care about? That it's just an income? That it's just something for me to do while I'm here, waiting to die? It pays the bills, and then I can move on?" There was no sarcastic tone, just a sad acceptance.

"To a certain extent, yes," she said carefully, trying not to offend him. "I'm sorry that you've spent your life here so unhappy. If you'd left, maybe you could have rebuilt a new life."

"Maybe," he said, "but I wanted nothing else. I just wanted her."

Something was almost creepy about that, but Gabby didn't have any energy at the moment to think about it. Just then the doorbell rang, and a customer walked in. She smiled at the young man and asked, "May I help you?"

"Are you Gabby?"

She smiled, nodded, and said, "Yes, I am."

"I'm Carl, Betty's boyfriend."

"Oh," she said, with a hand extended, walking toward him. "How's she doing?"

"Well, she's pretty angry. She's blaming you for this."

At that, Gabby stopped just short of approaching Carl and stared at him in shock. "Me? What have I got to do with it?"

"She says it's your fault," he said, getting belligerent and angry himself. "Otherwise she would have moved back into the apartment with you guys."

"But somebody was killed in that apartment," she said slowly. "Why the hell would she blame me for that? She lived there just as much as I did."

"But you're the weird one who did the tarot cards, and,

if you hadn't done that, none of this would have happened apparently."

She stared at him in shock. "What? So I'm to blame for the murder of my friends?" she asked, her voice rising in shock.

"Well, I asked her about that, and she said, *Absolutely*, and, if you hadn't been playing with the tarot cards, death wouldn't have found everybody."

Gabby shook her head. "The tarot card readings aren't reality."

"Well, apparently they are now," he said. "I came here to warn you."

"Warn me?" she said, stepping back slightly.

"Yeah. Stay away from her," he said. "She doesn't want to be the next victim. If you're doing this," he said, "you need to stop."

"If I'm *doing this*, as in you think I killed our friends?" She couldn't imagine anybody would have thought something like that, much less Betty and her boyfriend. To think they would even consider something like that just blew her away. "I didn't kill anybody," she cried out.

"Well, I don't know if I believe you," he said. "You are kind of weird-looking."

She shook her head, in shock. "Weird-looking?" She didn't even know what to do with that.

"Yeah," he said, "weird-looking. Now stay the hell away from Betty."

"That's fine," she said quietly, as he turned toward the door. "Have a good life."

He turned and snapped at her, saying, "Stop saying weird shit like that too." And, with that said, he stormed out.

It was all she could do to not run after him and see what

he was driving, just so she could tell Damon. Yet it made no sense to figure out what vehicle the guy had. Damon could easily track it all down anyway. She turned slowly and looked at her boss, who was back to looking as if he'd just had a heart attack. She raced over to his side. "I really think you need to go to the hospital," she said.

"No," he said, "but it's happening all over again."

"What's happening?"

"Things like that. Angry men coming in and making accusations for no reason."

"You mean, this happened back with your wife?"

"After she died," he said, "it happened all the time. It was just nonsensical stuff, as if somebody out there were just trying to torment me. As if I wasn't tormented enough already," he said hoarsely.

"I'm sorry. I don't even know what that guy is all about," she said. "Betty was one of the roommates I shared an apartment with. But I don't know why I'm supposed to be the weird one, or why I'm responsible."

"You aren't," he said, patting her hand. "People used to accuse me of it too, back then. They tried to ruin my life. And it had already been ruined because of my wife's death, but it didn't seem to matter to them. They all seemed to think that maybe I'd killed her and wanted her out of here. So I could steal the store out from under her or something." He shook his head. "It made no sense to me because she loved this store, absolutely loved it, and I loved her," he said sadly. "So none of their logic made any sense to me."

"I'm not sure they are using logic," she said. "When you think about it, they're just spouting nonsense, trying to convince others to believe it too. Then they cause the chaos they want to, based on that nonsense."

DAMON SPENT THE afternoon in the records room, accessing the full digital database, looking up old case files, even though he had been warned away from it. It wasn't something he could stop. As far as he was concerned, fear now prevented people from finding out the truth. He wasn't willing to walk away again, and they couldn't handle that. This needed to be solved, and it needed to be solved now. Otherwise it would just get worse.

And then to have another bout of deaths wasn't acceptable either. But he didn't know quite how to handle his own coworkers putting up a wall and not dealing with what looked to be a repeat serial killer. Still he had to keep going. He had to try something. When he came across another death on the mountain, he started searching for just mountain deaths, not deaths in town—which might have limited his ability to find everything related to his two current cases—but it was a place to start. He requested each of the relevant files as he found one.

When he went to pick up the cold case files, the front-desk clerk said, "That's a whole pile of cases."

"Yeah," he said, "I was just thinking it might be related to something more current."

"Well, there are a lot of mountain deaths. Several books been written about it."

Damon looked up, frowned, and said, "Really? Which ones?"

The clerk thought about it and then said, "I don't remember any specific titles, but my wife will know for sure." He quickly sent her a text and got a reply right away. He wrote down the two titles for Damon and said, "Here you go."

"Thank you," Damon said. "I appreciate that."

"No problem. Nice to have some young blood around here, shaking things up a bit."

"Well, you may be the only one who appreciates it," he said, laughing.

"Isn't that the truth? The captains never like it, but you know that shaky stuff has been going on here for a long time."

At that, Damon looked back at him and asked, "How long you been here?"

"Oh, forty-two years," he said. "At least next month it will be. Seen a lot in my time. Lots more I've forgotten too."

"That's a long time," he said.

"Yep, sure is."

"So you know all about these deaths on the mountains then, huh?"

"I know about a lot of them. Some of them were pretty scary. Some of them were pretty weird. Some of them were out there—like really out there. But we're not allowed to talk about those."

"And those are exactly the ones I want to hear about," he said.

"Ha," he said, "well, I'm retiring next month, so I'm not sure that they can do anything about that except retire me a little sooner."

"Well, I wouldn't want to do anything to put your pension in jeopardy."

"Nothing they can do at this point," he said. "I've got three weeks of vacation time to use, so I'm out of here in a few days."

"So, in a few days, can I come talk to you?"

He laughed. "Yeah, we can do it that way. But no need.

There's really not much to tell. The higher-ups put a gag on the cops in the initial case. Now they knew stuff. Otherwise grab the files. The rest? ... Well, that's just the voodoo factor of unexplained happenings. Read up, and, if you still have questions, you can call me. Not that I'll know more than the books and the files will show, though."

"Okay," Damon said. "I'll take these, and thanks for the book titles." He signed them all out and packed up everything into his car. Picking up the other ones from his office, he added them to the carload and headed to the bookstore. As he walked in, a client was just walking out. He looked up, saw Gabby staring at him, and he smiled. "Hey, you ready to go home?"

"Sure," she said. "This is getting to be a habit."

"A nice one," he said easily. "But a little business first," he said, handing over the handwritten note. "What about these two books? Do you have them?"

She glanced at the titles, nodded, and said, "Actually, yes." Then she walked over to the counter, right beside the cash register, and picked up both books. She checked the titles, shook her head, and looked up at him curiously. "Who told you to get these?"

"The guy on the Cold Case desk," he said. "Why?"

"I have a weird story about them," she said. "I'll tell you later."

"Perfect," he said, "let's grab them and go."

She rang them up, and he paid for them; then she called out to her boss, "Jerry, I'm going for the day." He'd been sitting in the back office, recovering from his earlier shock.

When he came out, she saw how he looked older and older as time went on. She frowned and said, "Are you sure you're okay? Maybe you should just go on upstairs now."

"I'm going up," he said. "Lock up the front, will you? I'll just call it quits for the day."

She nodded. "I'm really worried about you, Jerry."

He gave her a gentle smile. "I know," he said. "I'll be fine."

"I'm not so sure," she said, chewing on her bottom lip.

He waved at them both and said, "You go on. It's all good."

She nodded slowly and headed out, shaking her head.

"Problems?" Damon asked.

"Yeah," she said, "he had a shock today, and he turned white. I thought for a moment he was having a heart attack or something. But he wouldn't go to the hospital, wouldn't have anything to do with the idea. I'm really worried about him," she said. "Underneath that rough exterior, he's the sweetest guy."

"He's had a pretty rough time of it."

"We talked about his wife today. He's tormented by the idea that she might have thrown herself over the cliff to get away from him."

"That's enough to make anybody's head spin," he said. "My captain said Jerry's wife's death was originally classified as murder because, as far as they could tell, she was picked up and thrown over."

"Which would look similar, I would think, to a running jump, wouldn't it?"

"Possibly." He filled her in on what Captain Meyer had said.

"So they changed it to undefined, unknown causes?" she asked.

"Yeah, but she died of blunt force trauma from the fall," he said. "The old guy back in the Cold Case files says it's one of the things they're not allowed to talk about."

"What do you wanna bet it's more woo-woo stuff," she said quietly, "and nobody knows how to handle it?"

"Well, do you?"

"No, I don't," she said. "It's happening right now to me, and I don't know what to say to people."

"Did you tell your boss about last night?"

"No," she said, "he also doesn't think that he's the one who pulled out the tarot cards from under the counter."

"Meaning?"

"I just wondered at the time if maybe it was anything like me not remembering dancing in the cold last night. What if something like that had happened to him, and he didn't remember what he'd done either?"

"Interesting," he said. "Well, I brought a pile of files home with me."

"It will be interesting to see what shows up," she said.

"If anything," he said, "but I'm beginning to wonder if history is repeating itself."

"Sounds exactly like it's doing that. Jerry thinks so too. So how long ago did this originally happen? How many times did it go on? I wonder what caused it to stop and what triggered it again."

"I know. ... All good questions," he said, "and ones we need to get answers to. We should get some dinner first, though."

"I don't think we have anything for dinner, do we?"

"I have lots at my place."

"Or I can have another omelet or some toast or just make a sandwich," she said.

"You might as well come to the main house," he said. "I've got chicken defrosting, enough for two."

"That would be lovely," she said, raising her eyebrows at him.

"Well, no point in both of us cooking meals like that, when I have enough food for us," he said. "And good food. I don't want you just eating sandwiches, when you should have something more substantial."

"Well, more substantial would be nice, but it's not always doable," she said.

"When do you get paid again?"

"Friday," she said, "but honestly, after seeing Jerry today, I'm not sure I'm gonna have a job."

"Do you think he's that ill?"

"I think he's definitely that ill. He's only kept the bookstore all these years because it was her dream. He told me that he felt like he was waiting for her to come home."

"Weird," he said, "but I guess, when you've lost somebody in a shocking way, you don't really know what you're supposed to do, do you?"

"I'm not sure there's any right way to handle it. These instantaneous and unexpected deaths are all so disorienting," she said. "He did tell me that his buddy helped search and rescue retrieve her body from the mountain. So I'm not sure why he thinks she's still gonna come home."

"That's a good point too," he said, "since theoretically, by bringing her body home, she should have been home."

"Exactly. So I don't know. It seems like the more I get into this, the less it makes any sense."

"Of course. But we also have that lovely little encounter that you had last night," he said, "where what you did isn't something you remember doing, and yet we have proof of your actions."

"Yeah, great. Thanks for bringing up that whole *dancing*

out in the cold thing again."

"Well, what if Jerry doesn't remember parts of his world from when his wife died?"

"Or weird parts that he has rewritten because it's easier?"

"Meaning?"

"I'm just wondering if his wife's body was really ever recovered. Or, if he's still sitting there, hoping that his buddy will make another attempt and get her."

"*Hmm.* That's a good insight into Jerry," he said, "though Andrea's body was found, since the coroner found blunt force trauma from the fall as her cause of death. Although, if they will change one record, why not change another?"

"Well, if nothing else," she said, "you won't be bored investigating this case and any others of note."

"Oh, I'm not bored," he said. "I'm just trying to keep you safe at the same time."

"Speaking of which, I had a visit from Betty's boyfriend," she said. "He basically told me to get out of town and to stay away from her. He didn't want her turning up dead too."

"Ouch. Did he accuse you of killing the others?"

"More or less," she said, striving for a light voice.

"Because you can tell him to call the cops, and we'll back you up, if he's getting violent."

"But, as you well know, violence happens when nobody else is around to help," she said.

"Not necessarily. If you've got a problem with him, it's really important to nip things right at the start," he said, "so we don't have that same issue going forward."

"That would definitely make sense," she said.

"Sure it does. Basically, if he's gonna threaten you, he

needs to know that we're here."

"Okay," she said with a shrug. "I don't think he's harmful anyway. He seems kind of, … I don't know, … rude to say it, but kinda useless. But I think he cares about Betty, and that's worth a lot."

"But he came across as useless?"

"Came across as blowing hot air," she said. "So that didn't sound very good, but I don't know what else to call it."

"Well, it's an interesting theory anyway," he said.

"Still doesn't help us."

"Maybe not," he said, "but maybe we'll get some answers from these cold cases."

"I hope so." As they pulled up in front of the house, she got out, looked up at the big house, smiled, and said, "You're really lucky to have inherited this."

"I know," he said. "I had a small condo. Actually I still have it," he confessed. "I've got it rented while I'm here, but again it's all part of that *not sure what I'm doing with my life* thing."

"Well, there are worse things to fuss over," she said.

"True, very true." As he walked to the entrance, he unlocked the door, pushed it open, and said, "Welcome."

She stepped inside and gasped. "This is gorgeous!"

"My aunt was an interior designer. She knew where all the fabrics and colors and stuff should go, and I have to admit that I always loved her choices. It's very serene here."

"Makes a nice haven for you, when you get off the hard, ugly workday."

"Isn't that the truth? Nothing quite like humanity to keep you on your toes, which makes you wonder how we even survive all the crude violence that we do to each other."

"I hear you," she said softly. "On that note, I guess you have nothing new about my friends, do you?"

"No," he said, "not at all."

"Okay," she said. "I just keep hoping."

"You and me both. Everybody's been interviewed around the second murder scene. Nobody heard anything. Nobody saw anything. The cameras in the hallway were glitched at the time, so nobody was filmed coming or going."

"Parking lot cameras?"

"They're out of order," he said.

"It seems almost like this entity, this person, had some kind of electrical vibration that sent all the cameras offline," she said. "I mean that's a pretty cool trick, if you're a thief. But I don't know how realistic it is for something like this."

Just then a golden sphere formed in front of them.

She gasped and stepped back. Damon, however, handled it much better.

"Hello, Stefan. How are you doing tonight?" he said in a humorous tone.

CHAPTER FOURTEEN

G ABBY STARED AT Stefan's glowing energy form in amazement. "I still don't get it," she said. "I mean, I saw it before, but I almost deluded myself into thinking it was fake, but here you are again."

"Absolutely," he said out loud for both of them to hear. "And, if you think about it, this is where I need to be."

"Why?" she asked in confusion. "Why do you need to be here?"

"Because lots of action is here," he said, "of an entity kind."

"Do you think it's related to the cold cases from a long time ago?" Damon asked him.

"Absolutely," Stefan said. "When things cycle around, you know that you've got to go back to the beginning to find out what's going on."

"Would a spirit even stay around that long?" she asked in confusion. "I thought they were supposed to leave the planet after death."

"Well, that's true in most cases," he said. "But often-times they hang around because they don't want to be separated from somebody."

"So, like my boss's wife, if she really, really cared about him, she might still be hanging around, waiting for him?"

"Possibly, yes," he said, "but you never really know the

reason for somebody to hang around."

"Revenge, you mean? Do they do it for the wrong reasons?" Damon asked.

"All the time," Stefan said in a soft voice. "Unfortunately they do that all the time."

"Is there anything you can do to help them?" Gabby asked.

"Sometimes there is, and sometimes there isn't. What I spend a lot of my time doing is helping entities leave."

"Do they ever *not* want to leave?" Damon asked him.

"The ones trying to regain a chance at life? Absolutely," he said. "They never want to leave."

"Okay, so that's scaring the hell out of me," she cried out. "Is it even possible that they can avoid death?"

"They've already died," Stefan said, "but, every once in a while, they find a way to try and live again."

"Well, that's the epitome of what everybody wants, isn't it?" Damon asked. "If you think about it, eternal life is the goal."

"For some of them, they lock into this way of finding another way to live," Stefan said. "We've got all kinds of people who study the occult, looking for a way to cheat death, but it doesn't work—well, so far, I haven't seen any be successful."

"And you've seen lots of people try?" she asked softly.

"Many, and they use other humans to attempt to continue their existence."

"That's scary."

"It's not only scary but it's also dangerous for the other person," he said. "Because, like with evil possessions, it's draining their system at the same time. They're essentially feeding off the host's body, like parasites."

"And the host can't sustain it?" Damon asked.

"No, it makes them exhausted, tired, ages them easily, and they look, feel, and act way older than they would if they were just themselves."

Like Jerry? Gabby wondered. But the man was in his seventies, after all.

"But," Damon continued, "what about Gabby? She was superenergized after her near-death experience. And you thought she might be possessed. That's the opposite of the draining you just talked about. So how is that possible?"

Stefan laughed. "Welcome to my world. Yes, you can have a healing possession of sorts, a rejoining of positive energies of a sort. But, in Gabby's case, she seems to have two souls fighting for her, one evil, one benevolent."

"Oh my," Gabby murmured, her eyes wide.

"Can you see these extra entities?" Damon asked Stefan.

"Sometimes. Lots of times not. Sometimes they blend so well with the person—because they love them or care about them—that it's really hard to find them. Sometimes you'll find humans are perfectly willing to carry them out of love, thinking that they're doing a good thing. Often they carry around a piece of somebody who's died, thinking that they'll carry that piece with them forever because then they never let go. But it has the opposite effect. These evil possessions are ghosts somehow finding a way to be strong enough to take over a host and to halfway live their ghostly life with them. And not to the benefit of the host."

"So like a parasite-and-a-host relationship?"

"Yes, and, at some point in time, that parasite ends up taking over the host and taking the energy from the healthy person."

"That's a scary thought too," she said. She walked into

the living room and sank into the nearest chair. "That's just something I don't really want to think about."

"Well, somebody's in your sphere, who you think is normal and completely free and clear and safe, but she isn't," he said.

"Who are you talking about?"

"Your friend, Wendy."

Gabby stopped and stared. "What's wrong with Wendy?" she asked, bouncing to her feet. "What's wrong with her? I need to help her, if I can do something."

"There's nothing you can do," Stefan said. "Not only do you *not* have the same relationship that you thought you had with her but she doesn't have that relationship with you."

"I'm sorry. I don't understand," she said.

"The only reason she came here was because of you," he said. "And the only reason she's with Meghan right now is because of you."

She stared at the golden orb in shock. Gabby sat down again, shaking her head. "I don't know what you're getting at. Why are you being so cryptic?"

"Ah," said Damon, nodding slowly, a light of comprehension in his gaze. "I get it."

Stefan agreed. "Exactly. Wendy came here because she loves you," he said in that musical voice of his. "And the only reason she's with Meghan is that you don't love her."

DAMON WATCHED THE shock and awareness filter across Gabby's face, as she sagged back and burst into tears. "I gather that you didn't see it?" he murmured, walking over and sitting beside her.

She nodded slowly. "How could I not have though?

How could I not have known that's how she felt?" she asked. "What's wrong with me that I can't see this stuff?"

"There was no need to see it," he said, "so why would you? You were happy in the relationship as it was, and you didn't realize that she was looking for or needing more."

"No," she whispered, "I didn't. Oh, my God, I don't even know what to say."

"There's nothing to say," he said. "You're where you're at right now. But maybe it'll help you understand why she's gone back to Meghan."

"No," she said. "That makes it worse than before because now I know why she's doing it—because I'm not interested, so Meghan is like settling for second-best, a fallback option."

"So," he said, "what do you want to do?"

"I want to find out if it's true."

"I understand why you feel that way," Damon said, "but wouldn't that just embarrass Wendy, make her feel even worse?"

His words made Gabby pause. "That's what it would do, isn't it?"

He nodded slowly. "I think so. When you fall in love with somebody, who doesn't love you back, … but when they don't even know how you feel, … well, that's harder yet again. She already knows you don't feel the same way, but asking her about it will only bring up more hurt feelings."

"God," she said, "I'm absolutely devastated. I had no idea."

"And you shouldn't feel guilty about that. She obviously didn't approach you about it, or you would have known earlier. So she just stayed on the sidelines, kept hoping."

"That's not making me feel any better," she cried out.

"I understand," he said, "but now we have quite a bit to deal with." He turned to look back at Stefan, but the golden orb was gone. "In case you hadn't noticed, Stefan is gone now."

"He dropped a bombshell and walked," she said, her tone bitter.

"Not his fault," Damon said. "You can't blame the messenger."

She reached up and rubbed her eyes. "I just feel like coming here was such a mistake," she whispered. "Everything's gone wrong since we arrived. And we'd planned it, dreamed of this winter for so long."

"But has it all gone wrong? Or just in this last little bit?"

"Maybe just this last little bit," she said. "We loved being here for December and January and February."

"You've almost made it through the season," he said. "So you can understand why Wendy's questioning when you're going back, *if* you're going back, and what you're doing."

"And I have no answers for her," she said. "And here I sit, undecided as always."

"I don't know that you are *undecided*. You certainly have decisions to make, and you probably should make them relatively soon, but, like I said, I need you to stay in town while the investigation is ongoing."

She nodded slowly. "And that gives me an out for now, doesn't it? So I don't have to go home right now."

"Are you looking forward to leaving at the end of the season?"

"I wouldn't go if I had a choice in the matter," she said.

"If you love it that much here, why don't you try to find a way to stay here then?" he asked.

"Because I would need something other than a mini-

mum-wage job," she said. "I used to work for a large
company as a buyer, but nothing like that is around here that
I could take on temporarily, and I do have a job potentially if
I go back. I was maternity relief where I was."

"Was it well-paid?"

"Yes," she said with a nod. "With that job here, I could
afford a decent place to live in Aspen, and I could survive
quite nicely. Remember that I don't get tips. I'm working
strictly for minimum wage," she said. "Tips in some of these
places in town are great—like the bars, the restaurants—but,
if you're working at a bookstore, like I am, it's a whole
different story."

"Does the bookstore make money?"

"For all Jerry's complaining, I think it must do well," she
said, "considering he's had it for so many years. But a lot
could be done to make the business better, and he's just not
too interested."

"No, and, if it was his wife's store, you can kind of understand that."

"I guess," she said. "It's kind of depressing to think of it,
you know? That it's not his dream. It was hers. Yet he won't
talk about her. There's no pictures of her. There's nothing."

"There's also his guilt," he said. "In this case, Jerry
couldn't save Andrea. So he's doing what he can to keep her
dream alive because he couldn't keep her physically alive in
order to live out her dream. And if he's worried that she may
have jumped, that just adds to the level of his guilt."

"Wow, we humans are so messed up, aren't we?" she
murmured.

He nodded. "Absolutely."

"There's so much to adjust to right now," she said, getting up and walking around. "It's almost impossible to

handle it all at once."

"It's a bit overwhelming," he said, "but come on. Let's get some food, and then you can get a decent night's sleep."

"I could use that," she said. "I didn't sleep well last night."

He quickly finished cooking, and then the two of them sat down to eat. She smiled in amazement. "This is lovely."

"Good," he said, and the two of them turned their attention to the meal.

As soon as she was done, he escorted her to the garage suite. Turning to walk away, he said, "Lock up behind me now."

"I will," she said. "So you still think I'm in danger?"

He looked at her and, with a reluctant smile, nodded and said, "Yes. I do."

At that, she winced. "You could have lied."

"No," he said. "You need to know as much as you can. Frankly I'm not sure if you're a danger to yourself or from others, but I really don't want any more *dancing in the cold without a coat* scenarios."

"Me either," she said. "I don't want to have any time where it feels like I've blacked out again."

"Have you ever experienced something like that before?"

"I don't think so," she said, "although maybe Wendy would say differently."

"What do you mean?"

"I don't know, but she's the one who always kept watch over me. Which just adds to my guilt now. She was always looking out for me, but I apparently wasn't even seeing what she was there for."

"Stop the useless guilt," he ordered. "You can't conjure up those feelings when they don't exist."

"I know," she whispered. "The trouble is, I love her. I really do, but I love her as a best friend, the friend I thought was always there."

"So continue to love her that way," he said gently, "and don't make her feel that it's anything less or different because of what you now know."

She nodded, as she sagged into the couch by the living room window. "I still wonder if I should say something to her."

"I wouldn't," he said. "I can't imagine a scenario in which a conversation like that doesn't go terribly wrong right now."

"Great, that just piles on to my guilt."

"You get some sleep," he said, and he turned and walked out. He waited for the *click* of the lock and then walked down the stairs. As he stood outside, he looked up at the sky. It was clear and crisp, a beautiful spring evening in Aspen. But it would be a long time before it really got warm. He was good with that because he loved winter. Not everybody did.

So many people came here just for the ski season and then left, and he could understand why. That was what Gabby had planned to do, but, if she liked the city so well, she should stay. He wanted to say that to her but didn't figure it was the right time for something like that.

As he walked back toward his house, his phone rang. He looked down to see that Jake was calling. "What's up?"

"Coroner's report just came in on the two deaths."

"Cause of death?"

"He says they were garroted."

"Seriously?" He stopped in his tracks. "How the heck could he tell?"

"He found residue of some rust from a wire draped

around the neck of the first one and, on the second one, where she was decapitated, he found indentations of the digging-in lines from where the wire was."

"Somebody had to be strong to do that," Damon said.

"He said that may be the case, but also wires with handle grips that twist and tighten the noose make it easier to kill somebody."

"And chopping off the heads?"

"He still says a long blade. Wouldn't be at all surprised if we were looking for something like a sword. It was a clean cut."

"Any precision needed?"

"Not necessarily, no."

"Damn, so it still could be anybody."

"Unfortunately, yes."

"No forensic evidence? Nothing found to point to someone different, something different?"

"The women's apartment, the first crime scene, was full of fingerprints," he said. "But apparently they hosted lots of get-togethers and had a lot of people over. So any number of people visited with a completely viable reason for their prints to be there, even if they were the killer."

"In other words, no way to isolate those fingerprints as being from the killer."

"No." Jake sighed. "As for the second crime scene, seems Liz and her boyfriend kept to themselves. No other DNA found but theirs."

"Do you have any good news at all?" Damon asked in a humorous tone.

"Well, I wanted to ask if you went through any of those files yet."

"Which ones?"

"The ones you signed out of the records division."

"Oh, so you heard about that, huh? And the answer is, no, I haven't yet."

"Well, if you find anything, let me know."

"Sure," he said. "Do you know anything about the bookstore owner's case?"

"Nope. Before my time. Other than what you shared about the conversation between Jerry and Gabby today, I don't know anything other than that."

"The guy I signed out the files from has been working for the department all the way back to then and beyond. I'm just trying to get to the bottom of exactly what happened."

"I'm not sure anybody knows," Jake said gently. "Jerry's wife's case is one of those woo-woo files that never could be figured out. And each captain from the past to the present has handed down a gag order, demanding we don't talk about them."

"I know, but the minute anything comes in with a woo-woo element, it makes me want to sit down and to find the logic behind it all."

"Well, good luck with that," he said, "because you and I both know that, too often, we don't get any answers."

"I know, thanks. Let's just hope there are no more deaths."

"Well, just make sure that Gabby's locked down and safe from being a suspect or a victim."

"I'm on it," he said. He hung up the phone, turning to look back to see her standing in the living room window, staring out into the darkness. He hated that she was as open and readily available for everybody to see like that. He quickly called her. When she answered, he said, "Don't stand in the window like that. I don't want to scare you, but somebody could be watching you, so let's not make it easy for them."

"What are you talking about?" she asked. "I'm in bed."

"Don't lie to me," he said, in exasperation. "I'm right here outside, looking at you standing in the window."

"And I don't know what you're seeing," she said, her voice starting to tremble with fear. "But I'm in bed, and I've been right here since you left."

CHAPTER FIFTEEN

G ABBY BOLTED OUT of bed, and, instead of racing out to the living room, she hid behind the divider and whispered, "What the hell is going on? Who is that in my living room?"

"I'm letting myself in through the door," he said. "Don't freak out."

"Damn good thing," she whispered, "because I'm hiding behind the screen and intend to stay here."

When she heard him already walking inside, she peered around the divider to see him standing in the living room, looking at the same spot where he had thought she'd been standing earlier. She wanted to call out to him but didn't want to disturb him, as he turned to look around the living room. She didn't see anything. He didn't either, as he immediately started searching high and low. She finally stepped out of her hiding spot and said, "I didn't hear anything but you."

"No," he said. "I didn't hear anything either, but I definitely saw something in the window."

"And you're sure it was me?"

"No, I'm not sure it was you," he said. "Somebody was there though, a woman with long hair."

She grabbed her hair, measuring its length. It would be classified as long because it came down below her shoulders.

"My length?"

He looked at it and then slowly shook his head. "No, a little bit longer."

"You could see that from down there?"

"Yes." He frowned. "It was a little odd to see, just because the lighting was different. But I was looking up, and I could see her clearly."

"Clearly enough to recognize her?"

"No, just clear enough to see what I thought was you standing here."

"So, did you see our resident ghost?" she asked in a broken laugh.

He stopped, stared, and said, "I don't know. But if it wasn't you and if nobody's here, who else is there?"

"Did somebody race out while you were coming in?"

"The door was in front of me the whole time. Nobody came out." He sagged down into the living room chair and stared at her. "I've never believed in any of this before," he murmured.

"Who has?" she said, coming toward him. "None of this is very believable."

"And yet," he said, "how is it we don't believe it when it's right in front of us?"

"I'm not sure, but I think Stefan would say that our lives have been relatively unscathed up until now, and, for the first time, we're actually having to deal with it."

"What I can tell you is, somebody was standing near the window. Definitely a woman in the window."

"In that case," she said, "we'll assume that it was somebody you saw for a little bit who isn't here now."

"Sure," he said. "But that doesn't help in the sense that we don't know who this person is."

"I think the question is, who this person *was*," she said gently. "I think what we must do is acknowledge that what we're seeing is something that's not of this world. Or not any longer. Something bizarre is going on, and we're caught up right in the middle of it."

"I think we're caught up in it," he said, "because of you."

He was right. Chances were this all revolved around her. She just didn't know why. Except for that pack of tarot cards maybe. "That's quite possible, but that still won't answer or solve the problem we're dealing with right now."

"Maybe not," he said, "but we sure as hell need to figure it out … and fast."

"Even if I am being haunted by a ghost," she said, "what is that telling us?"

"That somebody has latched on to you. For whatever reason, for whatever connection, that person has seen you as a conduit to whatever it is that they're here for."

"Do we know for sure that this person, this entity, has a negative reason for being here?"

"While I'm sure Stefan would say there are benign ghosts, however, it's still not in their benefit to stay here."

"Maybe," she said, "and does that mean that we're supposed to do something to get rid of her?"

"If she's the reason that you're out dancing in the cold, getting hypothermia, then, yes," he said. "She needs to go back to wherever she came from or move on to whatever comes after this," he said, with a wave of his hand.

She nodded slowly and looked around her, and then she held up her arm and said, "I had goose bumps as soon as you left earlier," she said slowly. "That's one of the reasons I raced into bed."

"And I was standing outside, talking on the phone for a

moment," he said. "When I got off the phone, I looked up and saw her standing here."

"Could you see what she wore?"

"It looked like a long tunic," he said, "but I couldn't see any more than that."

"So you don't know how old she was or how old her image was?"

He stopped and asked, "What do you mean by that?"

"I'm just wondering. If somebody like that is stuck in time, is their clothing stuck in time too, or was she dressed modern?"

"I couldn't see that clearly."

"And I wonder how old would somebody look who'd been dead, say, ten years? Would they look older, or would they still be their age at the time of their death?"

"Who knows about the age thing, other than Stefan maybe? As far as clothing, I don't know that fashion has changed all that much," he said. "So maybe there wouldn't be that much difference."

"Especially ski gear," she said, "sweaters and leggings or jeans."

"Yeah, I couldn't see that level of detail at all."

She nodded slowly. "I don't know what's going on, and I don't know who you call in on a deal like this, but the only person who comes to mind would be Stefan. Besides, before he left us so abruptly tonight, he said I have two entities fighting for me. Remember? So maybe the ghost tonight is the good spirit? I don't know. I need to know more."

"What would you ask him?"

"How do we stop this? How do we get her to go on to whatever it is that she needs to go on to?"

Just then, a wind gusted through the entire apartment.

The corner of the blanket on the couch lifted, the curtains billowed, and her hair swung about. She raced to Damon's side, crying out, "What's going on? What's happening?"

He jumped up from the living room chair, already on his feet, one arm wrapped around her, holding her close. "I'm not sure," he said, "but I think our ghostly visitor is here again."

"Oh, my God," she said, looking around. "I can't see her. I can't see her."

"Maybe that's a good thing," he said, holding her tight. "Just don't make any sudden moves, and let's see what it does."

"What *it* does?" she said. "I can't believe we're even talking about this."

"Do you see any reasonable explanation for what's going on?"

"No," she said, "I really don't." She twisted to look around behind him and then back again to the front. But the hairs on her head had calmed down, and, although she still had goose bumps up and down her arms, she couldn't see any visible sign that the ghost was still around them. "Do you think she lives here? Maybe it's your aunt," she said, looking up at him.

He looked down at her in surprise. "Well, my aunt died of cancer after a three-year fight," he said. "So I'm not sure that it was the kind of death that would bring somebody back."

"I'm not sure," she said, "if the way they die matters. Not as much as maybe they are attached to something here. I tried to do some research today, but it's pretty hard to get away with it at work, since Jerry isn't very open to any of this … strangeness."

"Well, I wonder why," he said snidely. "Just look at this. We're all going a little bit crazy, trying to decipher what any of this means, and we have no answers."

"So who does?"

"Stefan," he said, "but we need something more than just him. I don't know that he has the time to sit here and help us deal with a ghost who's hanging around."

"But if this ghost is killing people …"

He stared at her in surprise. "I'm sorry to disillusion you," he said, "but whoever is killing people is very physical. The killer decapitates his victims with huge blades across the throat, after being garroted," he said.

She paled as she thought about that. "Oh, my God," she whispered, "that's so horrible."

"It is horrible. It also requires a certain amount of strength and speed and, in some ways, even skill, although the coroner doesn't seem to think any specific skill was needed for the decapitation."

"You mean, they didn't need to know how to do it beforehand? Because I wouldn't know how to begin."

"Maybe not," he said, "but there were no hesitation marks, let me put it that way. So they started out doing just what they wanted to do, and they managed to cut nice and clean with a powerful sword."

"Would a sword take a head off just like that?"

"Done correctly, yes," he said, "but it depends on the force of the blow, the angle, and all kinds of different factors."

"I guess that's how they used to kill people in the olden days, isn't it?"

"Not that much really," he said, "though several regimes in China preferred that method."

"So strange. Does that mean we have an Asian connection here?"

"I think it would be a mistake to go that far," he said. "You must think about people in our global world today and just how different all that is right now. Any number of people could have those different skills. Hell, it could even be somebody who just grabbed a huge sword and swung with all his might. You know? If done just right, he could accomplish that."

"I suppose," she said, shaking her head. "It's hard to imagine."

"Well, a few other details are involved," he said, "but I haven't read the whole report myself yet. So I don't know everything that's going on with the murders."

"And is the coroner always correct?"

"Nobody is always correct," he said, "but obviously we do the best we can to get the most accurate information, so we can build a case around it."

"Right," she murmured. "How do we capture someone who might not even be physical?"

"Well, first off we won't go on the assumption that a ghost did the killings," he said. "Remember that."

She nodded slowly but wasn't convinced.

"I get that it's easier for you to think that," he said, "because then nobody you know is responsible, but that doesn't make it so."

"Maybe not," she said. "I wish I knew why it was connected to me."

"That actually would be a huge help," he said. "Maybe at least then we could understand why this ghost, which is one part of our problem, is even here."

"And, if it isn't here, why is it hanging around this apartment?"

"But I'm not sure it's just the apartment," he said. "I think you're the connection. You're the one with the tarot cards. You're the one thrown down the mountain. You're the one having these weird dancing episodes."

"Fine," she said, taking a deep breath. "So I'm the connection. Did I touch something? Did I pick up something? Do I own something? I don't know how somebody can connect like this."

"I think just like that," he said, "either by being related to, connected to, picking up something, buying something, owning something, touching something. Like those tarot cards." He shrugged. "I don't know, but obviously that's an awful lot to consider, and we need to clarify just what and how."

"Yes," she said, "and sooner than later."

He smiled. "I didn't see anything vengeful about this ghost in the window though," he said, "so keep that in mind."

"Not very helpful right now," she said, "not when two people are dead."

"No, no, I hear you." Just then his phone rang. He loosened his arms around her enough to pull his phone from his pocket. He took a look and, stepping back, said, "It's my partner."

She watched as he answered, her mind still caught up on what she had just seen.

"What?" He turned and stared at her.

She wrapped her arms around her chest and waited anxiously for the bad news.

"No, I'm on my way," he said. "Be there in ten, maybe fifteen." He slowly ended the call on his phone, staring at it the whole time, and said, "We have another death."

She gasped. "Not one more of my friends? Please tell me it's not one of them."

"No," he said, "it's your boss."

DAMON HEADED TO the bookstore, after dropping that bombshell. He knew that Gabby had even more to sort out now because there went her job, and Damon didn't even know if she'd get her last paycheck. So that had to be another financial blow. He wondered at what was going on in her life where everything was just continuously coming down on her shoulders. As he arrived at the bookstore, he walked in to see Jake, standing there, looking around. "Where's the body?"

"That's the thing," he said, "the body is in the back alleyway."

"Why is he out there?"

"It was surmised that he was taking out the garbage."

"Is this the same kind of death?"

"No, not at all," he said, looking at his partner. "Sorry. I didn't make that clear, did I?"

"No, but I'm happy to hear it anyway," he said, "because another one of those beheadings would be too much to take in right now."

"Right. What a messed-up world we're dealing with right now," Jake said.

"And was it murder?"

"Well, the neighbor called it in, and we assumed so. The coroner is on his way. But I'm not sure. It's possible it could be due to accidental or natural causes."

"Can I see him?"

Jake led the way through the back, where several cops

stood, waiting.

Damon walked over to see the bookstore owner lying facedown in the snow. His skin already had an odd color, and blood was under his head but not a lot of it. Damon took a look around and frowned. "I can see the blood from a head wound but not the wound itself. It's on the other side."

"Right, as if he hit his head on his way down."

"Could be a heart attack," he muttered.

"Well, let's hope so," Jake said. "We have enough odd things going on just now."

"Gabby said he hadn't been very healthy lately. He was really worried and upset."

"Well, that would all play into this end," Jake said, crouching beside the body. "The coroner should be here soon, so we'll know before long."

Damon nodded, stepped back.

Jake continued, "If it isn't foul play, then we don't need to go investigate the rest of the place."

"Exactly," Damon said. "So who called it in?"

Jake pointed to a woman standing off to the side, shifting her feet in the cold.

"I'll go talk to her," Damon said. He walked over with a smile, introduced himself, and said, "Did you call in the body?"

"Yes," she said. "Poor Jerry," she whispered. "I've known him for years."

"Well, we don't know anything for sure yet, but it looks possible that he had a heart attack or something of that nature," he said to her.

Immediately she nodded. "I warned him about that ticker of his, but he just gave me that sad smile and said that he lost his reason for living a long time ago and didn't care if he headed on to the next phase."

"I know. Losing his wife was a terrible shock that it doesn't appear he ever got past."

"Very much so," she said. "I guess I should be happy that he went so peacefully."

"You didn't see anybody around at the time?"

She shook her head. "I heard banging around by the garbage cans. The pickup day is tomorrow, so I wasn't worried, but I looked out and caught a glimpse of him taking something out. It looked like he was carrying something else back out again, and then I heard a weird *thunk*, and I looked back out and saw he was down. I came out to check on him and called out to him. That's when I dialed 9-1-1. I didn't want to say so on the phone, but I was pretty sure he was already dead."

"Yes, he is deceased," he said quietly. "Thank you for waiting and talking with me."

She said, "I would go inside, but I didn't want to leave him alone."

"Not a problem," he said. "Go on in, and get warmed up. We'll look after him now."

She gave him a grateful smile, then turned and headed inside.

Damon turned to Jake, shrugged, and said, "Doesn't sound suspicious."

"Well, that'll be up to the coroner, I guess," Jake replied.

Just on the off chance, Damon walked over to the garbage can, lifted the lid, and checked inside. He found many old pizza boxes, a bag of kitchen scraps from whatever meals Jerry had prepared over the last few days, and, other than that, just a rolled-up stack of papers. He picked them up and pulled them out, then took a quick look.

"Anything in there to question?"

"No, looks like papers from the store," he said. "In fact,

it looks like tax returns from ten years or longer ago."

"Well, we better hang on to them, just in case," Jake said.

Damon tucked them into his pocket and said, "Other than that, the contents look pretty innocuous."

"Well, that's better than stuffed full of questionable items." Jake took a quick look inside, nodded, and said, "Nothing too interesting in here. Mostly pizza boxes."

"Which goes along with the fact that Jerry was a single old man and wasn't enjoying life much." Just then, the coroner arrived, and they stepped back. If it was an unexplained death, it was a whole different story. Damon looked at Jake and said, "I'll go home and try to grab some sleep tonight. We can always return tomorrow."

"You do that," he said. "Let's hope this isn't a case for us, after all."

"Well, it'll be a case either way, even if it's only to identify next of kin," he said. "I hope he left his affairs in order because that'll be a bit of a mess otherwise."

"I think he had a lawyer," Jake said. "I just can't remember the guy's name."

"Oh, right." Damon stopped, frowned, and said, "I remember hearing something about that too, but I don't remember who I heard it from. I think Captain Meyer said something about it. Anyway I'll check in with you in the morning."

With one final look at the deceased, Damon turned and headed home again. The only thing that bothered him about the whole scenario was the fact that, once again, this was somebody with close connections to Gabby. And that meant three in a row. Thankfully this one looked to be something she didn't have anything to do with, and, for that, he was grateful.

CHAPTER SIXTEEN

I F DAMON THOUGHT Gabby could sleep after that bombshell, he was wrong. She tried to; she tossed and turned in bed and then finally gave it up and sat outside with a mug of hot chocolate, watching the snowfall, waiting on Damon to return. When she saw him drive in again, she waited until he got out of the vehicle and then called out to him immediately. He turned to face her, as she got up and waved at him. "You should be in bed," he said tersely.

"I would be, but I was worried," she said.

"Well, you might be worried, but the bottom line is, it looks like Jerry died of a heart attack or at least natural causes. He wasn't murdered by the same guy who took out your friends."

She felt all her breath whooshing out of her chest. "Thank God," she whispered. "I was so worried and feeling guilty."

"No, it had nothing to do with you," he said. "One of the neighbors called it in. She saw him taking out the garbage, and then he went back out again. She looked out again after hearing a noise to find him in the snow. He passed away on the spot. I've just been waiting for the coroner to come to take care of the body."

"It's sad though," she whispered. "Behind the gruffness, he was such a nice man."

"That may be, but he's gone on to the next stage of whatever the hell this life is all about," he said.

She heard the fatigue in his voice. "Sorry," she said. "I didn't mean to keep you from a warm bed."

"Well, you get into yours," he said, "so I know you won't make yourself sick, sitting up, worrying about things you can't control. It'll be a long day tomorrow. I'll call you when I wake up."

With that, she had to be satisfied. Still, it was the best news she could hope for. Obviously she'd rather Jerry was alive and well, but, at least, he hadn't been murdered. He was certainly old and had not been in great health. So it was no surprise if he'd finally had a heart attack or something. It was just sad, like so much else in life was sad.

With that last thought, she crawled back into bed and curled up, feeling more alone than ever. Jerry had always been very friendly and gentle and kind to her, which was more than she could say for a lot of the locals. But then, for the townies, it was hard to separate the transients, the tourists, and those temps just here for a season's work. She couldn't really blame them if they held themselves back a little bit, off-putting as it was. That's just the way of the world; it took time for them to warm up to strangers.

Gabby closed her eyes, sure that she probably still wouldn't sleep, but, when she opened them again, she heard birds and saw the sun up. She was surprised to see it was as late as it was. She got up, took a look outside, and, seeing the fresh snow everywhere, she wished with her all her heart that she could go up the mountain. But she didn't have her board back. She headed into the kitchen to put on the coffee, and then her phone rang.

Picking it up, Damon asked, "What are you doing up

already?"

She looked at the phone, frowned, and then the realization hit, and her heart sank. "Shit," she said, "I forgot."

"Forgot what?"

"Forgot that I don't have a job to go to," she said. "How foolish is that?"

"It's a habit," he said. "You shouldn't feel bad about it."

"Maybe, but right now it feels pretty crappy."

"You could always go back to bed."

She looked at the bed she had yet to make and shrugged. "I might have a nap later. I'm still feeling pretty tired, but now I've got fresh coffee."

"Fresh coffee trumps everything, right?"

"Yes, it does," she said. "Well, almost everything. Honestly, right now, I'm a little worried as to whether I'll actually get a paycheck for the time I've already worked."

She heard him sucking in his breath. "Good point," he said. "I'll try to find the lawyer who's dealing with Jerry's estate. Let's hope everything is straightforward and clear."

"I hope so," she said. "That would be terrible if it wasn't."

"On many levels. Anyway try to have a good day," he said, and he hung up.

She sat here, watching the snow twinkle outside, wondering what was on tap for her. She needed a job, and she needed it bad. If that meant washing dishes, that meant washing dishes. Not her favorite but whatever. As she considered potential places to apply, her phone rang again. She looked down to see it was Wendy. Surprised, Gabby picked it up. "Good morning."

"Good morning," Wendy said, her voice a little hesitant. "I thought maybe I could catch you before you went to work."

"Oh," she said, "you haven't heard the news then."

"What news?" she asked in confusion.

"My boss, Jerry, had a heart attack or something last night," she said. "He didn't make it."

There was stunned silence on Wendy's side. "Oh, my God," she said. "We're just beset with bad news right now, aren't we?"

"There doesn't seem to be any end to it, no," Gabby said quietly. "I know that he was ill and wasn't doing all that great, and he was pretty depressed. But I didn't expect this."

"So you no longer have a job?"

"Not only do I no longer have a job but I'm not sure that I'll get paid for the time worked," she said.

"Oh, my God," Wendy said, her voice rising. "Is there anything you can do about that?"

"I don't know," she said. "I have to wait to talk to the lawyer or whoever is handling the estate and see if that's something that can still get paid to me."

"They should be able to. It's not fair otherwise."

"Yeah, but life hasn't exactly been all that fair lately," she said, trying hard to keep the bitterness out of her voice. But, despite her best efforts, her tone still had an edge to it.

"I know," Wendy said, "it's been a really weird winter."

"I had such high hopes for our fun getaway winter. That one winter holiday before I buckled under the endless drudgery of the lifetime of work that faced us."

"And I was right there with you," she said, "but, since we got here, it hasn't been what we thought at all."

"And I wonder why," Gabby said. "It's just so frustrating. In some ways the beginning of the season was absolutely terrific. We got lots of boarding in, and we had a great

Christmas, and then what happened?"

"Well, a bunch of things on my end," Wendy said. "I lost my job, couldn't find another one, and hooked up with Meghan."

"Right," Gabby said, wincing at that. "That was before Christmas though, right?"

"Yes, all of that happened before Christmas, but so close to Christmas that the impact hadn't really set in."

"So have you talked to your parents lately?"

"Yes," she said. "They sent me enough money to get through the month."

"Wow," she said, "that's lovely of them."

"It really is because I know how they feel about this misadventure of ours."

"And I'm sorry," Gabby whispered, wondering how she had missed so much happening in Wendy's life. "I didn't realize they felt so strongly about it."

"That's because I didn't tell you," she said. "That was my fault."

"You know you can tell me anything, right?" she asked.

"Well, I can tell you, but that doesn't mean that you'll be nonjudgmental about it."

At that, she whispered, "Oh, God, Wendy. I feel like I failed you at every turn."

"No, you didn't," she said, "but we're definitely not the same people we arrived as."

"Maybe not, I don't know," Gabby said. "It just seems like everything has gone so wrong."

"That's what I mean. It just didn't turn out the way we thought it would. So we must move on with the times."

"Well, I'm not sure what that'll mean for me," she said. "I've got to get another job really fast."

"Well, there's always housekeeping or restaurant work."

"I know. I'll spruce up my résumé this morning and start sending it out this afternoon."

"Well, I was calling to see if you wanted to do lunch today," she said. "I thought I could come at your lunch break."

"Well," she said, "as I'm no longer even working, I don't have a lunch break anymore."

"Right," Wendy said. "Do you want to meet somewhere then?"

"You know what? Actually I was thinking, uh, why don't you come here?" she said impulsively. "I don't have much for food, but a little bit is here. I'm sure we could rustle up an omelet or something," she said. "Hang on." And she got up, walked over to the kitchen, and continued, "Lots of coffee is here. If nothing else we can always have a sandwich and coffee."

"Well, I'll see," she said. "I'm totally okay to come wherever you are, as long as it's on a bus route."

"Actually I'm not all that far away," she said and gave Wendy the address.

"Well, that's walkable," Wendy said in delight.

"Yeah, and it's a gorgeous place. It's a suite above a garage, but it's high-end and quite luxurious," she said wistfully. "I wish I could stay."

"Any chance of them letting you stay?"

"I don't think so. I'm here basically as a charity case because of the murders."

"Ah," she said. "Well, that makes sense. You really don't want to push on people's largess."

"No, I don't."

"Well, I might run past the deli on the way," she said.

"I'll pick up stuff for sandwiches."

"Perfect," she said. "I'll see you around noon then."

"Right. Get that résumé of yours brushed up, so you're not in the same spot I was in," she said with a note of humor. "Unfortunately for you, you don't have a family to bail you out." On that note, Wendy hung up.

Gabby stared down at the phone for a long moment. "It's unlike you to say something like that," she whispered. "Kind of hurtful."

But it was also the truth, and maybe she and Wendy would have been better off if they had spoken more truth. Seriously, at this point in time, it was well understood that Wendy had friends and family to help her out when things got tough, whereas Gabby herself did not. She'd been alone most of her life, even when she was part of an adoptive family. And being alone hadn't been the easiest either. But she'd grown a whole lot more backbone and had learned to stand on her own two feet. Right now, if she needed money, there was only one way to get it, and that was to get a damn job. With that in mind, she grabbed her laptop and sat down to revise her résumé.

IN THE OFFICE that morning, Damon walked over to see Jake already sitting there. "You're in early."

"Yeah," he said, "couldn't sleep much."

"Sorry. I actually slept. Not long enough but, hey, it's something," said Damon.

"I hear you," Jake said. "What we really need is to get some action going on these murders."

"I was afraid last night the bookseller would be another one."

"We don't have too many deaths as a rule here, but those two mutilations have really shaken the community. They're looking to us to solve this," Jake said quietly.

"Sure they are," Damon said, "but it's not like we're shirking our duty."

"No, but we're not getting the answers either."

"Well, that's troubling. But where will we get the answers from if not through the locals?" Damon asked.

"And nobody seems to have anything to offer. We have no forensic evidence, no sign of forced entry, no plausible motive that we can come up with for these two women." With real concern in his voice, Jake continued, "The odd thing is, they're all connected to the three who are still alive, because they all lived in the same apartment, but nobody seems to have anything helpful to offer."

"No, you're right," Damon said. "I was afraid when you called with the bookseller that it would center around Gabby again."

"You're getting pretty chummy with her, aren't you?" Jake asked.

"Not on purpose," he said.

"You better watch it though," he said. "When you think about it, the captain won't likely be too happy if you end up having a relationship with her."

"But is she ... a suspect?" He sat here and thought about it. "She has no motive. She has no priors, other than being at the first crime scene. Besides, she was talking to me on the phone at the time of that murder, and I heard the animal noises going on in the background, and it certainly wasn't her voice."

"I know. I know," Jake said, "and she wasn't there at the time of the second murder."

"Right, so I hardly think she's a suspect. She could be a victim or at least be on the victim list."

"But what's the purpose of killing these young women?"

"I don't know, Jake. I don't know," he said in frustration.

"Well, you damn well better find out soon," a harsh voice said from the doorway.

Damon looked up to see Captain Meyer walking in.

"Do you know how many times I get stopped in a day by people asking if we have any updates?"

"Well, do you have any?" Damon asked. "Because I sure as hell don't."

The captain glared at him. "Well, you're supposed to," he said. "Forget about a dead old bookseller with a bad heart and get your ass on the street and start asking who had a motive for killing these women."

"We have been," Jake protested. "So far there's nothing."

"Well, get out there until you find something," he roared. "I sure as hell don't want to be the one stuck trying to explain why the hell we haven't solved it."

"It's not a case of why we haven't solved it, but, if we have nothing to solve, then we're stuck."

"I don't want to hear it," he said. "Find another angle, work another thread, but get at it!" And, with that, he stormed off to his office, slamming the door behind him.

"Wow," Jake said, "I haven't seen him in a stew like this before."

"No," Damon said, staring at the office door thoughtfully.

"This case seems to have really gotten him screwed up," Jake said. "Did you go through those old case files?"

"I haven't found the time yet," he said. "I'd love to go

home and do it now though." He checked around and asked, "Is there anything else on deck?"

"No. I've got a few more coworkers to run down and to talk to about the two victims," Jake said. "If I find anything, I'll call you. Why don't you run home and see if you can find anything in those files?"

"Good idea." Damon got up, grabbed his jacket, and slipped out of the office, so he didn't have to talk with his captain anymore. Everybody knew Captain Meyer was upset, but a tirade in the wrong direction wasn't helping anybody. They were all trying to find answers, but, so far, they hadn't had any break in the cases.

As Damon made his way home, he looked up at the garage apartment, and he could see her sitting at the desk, working away. He presumed she was working on a résumé, so she could get another job. But if anybody had been followed by bad luck, it was her.

Inside the main house, he put on a pot of coffee, sat down at the dining room table, and opened up the first of the oldest files. In chronological order, he slowly and methodically read through what there was. And there wasn't a whole lot. The case was thin on the ground back then, and it certainly hadn't grown over time. It looked like nothing had been added since. He frowned at that because normally, with cold cases, every few years they were pulled out and given another look to see if they could do anything further before they were filed away again.

If that had happened here, it was obvious that nothing had changed or was different. The cases were almost as bizarre as what he was currently going through. One woman died on the mountain; another one died in an apartment. And again their chests had been cut open. The cuts were different, but it was the same idea. And that was concerning in itself.

He made notes on the case numbers with similarities, and, armed with that, he headed back to the office. As he drove away, he saw Wendy walking down the block, probably to visit Gabby. He was startled with that at first, but why not? They were friends, and, of course, it was totally okay for Gabby to have a friend over. If anything, she needed something like that right now because, without a job, she was just that much more at odds.

Damon walked into the head office where his captain sat, dropped the case file numbers and the similarities list on his desk, and said, "Captain, we must open up these other cases."

"Like hell," he said, without even looking at the list.

"You don't even know what cases I'm talking about," Damon said in frustration.

"Yes, I do, and nothing was normal about those cases back then," he said, staring at Damon's handwritten notes. "We had no explanation back then, and nothing has changed. They are cases that do nothing but haunt us all, and the only way that we can carry on and can survive is to ignore them."

"Four women died back then," he said quietly. "Four."

The captain glared at him. "And I can name every single one of them," he said. "I knew three of them personally," he roared. "It's not that we ignored them. It's not that we didn't try," he said. "There was nothing to find."

"Mirroring exactly what's happening now," Damon said.

The captain stopped and went really quiet for a long time. "Well, you better hope it's not," he said, "because that would mean two more women will die soon, and we won't have any answers again."

He looked at Damon sternly and said, "You're young. You're smart. You were some big-city hotshot. You're not the first young gun who thought he could figure it out. The men who have tried have paid a high price, and we're still paying. If you're set on joining that club, you get your ass all over these files, and you find out what we missed, but I'll be damned if I stand over four more dead women and have not one answer for the families."

The captain looked at Jake, who had come in behind Damon, and back to Damon. "Pull in whoever the hell you need," he said, "but we need answers, and we need them now."

And, with that, he pointed at the door and said, "Go."

CHAPTER SEVENTEEN

WHEN GABBY HEARD a faint knock on the door, she realized it was probably Wendy, knocking on the door downstairs. She opened the upstairs door, skipped down the stairs, and opened up the bottom door, and there was Wendy. Gabby grinned at her and said, "Come on in."

"This is a pretty high-end area," she said, stepping in and shaking the snow off her shoulders. She held out a grocery bag and said, "I picked up a few things."

"Good, we get lunch then," she said, as she led the way upstairs. "I've got lots of coffee, so that's one thing."

"Well, that was always more important to you than me," Wendy said with a laugh. As soon as they got into the apartment, she stopped and stared. "Wow," she said, "now this is the Aspen lifestyle."

"I know. It's gorgeous, isn't it?"

"How did you get here?"

"The detective. After everybody left the first crime scene, and I had no place to go, he offered me this place. He inherited the house and this garage suite from his aunt and hadn't quite decided what he would do with it all yet, so this suite was empty."

Wendy shook her head. "Wow," she said. "You know what? I get that you feel like you've had a ton of bad luck, but this is a welcome relief. This is seriously high living."

"High living when you consider it's a suite over a garage," she said drily.

Wendy laughed. "Isn't that the truth?"

"But so much in Aspen is over-the-top anyway."

"That it is. I'm still glad I came here with you," Wendy said.

"I am too," Gabby said with a smile. She motioned at the coffeemaker. "Do you want one?"

"Sure," Wendy said, shrugging off her coat. "What have you been doing on the laptop?"

"Well, I should be working on my résumé," she said, "but I've been looking into the details of some old unsolved cases around town, wondering if they have any connection."

"*Ugh*," she said. "You're the one who always had that kind of fascination, not me."

"Maybe," she said, "but this all directly impacts us, and I would really like to have that shadow of doubt off our shoulders," she said.

"You and me both. It's pretty damn uncomfortable with people avoiding you because they know you're connected to that case."

"And yet we didn't do anything," Gabby said. "We're the ones huddled in the bedroom, calling for the cops."

"I know," Wendy cried out. "That was such a horrific night. I still have nightmares."

"You and me both," she said. "And I'm not sure that'll ever go away."

"I hope so," she said. "Meghan is getting pissed off about it."

Gabby winced at that. "I'm sorry. It's one thing if it's your sleep that's getting dragged through the mud. But it's another thing if it's somebody else's as well."

"She's usually pretty tolerant, but, when I wake up, bawling my eyes out, she's struggling with that."

"I can see that," Gabby said, trying for a noncommittal neutral tone.

"It's okay. You can say it. I know you don't like her at all."

"It's not that," she said, "but it's hard to like anybody who hurt my friend."

Wendy just nodded, almost as if she were ignoring Gabby's comment. "Have you decided what you'll do?"

"No," she said. "I haven't."

Wendy asked, "If you don't get another job, are you going home?"

"I don't know yet," she said. "I'd like to stay, but, if I can't, then I can't." Something was weird about the way Wendy had said the word *home*. Because of all the things that California was, Gabby no longer felt like it was home. Aspen felt like home. She'd only been here a few months, but she'd acclimated really fast. "What about you?"

"No decision as of yet," she said. "I have enough money to get through the month, and then I'll see."

"What about you and Meghan?"

At that, her gaze slid sideways. "I don't know what to do with that yet," she said finally.

"Okay, then we can leave that subject alone for a while," Gabby said. "No pressure."

And Wendy gave her a big grin. "Thanks for that," she said. "Normally you're more of a *nag until you get the answer you want* kind of person."

Gabby winced. "Apparently I've been pretty insensitive to a lot of things," she admitted. "And, for that, I'm sorry."

Wendy just stared at her in surprise. "Where's that coming from?"

"I don't know," she said. "It just seems like maybe I haven't been there for you as much as I might have been."

"Oh, baloney," she said. "I made mistakes, should have said something, should have stopped some things, and I didn't. Same for you. It's the same for all of us all over the world. We do the best we can in the moment, with the limited knowledge that we have at that point, but, yeah, we could have still done more things, and we only ever realize them in hindsight, maybe because we did find more info. The sad part is that, if you knew what three months down the road would bring, you would make appropriate plans now, but, because we don't know in advance, we're stuck with the decisions we already made."

At that, Gabby wasn't sure if Wendy was talking about hooking up with Meghan or their roommates getting murdered or their decision to come to Aspen. But Gabby decided she didn't want to get into those discussions. "I've got my résumé up," she said. "You've always been better at that stuff than I am. Do you want to take a look at it for me?"

"Sure." Wendy walked over to the laptop and looked over Gabby's résumé while Gabby made more coffee. "It doesn't look a whole lot different than the last time I looked at it," Wendy said. "You've only added in the bookstore."

"But I added in the customer service retail experience and a few other things," she said. "The bookstore gig wasn't much of a job, I suppose, but I really enjoyed working there."

"And that's worth a lot," she said. "To be happy in a job seems like nirvana these days."

"Only if that job pays the bills," she said with half a

smile. "And now that I don't have the job and the bills are still there, I'm not sure what I'm supposed to do."

"Do you think we're on the hook for the rent?" Wendy asked.

"I think we're probably on the hook for a couple months' rent," she admitted. "If you think about it, we paid for this month already, but we owe for next month. Plus we haven't given notice yet."

"But we can't even live there," Wendy exclaimed.

"I know, but I don't think that lets us off the lease."

"That's just—" Wendy stopped and shook her head. "And now there's only three of us to pay too."

"I'm not even sure Betty will pay her share," Gabby said. "Her boyfriend is pretty irate about the whole thing." Gabby then explained about the unpleasant visitor she'd had at the bookstore.

"But it's not like you did anything," Wendy said in Gabby's defense.

"I know. I know," she said. "And I don't know if the cops went and talked to him or not. But I wouldn't mind if they poked around a bit into his life and make him angry at them instead," she said with a smirk.

"Maybe they'll find out that something crooked is going on there and that he didn't want the cops brought so close."

"I don't know, but Betty had been going out with him for quite a while beforehand," she said. "So, in a way, it makes sense that she just moved in with him."

"Maybe so but I can't stand him," Wendy said.

"He is a little creepy," Gabby said, "but it's not that bad."

"I think it's that bad," her friend said, "but what do I know?" Wendy looked up, accepted the cup of coffee that

Gabby held out to her, and said, "Thank you." She then switched to one of the two chairs by the window.

Gabby looked at her, smiled, and said, "Almost like old times."

"Maybe," Wendy said. "At least the time when we were young and stupid. I feel old and jaded these days."

"Well, it's been an eye-opening winter," Gabby said, tilting her head. As she studied her friend, she could see an odd glow around her head. Gabby shifted so the light behind Wendy shone at a different angle, but it didn't change the shadow. She looked at it and frowned.

Wendy watched her and asked, "What's the matter?"

"Nothing," she said with a shake of her head. "My eyes are just really tired."

"I get that," Wendy said. "I didn't sleep any these last few nights."

"No, me either. It was thinking about my boss last night," she said.

Wendy winced. "That just adds to it, doesn't it?"

Morose, the two women sat here and sipped their coffee.

"We could go home at the end of the month," Wendy said.

"We still have to pay rent on the apartment for next month."

"I know, but all I can do is come up with my fifth. I can't come up with the rest of it."

"That's an idea," Gabby said, considering that angle. "I wonder if that's enough. But I still must find another place to live too. And I don't even know how to get that kind of money."

"I guess that's why I'm wondering about going back to the way we were."

"But I don't have a home back there," Gabby said. "You can go home. I can't. I still need a place to live, no matter where I go," she pointed out.

"You could stay with me for a few days."

"I don't think your parents would accept that," she said. "They're pretty upset with me as it is."

"I tried to explain to them that it wasn't your fault. But—" Wendy shrugged and said, "I don't think they want to listen."

"No, I'm sure they don't," Gabby said. "They're looking for somebody to blame, and I'm an easy target."

"Maybe," she said. "There's also something else I didn't explain to you before."

"What's that?" Gabby asked.

"I didn't say anything because I didn't want to ruin our friendship."

At that, Gabby stiffened. *Uh-oh, what kind of conversation will this be?* She was hoping to just avoid all that other stuff and cheerfully get out of it. Taking a deep breath, then another, Gabby finally said, "What are you talking about?"

"Well, I have feelings for you. I have always seen you as more than a friend, even before we came to Aspen," Wendy said. "But I hooked up with Meghan because, well, … you didn't feel the same way."

Silence. Gabby didn't know what to say.

With Gabby quiet, Wendy continued, "I had this talk with Meghan, and she has basically given me an ultimatum that I either need to commit to her exclusively or leave."

"I can't really blame her," Gabby said slowly, avoiding Wendy's earlier comment. "I mean, you want to be the one person in someone's life and not be worried that someone else is in the picture too."

"Regardless," Wendy said candidly, "I know you don't feel the way about me as I do about you," she said. "But I should have made my feelings known earlier."

Gabby stared at her in surprise. "That possibility only recently occurred to me," she said, trying to keep everybody else out of it. "And I'm sorry I didn't see it before."

Wendy gave her a ghost of a smile. "You didn't see it because you weren't thinking like I was," she said, "and I didn't say anything because I knew you didn't return my feelings. But I came here to Aspen for you. My mother knows that, and I think that's why she's angry with you."

"Did you tell her that I didn't know? That you didn't say anything to me?"

"I did, but she thinks you should have figured it out anyway."

"I'm not a mind reader," she said. "I can't figure this stuff out. Apparently I'm really dense when it comes to these emotions anyway."

"I don't know about dense," she said. "It just never hit your radar. It wasn't something that you've ever really dealt with, and that's fine," she said. "I've come to terms with the fact that you and I aren't an item and won't be an item. What I must figure out now is whether I want to be an item with Meghan."

"No," Gabby said. "You currently *are* an item with Meghan. What you must figure out is if you want to be a long-term item with Meghan. Because anything else is effectively cheating her."

"I know," she said with a sad smile. "I feel like I cheated myself by hooking up with her, but now I'm cheating her by being with her too."

"I know," Gabby said, "and now I feel like I cheated us

because I was looking for and thought we were best friends. Not seeing that you wanted more."

"We are best friends," Wendy said. "You have no idea how many times I beat myself up for feeling the way I do about you and not able to change it. But we can't always control this kind of stuff. So I'm asking for a little bit of time to deal with downplaying some of this, so it's not quite so prevalent in my world."

"Does that work?"

"I don't know," she said, "because the alternative is that I go home, and we stay friends from a distance."

Gabby winced at that.

"I know we've been friends for a long time," Wendy continued. "And I wouldn't want us to end up as estranged friends, but, if I can't stand to see you and not be with you, then I don't know what else I can do."

"You'll need to do whatever you need to do," Gabby said quietly. "I'm sorry I don't feel the way you do, but I can't change that either." The two friends looked at each other sadly, and Gabby didn't know what to say.

Wendy jumped up and said, "I'm hungry. Let's make sandwiches."

Gabby laughed. "You've always been the pragmatist," she said.

"That I am," Wendy replied, "that I am."

With her feelings churning and not sure how to completely avoid going back into that conversation, yet knowing that something had changed between them, Gabby helped Wendy make sandwiches.

By the time they'd finished eating, and Wendy was ready to go, Wendy reached out her arms and said, "One last hug."

"It doesn't need to be a *last* hug," Gabby said.

"Yes," she said, "if I stay here in Colorado with Meghan, it does."

"I'm sorry for that then too," she said. "I didn't realize I was such a threat to her."

"Because of the way I feel, you are," she said. They hugged briefly, and Wendy turned and headed back out the door. As she left the door downstairs, she looked up the stairway where Gabby stood and said, "You've got a good deal here, so, if you can make it work, why wouldn't you?" She continued, "You've always wanted to live here. It's where you seem to thrive. Me? I just want to go home where it's warm again."

"And Meghan?"

She hesitated. "I think that's done too."

"So let her down gently," she said.

"I will."

And, with that, Wendy closed the garage door and walked away. Gabby walked over to the window and stared at her friend as she walked down the street. Now she was more worried about Wendy than ever. Meghan had already attacked Wendy once. What would happen when Wendy tried to break up now? It didn't bear thinking about. Gabby sent Wendy a message. **Hey, just because of Meghan's tendency toward violence, maybe you should leave and then let her know.**

I'll work it out, she replied, clearly with a hint of *mind your own business.*

Gabby wished she could do something for her friend, but it seemed like every time Gabby turned around and tried to help something or someone, it blew up in her face.

She sagged into the desk chair with her second cup of coffee, and, as she turned back to look at her résumé, a weird shadow came around the corner of her laptop. It was similar to the one she had seen around Wendy. She frowned, thinking about what she and Damon had seen earlier and waved her hand over and above it. There wasn't any weird feeling, no sensation here, so she didn't know what to make of this exactly.

As she moved her hand around it, the shadow slowly dissipated. "What the heck was that?" she murmured. But there was no answer because nobody had seen it but her. Like so much else going on in her world right now, she could make no sense of any of this. She sipped her coffee and decided maybe a nap would help.

As she finished her coffee and laid down, she thought maybe the world would forgive her a few hot tears. She'd not only lost so much about her way of life and her job but she was also now losing her best friend. Nothing would ever be the same between Gabby and Wendy again. At that thought, the tears just poured.

AS DAMON WALKED from his vehicle toward the house, as had become his habit, he looked up and could see her sitting there, staring out the window, but she didn't seem to notice him. He lifted a hand, but Gabby gave no sign of any acknowledgment. He frowned at that and pulled out his phone and called her. She jerked and looked behind her. She got up and walked away, then moved back in front of the window.

"Hey," he said, "I just saw you sitting there, but you didn't seem to see me."

"No," she said quietly. "I just got up from a nap."

"Good," he said, "that's the best thing for you."

"Maybe." She hesitated and then asked, "Do you have any news on my boss?"

"Well, I was home, working for a few hours this morning, going over old case files. Then I went back into the office for a bit. I do have Jerry's lawyer's name, and I'm about to give him a call."

"Okay, could you let me know afterward, please?"

"I guess you really need that paycheck, don't you?"

"I need it in a bad way," she said.

"Okay, give me ten minutes or so."

Then he turned and walked inside the house. He dropped the extra files that he had picked up this afternoon and laid them out on the dining room table. Everything appeared to be completely normal in the house, just the way he left it, but he noticed an odd feel to the room, as if somebody had been inside when he wasn't here. Frowning at that, he went over, put on the teakettle, and checked out the contents of his fridge and freezer, thinking toward dinner. He took out some sausages, hoping they would thaw in time for dinner, then walked back over to the dining room table full of files. He picked up his phone and contacted the lawyer.

"Hello," he said, identifying himself. "A client of yours was found dead outside his home and bookstore last night," he said.

"Jerry is an old friend as well as a client."

"Yes, Jerry, that's right. At this moment, we do think the cause of death is natural causes, though we don't have a full report from the coroner yet. We also need to look into his will and determine who is handling his estate. Would that be you?"

"Yes," the lawyer said. "Actually he made a few changes

just a couple days ago."

"Interesting. Also his employee is wondering if she'll get paid as usual," he said. "She's got a couple weeks pay owed her, I understand. Are you designated to take care of the store bills as well?"

"Yes," he said, "and Jerry did mention Gabby by name."

"Oh, good," Damon said. "Her circumstances have put her in a bit of a bind, so she'll be glad to hear that, I'm sure."

"Actually she's now in his will as well. In a big way too."

"What do you mean by that?"

"She inherits his entire estate."

"What?" He sat down hard in the closest chair.

"Yes, he felt like she needed to feel grounded and to put down roots, and she was the only one who had ever truly been concerned about the store, among all the people who he'd hired over the years. So he wanted to leave it to her, since he had no family."

"Wow," he said, "I'm sure she'll be thrilled."

"Well, she'll also end up getting her outstanding paychecks, so that should make her feel better too. This will go through probate and all, before everything can be finalized and transferred, and there are debts to be paid as well," he said, "but she should do just fine."

"Did he lease the space for the business?"

"Oh, no," he said, "he owned the building. He could have leased out the space to another business if he'd wanted to, but he kept the bookstore open, honoring the memory of his wife."

"And it has an apartment above it, correct?"

"Yes," he said, "absolutely."

"Well, that'll be more good news for her. Do you want to tell her?"

"Yes, I was just waiting to make sure there was no foul play or anything suspicious about Jerry's death."

"Waiting for the coroner on that. The neighbor did see him go to the garbage bin, making a couple trips, and, at one point, she heard a noise and looked out to see him lying in the snow."

"He did feel like his time was coming," he said, "which is why he made the changes to the will."

"And it's all legal?"

"Yes, of course."

"So, if Gabby wasn't supposed to get his estate before, who did he have down to get the building and the business?"

"It was all to be sold and the proceeds to go to charity because he didn't have any family."

"That's kind of sad, isn't it?"

"Very sad. Once his wife died, not a whole lot was left for him."

"No, I hear that. That's good news though for Gabby. If you don't have her number, I can give it to you right now," he said.

"That would be great, though I'll still wait a little bit about the contents of the will," the lawyer warned.

"That's fine, but maybe you could set her mind at ease regarding the paycheck."

"Right, and she's in tough straits, as I understand from Jerry."

"Yes, that was her only source of income."

"He could have done a lot to bring in additional business, but he just wasn't interested anymore."

"I suspect she'll add some life to the place," Damon said drily.

"Good. That's what the business needs." And, with that,

they hung up, and Damon sat here for a long moment, thinking about the implications. It was a hell of a good turn for her, as long as no suspicions were raised about Jerry's death. The last thing she needed was for somebody to think she'd killed the man in order to get the bookstore, but then supposedly she didn't know anything about it, at least according to what the attorney had said.

Not Damon's problem unless it became his problem. And he hoped it wouldn't. Hoping it could be wrapped up quickly, he phoned the coroner. "Any update on the bookseller?"

"It's not like I don't have anybody else to deal with," he said in a testy voice.

"I hear you. I just heard the contents of the will were changed a couple days ago," he said, "and I was hoping that there was no conflict of interest or suspicion about to be tossed onto the young woman who's about to inherit."

"As far as I can tell at the moment," he said, "nothing sparks any controversy, but I haven't finished the autopsy yet, so you'll have to wait and see."

"Okay," he said. "I'll give you another day or two."

"Thank you," the man said in an overly sarcastic tone and abruptly hung up.

Damon wasn't sure what to think, but it just had to be waited out. He checked the assessment on the property. His eyebrows shot up. As a commercial property with an apartment above, all of significant size and in a good location, it was worth several million dollars. He shook his head. If Gabby had any idea of all this, he didn't know what she'd be doing with herself right now.

Damon wanted to ensure that everything was free and clear before she found out. It would just make life way too difficult for her if the town turned on her and suspected she'd murdered her boss. Especially after the other two murders. Not that she'd gained anything from their deaths at all. Or had she? He thought about that for a long moment, then quickly checked into both cases.

He made several phone calls, but, at the end of the day, absolutely nothing pointed to any monetary benefit to Gabby upon the death of those two women. And, with that, he sat back with a sigh of relief and dug into the cold case files.

He could only imagine what Captain Meyer went through some thirty years ago when the same thing happened. Damon didn't want a repeat of that. And, for his captain's sake, Damon would love to close the old cases as well. But absolutely nothing in these files revealed anything. Other than the victims' blood, no forensic evidence was found. All the blood collected had been retested, once DNA testing became more prevalent and accurate, and confirmed it was only the blood of the victims. So somebody had either been extremely careful or had somehow managed to kill these poor women and never got caught. And went silent for thirty years before resuming this cycle, which made no sense to Damon.

Now they had two murders. What would it take to stop this killer before there were three?

CHAPTER EIGHTEEN

THE NEXT DAY passed in a blur of confusion, sending résumés and waiting. Hour after hour after hour passed, but nothing came of it. Damon was holed up with the cold cases but called throughout the day, if not dropping in at random times too, usually to share a cup of coffee with her.

The following morning Gabby woke up and decided she had to get out of the apartment. It was Friday, and she'd really hoped to go up the mountain this weekend, but who knew if that would even be a possibility. She had no job, no money, and nobody had contacted her about her boss's death. She got up and had the last of the eggs and the bread. She knew she would need more food soon as well.

After her second cup of coffee, she bundled up and headed outside, happy to see a beautiful sunny day with a bright blue sky. She headed toward the bookstore, her feet automatically taking her in the direction she was accustomed to going. But, as she got there, a big sign in the window read Closed. Nobody was around. She peered in through the window, but it was all dark inside. She groaned. "What am I supposed to do now?" she whispered to herself.

Determinedly, she turned and walked on and then came back and checked that the front door was locked. It was. Relieved and yet also disappointed because she'd love to go inside, even though she probably wasn't allowed, so she turned and headed to the corner of the block.

As she got to the far side, she turned and came back again, noting she was basically pacing outside the property. And that made no sense either. She had no right to be here; it was closed. Jerry was gone. She had no job and just needed to deal with it and to move on. But why hadn't she received any requests for work? She knew the ski season was shutting down soon, but surely somebody needed help somewhere.

As it was, she hadn't heard anything from Wendy in the meantime either. On a whim Gabby called and heard her sleepy friend's voice answering. She said, "I'm sorry. I didn't even think that maybe you were sleeping."

"Yeah," she said, stifling a yawn, "I was. What's up?"

"I was wondering if I could borrow your snowboard so I could go up this weekend. I'm going stir-crazy right now," she said, "and that at least is free and would get me out of here."

"Is it safe?" her friend asked, coming awake. "Look what happened to you the last time."

"Ouch," she said, "I was trying to forget that."

"I may never forget it," Wendy said. "You didn't see yourself go across that mountain like a crazy woman."

"No," she said, "but I experienced it, and I'm trying to forget it," she said, trying to interject some humor.

"Well, you can have my board," she said, "but I don't want to go out and look after you."

At that, Gabby felt her own back bristling. "I don't need looking after, thank you," she said, striving for a neutral tone.

"Well, I didn't mean to insult you, but I'm kind of scared about a repeat of what happened."

"I hope not," she said. "Do you want me to come by

your place to pick up your board?" When Wendy hesitated, Gabby said, "Or do you want to meet me somewhere midway between us?"

"Where are you now?" Wendy asked.

Gabby heard rustling in the background, as if Wendy were throwing back bedcovers, and also a murmured voice beside her. Of course that would be Meghan. "I'm pacing outside the bookstore, thinking about going to a coffee shop," she said.

"Well, you probably need to do something because, unless you expect to get into the bookstore, I don't think that'll change immediately."

"No, probably not," she said. "It's just so frustrating. I need my paycheck, and so far nobody's giving it to me."

"Did you contact the lawyer?"

"I talked to the detective about it, and he said the lawyer would be contacting me."

"Well, I wouldn't give him a chance to wait," she said. "You're owed that money, and, as long as there's any money to pay you, then you should be paid out first."

"Well, that's the theory," she said hopefully. "That's one of the reasons for going up the mountain for another ski, another day to just kind of blitz. The weather is turning warmer, so I don't know how much longer the season'll last."

"Any luck with the job search?"

"None," she said, "not even a phone call for part-time or something temporary. Nothing."

"Because everybody's winding down probably," she said.

"Yeah, I just don't know what to do."

"Well, I'm likely to be leaving soon," she said, but her voice had dropped to a whisper, as if to say that she hadn't told Meghan.

"Well, why don't you come? Bring your snowboard, and we'll have coffee," she said. She felt the hesitation in Wendy's response, and then Gabby said, "Maybe pick another time. I wanted to go up on the weekend and all, but it doesn't really matter."

"Well, let me get back to you," she said, "and I'll meet you somewhere with the board." And, with that, she hung up.

Gabby stared down at the phone, as she wondered at a friendship that had to be done on the sly because her partner didn't approve. But then Gabby didn't approve of the partner either. Raising her hands in frustration, she said, "What difference does it make?"

Just then a vehicle pulled up and parked in front of the bookstore. A man got out and headed toward the front door.

She raced up to him. "Hey."

The guy looked at her with surprise.

"I'm not sure who you are," she said, "but are you related to the bookstore owner?"

"I'm the lawyer," he said. "Why?"

"Because I was the employee who hasn't been paid yet," she said in a rush. "Any chance of getting my money?"

He nodded. "I was coming to do a cash-out and to see what was left here," he said. "You want to come in? You can show me some of the stuff that I need to know."

"Sure, I'd love to. I was just out here, feeling wistful about the old place. And Jerry."

He held out his hand and said, "I'm Nathan Rutledge."

"Hi," she said, "I'm Gabby."

"He talked about you a lot," he said, and something almost searching was in his gaze.

"He was a sweetheart," she said. "A little scattered and

quite depressed, but I'm really sorry he's gone," she said sincerely.

"Yeah, we don't always get to choose our time, do we?"

"I think if he got to choose, he would have gone a long time ago," she said. "I don't think he ever quite recovered from his wife's death."

"It happens that way sometimes," he said.

The door was now open, and she walked in, feeling that wonderful sense of homecoming. "I know the store didn't have a ton of business," she said, "but it was very much a place I appreciated being. Jerry could have done so much more with it."

"Well, as soon as we can get his death cleared," he said, "I need to talk to you about that."

"Why?" she asked.

He gave her a shake of his head. "We'll talk once I get everything cleared up."

"Fine," she said, "so what do you need to know here?"

"Who cashed out at the end of the day?"

"I did or he did," she said. She walked over to the till, opened it up, and said, "It doesn't look like he even got that far on his last day," she said, "because the money is still here."

He walked over, took a look, and then he pulled out the money, counted it, and put it into a bag.

She watched it wistfully. "Look. This is awkward, but it would be really nice to be paid sooner rather than later," she said. "I'm pretty desperate."

"Give me twenty-four hours," he said.

She brightened at that. "I can make it through that. Thank you."

"I also have to deal with his apartment upstairs," he said.

"I haven't ever been up there," she said. "He worked hard to keep the business part down here. I asked him at one point about renting the room at the top of the stairs because I was so desperate after the murders, but we hadn't quite come to an agreement about it."

"Well, now it's not an issue anyway," he said.

"What'll happen to this place?" she asked, looking around. "I suppose it'll get sold."

"Maybe. It will be up to the new owner," he said, again that weird tone in his voice.

"I guess," she said. "I hate to see it sold though. But not everybody has a passion for books, like we did."

"Well, I'm sure he appreciated that," he said.

"I think so. We talked about books a lot," she said with a smile. "I'm not sure it was his passion as much as it was his wife's, but I appreciate the fact that he kept it open. It's a great spot for commercial development, but *argh*."

He just nodded and said, "I know you're dealing with the loss of your job and Jerry. So I'll head into the office and get busy on this. Thank you for your help."

She took that as a dismissal. She nodded and said, "Will you call tomorrow then?"

"I will," he said. She looked at him, and he smiled and said, "I promise. I just need to get the finances sorted out. I'll figure out the accounts, where the money is, and who all needs to get paid."

She nodded. "Okay, thank you then." And she had to walk out. It was really all she could do.

Outside, she stood here for a long moment, but at least she knew the joy of getting paid soon. She would have to wait for that check to buy more groceries, but she could probably scrounge enough at home to get through until tomorrow.

She needed to get a job that would give her so many more options right now, even though, at the moment, it seemed impossible. She understood that Aspen was closing down for a season, but surely some of the world functioned that way. She groaned as she headed home. By the time she got there again, her phone rang. She pulled it out to see Damon calling. "Hey."

"Hey, are you okay?"

"Well, once I get paid tomorrow," she said, "I will be. I walked to the bookstore and caught the lawyer just going in. He was looking at the state of affairs of the business itself, and he said he would pay me within twenty-four hours."

"Good," he said. "That's great news."

"Yeah, but just so you know, twenty-four hours is still twenty-four hours," she said with a sigh.

"That bad?"

"No," she said, "there's still coffee at your place and some leftovers."

"Well, there can't be very much," he said. "That was a few days ago."

"I haven't been eating a whole lot," she said. "I've been trying hard to find a job but not getting anywhere so far."

"No, Aspen is a place that's hard to crack this time of year," he said. "Have you got any plans to leave yet?"

"You told me that I couldn't leave," she said.

"Exactly. I just wondered what you were thinking."

"I don't know," she said. "I don't really have anything to go back to. If I could find a good job here, I would stay. I'll borrow Wendy's board and go up the mountain and just take a day to clear my head. That's what I came for, and I need to remember why."

"You're not going alone up on the mountain though, right?"

"Why not?" she asked in exasperation. "Now you sound like Wendy. She seems to think I'll go off the damn cliff again."

"Well, it did cross my mind," he said.

She glared into the phone. "I didn't do it. Remember?"

"Maybe not," he said, "but it happened, so what's to stop it from happening this time?"

She winced. "Well, I can't spend my life in fear. I mean, whatever that was," she said, "it could happen here and now as well."

"That's not making me feel any better," he said.

She groaned. "I'm going stir-crazy," she said. "I've got no job, and it seems like I'm spinning my wheels and can't get anywhere."

"I hear you," he said. "I'll be home early today. Maybe you can come over and have dinner. We can talk through some issues."

"Depends on what issues," she said. "You're not a shrink."

"I meant, the case," he said, laughing. "Have you seen any more ghostly apparitions?"

"Not really," she said. "Thankfully it's been quiet on that front." *Other than those two shadows earlier, one behind Wendy and one at her laptop.* Should she mention those?

"Good," he said, "that's good news."

"Or whoever and whatever this thing is, it's just building up power."

"That's not what we want to hear," he said.

Happy that she'd at least rattled him out of that compla-cent attitude, she smiled and said, "Maybe, but I don't know if anybody can do anything about it anyway."

"So maybe you should be running out of Aspen scream-ing then," he said, "and looking to get the hell away."

"Yet I'm oddly content here," she said. "And that's a little disconcerting too."

"Very," he said. "Anytime you feel out of the ordinary, you must consider that maybe it's that thing again."

"Maybe," she said, "but how does one even know?"

"I don't know," he said, "but we need to make sure you stay safe."

"There's been no other news?"

"No."

"Well, that's good, I guess," she said.

"Yes, but, at the same time, it feels like something's building there too."

"Don't say that," she said in alarm.

"Too late," he said, "and, if you were listening, you'd be feeling it too."

She glared down at the phone. "I am listening," she said. "I just don't know what I'm supposed to listen to."

Yet, ... for Damon, for him, it was all about whatever this apparition was. *Am I willfully being blind and not seeing what was going on?* That was an upsetting thought. It was possible. Gabby wasn't unaware of her surroundings, but neither had she been very aware of what was going on either. It was easier to blank it all out, relegating it to the back of her mind, as if nothing to be concerned about. She didn't know; it was all just so frustrating. "Anyway," she said, "I'm supposed to meet Wendy, but that doesn't mean that I will. Or that she will," she amended.

"Why don't you just go home? Find a good book and relax?"

"Where will I find a book?" she asked. "Just forget about it. I'm almost home again."

"I'll be there in a few hours," he said, and, with that, he hung up.

She finished the walk back to the garage apartment, enjoying being out in the fresh air. At the last moment, she decided to head over to the bridge, where she'd been acting so weird. She didn't know what the hell it was about that place. She felt something special out there with the water half frozen but still running underneath and the beautiful ice patterns being made.

It was a gorgeous day, and, as she walked onto the bridge itself, she stopped, stared down at the river, and smiled. Some of the ice patterns were starting to melt, but a lot of it was still stunningly beautiful. She looked around and said, "This is an absolutely gorgeous location."

Really, Damon was so blessed to have his aunt's house nearby. Gabby didn't have a clue how to get him to fully figure that out. But to have the house on his own was something, and then to have the garage suite that one could rent out to help with the bills was another stroke of luck entirely. To think that he got the house without a mortgage just added to it too. "Some people have all the luck," she murmured, "and don't even realize how lucky they are."

She closed her eyes and tilted her face up to the sun. She let go of several deep breaths slowly, trying to ease some of the tension quarreling inside her. The last thing she wanted to do was to ruin the last few days that she had here, but, every time she said that, even thought that, she felt this resistance inside at the thought of leaving Aspen. She had nothing to go back to. That was the real problem. It was okay for Wendy to go home—she had friends and family.

But Wendy was leaving friends here too. Apparently Wendy made friends easily, and apparently Gabby did not.

Over time, Gabby had noticed that it seemed that people liked her if she was around for a while, but nobody kept contact with her afterward. Maybe she was just difficult, or maybe she was just too weird, too different. She didn't know, but it was frustrating.

She wouldn't have thought that a problem, but apparently she just didn't have the same kind of friend base or ability to make friends that other people did. Sad, yet aware that she couldn't do a whole lot about it, she headed back to the apartment. She was just short of reaching it, when she heard a vehicle.

She turned around to see Damon coming toward her. She lifted a hand, as she stepped off to the side, and watched as he drove in. He pulled up to the front of the house, hopped out, and said, "I got off earlier than expected."

"This isn't getting off early," she said. "It's like skipping out entirely. It's only ten in the morning. Surely you're not done."

He laughed. "No, I came back to go over some of my notes that I've got here."

She nodded. "Right, I guess that makes sense."

"Come on in," he said. "I picked up food for lunch."

"You don't have to keep looking after me, you know?" she said.

"You're in a tough spot right now," he said. "It's just human decency."

She thought about how many other people she hadn't experienced such decency from and shook her head. "Not so sure about that," she murmured, as she followed him inside. Once there, he opened a bag and took out big take-out containers of what could be soup.

"This is from Chef Tom Hengie," he said. "He and I have been best friends for a long time. He told me that he had leftovers from yesterday and, if I wanted something, to come and get it."

She looked at him in surprise. "Wow. Your family gives you a house," she said, "and your friends give you food." She marveled at that.

He laughed. "Well, I don't think he would look at it that way. He hates throwing out food, so, if he can get me to take some, he doesn't feel guilty."

"Yeah, well, you could pass on my name, you know?"

"I told him that I was helping you out. It's one of the reasons he gave me this." And Damon lifted a second bag off the floor that she hadn't noticed.

She looked at it, frowning. "What's that?"

"That," he said, "is enough food to feed you for a couple more days. We got chicken cordon bleu with Greek potatoes, some leftover rice pilaf, a bunch of veggies. By the way, everything's microwavable."

She stared at the stockpile in front of her in shock. "Oh, my God," she said, "I can eat meat now."

He laughed. "Not only that but it also won't keep, so dig in."

She shook her head. "But it's for you too."

"There's more than enough for the two of us," he said. "I thought we'd have the soup today because it's fresh and would go down very nicely, and Chef Tom already heated it for us."

"Thank you. And thank the chef too," she said.

Damon nodded and opened up a cupboard, pulled out bowls, and slowly poured some thick potato soup into them.

Next he reached for a loaf of bread sitting off to the side and cut thick slabs.

"This looks divine," she said, her stomach growling.

"Did you get any breakfast?" he asked.

She shook her head. "Honestly I was saving it for lunch."

"Things aren't that bad, I hope," he said.

"Says you," she said with a laugh. "But, if I don't get paid, I don't have any food money. Plus the rent has to be paid on our apartment, even though we can't live there."

"Right. I keep forgetting that. Well, at least you got to talk to the lawyer today. You should call your landlord and ask him if he has insurance coverage for the last month's rent."

"All right, I can try. Why does the world always function at a slower rate than I do? I could use the paycheck today."

"I hear you there. I have a similar complaint all the time," he said. "It seems like when the world says it'll be two days, it's four, and, when I expect something in one day, it comes in three. Nothing is ever quite on time."

"No, it never is," she said. "Even the lawyer today, it's his first time being in the store. He didn't know where the cash was or even how to open the till or anything."

"Did he say anything to you?"

"No. Just that he would do my paychecks right away and would talk to me when he got through with the proceedings and got the death certificate and everything cleared up a bit. He needed time to check out the bank accounts, figure out the bookkeeping system, and figure out who he needed to pay."

"Right," he said. "Well, he should get the death certificate today. And I can confirm your boss died of natural causes."

She beamed at that. "Well, that's great news. It also means that hopefully the attorney could fast-track some of this through," she said, rubbing her hands together.

He placed a hot bowl of soup in front of her and pushed over the board with the slabs of bread and said, "Eat up."

"That won't be a problem," she said enthusiastically, as she lifted her spoon and took a taste. "Oh, my God," she said, staring at the soup. "This is excellent."

"Well, he is a chef," he said, "so, when he tells me there's food to pick up, believe me. I go pick it up."

"Yeah, I would too," she said. "Oh, wow," she said, and, murmuring happily to herself, she polished off the bowl of soup. When she looked up, he was only half done. She flushed. "I'm sorry. That's incredibly ill-mannered of me."

He looked at her, surprised, and then laughed. "I hardly think we need to worry about manners," he said. "Go ahead and get yourself some more."

She shook her head. "Oh no, but, if you don't mind, I'd love another slice of bread?" she asked hopefully. He pushed the board her way again and said, "Go for it. There's plenty. Eat up."

So she had two slabs of bread buttered in no time.

He jumped up and brought out a block of cheese from the fridge, then, cutting a few slices, said, "Try putting that on top."

Happily adding the cheese, she asked, "So, what are you working on?"

"Cold cases still."

"There were rumors about something weird happening way back when," she said. "I was trying to look into it online and in the books from the store. Jerry wasn't happy about it though."

"Probably because one of them was his wife's death," he said.

She nodded. "No doubt. I feel terrible I didn't know about it until so late in his life. I had no idea how sensitive he still was to it all."

"Makes sense to me," he said. "I don't think there's a deadline for when one stops grieving."

"I know," she said. "I just, now that I'm sitting here thinking about it, I wonder how much of it was actually born of guilt for not saving her."

"A large part of it, I'm sure," he said. "Don't worry. We've all considered whether it was guilt because he killed her."

"I don't know," Gabby said. "We have to almost consider that, since it's an automatic thing to question, isn't it?"

"Absolutely," he said. "It just makes good sense to look at everything with an open mind."

"How long ago did Jerry lose his wife?"

Damon checked his notes. "Thirty years ago."

"Wow. He has mourned her loss for a long time." She frowned. "Can I look at those old cases with you?"

"Sure," he said. "I've already done a summary about a lot of them. Let me just grab those notes," he said, looking around, as she munched on the bread. He walked off to the side and pulled the notepad to him as he sat again. He checked his notes and read, "We have four women, all between the ages of twenty and thirty."

"There were four cases from back then when Jerry's wife died?" Her gaze widened.

"Yes," he said. "And the question is whether it's really a repeat now because we still only have two cases."

"But how quickly did those four cases happen back then?" she asked.

"Good question," he said. He checked his notes, looking for the dates, then said, "So, the first two were fairly close together, and then the last two were a week after that."

"I wonder if that was random?" she said, mentally counting how long since her first roommate had been murdered.

"Again, we don't have any reason to believe one way or the other."

"Except that, if it is repeating this pattern," she said, "we're coming up on the seven days later, when the other two would have died."

He looked at her, surprised, then checked the calendar and nodded. "You're right. Sunday would be the earliest. If it's repeating, that is," he emphasized.

"Right, and, of course, we don't want to think that," she said.

"Nobody wants to think that. Obviously it's hard not to, but let's try and keep to the facts," he said.

And, with that, they carefully went through all four of these unsolved murders from thirty years back.

Damon noted, "They all had different jobs. One was a ski instructor. Tons of them in Aspen. One was a secretary for a local law firm. Another worked in a bank, and the last one was a seasonal worker who worked on the lifts."

"Right," she said. "So that doesn't necessarily sound like my two roommates who are dead, although one was a secretary and the other a waitress, although she worked multiple jobs at times. It was hard to keep track, since I didn't know either of them that well."

"I don't think the job title itself matters as much. But let's confirm that." As he looked up the details on the two latest murders, he said, "One worked at a restaurant, and one worked as a secretary."

"So I guess it depends whether you call waitressing seasonal or not," she said, tilting her head in thought.

"I wouldn't think so," he said.

"Okay," she said, "so what else? What about characteristics, such as physical descriptions, things like that, which are consistent now and back then?"

"They were all relatively slim, all relatively average height, between five foot five and five foot seven. They all had either auburn, brunette, or darker brown hair."

"So brown hair basically, just from lighter to darker shades?"

He nodded.

She frowned at that, thinking. "Well, both of the women from my apartment who died also had brown hair."

Grimly, he nodded and added to his notes. "Same age category too," he reminded her.

"Right," she said, wincing. "Not a good time to be that age, is it?"

"Nope," he said, "not really."

"So, what's next?"

"Back then, two were found at home. One was found out in the wild, and one was found on the mountain."

She stared at him. "You realize the first two recent deaths were found at home, right?"

He looked up, and they exchanged hard looks. "Yes," he said, "I did realize that."

She took a long slow deep breath. "So one was found where?"

"Outside, beside a river," he said, looking at his notes.

"That's a little freaky."

"Well, it is, particularly considering that you were outside along a river, and, if I hadn't been there, you probably would have died of frostbite."

She sucked her breath back and then slowly nodded. "I didn't feel like I would die," she murmured.

"No, but we don't know that these ones did either."

"Any witnesses?"

"None," he said. "Not only no witnesses, nobody had any motivation that the cops could find back then. The original investigators found absolutely no reason behind the killings. The murders started, and then they stopped."

She nodded slowly. "I know it's an odd thing to ask," she said, "but what are the chances of finding more cold cases like these some thirty years before them?"

He looked up and stared at her. "What?"

"I just wondered if we could have a pattern of every thirty years."

"Well, that would make the killer extremely old now."

She took a long slow deep breath. "Maybe," she said, "it could also possibly mean something more otherworldly than what we're prepared to really look at."

"Are you back to the psychic and ghostly stuff?"

"It is a little odd," she said, trying to work her way through it to think that somebody might have killed these women that many years apart. "But we also aren't seeing any rhyme or reason for the deaths or any witnesses to any of it," she said. "So, if what we have doesn't make any sense, maybe we should look at what does make sense, and we do have an oddly strange psychic thing happening here."

"If we believe any of the people involved in this."

"Well, I personally would believe Stefan, although I understand that you have some reservations about that."

"The reservations are the fact that this isn't a field anybody wants to know a whole lot about," he said.

"That's not true," she said. "I want to know."

"Maybe, but we still need some motivation or reason for this."

"Did you send any of this information to Stefan? Does he have any idea?"

"I didn't ask. He didn't ask either."

She nodded slowly. "Is it possible to check if there were more cases older than this?"

"I don't know," he said. "That goes back a long time. I'm not sure if our digital database covers sixty years or if I have to check the physical files."

"Right," she said, "well, I mean, the pattern should be theoretically the same. So you'd have to search for similarities."

"I can take a quick look, when I return to the office," he said. "Or ..." He stopped, looked at his laptop, reached for it, and dragged it toward him. "I guess I can log in from here."

She stood and gathered their dishes, then took them to the sink and began to wash them. She heard him in the background, muttering away. Finally she stopped, looked at him, and asked, "Finding anything?"

"Maybe," he said. "Just maybe."

She finished up the dishes, then sat down quietly, as she did not want to disturb his train of thought. Plus she did not want to be told that she had no part in this because she was so desperate to get answers herself. The thought that two more women could die, particularly in this violent way, was enough to make Gabby want to run for the hills. She didn't want it to be Wendy or anybody else at this point either. She was just a little desperate to make all this go away, in a good way.

Finally Damon sat back and stared at her. "*Huh*," Damon said, running a hand over his face. "It never occurred to me to look further in the past," he said, "but there are other unexplained deaths about sixty years ago."

"And?"

"Well, they seem similar but not exactly."

"Is that normal?"

"The experts supposedly say killers don't change, but we've all seen instances where they do, so it may be normal, or it may not be."

She nodded. "What happened?"

"There were three murders, at least that I found. Of course, for police records, they are each given a separate file, yet I consider them one case as they were all at one crime scene."

"And what did you find?"

"The husband was blamed for the trio of deaths, all found at his home. He committed suicide not long afterward, saying that he didn't do it, but, because the murders were never resolved, the case is still open, with no witnesses, no suspects." Damon frowned, focused on the data.

"What parameters did you use to find these?"

He shook his head, as if coming back to the present. "The flaying of the chest," he said. "That seems like something that's very indicative."

"Yeah, it would be. So the breasts were cut off or something?"

"Yes, the breasts were peeled back off the chest with a sharp knife."

"Decapitated?"

"Yes, but the heads were still there on site."

"So, maybe the killer got better thirty years later," and she winced even as she said it.

He looked at her with a wry smile. "I know what you mean," he said, "but you're not wrong. Serial killers often practice and improve as they go on."

"But now we're talking about somebody who was at least a teenager then. So, some sixty years later, in theory, would make them at least seventy-five right now."

"Potentially, yes," he said, still frowning. "But remember. This guy committed suicide at some point during the investigation, though I don't see a date for that." He still frowned, leaning closer to the file.

"What is it?"

"His name's been redacted. Even the names of the victims. He's referred to as James Doe, with Jane Doe #1, #2 and #3 listed as the victims."

Gabby raised her eyebrows. "That's unusual for the police, right?"

Damon nodded. "Hell, yes." The grimace on his face was evident. "This may be the originating file that the Cold Case clerk reminded me to not talk about. I can't even ask him about it until he's retired in a few more days." Damon hesitated. "And my captain already yelled at me for pulling these files from thirty years ago. He'd probably fire me if I mentioned this one from sixty years back. Hell, he may fire me once he finds out I've been using Stefan. Though the captain did tell me to do whatever I needed to solve the current cases."

"So what will you do?"

"I'll keep working these old cases quietly, trying to get answers. Hopefully answers that don't involve Stefan's line of work."

Gabby nodded. "Any other weird cases? Anything else that could even be close to this?"

"I don't see anything at the moment," he said, "but we do have a lot of cases, so I'm not sure."

"And I guess the other problem is," she said, "whether the killer would stay in this location. Or, in our case, our killer's ghost."

"Having found these cases," he said, "I would say, yes."

"Well, that's a good place to start then," she said.

"Maybe. We'll pull this data and see if anything is compelling. Any sort of motivation, I guess, is what we're looking for. What is the source of all this anger? What would make somebody repeat this every thirty years?"

"But I don't understand—"

"Something started this, made him mad to begin with," he continued, "and something instigates it all over again, every thirty years, it seems. Serial killers who go to sleep for so many years do so because something, some need inside them, has been satisfied. Then something happens to restart the cycle, and they deal with it all over again."

"I get that," she said, "but, at the same time, we must have a little more than that to go on."

"We often don't get any more than that," he said. "Cases are often built on the thinnest of evidence, and we just keep following the trails, until it makes sense."

She groaned. "But it's not exactly something I can do to help you." Then she held up her finger. "What about the three books you bought?"

"I have them, but I haven't had a chance to read them."

"Wait. Why don't I take them and read them?" she said, bouncing to her feet. "You have work to do, I know, so I need to get out of your way, so you can do it. I've cleaned up the dishes. Let me just grab those books and go home and get to reading, see if I can make sense of anything."

"I'm good with that," he said. He got up, walked over to the side, and grabbed the books. "I haven't even opened them, as you can see."

"Perfect," she said. "I was looking for something to read anyway." And, with that, she turned and headed back out.

"Don't you want to take some leftovers?" he called out.

She stopped, looked back at him, surprised, and said, "I forgot."

He quickly split up the leftovers and said, "Here. You take these."

She smiled and said, "It almost seems foolish, doesn't it?"

"Well, we could eat these meals together," Damon said.

"It's much nicer that way," she admitted.

"In that case," he said, "if you're good until dinnertime, come back around four or five."

"Done," she said with a big grin and ran out of the house.

CHAPTER NINETEEN

WITH A FRESH cup of coffee, Gabby crawled in front of the fireplace with the books. She'd browsed through a couple initial paragraphs in some of the beginning chapters without actually reading each one fully. Checking the Table of Contents, she immediately turned to the chapter covering the death of her boss's wife. It seemed almost wrong to read about it, but what else was she supposed to do? Besides, if any information was to be found in here, they needed it.

In the back of her mind, she wondered if the wife was Gabby's ghost, and that was kind of scary too. What would cause somebody like that to hang around and to torment people—or, in this case, murder people? Although Gabby didn't think that was even possible. After all, how could her ghost pick up a sword and cut somebody?

It didn't bear thinking about it because it brought up questions that she couldn't even begin to understand, and anything she couldn't understand was beyond what she wanted to look at. It was hard enough to understand the world around her without getting ahead into scary things along that psychic line. Finally finding the right chapter, she shifted her position, and the book closed on her.

Frustrated, she took another moment to get to the right chapter. This time she checked the page number, and, as she shifted her glance for a moment to look out the window, the book in front of her closed. Frowning, and much more aware of what she was doing, she opened it to the right page and waited. Sure enough, it slammed closed in front of her.

As far as signs went, it was hard to argue that this wasn't one. But was reading this chapter so bad? She couldn't imagine Stefan stopping this informal investigation on her part. Or would he? Otherwise, why would her ghost stop Gabby? *Maybe the ghost is Andrea. She wouldn't like the rehash of her death any more than Jerry did.* This made more sense to Gabby.

Even so, fear choked the back of her throat, and she started to hyperventilate. She could almost hear Stefan's voice in her head, telling her to calm down and to just relax. But she couldn't relax because the damn book was closing. Was it a joke? Was somebody just playing with her? Was it Stefan testing her? Trying to prove something to her? What the hell was going on?

She slowly and carefully opened the book to the right page, yet again. And waited. This time nothing happened. Feeling like a bit of a fool for even believing that something paranormal was going on, she relaxed and started reading.

Jerry and Andrea had been out skiing all day.

They were celebrating a special event in their life, and this was her first free day. Gabby frowned at that because it talked about a child. Andrea had given birth just a few months earlier, had a tough time of it, and this day was a gift from his parents—looking after the child so the new parents could go up on the mountain for a day. Andrea had been a ski racer when she was younger and was very experienced too. They were out to spend the day up there.

According to the book, Andrea had experienced postpartum depression after the birth of her child, but nobody had any inkling that she might have been suicidal.

Gabby wondered what would make someone suicidal. But clearly, sometimes postpartum depression did, even though—once nutrition and hormones were balanced, with time, adequate rest, and support—recovery was to be expected. She frowned, thinking about somebody who had just given birth, then choosing to throw herself off the mountain. It didn't equate as normal in her mind, but who knew? As she kept reading, apparently a good twenty to thirty witnesses were around Andrea. All had been interviewed afterward, but nobody had seen anything.

That was the part that really got to Gabby. How is that even possible? She understood how half of them didn't see anything, but was it really reasonable to think that *nobody* saw anything? Of course, that's where the doubts started to set in. Maybe Jerry had seen something. She didn't know.

As she kept reading, she went through the factual statements from everyone else who had been there, and the eventual outcome was that everybody just saw her flying through the air. There was absolutely no rhyme, reason, or motivation that they could determine.

Although postpartum depression had been brought up, Gabby couldn't imagine what Jerry had gone through. Not only to have lost his wife but having to raise a small child on his own. Speaking of which, did the child die too? Jerry never mentioned a child, and Gabby knew of no pictures of Jerry's child anywhere, so what had happened? Gabby didn't know, and, as she sat here, she pondered the question of who would inherit the bookstore. It was an odd thing, but, as she continued to read, she found a lot of backstory to the case.

Much of it was interesting, almost like a fictional story. Apparently Andrea and her husband, Jerry, had had some difficulties, and the baby was supposed to be a way to smooth things over. Yet Gabby wondered how anybody could think that the stress or the additional expenses associated with having a baby could possibly make things easier.

But supposedly Jerry's wife, Andrea, had wanted a child since forever, so getting the baby seemed to make her a lot happier. But then she suffered severe depression with the birth, which fueled the speculation of suicide. As it was, the chapter had nothing else to offer besides conjecture and rumors about Andrea's life, friends, and family, but nothing more.

Gabby picked up her phone and quickly texted Damon. **Did my boss have any children?**

He replied with a question mark.

She called him back instead of texting. "According to this first book, Andrea, Jerry's wife, had a baby not long before she died. The authorities were considering whether postpartum depression could have been a factor in the suicide theory."

"I don't remember any talk of a child," he said. "Let me look into it."

"Okay, talk to you later."

Gabby hung up and went back to the book, moving on to another woman's death. Gabby realized very quickly that it was a similar story, with the woman on the mountain, snowboarding with Andrea, but that this woman had died at home in particularly grisly circumstances. No conjecture about suicide, but it was also an odd death, saying that the police weren't releasing any of the details because it was an open criminal case. She quickly texted Damon the name. **Is Susan Volvod one of the four women from cold cases**

thirty years ago?

Yes.

She's in chapter twelve.

Then Gabby kept on reading. Again, it was more conjecture than anything. The book was obviously written for the purpose of sharing salacious details about Susan's private and personal life, rather than offering any meaningful clues about her death. And that was kind of sad—that people would profit off something like this, particularly when the author had nothing to actually say. Everybody had a theory, but nobody had any proof.

Then she reached the next chapter, describing the death of the third victim, Becca Jones, seven days later. As she read through those details, which indicated nothing specific, she reached a point that struck a chord: this grisly crime occurred after snowboarding. She stopped there, making notes. Becca had died on the mountain after snowboarding. With Susan? With Andrea? The same woman who had been conjectured to have killed herself?

Gabby wondered at that. She kept reading, looking for more details of the same oddities, finding that the third woman who had died thirty years ago had definitely been snowboarding on the mountain at the same time as Andrea and Susan. Gabby nodded and wrote down her name and the time frame.

Now Gabby got a shiver up and down her back as she read that Susan and Becca had both been in contact with Andrea. Gabby made further notes.

And, sure enough, the fourth of five victims, Jerri Appleby, who died seven days later, was in a different chapter. A car crash was listed, supposedly unexplained, that had killed two single men. There wasn't any record of them, other than the fact that they died in the car accident. Gabby put a bookmark in that chapter.

She kept on reading, looking for more on the women. The fifth woman, Haley Hart, who Gabby was pretty darn sure was also in Damon's cold case files, was also written about here, but she had died at home. Seven days later.

Gabby rechecked the five dead women from thirty years ago, including Andrea, confirming the dates of their deaths, then confirming two died at home—Susan and Haley. Two had died on the mountain—Andrea and Becca. One died outside—Jerri, the car crash victim.

Was Jerry's wife, Andrea, one of the four cold cases? That didn't make sense because Gabby had five dead women from thirty years ago. She picked up the phone to call Damon, and she heard the exasperation in his voice. "I gather that Jerry's wife wasn't one of the cold cases, correct?"

"No," he said, "she isn't."

"Okay, because there's the one who you said had been skiing with Andrea on the same day she died."

"And?"

"Well, counting Andrea, I have five dead women from thirty years ago. It just didn't make sense, when you've got four cold cases," she said. "I'll leave you alone now."

She continued through the book, reading several more chapters on other deaths in the area, but none were similar to these current deaths. Toward the end of the book, she found something else disturbing. A child who had apparently died in its bed with no cause or explanation. She shook her head, wondering why someone would write a book about such horrid things, muttering to herself, "How odd that the same cold cases were written up in this book."

She wrote down the author's name and looked him up

on the internet. He passed away ten years ago. She shrugged, checked for reprints on it, but it hadn't been reprinted. It wasn't a terribly popular book from a sales perspective, but why would it be? It was local lore more than anything. For the amusement of anyone visiting or for any of the locals potentially. She ended up speed-reading through the initial chapters, and they all involved some spooky case or an unsolved mystery, but nothing of the same ilk that she sought.

Finally she got up, made herself another cup of coffee, and heard footsteps on the stairs. She headed to the doorway and called out, "Is that you, Damon?"

When there was no answer, she frowned and waited. But no one appeared at the door. She shut the door, grabbed her phone, and texted Damon. **Where are you?**

In my living room. Why?

Somebody just came up the stairs, she typed, **but, when I called out, nobody was there.**

Hang on, he wrote. **I'm coming.**

She stood here, waiting, hoping that somebody would at least show up, so she wouldn't think she was crazy. And, sure enough, she heard Damon on his way over here. First, the door at the back of the main house slammed open and shut, then the crunch of his footsteps on the snow as he crossed over. The door down below opened up, and he came up the steps and called out, "I'm right here."

"Go ahead and open the door," she said. He opened it, and she peered behind him. "Is anybody there?"

"No," he said. "You're really expecting somebody, aren't you?"

"I heard footsteps," she said. "Clear as a bell, I heard footsteps."

He frowned, then looked down the staircase and said, "I didn't see anybody."

She nodded slowly. "But I did hear them," she said.

"I'm not saying you didn't," he said, holding up his hand. "Just one more of those bizarre experiences."

"Too many of them," she said. "Did you know that all four of your cold cases are written up in that first book?"

He looked at her in shock.

"I don't think that they're done in any great detail, and certainly without anything definitive that could be used to help solve the crime," she said. "I just thought it was interesting that somebody was writing the salacious details and hoping to make a profit from it."

"Well, I don't think the book is terribly popular," he said. "I've never heard of it before."

She smiled and nodded. "It's probably more of a curiosity piece than anything."

"Did the author say very much?" he asked.

She shook her head. "More about the victims' lifestyle, the families they left behind, and then the public details about the crime. Only that they died and, you know, in horrific circumstances. But it does mention that two women had been up on the mountain with Jerry's wife at the same time, Susan and Becca."

"Interesting," he murmured.

"It's a connection but not much of one," she said. "And it doesn't mention if the other two were as well."

"Well, I can tell you they were from my cold cases," he murmured. "I didn't know about the first two though."

She looked at him and said, "The book could be wrong."

He nodded. "I'll go back to the statements and see."

"Did you find anything yet?"

"Nope," he said, "boring and dry. Lots of families were together. Lots of friends were together. But nothing terribly conclusive."

"Of course," she said, "that would be way too easy."

He nodded. "You know what? If killers got away scot-free all the time, we would probably not even bother looking," he said with half a smile. "We are pretty good at our job, and, most of the time, killers do get caught."

"More so now," she said, "than before. DNA has moved you guys well ahead."

"As has genealogy," he said. "That's been a great avenue for us to explore new connections that we didn't have access to before."

"I've heard about that," she said. "Might be interesting to check."

"Maybe," he said, "but it's an extra cost, and we don't have a budget for it, unless there's a good reason with a solid theory behind it."

Gabby nodded. "I've been thinking about getting my DNA tested and put up on a genealogy site to see if I have any relatives."

"What do you mean, *if* you have any relatives?"

"Well, I'm adopted, although not legally," she said. "It's one of the reasons I came to Aspen actually. I just knew that my adoptive mother picked me up from somebody here in town."

He stopped and stared. "What?"

"I know, hard to believe isn't it?" she said, struggling, even now, to avoid the hurt and pain of not being wanted. "Back then a lot of things were informal, not done legally."

"Very true," he said thoughtfully. "You could probably check it out easily enough."

"Maybe, though it doesn't mean there'd be any answers."

"Well, if and when you become wealthy," he said, "you can get it done yourself."

She laughed at that. "How about if I just manage to pay my own damn bills?" she said with a shake of her head.

"Still no response on the job applications?"

"Nope, nothing. I'll start pounding the street soon," she stated.

"What about snowboarding?"

"That's still the plan," she said. "I haven't heard from Wendy yet though."

"Well, let's see if you hear from her tonight or tomorrow," he said. "You should go up when I'm there anyway. I'm scheduled to be on mountain patrol soon."

"Lucky you," she said. "You get to go up there and get paid for it."

"Actually it's a volunteer position," he said. "At least it is for me."

She rolled her eyes at that. "Nice to be able to do that for the community," she said.

He nodded. "You're right. It is," he said with a grin and didn't say anything else.

She smiled too. "Now, if only the lawyer would contact me."

"He said twenty-four hours," Damon reminded her.

"I know. I know," she said, raising both hands. "Doesn't mean he couldn't do it earlier, if he wanted to."

"Are you ready for dinner?"

She looked at him in surprise, and just then her stomach growled. "Maybe. I didn't realize how late it was."

"Oh, yeah, it's plenty late," he said. "It's after five-thirty already."

She looked at him, shocked.

"Didn't you just read that whole book this afternoon?" he said. "Surely you felt the passage of time."

"To a certain extent, sure," she said. "I just didn't realize how much. Oh, and I forgot to tell you something else."

"What?" He turned back from the doorway.

"I had a little bit of spooky trouble earlier. I think this place is really haunted. Are you sure your aunt is dead and gone? Like happily gone?"

He nodded slowly. "Why?"

"My book kept closing on me," she said quietly. "Without any justifiable reason."

He just looked at her and started to smirk and then laughed out loud.

"I get it," she said crossly. "It's funny for you."

"Well, I don't imagine it was too funny for you," he said. "But you know something? If that's the only thing that ghosts can do, I'm okay with it."

"You mean, outside of those heavy footsteps I heard earlier here." She snatched up her notes and the first book and said, "Come on. Let's go get some food then."

As they walked downstairs and crossed the driveway, entering Damon's place, she said, "It's weird to think spirits may actually be out here, you know?"

"I hear you," he said. "I think it just goes along with that comment of Stefan's, about a whole world that we don't want to actually know anything about."

"And yet you'd think we would. I mean, we're a curious species. We push the outer markers of our world and the boundaries constantly," she said. "You'd think going across the life-death divide would be something we would want to understand more."

"I think it scares people," he said. "I think, at one point in time, they don't really want to know."

"Plus just so much misinformation is out there too," she murmured. "You get one experience from one person that seems to completely contradict the story from the next, so nobody really knows what the truth is."

And, at that, a voice in front of them said, "Very good analysis."

Gabby jumped back with a small shriek and then glared. "If that's you, Stefan," she said, "a little warning would be nice."

"Well, I've been trying to talk to you," he said, "for the last bit, and then I gave up for a while."

"Was that you slamming the book in front of me?"

"No. I believe that was your ghost."

"So can you tell me anything more about … him?"

"Her," Damon and Stefan said together.

"Sorry, nothing I can confirm," Stefan continued. "I must have some connection with her to tell you more. However, I tried to get your attention telepathically," he said, "but you still ignored me. You just kept on reading."

"What was I supposed to do?" she said. "You could use a phone like a normal person."

"I could," he said, "but sometimes it's just easier to talk this way."

"But not as effective," she said.

He burst out laughing at that, his ghostly voice echoing around the house.

"God, that's just spooky when you do that," Damon said beside her.

"Maybe so," Stefan said, "but I can also do it from the

comfort of my bedroom, which makes my life a whole lot easier."

"Well, maybe, but, at the same time, an awful lot is going on right now that we're not too sure about."

"You need to dig more into Andrea, your boss's wife," he said to Gabby. "I read up on her, and I was there while you were reading part of her story and talking to Damon. I could see her partial silhouette."

"My boss's wife is here?" she asked Stefan, but she stared at Damon.

Damon shrugged, his palms up.

"So she's here?" She looked around. "Andrea, are you here now?"

"Do you feel her?" Stefan asked.

She shook her head. "I don't know what it feels like."

"What about that coldness you experienced at Dr. Mica's?" Damon asked.

"I'm not feeling that now," she said. "I did walk around the bridge earlier today, wondering if I would have a similar experience." Damon glared at her, but she shrugged and said, "But I didn't."

"It could have been timing, or somebody else could have been around," Stefan said. "Ghosts pick and choose their times. They're not always capable of coming when we want them to."

"Do they have a choice?" Damon asked. "Can they just wander at will, or are they tethered to a spot?"

"Yes, to all of that. And, no, to all of that," he said. "As Gabby said earlier, everybody's experience is different, and that is the important lesson here. Andrea could be tied to the garage apartment. Or to Gabby herself. It's just when you think you understand that you find out you don't understand anything."

"Well, that's not helpful," she murmured. She sat down at the table and said, "Can you see anything with these people?"

"I see a lot of them," he said. "I can see through time in some cases, but, if you're asking me if I know what's going on in this instance, I don't. I'm not connected to them. You are."

"Me?" she said, startled.

"Yes, you."

"And how am I connected?" she asked in surprise.

"I'm not sure," he said. "That's what you'll have to dive into."

"Are you saying it's by experience, by family genetics, by something odd, like those tarot cards, or what?"

"And again, it could be any or all of the above," Stefan said carefully. "Or none. There is no right or wrong here. I will tell you that generally the ghosts are connected by some feeling. Often somebody they love or hate."

"Well, that was my understanding too," Damon said.

"But, in this case, nobody even knows me," she added. "I'm the newcomer here."

"Maybe not, or maybe it's not what you thought," Stefan said.

At that, Damon turned to her and said, "But you were *collected* from this area as a child."

"Sure," she said, "but that was what? Thirty years ago?" At that, she stopped, and her jaw dropped. "Oh, crud," she said. "*Thirty years ago.*"

"The same time frame that we're looking at," he said, staring at her in complete surprise. "So you are thirty?"

"Yes," she said, "just over." She shook her head. "One of

the reasons I came here was because I felt a connection here, and I wanted to come before my, you know, ... before life got too old," she said. "I know that sounds weird, but it just seemed like it was passing by so fast, and I was doing everything I *had* to do, but nothing I *wanted* to do."

"So you took the winter off to come snowboard?"

"Yeah, selfish, huh?"

"Or thinking about yourself and your mental health," he said. "Nobody can judge that, even though they're all willing to line up to do so."

She started at that. "And I think the problem that Wendy's mother was having with all this was the fact that she thought it was a frivolous whim of mine, and her daughter was just being sucked along."

"Well, Wendy was," Damon said, "but she wasn't being sucked along willy-nilly. She was coming along because she cared."

"Believe it or not, we talked a little about that when she was here earlier too," she said. "Not the most comfortable of conversations, but she told me how she felt, and we cleared the air a bit."

"That's great," Damon said. "Now I want to know everything there is to know about your history."

"I don't know anything," she said. "I was raised by a husband and wife who had no kids. The husband died about three years ago, leaving the wife, whom I don't really have any contact with, other than the random Merry Christmas call."

"Why not?"

"Because I was a chore to them. When I turned eighteen, they told me that they'd done their duty, and that was it. Get out."

"How do you feel about that?"

"Well, it would be nice to have a family, but, if they didn't want me," she said quietly, "what was I supposed to do?"

"Good point," he said. "I want their names, their address, and anybody else who was family to you back then."

"It's just them, as far as I know."

"Do you have any idea why they adopted you?"

"No, I don't. I assume they always wanted kids, but, when they got one, parenthood wasn't quite what they thought it would be."

He started at that. "Wouldn't it be nice if people had a take-back option when it came to kids, when they discover they didn't want them?" he said. "Instead they tend to abuse them."

"Well, I didn't get abused," she said. "I just basically got ignored."

"I wonder what the connection is," he said, "and why?"

Stefan broke in and said, "You need to find that out because there is a connection, and there's a reason why it involves Gabby."

"But that would also mean," she said, "that there's a reason why it was those women thirty years ago."

"Absolutely," Stefan said. "You just have to dig it up. Think outside the box and you'll cut to the right answer, but it won't be simple, fast, or easy."

"As long as we get there, and we get there before somebody else dies," Damon said, "I'm okay with that."

Stefan's golden orb disappeared, and Gabby helped Damon reheat dinner for them. After cleaning the dishes, Gabby returned to her suite and left Damon amid all his cold cases.

It never occurred to Damon that this would have anything to do with Gabby personally. And why would it? Stefan had just told them that ghosts only hung around those they loved or hated, so Damon wasn't exactly sure what the connection was to Gabby. But now, armed with information on her adoptive parents, he sat down after dinner to dredge up whatever he could about her life. He had her social security number and her formal name. She didn't have a birth certificate, but he quickly uncovered one.

As he sat here and stared at it, he felt everything coalescing. Putting that off to the side, he quickly brought up the info on the adoptive parents and didn't find any formal adoption on file in the Aspen courts, but there had definitely been some kind of an agreement that they would come here and pick her up, that they would raise her until she turned eighteen. He felt it deep within his gut, without any written confirmation, just going by what Gabby revealed.

As he considered this further, he picked up the phone and called the lawyer. "Gabby is Jerry and Andrea's daughter, isn't she?"

The lawyer laughed and said, "Yes, I believe she is, although Jerry never confirmed it. Something about her really reminded me of someone, and I didn't figure it out until dinnertime. Her resemblance to her mother is quite striking," he said. "I was sitting here and realized that she looks a lot like how I remember Jerry's wife. I found some photos, and they seem to confirm it too."

"I only found out today that Andrea had a baby and that part of the reason people thought she may have jumped was postpartum depression," Damon said.

"That's what they said at the time. I know that, for Jerry, it was horrific to even think about, and he was left with a three-month-old baby that he could barely even stand to look at because she just reminded him of the loss of his wife."

"Some of the written accounts suggest they had some marital issues that they thought the baby would fix."

"She couldn't get pregnant," the lawyer said. "I was friends with him at the time, way back when, and it was a big problem within their marriage, and then, out of the blue, she got pregnant."

"Did he know Gabby was his daughter?"

"He didn't for the longest time, but he did wonder, asking me about a paternity test."

"Would he ever tell Gabby about that?"

"I think he was working his way around to it," he said. "He was still struggling to accept it himself."

"There's a huge age difference there, for a father and daughter," Damon said.

"There was a significant age difference between Jerry and his wife," the lawyer said. "Jerry himself just hit seventy, but Andrea was fifteen years younger. So she would have been fifty-five today. She was only twenty-five when she died thirty years ago."

"With her whole life ahead of her," he murmured.

"Exactly. But I know Jerry was incredibly devastated at her death. And he was completely overwhelmed with a baby that, I'll be honest, I'm not sure he ever wanted."

"No. That just adds to the pain for everyone, doesn't it?"

"Yes," the lawyer said, "it really does. So he made arrangements with his wife's best friend. They had just moved away a few months before Andrea found out she was pregnant, and Andrea was devastated over that loss as well. And, when Jerry told the couple what had happened, they agreed to come and get the child. He paid them for her upkeep until she reached the age of majority, and, as far as he was concerned, it was a good deal for all involved. But I'm not so sure that it was. As I look back on it, and I hear where Gabby is at in her life, I wonder. Clearly no one gave her any explanation of her birth family."

Damon said, "I don't think this environment was a very good family scenario. I'm pretty sure Gabby was more tolerated than anything else, and, when she turned eighteen, that was it. They were done and told her so."

"And, of course, she didn't know anything about her father to come look for him."

"But he did know about her," Damon said. "The least he could have done was look for her."

"Well, we can make judgments all we want," he said, "but there's really no way to know what he was thinking, even at the end."

"No, I guess not, but Jerry did seem to be in deep mourning over Andrea, even thirty years later. So maybe he didn't have room for guilt over Gabby too."

"I just don't think he knew how her life was," the lawyer said sadly.

"The fact that she found her way to him is just amazing in itself. It's almost like it was fated," Damon said.

"We hear stories all the time," the lawyer murmured. "You know? How brothers find out that they've been neighbors all this time but didn't know that they were brothers."

"You're right. I do hear stuff like that quite a bit," he said. "You need to tell her."

"You haven't?" the lawyer asked.

"No, not yet. I thought you would handle that, with the

distribution of the estate."

"Well, why don't you bring her in tomorrow morning," he said, "and I can tell her all of it."

"That's a good idea," he said, then hung up and contacted Gabby. "We have an appointment at the lawyer's at nine tomorrow morning."

"We do?" she said in surprise.

"Yeah. Are you okay if I come?"

"Sure," she said cautiously. "So it's an official visit?"

He heard the worry in her voice. He smiled. "Kind of. I have a bunch of questions I need to find out about too."

"Fine," she said. "I was trying to go to bed early, but I'm having trouble sleeping."

He chuckled. "I can understand that. A lot is going on."

"Well, and he still hasn't paid me," she said. "I'm really worried."

"Get some sleep," he said gently. "Tomorrow's a whole new day."

"It's a new day, but that doesn't mean it's a new *good* day though," she said in exasperation.

At that, Damon burst out laughing. She, of course, had absolutely no idea what was coming, but he was thrilled for her. "Just stay positive," he whispered. "Good night. I'll grab some sleep myself and hope there aren't any more crazy calls."

"By our calculation, the killers are not working tonight, are they?"

He stopped, and then he said, "Well, I guess, if they're on schedule, it would be tomorrow night, or early morning on Sunday."

"Right, so we should both sleep tonight."

"Yeah," he said. "We should have found somebody involved in this already."

"If it's a ghost, then nobody to find," she said. "And that's the problem."

With that, she hung up, and he sat here, staring at the files in front of him. If this ghost was connected to her, and it was connected to what was going on, was Gabby the possessed killer? Was this some kind of vendetta? But why would a mother, Andrea, go after her daughter, Gabby? Because there's no doubt that she had at one time. That whole dancing-on-the-bridge thing? At that, he picked up the phone, and he contacted Stefan.

"You decided to try it my way, huh?"

"I'm too tired to be rattled," he said. "Tomorrow night is the seven-day mark, if it follows the same pattern from thirty years ago for another murder to happen," he said. "I'd really like to avoid that."

"I'm sure you would," Stefan said.

"And we found the connection with Gabby."

"And it's familial, isn't it?"

"Maternal. Her mother was the bookseller's wife, who was suspected to have committed suicide from postpartum depression by jumping off the mountain. Although everybody said no way she would have done that. Given the time frame back then, nobody had any other explanation. But she appeared to fly through the air off the mountain."

"And she's Gabby's mother?"

"Yes. I just confirmed that with the lawyer. Gabby doesn't even know yet."

"Interesting," he murmured.

"So I suspect that's the reason for the ghostly visits to Gabby," Damon said. "Andrea, if she's the ghost, obviously knows who Gabby is, but I don't know if that's connected to the murders."

"Well, if Andrea was murdered it would be," he said. "If she wasn't murdered, then it could just be her need to reconnect with Gabby and to say that she's sorry."

"Well, Gabby's life would have definitely been different, if her mom hadn't gone over that mountain," he said.

"Exactly. And that would be what the ghost needs to say," Stefan said.

"Do they really hang around for something like that?"

"Absolutely, and she wouldn't necessarily have gone after Gabby. Andrea would have thought that her baby was here in town and could have been searching for her all this time."

"That's very sad," he said.

"A lot of these cases are sad," Stefan said simply. "These are just people who loved and lost, for whatever reason."

"And here I was thinking the ghost was the vengeful killer. I just didn't know how they went about killing."

"They can utilize somebody else, either through physical possession or verbal manipulation," Stefan said, "and we don't ever really understand how, but they do take possession and somehow make them act in a way that the host doesn't know about."

"Like, when Gabby was dancing out on the bridge here," Damon said.

"But remember. Gabby has two spirits attached to her. The question is, was that her mother back then on the bridge?"

"Would her mother do that?"

"Quite possibly," Stefan said. "Maybe she just wanted to experience life in her daughter's body, or maybe she thought it would help her to connect to her daughter again."

"By possessing her?"

"Ghosts don't think things through necessarily the same way we do," he said. "Some of them are very advanced, but some are just basically operating ectoplasms."

At that, Damon laughed. "I get more confused the more I even talk about this," he said. "You know how bizarre it all sounds, right?"

"Oh, I know," he said. "I spend my life trying to make sense of this."

"And it's not something that we even can make sense of. I mean, Andrea died thirty years ago, and I have four other unsolved murders back then, not including Andrea's death."

"And the fact that she wasn't included is also interesting," Stefan said, "because she could very well have been the first victim."

"Except we found more victims thirty years before that, so sixty years ago, but the information is very sketchy."

"Ah," Stefan said, "now that's interesting."

"Why?"

"I feel like it's all connected," Stefan said.

"Sure, but how long would a killer keep doing this?"

"I guess it depends on what the connection is to all these women."

"They look similar in appearance, but they weren't sexually assaulted. They were basically terrorized and completely brutalized," he said, "but it was over fast."

"Like an execution?" Stefan asked, curiosity in his voice.

Damon thought about it and said, "Potentially, but their chests were also flayed open. With a sword."

"What do you mean by that?"

He described the scene to him.

"That's a very distinctive mode of killing," Stefan remarked.

"Yes, and I can confirm that the ones from sixty years ago were the same. Rougher execution but same idea."

"Interesting," he murmured.

"You keep saying that, but I don't know what it means."

"Well, nobody does," Stefan said, "and you won't, until we can get a little further into this."

"And how am I supposed to get further into it?" Damon asked.

Stefan laughed at that. "We just keep digging. But we must dig into the mother-daughter relationship, and then we have to spread out to all those victims."

"Maybe, but I don't see any connection to all those victims."

"Well, it's there," Stefan said. "You just haven't found it yet."

With that, Stefan hung up.

CHAPTER TWENTY

THE NEXT MORNING, Gabby woke up and had the last of the bread and coffee. As she was getting dressed for the meeting with the lawyer, Damon sent her a text, asking if she wanted breakfast.

She responded, typing how she'd cleaned out the bread.

Her phone rang immediately after that, and he said, "Don't be a fool. Come over here, and get some real food."

"Hey, I had lots of bread," she muttered.

"That's not terribly healthy all by itself," he said.

"Maybe not, but it's what I had."

"Stop being so stubborn, and get your ass over here this minute."

She groaned because he'd already hung up, so nothing she could say would make a difference. Shaking her head, she grabbed her purse and a winter coat and headed over. "I don't think we have time," she muttered.

He looked at the clock and said, "We'll take my car. We're not walking, so we have time."

"Fine." And, with that, she sat down to see fluffy scrambled eggs and hot toast waiting for her. "You really can't spend so much of your time taking care of me, you know?"

"Why not?" he said. "I'm kind of getting used to it."

She snorted. "That's not exactly a good answer."

He chuckled. "Why not?" he asked. "I like you. I like

spending time with you. I was kind of hoping we could go boarding up on the mountain together."

"Sure. How about tomorrow. So you work ski patrol this Sunday? That would be good, if you want. I know Wendy doesn't want me to go alone."

"Why?"

"She thinks I'll end up in another weird possession case again," she said with a shrug.

"Well, I suppose it's possible," he said. He stared at her for a long moment.

"I don't know," she said. "I think it's all a little foolish."

"Maybe," he said, "but it's what we must deal with."

"Very true," she replied, as she quickly polished off her eggs and toast. Within minutes, they both stood, ready to go. "I just hope he gives me my check," she muttered.

He glanced at her, smiled, and said, "I don't think that'll be an issue."

"You say that, but you can't really understand until you've been on the edge of having no money and really see what they've got for you as a lifeline."

"Let's get going," he said, as they climbed into his car. Smoothly he pulled ahead and drove to the lawyer's office.

As they got out, she frowned and said, "It's a pretty high-end place."

"Lawyers offices tend to be that way," he said, laughing.

"I guess, but I know Jerry didn't think much of them."

"Well, for somebody who didn't think much of attorneys, Jerry certainly used Nathan's services."

"Interesting, isn't it?"

"Apparently they were good friends."

"Maybe," she said, smiling, but clearly unconvinced.

As they walked forward, he said, "So keep an open mind,

all right?"

"Sure, but I don't know what I'm supposed to keep an open mind about."

"All kinds of things today," he muttered in a cryptic tone.

She stared at him, surprised, but they were already inside. As she walked forward, she spotted the lawyer and said, "Good to see you again."

He turned toward her, gave her a long close look, almost blinked, and said, "The resemblance is really striking."

She frowned. "Resemblance to what?"

He smiled as they followed him into the back office. "Come on. I've got some photos for you."

"What kind of photos?"

He reached into a folder and pulled out a single photo of a woman. He held it up and asked, "Does she look familiar?"

She looked at it in surprise and said, "Well, it kind of looks like me."

"That's because it's your birth mother," he said.

She stared at him in shock. "What are you talking about?"

"Gabby," he said, "your mother was Andrea, Jerry's wife."

She sagged into the nearest chair. "What?"

"Yes, and, just like a homing pigeon, apparently your need to come back here to Aspen also brought you back with the same love of books to her bookstore and to your father."

She stared at him in shock. "Jerry was my father, and I didn't even know?" She couldn't get her mind wrapped around it. "What happened that—" And then she stopped, took a deep breath, and said, "that he gave me up?"

"He couldn't handle life after your mother's death, and

he didn't know what to do with a newborn. Your mother's best friend was Bernadette, the woman who raised you after Andrea's death. Jerry agreed to pay for your care, so she came and collected you and raised you."

"Oh, my God," she said. "And never once did she tell me."

"What would you expect her to tell you?" Damon asked at her side.

She looked at him in shock. "That my father was alive would be a good start."

"Well, I think in a way he secretly hoped she would tell you," Nathan suggested.

"But he could have contacted me himself," she said, her heart cracking from this revelation that she never thought to experience.

"And I get that," he said gently. "Of course it's just that much harder to accept, considering he's now gone."

"I was so close to having a relationship with a real relative," she said, "and, just like that, I didn't even get that opportunity."

"Well, isn't it a good thing that you did get to know him though?" Damon asked.

Reaching across, she gripped his fingers hard. Then she turned to the attorney. "Did Jerry know?"

"He came to me a couple days before his death and asked me to check. I did some searching, and the preliminary investigation, short of a blood test, seemed to confirm it for him. And that was the morning of the day before he died."

"I wonder if that's what brought on the heart attack," she murmured, staring at the window.

"Stop," Damon said. "You are not responsible for that."

She glanced at him with tears in her eyes. "Maybe not,"

she said, "but it feels like it."

"No, not at all," the lawyer said. "He felt horribly guilty for what he'd done all those years before to you, on top of the loss of his wife, so he was dealing with two losses. However, once he had already made arrangements for your care, he felt he couldn't reverse it."

"Well, he could have," she said. "I had a terrible life! It was cold. It was lonely. I was taken care of, but I was never loved," she said. "Even if he hadn't done a very good job of raising me, at least I think Jerry would have loved me."

"We can't judge him," Damon said. "Life isn't that easy, especially with Andrea's death thrown in there. Life's not that black-and-white. Nothing is ever clear-cut, and we don't always get the answers we wanted."

Tears cloaked her eyes, and she nodded slowly. "I get that," she said. "I just wish I'd had more time with him or had known so I could have appreciated the time I did have."

"I get that too," Damon said, then looked at the lawyer. "Do you want to tell her the rest?"

She looked up at Nathan. "Tell me what?"

"He did know about you at the end, and accordingly he changed his will. He left you the building with the business and any other assets in his will."

She stared at him, her jaw dropping. "What?"

"Yes," he said, smiling. "So the bookstore is yours, free and clear. He owned the building as well, in case you didn't know. He also owned the two buildings on either side and rented out space to those two businesses."

She shook her head. "What?"

Damon couldn't stop grinning.

She stared up from the lawyer to Damon and back. "Oh, my gosh," she said, focused on Damon now. "You knew?"

"I figured it out last night, after we talked, and I then called Nathan to confirm it last night," he said. "That's why I came in with you this morning."

She sagged in place. "The bookstore is mine?" In that moment, she could almost feel hope welling up inside her. But she'd had a lot of disappointments in life, and this was too big to get wrong.

"The bookstore is yours, as is the rental income from the other stores. You have an apartment above that you can live in yourself," Nathan said, "or you can rent it out."

She stared at him. "I can't believe it," she said. And then she asked, "Do you have my paycheck?"

Both men burst out laughing. "Yes, I have your paycheck," Nathan said, "and, from now on, you can write your own paychecks."

She just stared, thinking it was far too much to comprehend. "Who was supposed to get it instead of me?"

"There was no one, so it would all have been sold, probably to a developer, and the money would have gone to charity. Instead he chose to give it to his daughter," he said. "I think he would have loved to have had time to explain it to you himself, but he didn't get that time."

She nodded slowly. "That's something I'll deal with myself as well," she said. "I never even once tried to track down any of my birth family," she said. "I was told that they were all gone and that nobody wanted me."

"And, at the time, it was true in a sense," the attorney said. "I can't lie to you. At the time, Jerry was so devastated by the loss of his wife and by the possibility that she had committed suicide. He just couldn't handle any more, and the thought of being faced with the innocent but very real baby, day in and day out, was too much. He was torn between blaming you and blaming himself. He didn't want to be around the person that he thought had sent his wife off that cliff, and he couldn't deal with the self-loathing. In the end, he realized it was a dreadful mistake, one that he regretted very much."

She sagged in place. "God," she said, "this is just too unbelievable."

"Maybe, but it's a good kind of unbelievable," Damon said. "You got answers. You found your birth family, and you get to inherit enough to allow you to stay in Aspen."

"And that's why I've always been drawn here, isn't it?"

"That's because this is home for you," Damon said. "This is where you belong."

She felt the tears burning at the back of her eyes. Damon hastily reached across the desk, grabbed a box of tissues, and shoved it at her. "Here," he said. She wiped her eyes and blew her nose. "Thank you," she whispered. She looked up at the lawyer. "Do I have papers to sign or something?"

"You absolutely do," he said, "and it'll take us a little bit to get through it all. You'll also need to set up a will of your own."

She looked at him in bewilderment.

"The estate is of significant value. If you passed away," he said, "which one day you will, we all do, you'll want to decide for yourself what would happen to it."

She said, "It's all too much to take in."

"Maybe right now, but you've got some time," he said, "so don't worry about it."

She looked at him for a long moment, and it started to settle inside. She felt the tears, but there was also joy. She stood up, as Damon stood as well, and she wrapped her arms around his chest and hugged him close.

"Thank you, thank you, thank you," she whispered.

Laughter rumbled up his chest, as his arms closed around her, and Damon held her close. "Don't thank me," he said. "Your father left you all this."

She nodded. "But you're the one who helped me in the meantime. I don't know if we would have gotten this far without you."

"The lawyer confirmed your identity," he said, "so it's all good."

She looked at the lawyer. "Did you call my …" And she stumbled over the words. "… adoptive mother?"

He nodded. "She confirmed that she picked you up from Jerry, agreed to raise you, until you were of legal age. And I must admit, she sounded like she deserved a reward for it too."

She started at that. "She won't get one from me," she said. "I think she was always jealous of my mother."

"Well, that didn't help her any. She never had any other children herself?"

"No. I don't think they wanted any, after inheriting me," she said.

"Well, they didn't know what a blessing was then," Damon said. "I can't imagine you being anything but a beautiful child."

"Well, I was a heartbroken one, right from the beginning," she said. "Even though I was an infant, Bernadette and I never really bonded somehow. And, while this is all just incredible, it'll take a bit of getting used to."

"Give me a day to get the paperwork situated," he said. "I do have some of it right here, but we must get the property transferred into your name, and, like I said, we must sit down and sort out a will for you."

The next hour was taken up going over paperwork, and, by the time they finished, she was dazed. "He actually had money?"

"But he was old-school," the lawyer said. "He didn't spend it because he didn't think he needed to. And, though he'd changed the will only recently, I think, deep down, he'd always saved what he could because you might need it for later."

"So I'm not broke?"

"Not only are you not broke but I think a lot of people would say you're a very wealthy woman in your own right."

She shook her head. "Whoever would have thought it?"

Saying their goodbyes to the lawyer, they walked toward the car.

"Your parents had to be out there somewhere," Damon said. "I'm just glad that, after all of it, there was something left for you."

"I'd rather have had my father," she said tearily.

"I know," he said, "and that's what makes you special."

"He had such a broken life," she whispered.

"And he's happy where he is now."

"Do you think my mother's happy now too then?"

"Well, we can hope so," he said. "At least they should be together."

She frowned at that. "Not if she's still here."

He nodded slowly. "We'll ask Stefan about that," he said. "You never know. Maybe they can meet up and cross over together or however that works."

"Isn't it bizarre," she said, "to think of such a thing."

"Absolutely. But look. You have options now. And you're not destitute."

"And I should clean out Jerry's apartment, shouldn't I?"

"And open up the business," he said with a bright smile. "So you don't need those résumés after all. You have your own business to run now. Not only that, because you are the landlord to the other two businesses, you might have to brush up on how to handle it."

"I took business classes in college," she said, standing up a little straighter. "I'm really looking forward to this."

"So now you're working for yourself," he said. "Nobody else."

She started to laugh, threw her arms around him, and said, "Life seems so wonderful right now."

"Good," he said. "So it's eleven o'clock."

She looked at her watch, smiled, and said, "Meaning, you must go to work."

"I do, indeed," he said.

"Is that why you wanted my DNA?"

"That's partly why," he said. "Though those results take longer to come back."

She froze. "What if I'm not Jerry's daughter?"

"Well, legally everything passes to you anyway," he said. "And you are your mother's daughter. That photo confirmed that. As for the rest, well, I don't really know about that," he said with a shrug.

She nodded and smiled. "I'm still in shock."

"Well, I'm heading back to the office. Do you want a lift home?"

"No," she said, looking down at the keys in her hands. "I think I'll go to the bookstore."

He grinned. "I don't blame you one bit," he said. "Maybe avoid doing too much upstairs or going into his private stuff yet but consider opening up the store, so people know that everything's okay."

"I can do that," she said. "There'll probably be a lot up-stairs to clean or to toss or whatever anyway."

"Exactly," he said, "and wait maybe until I get there, and we can go through the upstairs together."

"You think that's best?"

"I think it might be emotional for you," he said, "so, yes."

"Okay," she said. "I'll go open the store and spend time in the office, just familiarizing myself with the business aspects, and I'll see you whenever you're off work then."

He nodded. "That sounds good."

She stopped and looked at him, then said, "Of course, tomorrow's the day, isn't it?"

He looked at her, his smile falling away, and said, "Yes, the seventh day, so please be careful and stay safe."

"There's no reason for anybody to come after me," she said.

"So you say, but there was no reason for anybody to come after your two roommates either."

She winced, nodded, and said, "Right."

And, with that, she headed down the street toward the bookstore. Her heart was heavy, but her steps were light, and she felt a completely different change in circumstances now. She was no longer destitute, for one thing. She had a paycheck in her pocket, which felt even weirder now that the bookstore was hers.

As the realization hit her, she started to dance and twirl on the sidewalk. She accidentally bumped into somebody walking past.

She apologized immediately, but he just grinned and said, "At least somebody's having a good day."

She beamed back. "You're not kidding," she said. "Life is

good, indeed."

And, with that, she danced all the way to the bookstore.

Her bookstore.

DAMON WAS HAPPY for Gabby. He was thrilled for her actually, now that she was clear of all the murders and suspicions about her tarot card readings, which had been just a bizarre coincidence, as far as he was concerned. At least at this point. Now if somebody like Stefan told Damon it was something other than that, maybe he'd listen to that theory, but, for the moment, he was completely content to go with coincidence on that one. Now she had a way to make a living, and she also had money in her pocket from the paycheck, and she had a place to live.

He smiled at that because it was pretty much everything she needed all at once. Good for her father for recognizing exactly what was going on there and doing something about it—even if he hadn't come forward and said something to her personally, maybe simply because he didn't have enough time. Damon didn't know, but it was an interesting conundrum. He drove to his office, and, when he walked in, Jake looked up and said, "Where the hell were you this morning?"

"At the lawyer's," he said, shaking his head. "In a weird coincidence, the bookstore owner, Jerry, is the father of the woman I've been helping."

"Gabby?"

"Yeah." He told him more of the story.

Jake stared at him. "That is beyond bizarre."

"It is. I know."

"You sure she didn't kill him?"

He looked at Jake in surprise and said, "And here I

thought it had already been ruled as natural causes?"

Jake nodded. "Sure, but it does make you wonder."

"Yeah, except she had no idea he was her father. The lawyer broke the news to her this morning. She was raised by her mother's best friend and her husband, and, although they took her and raised her, providing her needs growing up, she missed out on that entire loving family connection. They took care of her in a literal sense, but that's all, then gave her the boot when she turned eighteen."

"Right, so, in that case, she might very well have preferred to have had her father around."

"Definitely she would have. She also really loved the bookstore and has apparently inherited that trait from her mother."

"Well, things are looking up for her then."

"It'll still be a bit for everything to transfer of course," he said, "but the paperwork is done."

"Good for her. It doesn't help us with the murders though, does it?" he asked.

"Not that I can tell at the moment, and unfortunately tomorrow is the day."

"Meaning?"

"Remember how I said that, thirty years ago, there were two deaths and then, seven days later, there were two more?"

He looked up nodded and said, "And?"

"Well, tomorrow is seven days later."

"So, if we get another murder in the wee hours of Sunday or later Sunday night," Jake said, "we can pretty well be assured they're all connected because they are following the same pattern?"

"Absolutely, but of course that's the worst way for us to reach that conclusion."

"I hear you, but that doesn't mean it will be the only way though."

"I get it," Damon replied. "That's where our focus needs to be."

"Are you thinking about trying to protect the other women in the group?"

Damon winced at that. "Well, it would be a damn shame if Gabby was murdered now that she's finally getting a chance to live."

"And not many of us get a chance like she just got," Jake said.

"I know." Damon frowned at that and said, "But you make a good point." He picked up his phone and called her.

"Hey," she said, her voice almost singing.

He grinned. "Still on a high, I see."

"Probably will be for the rest of my life," she said. "I mean, it's a lot to take in, in the sense that I actually had a father and somebody who cared enough to leave me something," she said. "But it's also sad that I just lost him, but then, at the same time, there's the high that I have a way to stay in Aspen now and actually make a living."

"Did you open the bookstore?"

"I did," she said. "It's pretty slow though."

"Well, it'll take a bit for everybody to realize that it's back open again."

"True enough," she said. "Listen. Since I actually have some money now in my pocket, and you've been looking after me all this time, I thought maybe I could pick up some groceries and cook a meal for you tonight."

"Oh," he said, surprised, "that'd be wonderful. Thanks."

She chuckled. "I don't know how long the money will last before the rest is freed up, or when I'll move into the place, so I need to make some kind of arrangements with you—if you're okay to let me stay until I can get into the bookstore."

"Yeah, you should ask the lawyer about that," he said. "You can probably make that arrangement ahead of time, before the paperwork is processed or whatever."

"That's what I'm hoping for," she said. "I've tried to call him a couple times but, so far, no answer. I know he had a busy day scheduled, and that's one of the reasons we went in so early this morning," she said, "and I guess I still feel like maybe I should do a DNA test too."

"I'm pretty sure the lawyer already did one," he said.

"Really? Without a sample from me?"

"All it takes is a strand of hair or your saliva on a glass."

"Is that how my father knew?"

"Well, it would make sense. Particularly if Jerry would leave you everything, though I don't know how quickly they may have processed it."

"Well, a private lab can do it pretty fast," she said, "but I don't think he would have the results back yet. Jerry didn't think I was his until just a few days ago."

"Well, maybe Jerry didn't tell the lawyer until a few days ago. Jerry could have known longer than that. Maybe not. Regardless a report could be in potentially anytime now, depending."

"I can take a look for the results here at the store," she said. "I don't know what I'd do if I found out he wasn't my father."

"It doesn't matter," he said. "You've been left the place regardless. You are your mother's daughter, after all."

"But what if another woman's out there, who was expecting or hoping for this? Like Bernadette?"

"Don't borrow trouble," he said. "Your father left it to you because he needed somebody to leave it to."

"Ouch," she said, "that's kind of a slap in the face, if you look at it that way."

He groaned. "And that's not the way I meant it. You know that."

"I hear you. Anyway I have a customer," she said. "I'll talk to you later." And she hung up.

He smiled at that.

"So I presume Gabby's DNA was run against the forensics we had from her mother's murder, right?"

"I would presume so too. Nathan didn't get into that."

"So did the bookseller actually get a DNA test done to determine paternity?" Jake asked.

"I'll contact the lawyer about that."

As it happened, the lawyer answered Damon's call on the first ring. "Hey, what's up?" Nathan asked.

"Did Jerry do a DNA test on him and Gabby?"

"Yes, he did. He sent it off earlier this week for a rush processing, but he was pretty convinced regardless—what with the physical likeness and other traits Gabby and Andrea shared—and once Jerry confirmed with me that Bernadette and her husband had looked after Gabby, and I confirmed that loosely binding agreement between them, we didn't need the DNA results to verify at that point."

"So, there is still DNA coming? Gabby's a little worried that it'll all go away in a puff of smoke."

The attorney chuckled. "Nope, everything's hers. Not a lot of people would say she inherited much, you know? It's a pretty dusty old store."

"Maybe, but, for her, it's a gold mine. Plus it's something she really cares about."

"Well, she inherited that love of books from her mother obviously," he said. "Andrea was a bookworm, like you wouldn't believe."

"Did any particular genre hold her interest?" Damon asked on a whim.

"Everything metaphysical," he said.

Like those tarot cards? "Ah, lucky for her," Damon said.

"Why is that?"

"Because it seems like some very bizarre metaphysical event may have killed her."

"You don't believe that, do you?" he asked in surprise.

"No, of course not. I'm a cop. We end up looking completely at the evidence." When he was done with the conversation, he hung up to find Jake grinning at him, like a madman.

"You changed your tune on all that pretty fast, didn't you?" he asked.

"I don't know about that," he said, "but I didn't want to get into an argument about the merits of psychics with a lawyer."

"Well, Stefan is pretty damn convincing."

Damon thought about everything that Stefan had done and nodded. "He is, at that. I also saw some weird events happening that I just don't get," he said. "Once you see something like that, it makes it very hard to forget."

"Yep, it sure does. And you're lucky that lawyer is still practicing."

"Jerry and Nathan were friends apparently," he said. "I don't know how old the lawyer is, but probably in a similar age group. He has mentioned enough details about the wife, Andrea, to suggest that he knew her."

"Even if Nathan were no longer with us, it probably

wouldn't make a difference on our case. Aspen is a much smaller town, with a much more close-knit community, than say Denver or whatever. You probably would have figured out the mother-daughter connection eventually by talking to other old-timers."

"Understood. But now let's focus on the murders. I'll contact the other two roommates, put them on alert." Damon quickly texted the two other survivors, asking that they stay in with protection tonight and Sunday night, then to reply so he'd know they got the message. Both women replied right away, suitably warned. He phoned a couple patrol cops on duty this weekend and asked that they make frequent swings by the addresses where Gabby, Wendy, and Betty could be found tonight and tomorrow night. Damon would phone Gabby, speak to her in person.

As it was, in the back of his mind, Damon kept waiting for *that* phone call. But he knew instinctively it would be at nighttime, since that's when these murders always happened. But he didn't know what to do about it. He didn't know who else to protect because the first two knew each other, but the other three didn't really know the first two, despite all being roommates.

So, would that pattern hold, or would the killer just attack whoever for the sake of fulfilling whatever killings that he needed to do?

Damon frowned at that, worried sick that he'd completely missed something, and somebody would die this weekend because he couldn't stop it. The real problem was that he couldn't stop it because he didn't know for sure that it would happen. He also didn't have an intended target, someone who the killer had already threatened or whatever, so no one to intentionally protect, and all he could do was warn the other women and have cops make more patrols around the homes of Wendy, Gabby, and Betty.

With that thought in mind, he called Gabby back. When she answered again, her voice was still warm and bubbly. "I figured the shine would have worn off by now," he said jokingly.

"Nope," she said. "And I've had several customers in, all delighted that the bookstore will stay open."

"Good," he said. "I just wanted to warn you again, that tomorrow is seven days."

Instantly there was silence at the other end. "I was thinking of that," she said, "and, if there was ever anything guaranteed to shut down my good mood, that was it."

"Which is not why I'm warning you," he reminded her.

"No, I know," she said. "It's just one of those very sobering realities. Two people, two friends of mine, have lost their lives."

"So let's hope there isn't a murder this weekend," he said, "and I definitely don't want it to be you, so please take care."

"Well, I'm at the bookstore now, and then I'll spend time with you later," she said, "so you're in the middle of any happenings tonight."

"Good point," he said, "but, just in case I get called away or something, you need to stay safe."

"I have a lot of reasons to stay safe," she said. "I had a lot before today, and now I have even more. Do you think I'd be better off staying here then?" she asked as an afterthought.

"No," he said instinctively. "I don't."

"Okay," she said, "I'm not even sure that's an option yet anyway."

"You'll work all that out with the lawyer soon enough."

"Yeah, I hear you. I've got a customer coming in. Talk to you later."

They hung up, and footsteps approached him.

"Damon, you want to come in here for a moment?"

He looked up to see the captain motioning at him. Damon frowned but stood up agreeably. As he walked into the office, Captain Meyer said, "I'm not sure what's going on or how we ended up with all these cold cases being opened up again, focusing on the same scenarios right now. You want to explain that to me?"

Damon quickly went over the logic, going with what had happened thirty years ago, even sixty years back too, and then the parallels to the current situation.

The captain nodded slowly. "I get that, but what's all the buzz about tonight?"

"It's the seven-day mark. Well, technically tomorrow, Sunday, is the seven-day mark. But the killer works at night. And the seven-day break happened with the four murders from thirty years ago. So I'm just being extra cautious."

"Do you think that pattern's being copied?"

"We don't have any way to know," he said, "but I don't want to find another young woman dead tomorrow morning who we could have saved, if we'd been a little faster on the ball."

"That's never a nice feeling," the captain said tiredly.

"You're not sleeping much right now, are you?" Damon said, looking directly at him.

The captain looked at him in surprise, shook his head, and said, "No. Too many grim memories at the moment. Catch this guy, and I'll sleep nicely."

"Right."

"Were there any male killings or any other killings

around that time that you thought could be connected in any way?"

"No," Damon said, "these were clearly connected with the murder MO of the two recent women, and that's what we focused on."

"Right." He pondered that for a moment. "You aren't thinking he's still killing somebody else at the same time but in a different way, are you?"

"I'm not turning anything away," Damon said. "I'm just not seeing any answers yet."

"How do you think we felt last time?" the captain snapped. "You need to solve this before it gets even uglier."

"Working on it," he said mildly.

At that, the captain nodded again. "Sorry. I'm just really touchy over this whole thing."

"I get it," he said. "I really do. It's obvious that this set of cases has disrupted the town for long enough."

He nodded. "Anyway, take off, do your thing, but make sure nobody else dies this weekend if you can help it."

"I'll do my best but no guarantees." And, on that note, he left. He frowned, and it occurred to him that, if the lawyer had known a bunch of the people back then, who were still alive and in town today, that might shed some light on all this.

He went back to the cold cases from thirty years ago and wrote down a list of all the people who had been interviewed. A lot of names. The captain back then had been as thorough as possible. Then Damon took that list, put checkmarks beside the ones who he personally knew, then started looking up the twelve that he didn't know.

As he worked, Jake walked over and asked, "What are you working on?"

He explained his theory.

"Let me see the names," Jake said, and he quickly took four more off the list. "Those four are dead," he said.

"That'll save some time. What about the rest of these? Recognize any of them?"

He took another look and said, "This guy is still alive and in town, but I don't think he does a whole lot. This one here is in an old folks' home, I believe." He stopped and said, "And these other three, I don't know."

"So, let's find those three," he said, "and then I suggest we cross-reference everybody to the new murders."

"You want to find out where they were at the time of the latest killings?"

"Yes, and if they have any connection to these women at all."

"I'll get started at the top of the list."

And, with that, the men buried themselves in that process for the next several hours.

When Jake walked back over again, he said, "Two of them knew the women from skiing and a fitness club," he said. "They still go but not very often. They had seen the women but, other than that, didn't have much of a relationship with them."

"Okay," Damon said. "I found one of these other guys is dead. Nobody seems to know anything about this one, and this other one is also missing, but he probably moved out of state," he said. "I don't have any of that information available."

"And, of course, you also have to put down all the cops working back then," Jake reminded him. "Both the good and the bad."

Damon looked up in surprise and then nodded and

quickly wrote down everybody who had been involved in the court cases back then. "That would be a little disturbing," he said.

"Unfortunately it's happened before."

"I know," Damon said, rubbing his face. "I just hate to even think about it being a cop who kills."

"Hate away," Jake said. "Let's just make sure that we put a stop to this, whoever it is."

"Doesn't the captain have a family lineage of cops?"

Jake nodded. "A lot of captains in his family. Maybe his grandfather, his father, now him? Or maybe a great-uncle, an uncle, and him? I don't know the exact connection. We'll have to double-check that."

Damon nodded at that and kept working on the list.

"We have a lot of people on this list who still live here," Jake noted.

"A lot have moved away though too. If so, they're most likely not part of our immediate concern right now," Damon said. "Let's narrow it down by checking only on those still around Aspen."

"Do you want to go in person?"

"I think we better. We've got the live local witnesses narrowed down to ten names. How about we split them up and each take half?"

"I'm down with that."

Damon stood, grabbed his half of the list, and headed outside. The first one was just a few blocks away.

When the door opened, he found an older woman staring at him in confusion. And he realized, in that moment, that they hadn't prioritized these suspects. Given the ages of most of them, they would be too old to have the physical capacity demonstrated in the current murders. He frowned and introduced himself. "We're investigating the murders from thirty years ago."

The clouds cleared in her eyes, and she nodded. "That was a terrible time."

"You were one of the witnesses back then, is that right?"

"Well, not a witness to the murders, no."

He quickly amended that. "Sorry. I meant that you gave a statement back then."

She nodded. "Well, yes, we all did. Anybody who was involved with those women did."

"I wanted to ask if you happen to know …" And he named the two recent victims. He watched closely, but there was just a blank look in her eyes.

"No," she said. "I don't know those names at all. Were they killed at the same time?"

"No," he said, "they were killed just recently."

She gasped. "Oh my, those are the two young women who just died, aren't they?"

"Yes," he said. "We are investigating their deaths as well."

"Well, I've never heard of them that I know of," she said with a shrug. "So I guess I can't help you."

He nodded. "Do you live here alone?"

"My son lives here," she said, "and my grandson."

"Where are they now?"

"Hawaii," she said. "They didn't want to be here for the winter."

He smiled and nodded and got their information, so he could double-check their alibi, then crossed her name off, as he went to the next witness's house. He was on the fourth name on his list when he realized how late it was. He hoped he could get through his list and finish up soon, so he could have dinner with Gabby.

"WHAT WERE YOU thinking about when I walked into the bookstore just now?" Damon asked, as he and Gabby began the drive home.

"I don't feel any different," Gabby said, "but I know a lot of people would look at me as weird if they knew about all this crazy stuff going on."

"Honestly, if I hadn't seen it for myself," he said, "I'm pretty sure I wouldn't have accepted it. But, given that I did see it, I'm not sure what else I can do besides give you the benefit of the doubt and believe it."

"And you saw *her?*"

"I saw somebody in that window, and you were in bed, so it wasn't you. Nobody came out, and nobody was there, so it's logical to assume it was *her*, Andrea, I presume," he said. "The question is, do you really think she's the one who pushed you down the mountain?"

Instinctively Gabby's mind objected. She shook her head. "No. It feels different," she said. "The energy with her isn't like that."

"Versus?"

"The energy with that first person," she said, "and that voice in my head was male."

"What about *her* voice? Did she ever speak to you?"

"*Hmm,*" Gabby said. "My mind immediately said, yes, but I don't remember the ghost of the garage apartment speaking to me." She held up her pointer finger. "Those tarot card readings!" she exclaimed.

"What about them?" Damon asked cautiously.

"The voice in my head was female," she said, "definitely

female."

"Good," he said, as he led the way to the kitchen. "Stefan said you had two spirits, one good, one bad. This latest revelation of yours seems to confirm that."

"Which brings us back to what Stefan said. That maybe she's tethered here because of somebody else, not necessarily me."

"And that's possible," he said, "but is it likely?"

"I'm not sure I have an answer for you," she said. "It's just such a bizarre scenario. I don't have a clue."

"Well, that's fair enough," he said. "Let's go eat, and then we'll figure it out."

"Let's eat," she said, laughing. She gave her arms and legs a quick shake.

He looked at her curiously.

"Just a weird feeling," she said, "but it's all good." Then she winced. "I know I said I would go shopping and cook dinner, but the idea of walking around the store with the townsfolk kind of spooked me, considering this being so close to the seventh day."

"Good," he said. "I'm glad you made that choice. We still have lots of leftovers. I was actually looking forward to chicken cordon bleu for dinner anyway."

"That sounds wonderful," she said. She sat down across from him at the island while he quickly warmed up dinner.

"I never really did a whole lot of cooking at home," she said, "so microwaving seems to be the norm for me."

"I do cook," he said, "but, when you've got five-star-chef leftovers, it's kind of hard to turn them down."

"I'd never turn them down," she said immediately. "But then I've also been broke a lot."

He smiled. "That was before," he said. "Remember? It's

a whole new day."

"Exactly. I want to get into Jerry's apartment and get to know him," she said. "I know there's no rush, but, at the same time, it feels like there is, like the more time that passes from his death, I'm like losing the connection, you know?"

"Again, contact the lawyer," he said. "I highly doubt there's any issue."

"No, but doesn't it go through a legal process first?"

"Sure, but the store will keep functioning. You're the owner and the only employee of the store, so I don't see why Nathan can't give you a key to the apartment."

"I can ask," she said. As soon as the hot steaming plate was placed in front of her, she immediately pulled it closer and sniffed the air above it. "It smells wonderful," she said. He handed her a knife and fork, and the two of them sat down together. As they ate, they talked about what had happened and what to do about it.

She said, "The priority is tonight or the wee hours of the morning, isn't it?"

"It is," he said in a sober tone. "But since we have no idea if these murders are even connected to those from thirty years ago, much less the specifics on any potential victims or suspects, it doesn't really make any sense to me yet."

"Unless we solve it first," she said impulsively.

"Wouldn't that be lovely?" he said. "But I don't have any answers for you," he added.

"No, but my mother does," she said.

"Right, but she's not talking."

Just then they heard a noise in the house. Like the sound of something falling.

"Yikes, maybe she is," Gabby said with a chuckle.

Damon had gotten up to check out the source of the

sound. "Uh, Gabby, you want to come back here?"

Frowning, she headed down the hallway toward the sound of his voice. She found him in a bathroom, where he stared at the mirror. The surface was all steamed up, and words had been written on it.

I was murdered. Fendster.

"What the hell?" Gabby asked.

"Did you see anyone?" Damon asked her.

"No. Uh, Damon, I don't think there was anyone to see."

"What do you mean?"

"Well, the mirror is all steamed up, but the shower is dry. The sink is dry. Where did the steam come from?"

"So, what are you saying?"

"I think it was *her*, … my mother."

"Jesus," he said, running his hand through his hair.

"What is *Fendster*? Is that a name of a person?"

"Afraid so. I hate to say it, but my captain's first name is Fendster. Fendster Meyer."

"Do you think he could have killed Andrea?" she asked bluntly.

"I won't say no," he said, "because I think, under particular circumstances, everybody is capable of killing, but I don't know what the motivation would have been or why would he have gone on to kill four more."

"We're assuming he killed four more, but it could be that somebody else did the rest. Like a copycat murderer, trying to hide his actions, under the guise of the suspected murderer." She paused, tilted her head. "Or possession comes to mind. Again."

"Yeah," he said with an audible sigh. "But what are the odds of that really?"

"Meaning, how many murders does a town like this have in two weeks?"

"I'd have to check the database for that average. But don't forget that Andrea was considered to be an accidental death. Murders are rare here. Accidental deaths aren't that common either, but, given we're a ski resort, they do occur."

"Now, she was apparently killed," she said, pointing at the mirror. "We still don't know how she died."

"No, that's quite true," he said, raising his gaze to look at her. "What would cause somebody to jump off a cliff like that and have it look like she went flying, yet have it still be murder?"

"What if she was given a drug?" she asked quietly. "Something to make her think that was the completely safe and normal thing to do."

"Like a hallucinogenic of some kind?"

"That's one answer," she said. "Or consider the opposite. Something that would make her supremely depressed."

"I'm not sure," he said, "but it's an interesting conundrum. So who would have given her the drugs?"

"Well, of course, my mind immediately goes to her husband, except I wouldn't blame Jerry directly."

"True," he said thoughtfully. "In which case, no justice to be had there, so why did Andrea come back?"

"And then we're assuming she's come back because of that, to get justice or revenge or whatever."

"But that makes more sense now," he said. "She said that she was murdered and mentioned Fendster."

She nodded, looking stymied at that. "And I get that," she said, "but I still find it kind of odd."

He pondered it for a long moment.

She said suddenly, "Is there any chance ..." Then she

stopped and shook her head. "No, I don't want to go there."

"Go where? Come on. We're just brainstorming," he asked.

"Well, what if Andrea had an affair with Fendster or someone or something along that line?"

"Oh," he said, staring at her. "I hadn't considered that."

"And I don't want to consider that. But ... now that I'm thinking about it," she said, "it would be hard not to."

"What do you mean?"

"Because," she said, "it appears that I'm her child, but what if I'm not Jerry's?"

"Wow," he said. "I guess that's not too far of a leap to consider, but what would that mean in terms of what's going on here?"

"What if somebody killed her because she would tell Jerry about the affair?"

"As in telling him that their marriage was a mess long before she had the baby?"

"Or even just that he might not be my father."

"But maybe she loved her lover?"

"Maybe so. What if her lover was married?" She shrugged. "Who knows? The possibilities are endless really," she said. "It just occurred to me that if A were possible, then B could be possible too."

"Did you look for the DNA results?"

"No," she said, "I didn't."

"I wonder if they're in Jerry's apartment."

"Or it could be in an email," she said, shrugging.

"Do you have access to his emails?"

She looked at Damon in surprise, then nodded slowly. "Yeah. I used to do a bunch of clerical work as part of my job. I logged in and did orders and whatnot for him."

"So, could you log in now?" He'd gotten up and grabbed his laptop, setting it on the bar beside her.

She pushed her plate off to the side, brought up a browser, and logged into Jerry's email server. "Well," she said, "I'm in."

"So, take a look and search for DNA results in the emails."

She did a quick search for DNA and gulped. "It's here."

He came around to stand over her shoulder. "Interesting," he said. "Are you ready to open that?"

She nodded slowly. "Does it change anything?"

"If you mean, in the will, no. The estate is left to you by name, not by DNA," he said. "Besides, I would think that just the fact that you are Andrea's would matter to Jerry."

"I guess," she said nervously. When she double-clicked on the email, they could see the attachment. She opened that up, and they both quickly read through it.

"Oh, my God," she said. "Jerry wasn't my father."

CHAPTER TWENTY-ONE

G ABBY STARED AT the evidence in front of her, then turned to look at Damon with a stricken look on her face. "How is that even possible?"

"Well, we just discussed the fact that it was quite possible," he said, gently massaging her shoulders, as he read the rest of the document in front of her. "However, it does confirm that Andrea is your mother, so she did have a lover," he said. Gabby closed her eyes and sank back against him. "Gabby, we knew it was a possibility."

"Maybe," she said, "but I wasn't quite ready to see this."

"I don't think we're ever ready to see news like this," he said. "But now for the real question. Who is your father?"

She nodded slowly. "My guess would be the man who murdered her," she said.

"You're thinking Fendster?"

She nodded. "Yet, I don't know," she said slowly. "Andrea wrote that name for some reason. Assuming, of course, it was her and that's what she meant. Is there anybody else named Fendster, before we jump to conclusions?"

"That's true," he said. "Though it's not a common name, the first Fendster who comes to mind is my captain. Fendster Meyer. He comes from a long line of law enforcement family members. I'm not sure how far back it goes, like to cover these sixty-year-old cold cases too, but it may.

However, my captain's older brother was captain too. I don't know all the details, but my captain also had a nephew on the force who died in an accident or something. I'll check it all out tomorrow."

"So, this is really all just speculation. How do we find something out for sure?" she murmured.

"I know it's probably not something you want me to bring up," he said, "but have you considered asking the woman who raised you?"

She winced at that. "I could. I guess there is no reason not to at this point," she said, "but it's just kind of, you know, unsettling."

"Do you have any relationship with her at all?"

"Sort of," she said. "I do. It's just not something I particularly want to open up or expose myself to right now."

"She might be the one with the answers though," he said.

"Yeah, you're right." She picked up her phone and quickly called her adoptive mother, putting it on Speaker. When Bernadette answered, Gabby said, "Hey, it's me."

"Hey," she said, "quite a stir going on around your place, huh?"

"Yes. Apparently so. Look. I know that my father was the bookstore owner here."

"Yes, we heard all about that being revealed."

"The thing is, he had DNA testing done, and, as it turns out, he's not my biological father," she said in a rush.

At that, Bernadette gasped softly, and then she started to laugh. "Oh, that's too funny," she said.

"Why is it funny?"

"Because your mother was always one of those holier-than-thou kind of people," Bernadette said, in a tart tone.

"Do you know who might have been in her world at the time?"

"What? Are you tracking down your birth father?"

"Well, it did occur to me, yes," Gabby said.

"I wouldn't bother," she said. "It's not like he'll want to deal with an adult daughter at this stage."

"I know," she said. "It's just that we've gotten some answers, and now apparently there are more questions."

"Well …" And then she stopped and said, "Oh, I know why she did it."

"What do you mean?"

"I never even thought about it at the time," she said, laughing again. "But it makes a lot of sense."

"What does?" Gabby asked, wishing Bernadette would stop deliberately being so cryptic.

"Your father couldn't have children," she said. "It was a bone of contention between them, something about an extremely low sperm count from a childhood illness or some such thing."

"Oh. Well, that would make sense."

"So, that's why she went and had an affair, … to get pregnant," she said. "And wouldn't that figure? Then she goes and kills herself and leaves the rest of us holding the bag."

Gabby shook her head at that. "Well, let's hope she didn't actually kill herself," she said.

"Well, the only other thing it could be is an accidental death," Bernadette said. "Neither will help you at all."

"No, I get that," she said. "I guess I'm just wondering if you know anybody in her world who she cared enough about to have had an affair with."

"Oh, lots of men were in her world. Everybody was always sniffing around her," she said. "I can't believe that, even after all these years, all I ever get asked about is her."

"I'm sorry. I know this can't be terribly pleasant for you."

"No, it sure isn't," she said. "She was my friend, but it's been a friendship that I have regretted many a time," she said wearily. "It's like I'm never free of being in Andrea's shadow."

Listening to her adoptive mother, she looked at Damon, who just winced and shrugged. "So, you don't really have any idea?"

"Well, you can talk to Jerry's best friends. There were two of them at the time. I can't remember what their names were just now though."

"Do you remember what they did?"

"Well, one was a lawyer, and one was in the police force, I think," she said, "but I don't really know. Believe me. I'm more than happy to forget that stage of my life."

"And, once again, I'm grateful that you took care of me, and I just want you to know I appreciate everything you did."

"Well, as long as you're done needing me now," she said, "I feel relieved of a burden. So it's all good." And, with that, Bernadette hung up.

Damon stared at her. "Relieved of a burden?"

"Yep. That's how I was raised," she said, "always to remember that I was a burden," she said with half a smile. "Not exactly the easiest way to grow up."

"Well, that was interesting, but I don't know that it was really any help. I'm sorry I put you through that."

"It's fine. I knew what I was in for. I'm never to ask her for anything, even information it seems. But, at the same time, it does bring us back to two people."

"Right," he said and picked up the phone and called the lawyer again. When Nathan picked up, Damon said, "Hey, we're still looking into a lot of these unsolved murder cases. Did you happen to know Jerry and his wife way back then?"

"I told you that I did," he said. "We were good friends, even back then."

"Sorry. I forgot about that. So this is an awkward question to ask," he said, "but I feel like I need to."

"What's this all about?" the lawyer asked in a testy tone. "I'm cold and tired after a very long day."

"Did you ever have an affair with Gabby's mother?"

There was a long silence on the other end. "Is it really necessary to bring this up?" the lawyer asked.

"Yes," Damon said, "it is."

"Fine," he said. "Yes, I did."

"And was she looking to leave her husband for you?"

"That was never on the table," he said. "She wanted to get pregnant, and Jerry couldn't do the job. We all knew Jerry was sterile, but apparently she didn't seem to think it was an issue, until she married him, and then her biological clock started ticking away."

"So you were trying to get her pregnant?"

"Honestly there were several of us," he said, "and I don't want Gabby to think less of her mother because of it. She desperately wanted a child. That's all it was."

"In which case, why would anyone think that Andrea would have killed herself?"

"I never did think that. I actually thought Jerry might have tossed her off, but nobody saw him, and everybody said he was inside the restaurant."

"Interesting," he said. "Do you know who else might

have had an affair with her?"

"Does it matter? The poor woman is dead. Let's not sully her reputation."

"Well, the DNA came back, and Jerry isn't her father, so obviously Gabby wants to know who is."

"Ouch," the lawyer said. "That's not exactly what anybody wants to hear."

"No, but she's struggling, and it would be nice if she knew who her family truly was."

"Well, I'm happy to take a DNA test for her, if that's the issue."

"Okay, I'll check with her on that." He looked at her with an eyebrow raised, and she immediately nodded. "That's a *yes, please* on her side."

"Fine," he said. "I'll send it to the same lab, and they can compare it against hers."

"Thank you," he said, "and I still would like the names of who else might have been involved in this."

"Sure," he said, "that would be your police captain, and then there was Jimmy at the resort." Nathan stopped to think about it and said, "I don't know about anybody else. But it's quite possible there could be a couple others."

"Thank you," Damon said.

"Honestly, it was, I don't know, … a weird situation. Andrea was so determined. She didn't enjoy the process and knew she was cheating, but she just had to have that baby."

"Which all adds credence to the theory that she probably didn't commit suicide," he said, "and that helps too."

"Not if it brings it all back up again," he said. "It was pretty traumatic for all of us at the time."

"Because you actually cared for her, didn't you?" Damon asked, hearing something in the man's voice.

"Yeah, of course I did. Hell, most of us were in love with her, but she only had eyes for Jerry. So we all danced to her tune, just to make her happy."

"And deep down you were hoping that maybe, just maybe, she would leave him for you?"

"Isn't that what every man does when he's in love? You should understand that, since you feel pretty strongly about Gabby yourself." And, with that, the lawyer hung up.

She looked at him in surprise. "Is that how you feel?"

"Well, since he brought it up, I will tell you that I'm definitely interested," he said, feeling heat on his cheeks.

She nodded slowly. "Well, I'm really glad to hear that," she said, "because I definitely am interested too. I felt like we were getting closer and just hoped the relationship wasn't all about the case."

"Nope, not on my side for sure," he said. "When I first met you, I thought you were a scam artist who was out there just to cause trouble. But obviously I was completely way off there."

"Maybe not," she said with a cheeky grin. "Apparently I'm my mother's daughter and still cause trouble, no matter where I go."

"Well, there is that truth too," he said, smiling.

She looked down at her hands. "I don't think any less of her, you know."

"Good," he said, "because you can't judge anybody's life until you've walked in their shoes. Clearly she wanted a child very badly."

"Exactly," she said. "But is that why she was killed? Did somebody tell Jerry that she was pregnant? No, that doesn't make any sense because she'd already had the baby."

"The only thing I can think of is that she might have

decided that she wanted the biological father to be involved. Maybe she decided it wasn't fair to you or something."

"You know what? That just brings me back to thinking it may have been Jerry who killed her." She paused, cocked her head. "Like in a moment of jealousy. Yet I know he deeply loved her."

"Maybe. I just don't know what to say about it."

"So which one do you think?"

"I don't know," he said. "Honestly I don't know what to think." He looked at her and said, "But I do have a hot tub out back now, installed just for you. That could clear our heads. Are you feeling up to it?"

She smiled up at him. "Now a hot tub would be lovely," she said, "and, if you have any wine, I'd take that instead of that wretched whiskey of yours."

He started to laugh and said, "Well, we're just about done with the dishes, and so far everything is quiet in my world, so let's head for the hot tub, and I'll see if I can find a bottle of wine to bring with us."

She waited, while he checked. Finding a bottle of red in the cupboard, he held it up. She grinned and said, "Now that's more like it."

He nodded, then opened it up, and said, "Let's go."

Together they walked outside, and she stopped and stared at the beautiful winter wonderland and the covered hot tub. "This is beautiful," she said.

"Yep, it sure is." He motioned at the site. "My aunt used to live quite well here."

"Was she a gal who liked to have fun?"

"That she was," he said.

"Maybe she knew my mother."

"Quite possibly, but I don't get to ask her questions," he

said, "because she's dead and gone."

"Well, I thought dead and gone was a given," she muttered, "but apparently it's a choice in the ghost world."

"I don't even know if it's a choice," he said. "I think it's more like a passion that they can't let go of or something."

"True." She looked at the hot tub, looked at him, and said, "So ..."

"What?" he asked, as he set the glasses down.

"Well, since you've already seen me in the bathtub, are you okay if I go in without clothes?"

He raised his eyebrows and said, "That's the preferred way."

She grinned and quickly stripped off in the chilly Colorado air and stepped into the hot water. As soon as her body sank in, she tilted her head back and moaned. "Oh, my gosh," she said, "this is so much better than the bathtub."

"It's not that I don't agree with you," he said, "but there's something very fascinating about somebody completely comfortable in their skin, like you are."

"You mean, the fact that I'm not trying to cover myself up or anything?"

"If your adoptive mother did one thing for you," he said, "she gave you self-confidence."

"That she did, and the confidence to try new things. She also gave me a backbone, and, when things hurt, I didn't let them get me down. I just kept pushing through, until they didn't hurt as much."

"So there are good things to be said for the way you were raised. Let me rephrase that. You took a terrible situation and came out of it strong and independent."

She thought about it for a moment. "Thank you, I would agree," she said. "So now what will we do?" she asked, stretched out in the hot tub.

"What do you want to do?"

"I want to contact the men who could potentially be my father."

"And get DNA from them?"

She nodded.

"You might want to talk to the lawyer first," he said.

"Why is that?"

"Just a hunch," he said. "Besides, he already agreed. And you don't want to wait for the results from him?"

"No. He did sound like he thought maybe it was him though," she said.

"I wonder because he named a couple others, then suggested the potential for even more as well."

"Was he was just trying to throw us off the scent?"

"But he's not a murder suspect," he said. "Although, if he has a wife and kids, they might not like it if you have rights to a share of his assets."

She stared at him in shock. "Is that all people ever think about?"

"From my perspective as a cop, absolutely," he said. "When it comes to inheritance, the lawyer is not quite as old as Jerry, I don't think, but he's not that much younger."

"But he could still live like twenty more years," she said hopefully. "It would be lovely to get to know him."

"Even if he was only a sperm donor?"

She smiled at that. "I guess he might not be interested in playing father to me," she said. "But maybe I'll see if he brings it up."

"Yep, and I don't think that relationship would be terribly easy."

"No," she whispered. "Probably not." She sank back,

closed her eyes, and just relaxed.

"And what if you never find out?" he said.

"I don't know," she said. "It's not like I can do anything about it."

"Are you feeling guilty about the property?"

"No," she said, "because it was my mother's. Because I feel so at home there. Because I met Jerry there. No, I don't have a problem with that anymore."

"Good," he said, "that's the right way to think about it."

She smiled. "I do wish I had gotten to know Jerry better though because, if Andrea had lived, he would have been my father."

"That's a very good point," he said, looking at her.

"And, as I think about it," she said, "I really do want to get into that apartment early."

"We should have asked Nathan about that earlier."

"True." She frowned. "Can you send him a text about it?"

He grabbed his phone and texted the lawyer, asking if she could get into the apartment, and then said, "Okay?"

She nodded, then slid closer to him. "I liked what the lawyer said, about you and me. So do you understand what he went through with Andrea?"

"Ha," he said. "That was pretty brazen of him."

"He probably just figured that, if you were getting him in hot water, then he would see you in hot water too."

At that, Damon burst out laughing. "You know what? You might be right there. I was about to tell you how I felt anyway, but I was trying to get the cases cleared up first."

"I guess it's best not to get involved with me while the case is ongoing, is it? But then, if you think about it," she said, "that's like thirty years we'd have to wait."

"And that's not happening," he said, as he tugged her into his arms and gently kissed her. She sagged against his chest and smiled. "Have you heard from Wendy?" he asked.

"Not since I called, asking to borrow her board. She's supposed to let me know where and when to meet her, without Meghan knowing, I assume. I just hope she and Meghan either figure it out or decide what they'll do."

"I think Wendy will probably go home," he said. "I wonder how Wendy will react when she finds out about us."

"I feel so bad about that part," she said in a low whisper. "She's been hurting over our relationship for a long time apparently."

"I get it, but, if you're not leaning that way, what are you supposed to do?"

"I know. I know," she said. "It doesn't make me feel any better. If I would have caught on, we could have at least resolved it a long time ago."

"Understood." He smiled and kissed her again.

She chuckled and leaned over until she was floating up against him, her hot flesh pressed against his chest. "This is definitely much nicer than a bathtub."

"This is a bathtub built for two," he murmured against her lips, gently tracing the shape of hers with his tongue.

"And I like it," she said. "I've never really been in a hot tub like this, alone with a guy."

"Ah, so, in other words," he said, as he slid his hands down her back to her bottom and pulled her up tight against him, "you've never made love in a hot tub?"

She shook her head, feeling excitement stirring inside. Just something was so sultry and sexy about being in a private backyard, out in the freezing fresh air, while soaking together in the steamy hot tub like this. "That is true," she said. "I have not."

"So, something new today too."

"It's been a day of new on several fronts," she said, shaking her head. "But a good day overall."

"Well, let's make it better," he said, and he pulled her down and gave her one hell of a kiss.

"You, sir, are lethal," she said, when she could breathe again, gently rubbing up against his erection between the two of them. "And that is a dangerous weapon," she said, gasping. She couldn't really see through the churning water, but she slid her hand down his body until she could grasp him in her hand. He moaned gently and lifted his hips, tilting his head back. She gently stroked the length of him, exploring and testing. "There's something very magical about being out here right now," she whispered.

"Absolutely," he said. "But, if you think I've been in hot tubs like this before, you're wrong. You're christening this one with me."

She chuckled with joy. "Now that sounds even better," she said. "I'd hate to think of you out in Aspen's hot tubs with a bevy of gorgeous ski bunnies."

He burst out laughing, until she plunged herself down hard on his shaft. "Jesus Christ," he said, "give a guy a little warning." But his hands held her there, as she wiggled into position. He shuddered and said, "Stop moving. I need a second to regroup, before I embarrass myself."

"Nope," she said, "I won't do that." And she twisted gently and then a little bit harder before sliding up and then coming down hard.

He groaned and said, "You'll kill me. You know that, right?"

"Maybe," she whispered, "but what a way to go." She

leaned forward and kissed him.

He crushed her against his chest and whispered, "Wow, this is well beyond what I was thinking."

"Ha," she said, "you were hoping for this."

"No," he said. "I didn't even think that far ahead. I was just going with the flow."

"Well, guess what? This is where the flow is taking us."

He asked her, "Do you ever shut up?"

"Only if you kiss me," she said. With that, his lips slammed tight against hers, and, holding him close, she started to rise and fall in the water, the water slapping against them with her movements. She giggled as it splashed into their faces, but then she saw his face twisted with passion, and all thoughts of humor disappeared. She grasped his shoulders and started to really ride him. He groaned and tried to help but couldn't because of the splashing water.

Finally he whispered and said, "This is all on you, sweetheart."

And, with that, he just held her hips, as she plunged up and down, faster and faster, until the waves were pounding against them, and he was crying out beneath her. She sagged against him, as explosions rushed through her, wrapping her arms around his neck. "Oh, my God," she whispered, "that was divine."

He crushed her tightly to him and said, "When I get the energy," he said, "I'll show you another way."

She moaned. "We do have all night."

"God, I hope so," he said fervently, then kissed her long and hard.

She snuggled up close and wondered how the day could possibly get any better. Then she realized the day was damn near done, and it was one that topped every other day in her world. She closed her eyes and gently relaxed into his arms.

"You going to sleep?" he asked.

"No," she said, "I'm just resting."

"How about your wine?"

"Oh, that's a good idea," she whispered. He reached over and picked up the glass and handed it to her.

HOURS LATER THE phone woke Damon up. He rolled over in his bed to see Gabby curled up at his side, sleeping, her hair still damp from the hot tub, but she had crashed pretty well, hogging the rest of the bed. He reached for his phone and saw it was Dispatch.

"Body found in an apartment," she said, then quickly gave the address.

"Dammit!" he said, as he bolted to his feet, grabbing his clothes.

Gabby murmured and rolled over to look up at him. "What's the matter?"

"They found a body."

She stared at him, her heart in her eyes. "Oh, God," she said. "What's the address?"

He pulled up his notepad and read it off. She looked at him and shrugged. "That means nothing to me."

"Good, hopefully it's completely unrelated." He looked at her and asked, "Do you want to go back up to your suite or stay here?"

She yawned and said, "I'll stay here, if it's okay."

"Fine, but I'll lock the doors."

"Okay," she said and pulled the blankets around her. Once he was dressed, he raced downstairs, grabbed his keys, his wallet, and his winter coat, and, after locking up, he headed out. When he got to the address, he stopped, looked at the apartment building, and frowned. Jake met him outside. "This is where Meghan's apartment is."

Jake just nodded.

Damon asked, "Who is our victim?"

"We don't have a positive ID yet," he said, "but it's a female."

Damon stared at him in shock, a grim feeling ripping through him. "Well, I hope it's not one of the other two women from the apartment."

"I was kind of hoping that it wasn't anybody," Jake said quietly. "The last thing we need is to have the third victim now."

"And worry about who'll be the fourth one to follow tomorrow night?" he said.

"Or they'll ratchet it up and make it today, because it's already past midnight?"

"Damn," he said, shaking his head. He approached a uniformed cop and asked for the crime scene location. Getting that, Damon and Jake reached the apartment in question. Damon stopped, turned to Jake. "This is Meghan's apartment. This is where Wendy was." They raced quickly into the bedroom. Forensic techs were already on the scene. "Do we have an ID on the victim?"

"Yes," he said. "Meghan somebody."

Damon stared at him in shock. "Seriously?"

The forensics guy nodded slowly. "I actually know her. She works at the gym that I go to," he said. "Jesus Christ, we've got to get this guy."

"What about her roommate?"

"What roommate?" He gestured around and said, "No other body is here."

"No?" Damon said. "We need to find her though." He pulled out his phone and looked up Wendy's number and called it. When a sleepy voice answered, he said, "Wendy, this is Detective Damon Fletcher. Where are you?"

"I'm at a hotel," she said. "I'm leaving in the morning."

"Oh, and you aren't telling Gabby?"

"No, I figured I'd tell her afterward," she said, tears choking voice. "I know I'm not supposed to leave here, but I just can't stay…"

"What about Meghan?"

"We had a hell of a fight last night," she said. "I moved out early in the morning and just kind of wandered for most of the day. Remembering your text from earlier, I decided to get off the street and grab a hotel and get some sleep before I left in the morning."

"When did you last see Meghan?"

"Last night, when she was pounding the crap out of me."

"Oh, shit," he said, "that's why you didn't call or see Gabby, isn't it?"

"Yes," she said and burst into tears.

"I'm so sorry."

"I am too," she said. "I never want to see Meghan again."

"Can you do me a favor?" he said. "Can you take a selfie right now and send it to me?"

"I don't want to get her in trouble," she said. "I'll just leave and go back home."

"Well, you need to tell me what hotel you're in and your room number. And I want that photo and I want it now."

"Fine," she said, sniffling. She hung up the phone, and moments later he got a text message with a picture. Sure enough, her face was puffy; her nose was possibly broken, and her eye was black and swollen.

He called her right back and said, "You need to go to the hospital and get checked out."

"I don't think I can," she said. "You know what that will cost me."

"Go get it checked out," he said. "Your nose looks like it could be broken."

At that, she started to wail. "I figured Meghan would find me there," she said.

"I'm sorry to tell you like this, but Meghan isn't finding anybody ever again."

At that, she blew her nose, then asked, "What do you mean?"

"Meghan is dead," he said, "and it looks like she was killed by whoever killed your other two roommates."

"Oh, God," and then Wendy really started to cry.

He spent a few moments calming her down, and then he said, "Look. I'll phone Gabby and get her to talk to you. You meet her at the hospital. Do you hear me?"

She nodded, swallowing her tears. "I'll try," she said. "Don't worry. I'll call her myself right now."

"Okay, but make sure you do. Promise?"

"I promise," she said.

He hung up the phone and started swearing. Jake looked at him in surprise. "So Wendy was here," Damon said. "Night before last Meghan here beat Wendy up pretty bad. I'm trying to get her to go to the hospital now. It looks like her nose is broken, and the rest of her face was punched up pretty good too."

He stared and said, "Meghan's a beater?"

"It's what broke them up once before. It's also became the wedge between Wendy and Gabby because Gabby was pretty upset over it all. She got her friend safely away, but Wendy went back to Meghan and didn't tell Gabby, and that all came out after the other murders. They've been on the outs because Meghan saw Gabby as a problem."

"That'll do it. How many times have we seen it happen, time and time again?"

"Exactly." Damon watched as the coroner checked her over and asked him, "Is this identical to the previous two?"

He looked up and nodded.

"This is the third victim," Damon said to the coroner, "and then supposedly a fourth, and then he goes silent. I don't want to see a fourth."

"Neither do I. Nor do I want to see him go silent and get away with this shit."

"Nope." Damon turned to look at Jake. "We need to check up on the other roommate. It's after midnight already."

"I'll call her and get her out of bed," he said.

"I wonder if he expected this to be Wendy."

"That's what I was wondering." Jake kept dialing on the phone. "It's not going through," he said.

When he started to swear, the coroner looked at him. "What's the matter?"

"Well, the other roommate was living here. We're wondering if this is a case of mistaken identity, and we can't reach the fourth one."

The coroner shook his head. "You better find those women and find them fast," he said. "I don't know what the connection is between them, but somebody's got it in for them. Get out of here anyway. I'll give you a report as soon as I've got something."

"Anything on time of death?"

"Somewhere in the last few hours, I'd say."

Damon nodded, and, as they went out, Jake said, "We need to find Gabby and check up on her alibi too."

"I'm her alibi," he said. "I just left her in a warm bed."

Jake looked at him and stared. "Jesus Christ!"

"I know. I should have waited until the case was over, but, well, the time frame changed."

Jake shook his head and said, "I'm going over to the other one's apartment."

"Good," he said. "I'll go grab Wendy, make sure that Gabby meets her."

"Honestly why don't you go home and grab Gabby, then pick up Wendy, and take them both to the hospital where they'll be safe?"

He thought about it for a brief second and said, "You're right. Thanks." He raced back home. Once he got there, he opened up the door and stopped because it hadn't been locked. He was positive he had locked it. Instantly he raced upstairs to the bedroom.

And froze.

Gabby stood against the wall, but an odd look was on her face, as if she weren't quite here. Having seen it before, he took a long slow deep breath. "What's the matter, honey?" he asked.

She tried to open her mouth but couldn't seem to get anything out.

"Talk to me," he said. He looked around the room. "I don't know what spirit you are or what problem you have with Gabby, but I'm here now. So why don't you pick on somebody your own size?"

With that came a huge blow to his gut, and he was slammed against the wall. He heard Gabby scream in his mind, and he didn't quite understand where her voice came from. But he was still gasping with the pain from the blow he'd taken. He cried out to Stefan, "I don't know what's going on, but we need help."

He didn't know if he got through to Stefan because another blow smacked Damon's head sideways. And then another one that went the other way. Trying to remember the little bits and pieces he had learned about fighting an invisible enemy, Damon tried to center himself, as he straightened and said, "No!" The next blow seemed to stop just inches from his face. He raced to Gabby, and he looked into her eyes and said, "You can fight this."

She stared at him, terrified from the inside. It was like looking down a long tunnel to see her at the far end.

"Gabby, listen to me," he said. "You know this person is all about power. You know that they're trying to control you. You don't need that."

I know, she said.

But he stopped and frowned. "Did you just say that in my head?"

She could only stare at him, wide-eyed.

Not wasting any time, he picked her up and dropped her gently on the bed. But immediately she bounced out and slammed up against the wall again, and Damon frowned.

"Leave her alone!" he roared.

A burst of weird laughter filled the room.

"I don't know what you want with her," Damon said. "She didn't do anything to you."

"She's mine," came this terrifying cry from inside Gabby's throat.

He looked at her. "Is that the voice you recognized?"

She nodded slowly, as if fighting against hands trying to

stop her.

"Is that the man who pushed you down the cliff?"

She nodded again.

Damon could see the terror in her eyes. "What do you want with her?"

"She's mine," the voice said, "now and forever."

"Why?" he asked.

"Because I can, because it was done to me," he snapped. "And it's not fair."

"I don't understand," Damon said. "Why are you doing this?"

A weird ghostly overlay of a male face appeared on top of Gabby's face.

"Separate from her," Damon said. "Show me who you really are. Only a coward uses a woman like this."

"I'm no coward," he said.

And Damon watched as this huge form pulled up and out of Gabby, as Damon stood in stunned amazement. She collapsed on the bed, moaning, curling up in a small ball, as if finally freed from something. He turned to look at this massive specter in front of him, but, in the background, he heard Stefan's voice.

"He's just enlarging his energy to scare you, Damon."

"It's fucking working," he muttered.

"Don't let him see your fear," Stefan said.

Immediately Damon lifted his chin. "You're just a piece of marshmallow," he said. "You don't even have a fucking body. You had your chance at life, and you lost it."

At that, the ghost slammed against Damon, throwing him up against the wall again. Now he realized that the ghost could literally use Damon's physical body against him. He shook his head. "Not good enough, asshole." And he tried hard to push him back again. "Stefan, I can't even grab him."

"You can't grab him physically," Stefan said, "but use your mind."

He didn't even get a chance to understand what that meant, before his mind was pushing back.

"Think of a steel wall between you and him," Stefan said, "and use that, use the visual imagery to get him thrown off you."

Damon immediately saw a great big sheet of steel come down between the two of them, and a giant piece of machinery slammed the steel sheet back against the wall, pinning the evil spirit against it. At the edge of Damon's hearing was almost a roar. He shook his head. "Did you hear that, asshole? That's what happens to guys who abuse women."

"I never abused any women," he said.

"Never?"

"Never," he said bitterly. "But they thought I did, so I killed them."

"So now you're back here to get even with everybody else because of that?"

"If that's what they think I did, you can bet it's what I'll do," he said. "I've already been punished an entire lifetime for it."

"Sounds like you've been punished for several lifetimes," he said quietly. "Isn't it time to stop the torture?"

"No, not as long as any of them live," he said.

"Who?"

But there was no talking to whoever it was on the other end of this spirit.

"What did these women ever do to you?"

"They laughed when I found them in bed together.

They laughed!"

"Maybe your wife and her lovers did that, but these women weren't alive back then."

"Others are just like them," he said. "It doesn't matter now which females I choose. They're all to blame."

"Okay," he said, "but you chose these women this time. Why?"

"Because they were surrounding her," he said.

"Gabby?" Damon asked. "The woman you possessed here?"

"Yes. That made it easy to get to them."

"And you pushed Gabby on the mountain?"

"Yes," he said. "It had to be the perfect opportunity."

"I still don't understand."

"The tarot cards opened the door last time," he said. "It opened the door this time too. She pulled the Death card, which was me. Once I saw her coming, I knew I had the one opportunity to regain that same power I had when I was alive."

"When you killed the first three women, some sixty years ago?"

"They deserved it."

"You said you never abused them?"

"I didn't. I taught them a lesson," he said. "It's not my fault if you don't understand. Nobody understands."

"It's a little hard, when the end result is dead women."

"The women are nothing," he said. "They're useless."

"How long have you been doing this?"

"You don't understand," he said. "I killed the first ones when I was alive, but then, when the police caught me, I knew they would kill me in jail. So I took matters into my own hands."

"What?"

"Yes, I committed suicide. And now I must wait. Wait for the timing to get somebody back again."

"So, were you physically the one who killed these women thirty years ago?"

"Well, I did it, but using somebody to do it for me," he said. "There's no end to the amount of power that you can get on this side," he said. "At least for a little while. Then I burn out, and I can't do it anymore. It takes me a long time to build back up again."

"As in thirty years?"

"Yes."

"But you killed the first three on your own? The ones from sixty years ago?"

"And got caught for it, yes."

"Why did you kill them?"

"Because they were lovers and one was my wife," he said. "They laughed at me. Others knew about their affair too. I couldn't stand that humiliation, so I took care of the trio first, would take care of the other four women in their group, two at a time, soon afterward, like in a week."

"Then you were caught, and you committed suicide, and then what?"

"Well, I was caught too soon. Didn't have time to take out the rest of the women," he said. "I committed suicide to escape my fate. But then I came back! So I had to use somebody else to finish my plan, and that was easy for me."

"I don't understand," Damon said, and honestly he didn't. He heard Stefan in the background, trying to figure it out himself, and Damon watched Gabby on the bed, listening in, trying to figure it out too.

"It was my son," he said. "As spirits, we always have access to our children because they have doorways they don't know of. So, I used my son to kill again thirty years ago."

"And that was Fendster?"

"I am Fendster," he said.

"Oh, my God, the son and then the grandson were named after you. You're the grandfather?"

"Exactly," he said.

"But you were all captains," Damon pointed out.

"I raised my sons to be good law-abiding citizens. But they used me to get into office, so I used them. By the time I could manage to get a hold of one of them, it was always my oldest son. I used him to kill the women."

"And your younger son didn't know?"

"Not back then, but my grandson knew. Once he started digging into the cold-case files, he knew. I don't know what he found or how he found it, but I had to kill him," he said. "That took a long time and all my energy. I would have been back here earlier, but I couldn't. I couldn't get either of my sons to do the job because it meant killing one's own son, the other's own nephew. All my sons wanted to do was keep my grandson alive, even though he could convict us all."

"Imagine that," Damon said. "All he wanted was to keep his own alive. But you managed to convince him?"

"No, I managed to overpower the father. He was a drunk, and, when he drank too much, it was easy for me to take over."

"So you had the father drive his own son into the wall, killing him?"

"We cut his brakes," he said, "and then did a high-speed chase on a road where we were chasing him for fun. Of course it wasn't for fun, and he didn't know his brakes wouldn't work. By the time he slammed into the wall like that, everybody was pretty convinced it was suicide. My son didn't like his life after that, and he drank too much soon afterward."

"And your other son? The captain?"

"That one is useless," he said. "A do-gooder. Too honest to be useful."

"Does he know what happened?"

"Nope, he has no idea."

"But that still doesn't make any sense," Damon said. "You're just a ghostly form right now. Who have you been using to kill these women this time?" he asked. "You're obviously here with Gabby, but she didn't kill them."

"No," he said, in frustration. "I've been using the only one I could use," he said. "With my other son a worthless drunk and my grandson dead, that only left the one. But he isn't controlled as easily."

"Jesus Christ," he said, "you're using the captain now, aren't you?"

"He's old, and he's worried. He doesn't know what happened last time, but he's afraid it's all connected and is fighting me even harder."

"Because you're using him to kill, aren't you?"

"Maybe," he said, and then he started to laugh. "It's great, you know? The more I get control, the faster and easier I'm managing to do this. Look at how quickly I took a hold of Gabby. I don't even have to go back into silence now," he said. "Somebody like her, we can do all kinds of stuff in this world."

"You mean, kill people?"

"If need be, yes. I'm sure she can drive us to California, and I can enjoy life again," he said. "There'll be other victims, other people. It's not the same or quite as good, but, given the alternative, this is freaking awesome."

"And, if you can't kill people, then what?"

"Oh, I can kill people," he said. "I came to kill her but realized that, because I could actually possess her quite easily, it's one of the things that I'm looking at prolonging. I'll just take over and live her life, while I find another host. It's a perfect solution. It took me fucking long enough to get here to do this, and I won't let some little piece of shit, like you, take that from me."

"What about me?" Gabby asked from the bed, sitting up and staring at the ghostly image.

"You have no say in the matter," he said. "You're weak. And weak means victim. That's a lesson you should have learned a long time ago. Besides, you're female."

And, with that, Gabby gasped in anger. "And so, just like that, I don't count?"

He sneered. "I wouldn't worry about it," he said. "Not everybody counts in this life."

"Maybe not," she said, "but I do. I've spent an entire life trying to live, and you won't take it away from me now."

"That's right," he said. "You're the one who got—" And then he stopped and whispered, "Oh, my God. Oh, my God, that's absolutely perfect."

"What?" she cried out.

"That's why I can take over your system so well. You actually have my genetics."

She stared at him in shock and then quickly shook her head. "No, no, no, I don't."

"Yes, you do. Wow, look at that. ... My do-gooder son. He went and had an affair and actually produced an offspring." He smiled.

"Did you kill my mother?" she asked.

"Well, yes. It was something my son Fendster wanted, I thought. I didn't really understand why, but he kept talking about how she would ruin him. He needed her to disappear, so I obliged. I don't think he really understood what was happening, and I didn't expect him to be so upset. But he was weak, and weak people are victims. So, he's my victim, but that's the only one I managed to get him to do back then. Fendster got really strong and fought me after that. I had to possess other bodies to get the rest done back then. That takes a ton of energy from me."

"And now he's gotten weak again?"

"He got older, so whatever," he said. "But look at that? I'm fascinated," he said, "and that explains why I have access to you. Oh, my God, we should get you pregnant," he muttered.

She stared at him in shock. "No, we shouldn't, not so you can inhabit him and make my child your lackey."

"Well, I'll need a host in another thirty years when we're done," he said, "because your organic body will wear out. Besides, a son would be better. It gives me more physical strength."

"And that's how you managed to kill all those women and to flay open their chests. But why?"

"That's what I did to my first one, my wife. When I found her, she had two other women suckling her breasts in some godawful evil manner," he said. "I decided it would be better to cut them off. But I actually ended up flaying her alive." He smiled at that. "She screamed and pleaded and begged, but it didn't matter to me. I was getting the punishment I wanted for her. And now she and her lovers are dead and gone."

"So, she didn't get to live as a spirit past her death?"

Gabby asked.

"They don't usually, you know?" he said. "I've seen a few, like your mother, and she's tied to me because I killed her, but the other ones I've killed, they didn't stick around. I don't know what the problem was with Andrea."

"The problem is me," Gabby said, "but really the problem is you."

"Well, I'm already dead, so what will you do about it?" he said, then he started to laugh.

Damon whispered in the back of his head, "Stefan, what can we do?"

"We'll destroy him," he said.

"Sure, but how?"

"Well, for one, we need to cut the link. Without a host he can't stay strong."

"How long can you stay out of a body?" Gabby asked Fendster.

"Well, I must be close enough to get energy from you all the time," he said, "which is what I've been doing since the mountain. You freed me up there. I was pretty frozen that whole time."

"So, you were just waiting for somebody you could connect with?"

"Yep, I thought it was the tarot cards, but really it's not. It's the fact that I know the energy," he said, shaking his head. "Wow, there are things that I still have yet to learn over here."

"So, just because of my energy, the energy coming from my mother's lineage, you managed to attack me, throw me down the mountain, make my life miserable, kill my friends, and now you're still sitting here to torment me again?"

"Well, I probably won't do very much of that," he said,

"because I'll take your system over real fast."

"But what if I don't let you back in?"

"Well, if that were a possibility," he said, "I'd probably fade away into nothing because, without energy to sustain me, I would just get cold and freeze up again."

"I don't understand," she said. "Explain it to me."

He groaned. "You see? Maybe you're just too stupid for all this, but then that's just easier for me to deal with you. I told you already. Without a connection between us, I probably couldn't sustain it."

Just then her mother stepped into the room.

Fendster looked at Andrea and smiled. "See? She can't leave me alone. I'm the connection she has to you."

"Do you really think she wants to be connected to you now?"

"I don't really give a shit," he said, "because that's not my problem."

"I don't get it," Gabby said.

He just groaned. "God, are we back to that? See? You're too stupid to understand the simplest concept."

Damon looked at her, but she was up to something.

"So show me then," she said.

"What do you mean, *show you?*"

"Well, we're not connected right now, correct?"

"Yes, we are, dummy. I've got an anchor in your system," he said. "I can't get an anchor into these guys. It's not as acceptable, but now I know why, with you," he said and started to laugh. He popped the anchor out, and both Gabby and Damon saw it slide along the floor. "See? Just like that."

Gabby looked at her mother and said, "Now, Mom!"

Immediately her mother raced toward the entity in front of her and said, "You killed me!"

"Fucking bitch, of course, I killed you," he said. "I'd do it again too."

Only her mother started to grow and to increase in size. And, with an astonishing speed, she wrapped herself all the way around Fendster and fenced him in and held him tight. It was almost like watching a cartoon because the Fendster spirit held inside was trying desperately to punch out. But he couldn't escape.

Damon cried out, "Stefan, what can we do?"

"Wrap your arms around them and hold each other close. Gabby, tell your mother that you forgive her. Let her go, and tell her that she can take Fendster with her."

"She can take him with her?"

"Yes, but we'll all work together and help."

Damon and Gabby wrapped their arms around this crazy energy fight going on between them.

Stefan joined the circle too. All of a sudden, he said, "On the count of three, visualize that we're helping Andrea cross over this big divide. Think of a great big light coming from it, and we'll kick them both right into it." He said, "Ready? Three, two, and one!"

With the weirdest energy ever, Damon could almost feel his right leg lifting to boot this energy ball, which lifted straight up and over and through the room and into this light.

Stefan smiled and said, "I'm directing him. And now it's off and into the light."

Only the ball had a golden glow, even as part of it beamed in front of them.

"But I don't understand," Gabby said, stepping close to Damon. He wrapped her up in his arms and just held her close.

"But feel the room," Stefan said. "Feel the energy right now."

"It feels completely different," she said.

"It is very different. That's because he's gone."

"I don't get it," she said.

"It's okay," he said. "You don't have to. The bottom line is," he added, "they're gone."

"But, if Andrea went into the light, what about him? Surely he's not going where my mother goes."

Stefan smiled and said, "That will all be sorted on the other side. It's not for us to know. But, as long as Fendster can't come back, we're good to go."

"How do we know he can't come back?" she cried out.

He smiled gently and said, "All I can tell you is that he's gone. You should feel it. Your mother is gone as well. And that's what she's been waiting for. She'd been waiting for an opportunity to save you and to get back at him, once and for all."

"Wow," she whispered.

Damon just held her close. "It's over. That's all we need to worry about."

She smiled and said, "So, is it just us now?"

"Well, it will be," Stefan said. "I'm leaving."

Just then Damon's phone rang. He looked at it and said, "Jake, what's up?"

"The captain just had a heart attack," he said. "The EMTs are there, but it's not looking good."

After thanking him for the call, he looked down at her, and she whispered, "I think it makes sense actually."

"It does," Damon said. "Grandpa Fendster's probably been utilizing so much of his son's energy, that he didn't have a chance to live fully either."

"What's he been like lately?"

"He looked really tired and stressed the last few weeks. He wasn't happy when I started looking into the old cases, but, once I had, he just wanted it all solved, so it would be over."

"Do you think he knew?"

"I don't think anybody could really know. Did he worry? Yes, I think so," he said. "But the bottom line is, it's no longer our problem."

"How will you close the cases?"

He winced at that. "I don't know. It might just go into the annals of the cold-case files forever."

"That would be a shame," she said. "I mean, it'll waste a lot of man-hours down the road."

"Maybe, maybe not," he said. "We'll figure it out. I don't know what, but we can come up with something. Maybe somebody who doesn't exist can take the fall."

"I know what you mean," she said, "but I have complete faith in you to figure it out."

"Really? And here I thought you put your faith in tarot cards."

"You know what? I should pull a card to read my future."

"Oh, hell no," he said.

"Why not?"

"No way. I'll take my chances in the real world with you," he said, "but no more cards. Promise?"

She looked up, smiled, and said, "Promise."

Of course she didn't tell him that she'd already pulled the Lovers card earlier in the day. But she laughed to herself and smiled gently, as she cuddled in close. It was a hell of a good day.

"Did Wendy get a hold of you?"

"Yes," she said, "she called me from the hospital."

"Good," he said. "You must be easy with her."

"I will," she said.

"So I assume she told you that this guy killed Meghan."

"Yeah, but I had no time to process it before all hell broke loose. So that was the third death?"

"Yes, and you were likely to be slated as the fourth, until Fendster realized what the connection was and how easy it was for him to control you."

"Wow," she whispered. She shook her head. "And, if he couldn't get me, then he'd have gone after Wendy."

"Quite possibly," he said, "but it's over now."

"Thank goodness," Gabby said on a big sigh.

"And I think I know how to close all these cases without too much emphasis on the stranger parts of the investigations."

"Really? How can you manage that?"

"I'll add three things to each related file, going back to the original one some sixty years ago. One, I'll link each of these older cold cases to each of the recent three murders. Two, I'll note that further investigation likely reveals this serial killer to be dead. And three? In really small print I'll add in Stefan as a consultant."

"Wow. Would that actually work?"

"Let's hope so. I just don't know if I'll add in Grandpa Fendster's name to the original case. He was the captain back then."

"I say, just think on that one some more. And I still need to get to the hospital," she said.

"And I need to deal with the bodies," he said.

She reached up, gave him a kiss, and said, "We'll pick

this up later."

"At least we have all the time in the world now," he said. "You're not leaving, right?"

"I don't think I planned on leaving from the moment I saw you," she said, laughing. "I mean, I know I fell at your feet as one big snowball," she said. "But honestly, you are the cutest cop to ever interrogate me."

He burst out laughing, grabbed her face with both hands, and said, "As long as I'm the only one, I'm good with that." Then he gave her a resounding kiss.

This concludes Book 18 of Psychic Visions: Ice Maiden.

Read about Snap, Crackle…: Psychic Visions, Book 19

Snap, Crackle...: Psychic Visions (Book #19)

Remember ...

The haunting refrain torments Bethany, almost as much as the horrors of what she's forgotten. Chased, terrified, and injured, she races away from a gunman into the woods, determined to once again escape those after her.

Hunter's first meeting with Bethany reveals an injured, exhausted, and possibly dangerous psychic. Plus she uncooperative, barely civil, keeping everyone at arm's length. Only she needs help, ... and he is the one available. Time for the hunted to turn hunter, and that is his domain. Especially if he gets to champion the underdog, which, in this case, is a prickly and way-to-beautiful woman, who he doesn't want to let out of his sight.

Not only is she being tracked but they want her back as a captive. A captive to do their bidding. And they've enlisted another of their group, her ex-best friend Lizzy, to hunt down Bethany.

They want, no *need*, her to remember who she really is ...

With Hunter at her side, Bethany fights for survival, racing toward an explosive reveal that leaves them all gasping, as their world turns upside down.

Find Book 19 here!
To find out more visit Dale Mayer's website.
smarturl.it/DMSCrackle

Excerpt from Snap, Crackle...

"THEY WERE CLOSE, too close. *She* was too close, Izzy, her nemesis." Bethany Metlomar murmured, fear and panic sneaking through her body, exasperating her already fragmented energy. She tried hard to pull herself together but could feel bits and pieces of her disappearing into the ethers. Her already low energy being further depleted.

"No," she cried out, "stop. Get back here."

The pieces refused to obey. But then her energy had been getting worse and harder to control these last few days. Directly correlating to her waning energy. As soon as she'd been found, her long-lost control and hard-won ability to move in this world around her were instantly shattered.

It was all she could do to keep herself together. At that, she laughed bitterly because, of course, she wasn't keeping herself together. Finding out she was being hunted did that to her.

She shifted her sore feet, struggling to huddle underneath the tree boughs. No way anyone could have followed her here. Hell, there was no reason for them to have tracked her down in the first place, but they had. How had they known where to find her? That had to be Izzy's doing.

Instinct pushed Bethany forward. One foot in front of the other—following that one thread that she'd kept close all these years. He was the only one who could help. But would he? Would he remember her? He'd helped her a long time ago, and she'd never forgotten his compassion and his truth. He'd been that older brother to the young scared child she'd been… but they'd only been at the compound together for a short while before he'd escaped. It had taken her fifteen years to manage the same feat. Had he changed? She had. So why not him?

She was staking everything on her memories of him. But then she had no choice. Not if she wanted to survive. She'd been running for days. Was it only that long? It felt like months, years. Seven long years since she'd escaped that prison.

She could feel the blood seeping down her side, from a bullet hole two days ago out of the blue. A shot fired from behind her while she had enjoyed the morning sun. She'd managed to disappear into the woods, but it had been hard-won victory. Even now she looked down gratefully at her huge jet-black Maine coon mix at her feet. He wouldn't leave her side, even though she'd tried to get him safely away. He refused.

Then he was stubborn like that. Nocturne would survive, if she didn't make it. She wasn't sure she would, should their roles be reversed.

Shudders racked her slight frame, stronger than before, as she struggled to pull facets of herself back together again. She needed to find a source of warmth. Survival meant staying warm. She searched the darkness enveloping her world as the wind whispered around her. Other energies were tracking her. She could feel them reaching through the darkness, searching the ethers to find her. And then there was *him*.

Someone she could see—or rather feel. Someone she

thought should have seen her. Should have been able to feel her, yet he didn't.

Was he an innocent? Someone who had no idea of this insane shadow world? Or maybe she was sending signals, but they weren't strong enough, for him to push up as she was fading quickly. She slumped against the tree trunk, wishing she didn't need yet another rest. The night wouldn't last forever, and she needed to make headway while she could.

Just the thought of getting back on her feet defeated her. Still she was so damn close.

Just not close enough.

A few vehicles were on the road below, traffic moving smoothly, zipping along in the darkness. Normal sounds of civilization around her. Except everything felt, sounded off.

Her senses strained for signs of the danger she knew surrounded her. Only her ears couldn't be trusted right now. None of her senses could. Everything was too fragmented for that. She was desperate to pull them back, but it seemed almost impossible. She couldn't use her energy for that and also make it down to the house.

After all this time, after all the crazy energy she had put into hiding in plain sight, appearing to be normal, appearing to be one of them, even after everything that had happened to her …they'd still found her.

She struggled to her feet, wincing as her energy drained into the puddle of blood at her feet. She was dying, and the window to stop that was closing. Only he could help…

She gave a bitter laugh as she pulled her hand free from the oozing bloody wound in her side. Forcing herself to move, she trudged forward one more step and then another, leaving a heavy blood trail behind.

Nocturne at her side moved quietly, his ears up, his tail

twitching, as he searched the surrounding area. Nobody would see him. Nocturne was the darkness of night, but then so was she.

She tossed her jet-black waist-length hair over her shoulder, wishing she had a moment to braid it. But lacking food, water, and even a bandage to hold in her blood's life force, a braid was the least of her worries.

"Nocturne," she murmured. "You go to him, if I don't make it."

A tiny meow came from beside her. She felt it more than heard it. They'd always been able to communicate, like they were soul mates. So here they were, her a broken-down fugitive and this precious soul that stayed at her side no matter what.

A SURGE OF electricity shot through the room, shocking Hunter who'd been sitting comfortably in Stefan's living room. "Whoa," he exclaimed, jumping to his feet.

An electric influx had the power surging, then sparking. Hunter looked over at Stefan and Celina. "That storms is going to cause a power outage."

He'd only stopped by for a quick visit, not even sure of the impulse that had brought him here. But he was long used to listening to it. These power surges that had been going off and on over the last hour, … building in static and flares to whatever this was … something he'd never seen before.

Celina shook her head. "What is going on?"

Stefan walked to the massive wall of windows at the back of the living room, "It's not an electricity issue. Something, … someone is out there."

Another spark lit up the room.

"Did you see that?" Hunter walked closer to the window studying the energy. Bizarre. And that said a lot of him, a man who lived bizarre.

"I did," Stefan murmured thoughtfully. "But I'm not sure what it was."

Another flash lit the room.

In the fading light, Hunter caught sight of a woman.

"Is she … a ghost?" Celina asked, stepping closer to Stefan.

"No."

Stefan's words synced with Hunter's. "But it's like a holographic image."

"She's young."

"Mid to late twenties, hungry, afraid, … and … injured." Hunter wished the image had stayed long enough to learn something else. Something helpful outside of the massive dark wells of pain gazing out from her white face. What was unmistakable was the metallic smell of blood, her blood. He turned to look at Stefan. "I've never seen anything like this. Have you?"

"Yes and no."

"A little more detail would help," Hunter said with a note of humor, even as the light flashed again at a different location, showing the same woman, only slightly different. "Can we tell if this is real time? Is this slices of her past? Is she close? Is she trying to get here? Lord, she's not teleporting, is she?"

He seriously hoped not. It looked like something out of a horror show, and the end result couldn't be good. The next flash came faster, then another and another, completely surrounding them in the living room, as the three stood in wonder and, yeah, on his part at least, … in horror. Each with a macabre flash of the same woman.

The images and flashes were constant now.

"Is she dangerous?" Celina cried out.

Stefan wrapped an arm around her and held her close. "We all are in different circumstances," Stefan said, but his voice was barely legible over the crackling electricity.

Then suddenly it all stopped.

And silence reigned.

Until a knock sounded on the door.

BETHANY LEANED AGAINST the wall adjacent the doorway, sagged against it was more like it. But she was vertical. The trip had been horrific, but what waited for her? ... Other energies were here. She hadn't expected that. Hadn't allowed herself to consider that. She'd been so focused on him.

Nocturne meowed at her feet.

"Sorry, buddy. I just need a moment."

What if she was wrong? What if this person wasn't who she thought he was? What if he didn't care? What if he didn't remember her? What if he couldn't help? She leaned heavily against the wall—as her own vision narrowed down to a small pinpoint of light. And now the effort to stay upright was too much, and she did a slow slide to the ground outside the door.

Of course outside. She was always outside.

In the far recesses of her consciousness, she heard a hard knock on the door. She wanted to run, to cry out a warning, but it was too late ...

The darkness choked her before she could say a word.

Strong arms reached for her. She was shifted, carried inside. Light warred with the darkness. Softness warred with the extreme hardness of her world. Compassion, caring, opened up old wounds that leaked with pain and sorrow.

She wanted to cry out a warning, but somehow they already knew.

She wanted to let them know why she was here, but somehow it didn't matter.

She wanted to tell them who she was, but somehow they didn't seem to care.

With the last of her strength, she opened her eyes, trying to see if she were safe or had bet on the wrong door.

Fear struck her heart as she struggled to free herself from the man who carried her. "No," she cried out. "No, it can't be."

"*Shhh*, you're hurt," he said gently. "Let me help."

"No, ... it's you. You're the hunter." There she'd said it. The reality of losing crashing into her, tears leaking from her eyes. It was over. The war was won. She'd lost.

"I'm Hunter, yes," he said, staring down at her in his arms. "That's my name. I'm not, however, hunting you."

"No," she whispered. "Not yet."

With the last of her energy, she whispered, "But you will."

Find Book 19 here!
To find out more visit Dale Mayer's website.
smarturl.it/DMSCrackle

Simon Says...: Kate Morgan (Book #1)

Welcome to a new thriller series from *USA Today* Best-Selling Author Dale Mayer. Set in Vancouver, BC, the team of Detective Kate Morgan and Simon St. Laurant, an unwilling psychic, marries all the elements of Dale's work that you've come to love, plus so much more.

Detective Kate Morgan, newly promoted to the Vancouver PD Homicide Department, stands for the victims in her world. She was once a victim herself, just as her mother had been a victim, and then her brother—an unsolved missing child's case—was yet another victim. She can't stand those who take advantage of others, and the worst ones are those who prey on the hopes of desperate people to line their own pockets.

So, when she finds a connection between more than a half-dozen cold cases to a current case, where a child's life hangs in the balance, Kate would make a deal with the devil himself to find the culprit and to save the child.

Simon St. Laurant's grandmother had the Sight and had warned him that, once he used it, he could never walk away. Until now, her caution had made it easy to avoid that first step. But, when nightmares of his own past are triggered, Simon can't stand back and watch child after child be abused. Not without offering his help to those chasing the monsters.

Even if it means dealing with the cranky and critical Detective Kate Morgan …

Get a Free Cozy Mystery Now!

Download the first book in the **Lovely Lethal Gardens** series for free!

Go here and tell me where to send it!

https://dalemayer.com/arsenic-azaleas-free/

About the Author

Dale Mayer is a *USA Today* best-selling author, best known for her SEALs military romances, her Psychic Visions series, and her Lovely Lethal Garden cozy series. Her contemporary romances are raw and full of passion and emotion (Broken But ... Mending series). Her thrillers will keep you guessing (By Death series), and her romantic comedies will keep you giggling (*It's a Dog's Life*, a stand-alone novella; and the Broken Protocols series, starring Charming Marvin, the cat).

Dale honors the stories that come to her—and some of them are crazy and break all the rules and cross multiple genres!

To go with her fiction, she also writes nonfiction in many different fields, with books available on résumé writing, companion gardening, and the US mortgage system. She has recently published her Career Essentials series. All her books are available in print and ebook format.

Connect with Dale Mayer Online

Dale's Website – www.dalemayer.com
Twitter – @DaleMayer
Facebook – facebook.com/DaleMayer.author
BookBub – bookbub.com/authors/dale-mayer

Also by Dale Mayer

Published Adult Books:

Kate Morgan
Simon Says… Hide, Book 1

Hathaway House
Aaron, Book 1

Brock, Book 2

Cole, Book 3

Denton, Book 4

Elliot, Book 5

Finn, Book 6

Gregory, Book 7

Heath, Book 8

Iain, Book 9

Jaden, Book 10

Keith, Book 11

Lance, Book 12

Melissa, Book 13

Nash, Book 14

Owen, Book 15

Hathaway House, Books 1–3

Hathaway House, Books 4–6

Hathaway House, Books 7–9

The K9 Files

Ethan, Book 1

Pierce, Book 2

Zane, Book 3

Blaze, Book 4

Lucas, Book 5

Parker, Book 6

Carter, Book 7

Weston, Book 8

Greyson, Book 9

Rowan, Book 10

Caleb, Book 11

Kurt, Book 12

Tucker, Book 13

Harley, Book 14

The K9 Files, Books 1–2

The K9 Files, Books 3–4

The K9 Files, Books 5–6

The K9 Files, Books 7–8

The K9 Files, Books 9–10

The K9 Files, Books 11–12

Lovely Lethal Gardens

Arsenic in the Azaleas, Book 1

Bones in the Begonias, Book 2

Corpse in the Carnations, Book 3

Daggers in the Dahlias, Book 4

Psychic Vision Series

Unmasked

Deep Beneath

From the Ashes

Stroke of Death

Ice Maiden

Snap, Crackle…

Psychic Visions Books 1–3

Psychic Visions Books 4–6

Psychic Visions Books 7–9

By Death Series

Touched by Death

Haunted by Death

Chilled by Death

By Death Books 1–3

Broken Protocols – Romantic Comedy Series

Cat's Meow

Cat's Pajamas

Cat's Cradle

Cat's Claus

Broken Protocols 1-4

Broken and... Mending

Skin

Scars

Scales (of Justice)

Broken but… Mending 1-3

Glory

Genesis

Tori

Celeste

Glory Trilogy

Biker Blues

Morgan: Biker Blues, Volume 1

Cash: Biker Blues, Volume 2

SEALs of Honor

Mason: SEALs of Honor, Book 1

Hawk: SEALs of Honor, Book 2

Dane: SEALs of Honor, Book 3

Swede: SEALs of Honor, Book 4

Shadow: SEALs of Honor, Book 5

Cooper: SEALs of Honor, Book 6

Markus: SEALs of Honor, Book 7

Evan: SEALs of Honor, Book 8

Mason's Wish: SEALs of Honor, Book 9

Chase: SEALs of Honor, Book 10

Brett: SEALs of Honor, Book 11

Devlin: SEALs of Honor, Book 12

Easton: SEALs of Honor, Book 13

Ryder: SEALs of Honor, Book 14

Macklin: SEALs of Honor, Book 15

Corey: SEALs of Honor, Book 16

Warrick: SEALs of Honor, Book 17

Tanner: SEALs of Honor, Book 18

Jackson: SEALs of Honor, Book 19

Kanen: SEALs of Honor, Book 20

Nelson: SEALs of Honor, Book 21

Taylor: SEALs of Honor, Book 22

Colton: SEALs of Honor, Book 23

Troy: SEALs of Honor, Book 24

Axel: SEALs of Honor, Book 25

Baylor: SEALs of Honor, Book 26

SEALs of Honor, Books 1–3

SEALs of Honor, Books 4–6

SEALs of Honor, Books 7–10

SEALs of Honor, Books 11–13

SEALs of Honor, Books 14–16

SEALs of Honor, Books 17–19

SEALs of Honor, Books 20–22

SEALs of Honor, Books 23–25

Heroes for Hire

Levi's Legend: Heroes for Hire, Book 1

Stone's Surrender: Heroes for Hire, Book 2

Merk's Mistake: Heroes for Hire, Book 3

Rhodes's Reward: Heroes for Hire, Book 4

Flynn's Firecracker: Heroes for Hire, Book 5

Logan's Light: Heroes for Hire, Book 6

Harrison's Heart: Heroes for Hire, Book 7

Saul's Sweetheart: Heroes for Hire, Book 8

Dakota's Delight: Heroes for Hire, Book 9

Michael's Mercy (Part of Sleeper SEAL Series)

Tyson's Treasure: Heroes for Hire, Book 10

SEALs of Steel

Eton's Escape, Book 3

Garret's Gambit, Book 4

Kano's Keep, Book 5

Fallon's Flaw, Book 6

Quinn's Quest, Book 7

Bullard's Beauty, Book 8

Collections

Dare to Be You…

Dare to Love…

Dare to be Strong…

RomanceX3

Standalone Novellas

It's a Dog's Life

Riana's Revenge

Second Chances

Published Young Adult Books:

Family Blood Ties Series

Vampire in Denial

Vampire in Distress

Vampire in Design

Vampire in Deceit

Vampire in Defiance

Vampire in Conflict

Vampire in Chaos

Vampire in Crisis

Vampire in Control

Vampire in Charge

Family Blood Ties Set 1–3

Family Blood Ties Set 1–5

Family Blood Ties Set 4–6

Family Blood Ties Set 7–9

Sian's Solution, A Family Blood Ties Series Prequel
Novelette

Design series

Dangerous Designs

Deadly Designs

Darkest Designs

Design Series Trilogy

Standalone

In Cassie's Corner

Gem Stone (a Gemma Stone Mystery)

Time Thieves

Published Non-Fiction Books:

Career Essentials

Career Essentials: The Résumé

Career Essentials: The Cover Letter

Career Essentials: The Interview

Career Essentials: 3 in 1

Made in the USA
Coppell, TX
28 January 2021